Hemispheres

Stephen Baker was born in Stockton-on-Tees in 1969,
and now lives in Derbyshire. This is his first novel.

Hemispheres

Stephen Baker

ATLANTIC BOOKS | London

First published in Great Britain in trade paperback in 2010 by
Atlantic Books, an imprint of Grove Atlantic Ltd.

This paperback edition published in 2012 by Atlantic Books,
an imprint of Atlantic Books Ltd.

Copyright © Stephen Baker, 2010

The moral right of Stephen Baker to be identified as the author of this
work has been
Designs and Pa

All rights reser
stored in a retr
electronic, mec
the prior perm
publisher of thi

This novel is en
incidents portr
not to be constr
dead, events or

COVENTRY CITY LIBRARIES

3 8002 02026 716 9	
ASKEWS & HOLT	19-Mar-2012
	£8.99
CEN	

10 9 8 7 6 5 4 3 2 1

A CIP catalogue record for this book is available from the British Library.

ISBN: 978 1 84887 221 9

Printed in Great Britain by CPI Group (UK) Ltd, Croydon, CR0 4YY

Atlantic Books
An imprint of Atlantic Books Ltd
Ormond House
26–27 Boswell Street
London WC1N 3JZ

www.atlantic-books.co.uk

Hemispheres

1. Flightless Steamer Duck

(Tachyeres brachypterus)

Only six degrees outside but Dave's already damper than a glass-blower's arse. There's a sheen to his slick face like paraffin, like the sweat that starts from a lump of meat when you put it to the fire. Fidgeting the cards in his hand, left and right, over and under. A cigarette perched on the scalloped edge of his ashtray, the ash beginning to lengthen and the clotted smoke spiralling upward. Whisky in a stained glass, at least his fifth tonight. A cheap Canadian brand. I can taste the heartburn.

I smell you, says Joe Fish, elongated face and slicked-back hair flickering in the wash from the hurricane lamps, like a snail has run over him. The room is cavernous, a farmhouse kitchen with that sour milk smell of damp. Paraffin light trembles like a moth, skitters away from the corners where sinkholes of dark are welling up. Joe splashes a rumpled note into the centre.

The Falkland Islands, he says. *Islas Malvinas.* Whatever you call it, it's still the arse end of the earth. We're fighting over the scraps here boys.

He rattles his fingernails like a snare drum against the table. It's a battered thing, cobbled from ancient timbers. Gouged and scorched and pitted and tattooed and rubbed smooth by the passage of elbows and forearms, the buffeting of lives gone elsewhere. But the elbows on the table now are Joe's, pale twisted things like roots.

I'll go another twenty bar, he mutters, a second note following the first.

Joe plays distractedly, the game getting tangled up with his internal monologue. He bluffs aggressively, destructively. He sits on his hands. He chases his tail.

Working men. Aye, the great party of workers. We should stick together. Stick together like brothers.

He unscrews the top from a bottle, sniffs, grimaces, and slops a good three fingers into his glass. I take a yeasty gulp of beer. It's very cold. My eyes are stinging with the smoke.

I'm in man, says Horse Boy, tipping a note in.

He's almost gone, eyes darting wildly around the room, voice slurred. This is why I stick to beer. It's cold and calming. It slows everything down, makes everything clear. I'm assembling a cigarette. A screw of dry tobacco on the paper, curled between the fingers, a deliberate dab of saliva. It's tiny, not much more than the thickness of a match. Just enough to deliver the required jolt.

Fighting over a rock, in the middle of the drink, rambles Joe. Me against my brother. I've no beef with him, not me. I never thought the witch would send us down here. Never in a million years.

No, not me, says Fabián Rodriguez, laying his cards face down. I fold.

He closes his hooded eyes for a moment and fronds of his long hair trickle down either side of his face. Brow ridges, cheekbones, septum.

Look out there, says Joe.

We strain to see out of the window but only our faces splash back at us, foolish lanterns swimming in darkness. Joe leans towards me, shadow congealing in his deep eye sockets.

Nobody knows where the lines are, he says. Our boys and the spics. They're all out there lost, wandering about in the night.

I shrug.

I'm in lads, I say. And I'll raise you two hundred.

I reach over for Joe's lighter, a big brass thing like a shell case, and relish the oily smell of paraffin as I spark up, suck in a lungful. See, you got to have some discipline in this game. That's what Branigan taught me anyway, them rainy afternoons in the County. Two pair, jacks up, is the minimum hand. Anything less is a fold. It's foolproof. Play it to the letter and you'll make at least a modest buck.

You got to have some discipline in this game. Shame I never fucking listened to Branigan.

Dave is sweating like a nun in a cucumber field and I'm sure he's on the hook. I've been bluffing hard and losing on crap cards. He thinks I'm a tool and that's the way I want it. I'm egging it up on a pair of queens here and I've started this nervous blinking every time I raise. And I see him notice, his eyebrows twitching and settling again. I see him notch it away for future use. Blink means bluff. He opens and closes the buckle on his watch, worrying at the hairless white flesh of his forearm.

And now everyone is looking at him. The little eyes in the heavy face dart about, searching, appraising. He plays with his watch, a big heavy designer thing, the kind you need a mortgage to buy. His cigarette froths on the edge of the ashtray, the untapped finger of ash growing.

It's an ugly business, Joe rambles. See, in the old days, it was single combat, right? Champion against champion. Achilles and Hector. Them lads were bred up for war, see? Hard as nails they were.

It was the Bronze Age Joe, I say. They never had nails.

Hard as bronze, then. Not like now. Podgy lads straight from school, with the stink of fear on 'em.

They were still fighting for the man Joe, I say, winking at Fabián. It was his woman.

Joe looks blank.

The Greeks man, I persist. They went to get Helen back. The big man's trophy wife. Ten years fighting, all because the lady scoffed too much of Paris' Milk Tray. Now I hear she was a canny splitarse, but in my book a decade of all-out warfare could be seen as over-reaction.

A slender smile creeps across the face of Fabián Rodriguez. Dave picks up his cigarette, taps the ash, takes a big drag.

Okay boys, says Dave. Fuck it, I'll play.

He's dicking around with that watch again, over and over. He's got the cards. Definitely. I wait for him to raise, pressure building in my bladder. But he doesn't. Tips two hundred in.

See you.

As I expected, Joe has nothing. Bluffing, king high. Dave has little greedy eyes like a penguin and a wobble to his chin. Plenty of penguins on the Falklands – gentoo, macaroni, magellanic, rockhopper.

Chuck the man a sardine.

I lay down my pair of queens with a foolish grin. Beat that David. Dave lays his cards down, one by one. Three kings. Gold, frankincense and myrrh.

It's a pleasure taking money off you ladies.

He scoops the pot from the table.

Next hand, Yan to deal?

Actually Dave, I'm going to get some air. Jimmy riddle. I'll sit out a couple.

I stand up, glue the roll-up between my lips and head for the door.

Outside the farmhouse it's cold, the southern winter thickening. I walk away from the faint light of the windows, down towards the shore, tobacco smoke blooming almost crystalline in the night air. Stop at the bottom of the jetty and piss into the sea, steam rising, the bladder relaxing. Simple pleasures. The darkness is viscous, complete. I breathe it in. No lights at all, only the impossible chaos of stars brushed across the night sky like silver sand. Alpha Centauri blinking. Somewhere a raft of steamer ducks rising and falling on the swell, gabbling and sighing in their sleep. They're flightless. If you don't use your wings then they will shrivel up to stumps.

Shoals of islands out there. Keppel and Pebble and Carcass and Sedge. North Fur and South Fur. Elephant Jason, Flat Jason, Grand Jason, Steeple Jason. Long low grey seals lying stretched in the white-furred sea. How long have they been here, losing their wings?

We've only been here twenty-three days. I draw hungrily on the nub of my cigarette and it sears into the roach and the smoke turns bitter and mealy.

When I go back into the farmhouse I think of *The Dice Players*. Georges de La Tour, isn't it? We saw it at Preston Hall, when you were just a kid.

Aye, I remember.

Really?

Think so. It's going back a few years, mind.

Entombed underground, almost like a burial chamber. A crypt. It stopped the sunlight fading the colours I suppose. Down a flight of stairs and along a dark corridor and a small room glowing at the end.

That painting. It was like a chunk of time had frozen and never thawed out. It didn't move on.

Danny, you've hit the nail on the head. Five blokes stood around the table. You're right there in the room with them, in this rich and smoky and port-and-tobacco-scented sixteenth-century darkness. But they aren't looking at you. Candlelight shivers over your skin like goose-flesh, touches the face of a man sucking at a long clay pipe, touches the open palm of a hand. Candleflames ripple in the tabletop, in that deep mahogany sheen and the dice frozen in movement. You've stumbled in, just when everything's in motion and nothing is settled. These living, breathing men, awake only to the racing dice. Tumbling like the planets, like the spheres of the universe. And soon enough they'll come to rest. But for now. For now the night is endless and the candle will never burn down and the dice will never rest.

I stop in the doorway for a moment and look at them. Paraffin light washes over their faces. Eyes lidded, turned down over the cards. I lean on the doorframe, breathe in their tobacco second hand. The face of Fabián Rodriguez is framed in the light. He's about to show. The cards are in motion.

Look, says Joe Fish, who has already folded. They'll find us in the end. You can't just walk away in the middle of a war.

I just fancied going for a wander, I say. In them new boots.

Joe cracks a broad tombstone grin and Fabián spreads his cards on the table. A run, six through ten. It's an intimate business, peeling the boots from a dead man. Puttees and socks underneath, the delicate flexure of the toe bones.

You took a dead man's boots?

Aye. We all did. Our issue boots were shite and they fell to bits in the field. I started walking, through this strange blue sunlight, bright but bitter cold. Ringing in my head like a Tibetan singing bowl, someone running a moistened finger round the rim of my skull. And snow came, scribbles of it across the russet flanks of the mountain, and my feet rattled down stone runs, tramped through tussocks of whitegrass and pigvine, squelched over cushions of oreob and sphagnum. Scribbles of snow descending across my vision, swarming across the surfaces of my brain. It swallowed the others, blanked out the mountain, and I kept walking. Berkeley Sound down below, the long firth crawling away to the ocean, water bickering in the steady wind. And I walked towards it, towards the sea. When I got there, I would carry on. Icy water mounting to my chin, swallowing me. Walking down onto the deep ocean floor until the pressure burst me.

There's no shame in it, says Joe Fish. Who's to know, anyway? The fog of war. If you come back with us now Yan, no fucker will ever know you were missing.

I notice Horse Boy on the floor, asleep. A happy knack. The lamp casts a sheen over his bare back where muscles shiver in the blue autumn night, and his close-cropped head ripples like rabbit fur. Only Dave is left in.

Joe yawns and stretches. We are the proxies, he says. For the real villains. They need mugs like us to fight it out for them because they lack the *cojones*. We are exploited, man. Pure exploited.

Men like us, I say to him. Coal hewers and crucible pullers and farm navvies. Ripping the guts out of hawthorn hedges in raw November. They think we're just doing what we're told. But all along we're creating ourselves. It's in our blood to mine our own history in the dark, black and glittering carboniferous lumps of it.

That's what I'm saying, he persists. We do the dying, and they get the glory.

But none of it matters man. It's over in the blink of an eye. Steamer ducks spent a hundred million years down here evolving flightlessness.

Metaphysics, says Joe Fish, I'm trying to dig you out of a hole here, and you start in on the metaphysics.

He lights a fag, a straight, and the smoke gurgles upward. When I say it doesn't matter what I mean is it doesn't exist. There is no war. Just the five of us, and the cards, and darkness outside.

Dave lays down his cards, one by one. A flush. Five spades like ripe, black fruit. He scoops the pot again, and yawns, like an elephant seal.

Call it a day? Or should I say a night?

He proffers a queasy smile, begins to get up. Must be up hundreds on the last few hands.

The night is without end, says Joe Fish. And sleep is not for men like us.

He grips Dave's forearm and looks at him steadily from the ruined face. His eye sockets loom enormously, teeth like tombstones.

Play, he says. You deal.

Almost apologetically, Dave sits. Joe releases him. He deals. Five beatific faces in the lamplight, one cloaked in sleep, four hooded over the cards.

I have two jacks and some fluff, but Fabián Rodriguez is pushing things before the draw.

Two thousand, he says, his eyes black.

We take this on board silently. Dave has lit another cigarette and like its predecessor it clings to the notch of the ashtray, smoke blooming upwards. The beer is bitter and citrus and clear. Joe Fish beaches his cards with a grunt of disgust.

Fabián has something up his sleeve, I say, pushing notes into the middle.

His eyes remain black, unreadable, a dancing mote of lamplight in the pupil.

This is more like it boys, says Dave. Proper wedge.

He too shuffles some paper into the pot. His hands go under the table. I can't see the watch, can't read him at all.

Dance for tha' daddy, sing for tha' mammy, croons Joe, leaning back, scrolls of smoke issuing from mouth and nostrils.

One card, says Fabián, jerking his head like a horse as the card slides across to him.

One card. The probabilities churn inside my head. If he's holding two pair and drawing to a full house it's one in six and a half. If he's drawing one card to a flush it's one in four.

I'll take three, I say. Makes it obvious I'm holding a pair or nothing, but it can't be helped. Empty my head and let the cards come to me, sliding across the table. Stretch out this moment of not knowing. Of not being.

No cards, says Dave. Smugly.

His dimpled hands come out from under the table, fluttering like flames. He unscrews the cap from the whisky bottle. Pours himself a generous measure, trying not to spill. He must be holding full house or better. Unless he's bluffing. The hands go back under the table. I look at him and blink three times and he sees it. His cigarette in the ashtray, untouched, the ash tongue beginning to grow.

Dance for tha' daddy, for tha' mammy sing. Joe drums on the tabletop with those clubbed fingertips, the nails ridged and stripped back.

I raise. Five thousand, says Fabián. His pupils are becoming more dilated, tunnels into the centre of his head.

Thou shalt have a fishy, on a little dishy.

I will smell you Fabián, I say. This is the last of my cash, though the others don't know it. I can't raise any further. Blink. Blink.

See your five, and raise another five, says Dave. He's bluffing. Must be. Three or four solid hands in a row and it can't go on for ever. Probabilities. Hands under the table. Tobacco being slowly consumed, the untapped ash halfway to the filter.

Fabián is unblinking. Very well, I match your five.

They look at me.

Joe, I say. He holds my gaze. Joe.

Throw for it, he says, and slaps a hand onto the table, flat, with his palm upwards. He looks at my hand, with the forefinger and middle finger extended. The paraffin lamp picks out his palm, my fingers, the sheen on our faces.

Scissors cut paper, I say.

Joe reaches somewhere deep into his kit bag, and pulls out a metal cylinder, a thermos flask. He unscrews the lid and delves inside, withdraws a fat roll of notes.

Scissors cut paper, he says, passing it to me. But if you lose it, you come back with us tonight.

And if I win?

Joe doesn't answer. I turn back to the others.

Dave, Fabián, I match your five, and I raise you fifty thousand American. Blink. There is an audible squawk from Dave.

I watch a moth brushing at the window glass, drawn by the lamp, gentle and insistent. I watch a gob of sweat come adrift from Dave's hairline and sway down the side of his face, making a neat detour round the eye socket and the corner of the mouth, disappearing below the neckline of his shirt. His hands appear on the table, cards in the left, the right hand tugging insistently at the watch strap. He has the cards.

Thou shalt have a fishy, when the boat comes in.

I fold, Fabián says. It is too much.

His pupils are deflating to small, sharp coals. Blink.

I don't have that much with me, says Dave. Could get it in a couple of days, maybe.

Nobody says nothing. Dave buckles and unbuckles the watch strap. The ash on his cigarette is almost to the filter, beginning to bend under its own weight, about to drop.

Okay, he says, the boat. It's ocean-going. You boys might need that. It must be worth the money.

Blink. Blink. Blink. He has the cards.

We'll take the boat, I say, but you must show first.

Dave nods, and then he begins to lay his cards down, one by one. The dancing light of paraffin, cards in motion, nothing decided. I try to stretch it out. I try to make it last for ever. One heart after another, fat red berries. He has a heart flush. Must have been dealt it straight.

I drain my glass of beer. Astringent, medicine for the heart. Their eyes are on me, shining. The deep mahogany sheen of the tabletop. I begin to lay my cards down, one by one. Matthew, Mark, Luke and John. Four jacks.

Softly and soundlessly, the pillar of ash drops into the ashtray and the cigarette dies. A moth still presses at the window, patiently and persistently, looking for the moon.

2. Red-Throated Diver

(Gavia stellata)

The cold moon burned like a thumbprint smeared on the windowglass of the sky. I leaned back against the shutters of the pub and teased bitter cigarette smoke into my lungs. It was three years to the day since Yan went missing on the Falklands. I remember the phone ringing in the bar that day and Kate running to get it. She looked happy as she went, the smell of hairspray trailing behind her.

Back then it was all clunky mechanics, before fibre-optics and satellites and that. The baffling sequence of tiny relays and micro-switches it took to patch a phone call through the exchanges from one place to another. And if one switch among thousands flipped in the wrong direction you could be diverted to the far side of the world. Me and Paul used to play this game with the phone book. You pick an international code and dial a random number. Sometimes you get number unobtainable or the phone just rings and rings. But once in a while there's a click as someone picks up and then you hear a voice. A real person, from Uzbekistan, or Tasmania, or Tierra del Fuego, someone you'll never see. Someone you'll never meet.

When this happened we pissed ourselves laughing and slammed the receiver down.

Kate didn't like to see me smoking. Even though I was sixteen and she chained herself hoarse on them Superkings. You know the ones, look like a magician's wand when you wag them between finger and thumb.

I'm your mam Danny, she said. It's a do as I say not as I do thing.

Not my fault, I said. It's the absence of a father figure.

I leaned against those blistered shutters and tried to get my technique right. How did he smoke? There was a thumb and forefinger raise to the mouth, then a quick sucking of breath, the cheeks concave. Pursed lips and a furtive look around like a schoolkid smoking in the bogs.

I watched the early traffic on Port Clarence Road, winding down towards the Transporter. My cigarette died in the raw blustery wind rattling down the river, and inside the pub the phone began to shrill.

Phones get me thinking about life, about the complexity of patching yourself through from there to here like an electron singing in a wire. Each time you make a choice – no matter how trivial – you flip one of them micro-switches, you make a new connection. And maybe that's enough to derail the future onto some inscrutable new track. Maybe that's enough to send you to Uzbekistan. And maybe your old track – your old destiny – just shrivels up and dies right there and then and you never even know it was laid out ready for you.

It was dark in the bar with stacks of chalky unwashed glasses, dead and wounded butts mounded up in the ashtrays. The sharp smell of stale beer like vomit, like kissing a girl with rancid breath. Hagan never cleared up after a stoppy-back.

I gripped the receiver, one of them old bakelite things.

Cape of Good Hope.

A trickle of electrons rattled into the earpiece and came out as a familiar voice, the accent so thick it was almost Scouse.

Now then daft cunt, it's Jonah.

Now then Uncle Jonah.

I'd been half expecting him to ring today. Mark the anniversary somehow.

Red-throated diver, he said. Hartlepool Fish Quay. Worth a gander?

Aye. I'll meet you down there. Do you know what day it is?

He was silent for a moment. Gusts of static on the line.

I know, he said.

I fumbled for a tab and flipped the lighter, flame fluttering like a moth in the ugly darkness of the bar. Franco was over there, stretched out asleep on the fake leather bench under the window. Must have drawn the short straw and missed out on a bed. I walked over and looked down at him, knotty and pickled like a conker that's been in vinegar, fading tats on the forearms and a little tache bobbing gently on his upper lip. He snuffled, tugging the leather jacket further over him, eyeballs swivelling in sleep behind the wrinkled lids. I sucked long and hard at the cigarette, extended it carefully above his face. I smiled at the thought. I was going to tap a gobbet of ash onto his eyelid, soft and bristling like a woolly bear caterpillar.

But I didn't. I let the ash fall on the floor and walked out into the morning.

Haverton Hill was a ghost town, them days. Used to be a thriving little place round the shipyards on the Tees. Then they built the ICI at Billingham, right on the doorstep, the biggest chemical complex in Europe, and the pollution knackered Haverton. The people had to go, even though they were here first. So a few year before I was born they knocked most of it down, moved people onto estates further out.

Now there was just the Cape, beached on its corner plot like a ship on a reef. And the railway bridge, a second-hand car lot and a scrapyard and an old gadge called Decko who lived in a caravan in the middle of his pigeon sheds. And further out were the pikeys with them threadbare horses chained up in the fields around the Hole and then the saltmarsh and the sharp wind crackling with sea and impending rain.

Along Port Clarence Road the hoardings groaned in the wind in front of the railway embankment. The River Tees over there, flat and brown, slipping quietly to the sea.

Now then Danny charver, do us a ciggy.

Paul lurched out of the bus shelter and fell into step with me.

I've left the tabs at home marra.

He started wheedling.

Away, I'm fucking gasping here.

I shrugged and we carried on and the tramp of his boots echoed from the pavement.

Me and Paul were near enough the same age but you wouldn't know it to look. He was half a head taller than me and grown into his muscles with a bonehead haircut that made him look like an Easter Island statue. He was fledged from rubble, from bramble and thorn, dragged up by his mam in one of the houses behind the Social Club. When we were at Port Clarence Primary he was the kid everyone was scared of, who got slippered for calling Mrs Reresby a saggy-titted old bitch and then just walked out of the gate and went home. He got away with murder cos he had these cool green eyes like unripe sloes and full raspberry lips and brown skin with a bloom behind it that made you want to touch. He just grinned at teachers and they melted. Even now, sheared and bagged off his head with lighter fluid on his breath and pupils the size of dinnerplates.

Rain began to whirl out of a sky which was bulging and thickening like a varicose vein. Icy drops swarmed over Paul's rosy, shorn head.

You've been through that lass, then. The Paki one.

Raz?

Aye. Carlo said.

She's Bangladeshi. I go there to do homework. Can't get any space in the pub with Hagan and all them.

Homework, he erupted, with a barking laugh. Shook his head. We crossed over these little stumpy streets of terraces, fifty yards of houses and then Back Saltholme. Half of them were empty and the council had cages on the windows.

That Gary Hagan, said Paul. One of these days he'll get his napper tapped off.

Our feet tramping in the wet, the huge metal sheds of Swan Hunter looming ahead.

Has he nailed yer mam yet?

Kate? He wants to. I don't reckon she's having it, mind.

She keeps him hanging round, though, eh?

She likes having a man behind the bar.

I've seen her looking, he said. She wants me.

Fuck off.

A bus shimmied past us, headlights rippling like moonlight on the wet road. We swerved to avoid the spray.

I might fit her in me busy schedule, leered Paul. One of these days.

Go on then, I said. You're going to tell me anyway.

Paul's Munchausen sexual adventures. I assumed they were fiction, I half feared they were true.

Well, he said. There's this one. Hazel, from Pally Park. Went through seventeen squaddies in one go, what I heard. Me and Dog were up there the other night, panelling fuck out of it, one end each. Get yourself down with us sometime, you could squirt your beans in there as well.

There was a pause while I considered this tempting invitation. We were nearly at the bus stop.

I'm on the bus, I said. I hoped he wouldn't come along.

On the bus. There's cigarette smoke lazing through a shaft of sunlight and you lean your head on the window and the rattle of the diesel makes your thoughts dance away on a tide of vibration. Reclaimed fields on the estuary, unearthly green where the spring grass is beginning to stir, and below them the black earth and ballast and the alluvium of the old estuary in volume on volume like the pages of a damp book. A pair of teal rise on stiff wings and the air thrums in their tailfeathers and they fly for the shelter of a pair of cooling towers where steam blossoms high above the rim.

I called Jonah my uncle but he was just a mate of Yan's, back to when Noah was a lad. We went birding together, now and then, but his heart wasn't in it. He did it because it kept us in touch, and because of Yan. Like there was a thread he had to keep spinning.

Yan and me did the circuit two or three times a week, when he wasn't on base or on a tour. Haverton Hole, Saltholme and Back Saltholme and the Triangle, Dorman's and Reclamation, Greatham Creek and Calor Gas and Seal Sands and the Long Drag. Plus we turned out when a real crippler came in.

It's got to be some of the best birding in the country – one of the few consolations for living in this shitheap, said Yan. Maybe that's why he did what he did. But I always liked it here, where the river runs out of energy and the pylons are stalking their prey across country and the refineries and petrochemical plants come to fruition in giant rock formations, in hard cliffs and crags above the reclaimed land. I like the Cleveland Hills making a bunched fist on the horizon, shafts of cold sunlight sweeping across their flanks, across the distant estates of Middlesbrough.

I like hanging on by the fingernails. The honesty of it.

It wasn't the battery of telescopes you get for a real rarity, but a few of them at the edge of the dock with nowt better to do on a Saturday morning. I recognized a couple of the blokes and we nodded without speaking. I pulled my bins out and focused on the diver down there beyond the staithes, long and low and the water gulping right over its back. Right on the membrane between two elements. Sea and sky. Water and air.

You always find them at the front of the bird book because they're supposed to be the most primitive family, the furthest back towards reptiles. A seamless curve of bill and head and neck, sharp and snaky as a new pencil. Sea grey above and ghost white below and the eye like a bead of blood.

The bird blinked upside-down, silver membrane wiping the eyeball from below. Humped its back and dived. We glanced around and some-one lit a cigarette. I thought of mine, still sat on the bar in the Cape. Rain stippled the surface of the water, soft and insistent, and the bird bobbed back to the surface with a shrug. It didn't notice the rain. The eye, like a berry.

Blink.

Water.

Blink.

Air.

They winter at sea, red-throated divers. Range all over the Arctic and the north Atlantic and only bad weather brings them to harbour looking for shelter. They're out there now, weighing about the same as a bag of sugar.

Blink.

Water.

Blink.

Air.

A hand clapped on my shoulder and I whirled round to see Jonah.

Danny, he said, with a grin. A brown face creased like a well-worn slipper, the mouth baggy but the eyes sharp. Rain-beaded grey hair on his skull like coal ash.

Saw these nesting up in Shetland once, he said. On Fetlar. Handsome things in breeding plumage, like. They call it the rain goose up there. Used to believe it could predict the coming of storms. Some still do, I dare say. When you see the rain goose there's a storm on the way. Close up the shutters, get the livestock inside.

The bird dived again, rain becoming harder.

Is there a storm on the way? I asked him.

There's always a storm somewhere, said Jonah. He pulled the tatty denim jacket closer round himself and shivered.

We stood in silence for a while and watched the diver working its way back towards open water. Jonah shook his head.

Birders, he said, with a grin. Are we a bunch of fruitloops or are we the sanest bastards on the planet? Or is it just a good excuse to get away from the ball and chain?

All of the above, I said. And none of the above.

Jonah pulled out a pouch and began to roll a cigarette one-handed. It was like watching a card sharp, fingers blurring, flying. He tore a cardboard roach and notched it into the end, lit a match behind his hand. The smoke billowed from his mouth.

I taught your dad how to skin one-handed, he said. We would have been about fifteen. Mind you, he always rolled too thin. Like a fucking convict, he was, sucking at them little straws.

What was Yan, then? Sane, mental, or itchy feet?

Loony, said Jonah. Always a storm brewing, always a high wind racing behind them eyes.

I laughed.

Nah, he was a strange one. It was almost like he was a rare bird himself. One of these vagrants and passage migrants, blown around the place.

You know these birds, the journeys they make, I drawled, in imitation of Yan's voice. Makes Marco Polo look like a travelling salesman. Makes Neil Armstrong look like an average high-jumper. If you want a mythical hero, he's wearing feathers.

Jonah smirked. That's exactly what he used to say.

I know.

See, he said, we both had this restlessness thing – the itchy feet business. It was straightforward for me. Easy come, easy go, a woman in every port. The old cliché. Simple enough in the merchant navy. But your dad, he wanted it every which way.

Rain streaming down now, droplets worming down the back of my collar, twisting at the corners of my mouth.

I mean, he wanted the adventure, Jonah continued. But he wanted the home life as well, the family. Later on, when he had Kate and you, I couldn't help thinking that he'd got it right. All I had was an empty council house to rattle around in every few months, and a few extra notches on the bedpost. A few ships, a few tinnies and a few fucks. Not much to base a life on.

He grinned sheepishly, dragged hard at the cigarette which was struggling in the rain.

Anyways, he said, glancing at his watch. I've got a young lady to entertain. But I thought I might nip into the Cape tonight, for a quick one. We can have a pint on the old bastard if nothing else. Nine-ish?

Aye. See you then.

He buffeted me on the shoulder again and stumped away, disappearing quickly in the monsoon. Out in the harbour the bird dived, the black surface of the water untroubled. I didn't wait for it to surface.

I was drenched when I reached the pub. Paul was leaning against the wall equally sodden, snakes of water twining over his oxblood Docs. Pushed himself off as I approached, with a shake and a sneeze like a wet dog.

Hang on out here.

I cracked the door and swung into the bar. Still blousy, uncleaned, bilious. Franco had vanished from the bench. I stood a moment and listened. Thumping from upstairs, somebody blundering about, bath taps thundering. That was probably Kate. Ten thirty and the bar still a swamp. The pack of Embassy lying on the bar unclaimed. I swept it up and made for the door, then turned on second thoughts and dived behind the bar. Crisps, chocolate, cans from the chiller.

Nice one, said Paul, as I emerged. Special Brew. You know how to treat a lady.

We took shelter in one of the abandoned lots along Cowpen Bewley Road, found a portakabin, gutted and derelict but still almost watertight. Used to be the office for a car dealership, moved out two years ago. Old filing cabinets spilled their guts, paperwork strewn over the floor, the carpet sprouting mould.

Listen to your Uncle Paul, he boomed, several cans later, already leaden-faced with the alcohol. You want to get out, start living. I'm looking after your best interests here son.

I tossed over a can, the last one. I was pole-axed, sprawled on the floor, holding on to shreds of consciousness.

I've got a job now, chuntered Paul. On the landfill up the road here. Cash in hand. Better than the YTS – know what that stands for?

Youth Training Scheme, isn't it? I tried to focus on an old works calendar. A woman's body with a tyre tread rolling down her spine, between her buttocks.

Your Tough Shit, that's what it stands for. Twenty-six fucking quid a week, I ask you.

I made what I hoped was a noise of agreement.

Look at yourself Danny. Your dad's gone for good. Yer mam – she wants to move on. She wants a new dick. You got to look after number one. Empty the fucking till and get your own gaff. Forget about school and exams. Exams is just pieces of paper. Here, look.

He picked up a stray sheet of paperwork from the floor, brandished it at me, then turned his back and peeled down the skin-tight jeans to expose a pair of rosy buttocks. He balled the paper in one hand and ostentatiously wiped his arse with it, dragging it down his crack from front to back, then pinging it against the wall.

That's what you do with fucking exams, he grinned as he hauled up his jeans, eyes bulging. Learn how to party son, because you're only young once. You don't want to look back and ask yourself where it all went.

He was silhouetted starkly in the doorway, braced against either side. Behind him a flock of lapwings rose like smoke from the flooded pools of Haverton Hole, the piping call taken up by every bird, echoing over the marsh. They blew over on rain-softened wings. People were full of advice these days, full of certainty. I was too mashed to come up with any answers. In the end Paul lurched off in search of more entertainment. I could hear his boots receding across the cinder yard. I could hear Yan's boots coming up the stairs of the pub. Rise and shine me hearties. No rest for the wicked. Have you ever seen a paddyfield warbler? The scratch of the fingers rubbing the stubble on his chin.

The sound of him coming up the stairs, the clatter of his feet filling the stairwell, swelling out into the world.

I woke up, mouth burning with acid, with rust and chemicals. It was dark, and I was in the tiny box room at the back of the pub. I couldn't remember finding my way back from the portakabin. Noise bursting from downstairs, loud inflamed voices. I looked at the red, blinking eye of the clock radio. Half past nine. Nausea rumbled through me like a distant train.

Jonah. Nine-ish, he'd said.

I stumbled out onto the dark landing. Squalls of noise from the bar downstairs. On the stairs in the dark, hand on a wooden banister smoothed by countless other hands. Kate thought the pub was haunted. Like someone watching me, she said. And when I turn round, there's nobody. Yan laughed at her. I'll take any customer, living or dead, as long as they pay for their ale. You can only have a tab if you've got a fucking pulse.

Ghosts, I thought, that day on the stairs. Every pub must have ghosts. All the feet that have traipsed through it, all the lives that have been threaded through it. And Yan, too. Perhaps he's one of them now.

They were crowded round the pool tables. Watching, jostling, thumbs in waistbands, smoke billowing up from cigarettes clamped between lips and wedged into ashtrays. Gary Hagan himself was behind the bar, back to me, laughing at some harsh banter. A stark shaft of light roared down onto the green baize, solidified the dribbles of fagsmoke like candlewax poured into cold water. The rest of the bar was dark.

Fuck off, bellowed Jonah. You're underage.

He punched me on the arm and burst into ringing laughter, face creasing like a leather glove. Michelle served us, beer slopping into the pint glasses like whipped cream. Dark rodent eyes kept flipping dumbly up to mine as she waited for them to fill. You shouldn't be here, they said. She swiped the crumpled greenies from Jonah's fingers and turned away.

We found a table and sat down. Jonah raised his pint.

Here's to your old man, then.

He sipped thoughtfully, brow knitting.

Where's Kate?

Upstairs. Go up and have a word, if you like.

Still on the smiley pills?

Aye. She's camped in front of the telly most of the time. Like a kid gawping at the fishtank in the dentist's waiting room.

He frowned and lifted his glass, swirled the brown liquid round and round.

Keep expecting him to walk back through that door, he said. He had plans for this place, once he was out of the army.

Funny, that. He was always slagging the area off.

That's the paradox, said Jonah. When you're here, you want out. But when you're on the other side of the world you get this ache. It's like migration. You don't understand why but you have to do it.

He sipped his beer.

Your dad certainly did the rounds, he said. Germany, Belize, Norn Iron.

There was an old gadge at the bar, waiting to get served. Decko – the one who lived with his pigeons. Michelle kept cutting him a glance and then serving someone else. Magoo hauled himself over from the pool table, shiny-faced with the beergut thrust in front of him.

Do you know who this fucking is? he yelled at Michelle across the bar. He clapped a meaty paw on the old feller's shoulder, gold rings clustered on the swollen fingers. Light flickered though his sparse blonde hair as he turned to address the bar.

This ladies and gentlemen, he roared, face an ugly mask under the hard overhead light. This is the hardest man on Teesside. This is the bareknuckle champion of County Durham, Mr Declan Leary.

Decko glanced round, embarrassed. Thick white hair Brylcreemed back and stained yellow, dandruff on the shoulders of the shabby suit. You hardly ever heard him talk, except to his birds.

Took on allcomers, this gadge, announced Magoo. Nineteen forties, nineteen fifties. Me old man told me the stories.

He set his jaw forward like a bulldog and let an explosive belch go. Kurt sidled over to the bar, big blue eyes, cheekbones and a psychobilly quiff. Him and Magoo bookending the old man, towering over him.

Now mate, he said to Decko. Never knew you were a fucking brawler.

Not just a fucking brawler, roared Magoo. He was the fucking best. In the upstairs rooms and the backlots. Put any cunt on his back for half a crown, eh? Every gold-toothed pikey bastard, every plastic hardman in Boro.

Kurt grinned, turned and scanned the bar, one of his unearthly blue eyes squinting off to one side.

D'y'ever kill a man Decko?

Decko shook his head.

Aye he did, yelled Magoo. Some gadge who swallowed his own tongue. Me dad said he was on his back with foam coming out of his gob, eh? But his feet kept tapdancing for a full twenty minutes. Twenty fucking minutes.

Decko shook his head again.

Ow Michelle, said Kurt. Get the man a pint in, eh? On the house, like.

She turned and looked at Decko.

Mild, he said.

Jonah swirled his glass round.

You were born with a caul Danny, he said. You know what that is?

Aye.

It's the sac you're inside. In the womb. Keeps you from drowning in there. Most times it breaks up during the birth, but you were born with it right over your head. They had to strip it off so you could start breathing.

Aye, I know.

Jonah dropped his voice.

I kept it, he said. Asked Kate if I could. I've still got it.

Why?

Michelle plonked the pint down in front of Decko but Kurt lifted it up from the bartowel and had a good gulp.

Away then champ, he said, tapping his chin. Let's fucking go. Let's fucking 'ave you.

He started to bob and weave and throw imaginary punches. Magoo roared with laughter.

It's a powerful talisman, that's why, said Jonah. Against drowning.

I snorted.

Been a merchant navy cook twenty year, Jonah went on. Hard as nails, been called all the names under the sun for the state of my food. But what fucking terrifies me Dan, is going down with a ship.

I watched the creases dance around his eyes, the way his nose bobbed up and down when he was animated. He reached across the table and gripped my forearm. I looked into his eyes, steady and brown.

It keeps the terror down, he said. Just having it tucked away, stowed in my kitbag. I know it's just a barmy old superstition.

But.

Aye. But.

He laughed.

Franco leaned back against the bar with his cue. He had these deep hungry eyes like wormholes, sunken cheeks you could measure between thumb and forefinger.

Makes you think, he said. The old hardmen, they're all coffin dodgers now.

Magoo leaned back next to him, tee-shirt riding up his kite.

Back then like, said Franco. It was all white, eh? None of your monkey men over here. Coons.

He was looking at Jonah.

Did you ever try to find out what really happened to your dad?

His voice was low and urgent.

I shrugged. The army just told us the bare bones, I said, flatly. He was in action at Mount Longdon, not long before the surrender. It was a mess, close quarters and that. Afterwards, well, he'd just gone. Never seen again. No body, no nothing.

Spoken to anyone who was actually there?

Jonah's eyes were focused on me, large and dark like an owl's.

Nah. I never tried. Look, if he was alive, he'd have been in touch, wouldn't he?

Jonah studied me. I used to have a map of the Falklands up on my bedroom wall, when the war was on. All them little islands round the coast, Keppel and Pebble and Carcass and Sedge. North Fur and South Fur. Elephant Jason, Flat Jason, Grand Jason, Steeple Jason. I looked at that map every day, those long weeks while they were crawling south, wondering where Yan would be, which of those names would become real places. And then some of them did. And then I took the map down and folded it up and put it in the bin.

It was a premature ejaculation, that war, Jonah smiled. Too much foreplay and not enough action. The sabre-rattling from Maggie after the Argies invaded, the Task Force crawling down the Atlantic. Weeks and weeks of it. But when they landed it was over in a flash. Wham bam thank you ma'am and we're lying back on the pillows lighting a bifter.

Any bananas back there Michelle? Kurt's voice sailed over from the bar. We got a monkey sat over here.

The problem with wogs, said Franco, conversationally, is when they start interbreeding with white women.

Ignore him, said Jonah. I've had worse from toddlers. The thing is Dan, you need to know. One way or another. You remind me of Schrödinger's cat.

Who?

Ah. It's a scientific parable man. Supposed to describe how particles behave. How different possibilities can exist at the same time.

I looked blank.

There's a professor, right? And he locks his cat in a box.

Poor pussy.

Jonah grinned, but pressed on. Now this is the clever bit. In the box there's a vial of some radioactive shit. And there's a fifty-fifty chance that an atom of this stuff decays over the next twenty-four hours. If that happens, it sets off a chemical reaction, produces a poisonous gas, and the cat snuffs it. But if that atom doesn't decay, the cat lives. Confused, hungry, and mighty pissed off, but alive.

There were monkey noises at the bar, but I tuned them out, focusing in on Jonah. His quiet, insistent voice.

Nobody can predict the outcome, he was saying. Nobody knows what's happened until they open the box twenty-four hours later, and when they open the box there's got to be an outcome. The cat is a hundred per cent alive or a hundred per cent dead. But *before* they open the box, before they know the outcome, the cat is flickering in between. Like a strobe light. Alive. Dead. Alive. Dead. Alive.

I don't get it.

You got to open the box to make it stick. Until then all the possibilities are floating about, shifting, like ghosts. Ghosts of probability.

He looked pleased with himself.

See, he said. You and Yan are the ghosts. Half alive and half dead, and the box is still shut. You know what you got to do Danny.

Let me tell you a joke, said Franco, pushing back a chair and sitting down at the table. They were standing around us now. Kurt picked up Jonah's pint glass, cleared his throat, spat in it, put it back down on the table. Phlegm wobbled like eggwhite on the surface of the beer. Jonah leaned back, put his hands behind his head.

What, said Franco, is white, and floats face down in the river?

He put his forearms on the table, sinews bunching and knotting under the bluestained skin. Jonah shrugged.

A nigger, said Franco. With all the shit kicked out of it.

Jonah smiled, thin-lipped, and the lads around the table erupted in laughter. Hagan just kept watching from behind the bar. He was a steroid case, pumped solid from the weights. Had these pudgy features that were goodlooking in a bulky way, a floppy blond wedge cut and a single gold hoop in his ear. He stood there, surrounded by glass. Glass mirrors on the wall, pint glasses nesting on the shelves like seabirds, glinting.

Didn't know you were a rent boy Danny, he said. You should have told me times were hard. I could have lent you some of your dad's money out of the till. Or maybes you just like taking it up the wrong'un.

He looked at Jonah. You should know better, grandad. He's underage for a start.

Jonah blinked.

I better be going Dan, he said, standing up and pushing his chair under the table. He turned to Hagan and raised his glass, studied the thick swirl of phlegm.

Not a bad pint pal. I've had worse. A lot worse.

He lifted it to his gob and necked it down in one, phlegm and all. Banged the empty glass down on the table and turned for the door.

Lads, said Hagan.

Magoo went for Jonah, face twisted like a hound dog reaching the end of its chain. Jonah stepped back and sent a stool flying and we watched it bounce across the tiled floor and stop.

And everything stopped, because Kate was stood in the doorway and Trajan was braced against her calves with a snarl stuck in his gullet. She was still beautiful, black hair flowing down her back like a Persian princess. But there was something taut about her these days, skin stretched too tight over the bones.

What's going on, Gaz?

She looked at Jonah.

What are you doing here?

Jonah grinned and raised his palms. Hagan's face flowered into an idiot smile.

There's glass on the floor, she said.

Hagan dived beneath the bar for dustpan and brush. Jonah had gone, left the door gently vibrating behind him. I pushed out into the street where the rain had stopped and there he was, leaning against the pole of the traffic lights, hands thrust into his pockets. I let a taxi glide past and jogged across to him.

Have we got any more business? he said. Red light flushed across his face from above, gave him the bulbous glow of a Halloween apple. I kicked the kerb, hard.

I don't know what to do.

Yeah you do.

How do I start?

Find out who was there with him. There must be some of them who came back. His mates.

But how can I trace them?

Did he have a diary or owt? Somewhere he wrote down names and numbers and that?

Aye. Come to think of it he did have this old address book.

Do you reckon it's still lying around somewhere? Back of a drawer, up in the attic?

Dunno. It might be.

There you go then.

Jonah beamed. Above him the lights changed and green light flooded across his face. Molten sunlight dripping through new leaves, transforming him into a mischievous satyr.

Upstairs in the box room and you don't need to switch on the light because the orange gloaming of Teesside and the gas flares on Billingham are beaming back off the cloudbase and the hangover kicking in behind your eyeballs. Yan clumping up the stairs in them steelcapped boots and the little click at each step from the tendon in his ankle. Yan dead on the Falklands, white shinbones in the peat. Ghosts of probability. Alive. Dead. Alive. Dead. Alive.

Put your hand down on the bedspread with the bitten-down nails and tell yourself it's real and solid.

3. Wilson's Storm Petrel

(Oceanites oceanicus)

I put my hand down on the wheel and look at the white flesh and bitten-down nails just to convince myself I'm real and solid. The wheelhouse door is swinging on its hinges, yawning open at the top of a crest and slamming shut in the guts of the following trough. And the weather gets worse, wind, spray and rain streaming across the open deck and bursting against the glass.

Can't make headway, yells Fabián Rodriguez. The weather full in our face. He moves the dials of the radio and the static howls and pops. Horse Boy curled on the floor in the foetal position with that coverless paperback up close to his coupon. Lips moving soundlessly.

South Georgia, says Joe Fish, hunkered down over the charts, his pocked face glowering from wet oilskins. We can sit it out there, in the lee of the island. Head back west when the weather clears.

Fuck me, a sentence without profanity, I mock. Aren't there Marines down there?

The imminence of death smartens up the tongue, he counters. They're at Grytviken only, I think. And it's a big island – a hundred miles long.

South Georgia, I say, shaking my head. What do you reckon Joe? Reckon there's another reality where I lost that hand, and right now the redcaps are getting started on me?

Pure shite, he says.

But chance is the breath of the universe marra. It's what keeps us sharp, eh?

No such thing as chance, he says. If you wound the world right back to the beginning and set it all off again, them cards would still come out the same. Every time.

I give him a slap round the chops, nice and gentle like.

That slap was predestined, I tell him. Nowt I could do about it.

Dave smells of sick, slumped on the bench seat with his mouth gaping. Wishing he never came along, I daresay.

Hang on, so who's Dave? He was a civvy, right?

Aye, he certainly wasn't a fucking para with that kite on him. Nah, he was hiding out at Berkeley when the rest of us pitched up.

Fabián as well?

Yep. The deserter from the other crew. Like a mirror image of me. Got on like a house on fire. Dave was in some sort of bother, I reckon, cos he was a right snidey customer.

But the boat was his?

Not after he lost it at cards, it wasn't. It was a decent bit of kit, mind. Four square sturdy metal tub, an ocean-going trawler with all the fishing gear ripped out. Dave reckoned he used it to run cheap snout and brandy over from South America into the Falklands. Kind of latter-day smuggler.

Sounds like bullshit to me, Yan.

Aye, maybe it was. But that old fish hold was still brimming with the sweet earthy scent of tobacco. Makes me want to spin a bifter up right now.

You can't. Not in here.

I know.

See, the idea was to just run south around Cape Horn and make landfall in Chile. Somewhere on that long coast north of Punta Arenas. But we reckoned without the weather, and now it's driving us south and east into the Southern Ocean. I begin to conjure up a cigarette between my cold fingers and the door rips open again with a splash of Antarctic air.

Vamos! yells Fabián Rodriguez. A squeal of static, a splurge of Spanish, and a soft rock tune starts among the spits of white noise. Not my taste, says Fabián, but it's the best I can give you.

Jesus wept, complains Joe. Is nothing sacred? Do we have to drown listening to this shit? Give me some decent music Fabián. Gene Vincent, some rockabilly. Something with a bit of fucking twang.

Unfortunately we can't receive redneck America this far south Joe, says Fabián, with his expressionless face. Otherwise I would be delighted to oblige you with some hillbilly shit.

Rockabilly man, not hillbilly.

Fabián has a sly smile flitting across his face. He loves to needle Joe, already. The cigarette bursts its sweet cargo into my lungs, and I swim with pleasure, think about the radio waves lapping around the earth.

Wavelength and amplitude. Radio waves, sound waves, ocean waves, the longer the wavelength, the deeper the note. South of Cape Horn the ocean circles the planet endlessly, never makes landfall. A wave can travel for ever, a hundred years and a thousand times around the planet, sucking the wind's breath since before you were born and bloating up into a monster. And the immense wavelength of the Southern Ocean creates a sound, a single enduring note beneath the percussion of wind and water. Impossibly deep, too deep for the ears, but you can sense it in your spine and your piss and the base of your skull. It can be sensed by Joe Fish, swimming over the charts, by Horse Boy, grimly thumbing his pages, by Dave, quivering on the bench, and by Fabián Rodriguez, twiddling at the radio. It can be sensed by me, hauling on a tiny cigarette. It is the sound of despair.

Suddenly the boat lurches to port, springs back again, as a rogue wave tilts her over. Dave shoots across the wheelhouse and slides down the opposite wall, groaning. He isn't badly hurt. Horse Boy flicks over another page, the movement of a moth's wing.

She'd better not crack Dave. She'd better not fucking split, says Joe, the coal of a cigarette jammed between his teeth.

She's solid Joe, he says, but I never had her in seas like this.

The seas are growing by the minute. You've seen an October storm at Hartlepool, the waves coming in off the North Sea. Green and grey and intricately muscled, exploding on the breakwater. Well this is something else, another order of magnitude. The water isn't grey and green but black. An absence of colour. Sculpted from coal and glittering with a million sharp and shifting facets.

I'm going to turn her into the wind, I yell. We'll have to try and ride it out. Going to capsize if we stay quarter on. Won't make any headway, but at least we can stay afloat.

I remember snatches of the next forty-eight hours, before the wind dropped and we ran before it like ocean birds, glimpsing South Georgia like a row of rotten teeth on the horizon. I fought sleep grimly, keeping the boat head on to the seas.

There's a cycle to it. Megahertz and cycles per second. Rapid eye movement and slow wave. The boat wallows in a sunless deep, a smooth glacial valley, and the hills are singing with landslide. And you glide across shimmering waterlands until the scarp slope looms and hurls you upward through sea meadows and crags and arêtes and the air is shrinking and your ears are popping. And a mudslide screams around the bows and swamps the deck and the boat disappears until there's only a wheelhouse standing alone in the middle of the Southern Ocean. The air thin and cold and the ranges of water unfurling to the rim of the world. The curvature of the earth, that narrow girdle.

You wait.

And the boat explodes from the sea bucking like a horse and shaking off the furious water with great sighs and whipcracks from the steel. But she doesn't have time for breath before the ground drops away into nothing and her feet are skittering on the edge and we plunge down the screes in a tangle of limbs and sea is sky and down is up and we drown in air and breathe ocean until she points her bows up and we emerge into a sunless deep and the boat wallows.

That's it. Megahertz and cycles per second. Once is terrifying and a thousand times is numb. Rapid eye movement and slow wave, while sleep grips your eyelids with unrelenting teeth and you roll and smoke cigarette after cigarette in unending rhythm.

Don't stop reading, I shout to Horse Boy, who is still crouched on the floor, braced against the leaps of the boat. Water, wind, chaos, batter at the wheelhouse with lumpen fists. We've taped the door shut to keep the sea out, but water is squeezing through the gaps like shameful tears.

What's the book? I yell. He's been reading it since the Task Force, on the slow limp southward, and it's the first time I've asked him about it. He shouts something back and I only catch a single word. Crime.

What, Agatha Christie? It was the vicar, with a pickaxe, in the ladies' bogs, I bellow.

No… Punishment, I hear, above the crunching water.

Do you want to know what happens? I shout, mischievously.

The boat submerges at the top of the swell, which rises momentarily over the windows of the wheelhouse. Water squirts through the cracks. I see Horse Boy mouth the words fuck off. The boat bursts clear.

Keep reading it anyway. It's about redemption. Redemption for a man who's committed a terrible crime. Do you think that's possible? No matter how ugly the deed?

I'm talking to myself. He can't hear, doesn't even look up. Keep reading it anyway. If you stop, we will drown.

There's water in the fucking hold, we're going down. Joe bursts into the wheelhouse, drenched. She's riding lower in the water man. Can't you feel it?

The steel structure moans in agreement. There's no way she's going to survive this. She's taking too much punishment, too many stresses. Before too long the boat is going to disintegrate. How long will we last when that happens? A minute or two in the water perhaps, or a long slow plunge inside the boat.

We can pump it out, yells Dave, I've done it before. Water gets down there through the hatches and the companionways. Doesn't mean we've sprung a leak.

Aye, she's fucking burst, snarls Joe. It's pouring in somewhere, mark my words.

Whatever, shouts Fabián. Get the pumps working. It will give us more time.

They duck below. Their eyes are yellowed and there are bruises all over them from slips and falls when the boat thrashes about. The deep note of the sea underneath us all like the deep bell of a cathedral baying in the murk.

Jonah said this was his worst nightmare. I remember him talking about it one stoppy-back in the Cape when the cards had gone away but the whisky had stayed out. Talked about the fleet lost off Scilly back in the seventeen hundreds, the flagship plunging towards the bottom, stern windows still burning green in the phosphorescent depths and the hands of the admiral's little daughters clawing at the glass. Partial to a bit of gothic horror, was Jonah. But when he talked about taking that dive towards the seabed in some old tin can, the pressure building and the metal screaming and the rivets popping, you could see the sweat springing from his pores and the terror in his eyes and that was real enough.

They were white, those little hands. Muslin falling away from the forearms, white as a pelagic bird.

And I drag up from near sleep to a bird hovering at the glass, almost pattering against the window. Tiny and dark with a pale rump and ghostly crescent moons on the upper wings. It hangs there like a bat, flimsy legs dangling beyond the end of its tail, knit together with hollow bones sharp and white as ivory needles.

Wilson's storm petrel. See, I've still got it, even here.

These little beauties are super-abundant, the commonest seabird on the planet, but most of us will never see one because they're deep ocean wanderers, from the Subarctic to the Southern Ocean, from the Davis Strait to the Weddell Sea. Their bubble and our bubble don't often coincide. When they're feeding they walk on water, tiny feet treading the swell, pattering like black moths on the ocean. And here we are, in the trough between two monster waves, in the trough between two heartbeats. The man in the wheelhouse and the bird at the glass. The tiny black eye like a miniature planet, the strange little tubular nostrils. One of us is found and one of us is lost. One is solid and one is frail as wastepaper. One is everything and one is nothing. We study each other just for a moment until the boat rides up on the surge and the petrel is plucked away into the storm. It becomes part of the wind and the sea and is lost to us.

On the foredeck one of the inflatable boats is working loose. We lashed them down hard before the weather closed in, but some of the lashings have come adrift. Dave squints at me through bloodshot eyes.

We need those boats Yan. Can't get ashore without them. We can't just run up on the beach like the Vikings.

We're going to lose them pretty soon. Better than drowning out there trying to secure them.

There's a harness and lanyard. We could rig someone up to the safety cables. You couldn't get washed overboard.

I look at Joe.

Fuck off, he says, then shows me a clenched fist, looking at my hand, which is extended, flat.

Paper wraps stone, I say, briefly enfolding his fist. Joe rolls his eyes.

I'll go, says Horse Boy, looking up from *Crime and Punishment*, for the first time in hours.

He works his way slowly forward along the deck, towards the bows. We remain focused on his receding figure, with the boat pitching and rolling and the ocean swinging alarmingly behind him. A couple of times the sea comes over and he crouches down for stability, disappears under, and then emerges again as the boat bucks clear. I'm holding on to his book. It's served us well and I'm not going to break the spell.

I flick to the end and skim through because I've forgotten. Forgotten how Sonia follows Raskolnikov to prison, all the way to Siberia, waits for him all those years until they let him go. It makes me shiver. Faced with that mute and unconditional love I'd put my head down in her lap and beg for her forgiveness. But then maybe I'd slap her dumb fucking doughy face away and run to the hills.

Horse Boy makes it to the bow, bends to fumble with the lashings. It takes an age to secure the inflatable with wet rope and numbed hands. But now he's working his way back towards us along the centre of the deck. He is there as the boat crests a sickening wave and wallows right under. The sea swamps the entire bow, the rails and the deck disappearing below the water. And all we can see from the wheelhouse is Horse Boy, facing us, standing up to his waist in water, with a thousand miles of Southern Ocean howling around him and another thousand fathoms beneath his feet. He hangs on to the lanyard, and as he looks at us his mouth opens in a scream of terror. We think it's a scream of terror, but then he shows his teeth and he's laughing wildly. He stands alone like a figurehead in the middle of the ocean, laughing like a lunatic and raving incoherently at the storm.

Fabián and Joe Fish emerge from below, smeared with oil, but their teeth are glittering in their beards.

We're fucking dry boy, roars Joe. There's no leak, we're fucking dry.

I'm starting to fall apart. The vibration of the sea shaking me to pieces, the deep note beneath the storm. They've lashed me upright at the wheel with spare electrical flex. It stops the crazy bucking of the ship flinging me about inside the wheelhouse. I've already smashed a hand against the deck. Tobacco is running low and I'm shaking and I'd do anything to stop that sound. Begin to think that the flex is holding me together.

I grapple with the radio, turning the volume to max, bringing it into competition with the storm and the vibration.

And there's a woman's voice, big and meaty and almost masculine, jumping straight to your head like a jolt of raw vodka, cold and crystal clear. I don't know the singer, don't understand the words, but Fabián tells me later that she's Mercedes Sosa and that the song is called 'Las Golondrinas' – the swallows. And the song puts swallows in my head. Swallows racing gleefully above the chimneys of an Argentine town and storm petrels pattering above the Southern Ocean. The voice of Mercedes Sosa is infused with joy and with regret – infused with life – and the deep drone of the ocean no longer matters. And I know in that moment that nobody is lost, that redemption is possible for everybody. Whether we are convicts in Siberia or lost on the Southern Ocean. Birds are over the sea, and they are calling to us.

4. Snow Bunting

(Plectrophenax nivalis)

There are gulls blowing over the house, their shrill barking tangled with the alarm's electronic yelp. Five minutes ago they were over the sea but now they're headed for some damp playing field inland. I'm quick to hit snooze but Kelly stirs and turns over.

Dan, she murmurs. Drops back into sleep, her breath dark and muggy. I place my hand on the lump of her back to feel her lungs fill with air, expel it again. And then I unpeel the tangled covers and lever myself from the bed.

Down in the kitchen there's a reluctant light crawling beneath the blinds. I boil water in the stainless pan and then let it bubble on for a while just so I can listen to it plink. Unhurried and reassuring, the companionship of boiling water while dawn grows imperceptibly outside. I bolt my tea and let myself out into the street with stomach growling and feel the latch slip gently back into place behind me. Silent, these modern brick boxes with plastic windows, the same identikit streets all over Stockton. I almost wish myself back at the Cape, with lads on billy kicking off in the bar and ghosts in the stairwell. But the Cape has gone – I've driven past the cleared site, the mounds of rubble and buddleia. I've never stopped.

I've seen on the forum there are snow buntings down at North Gare. It's the right kind of weather for them, a biting northeaster coming from the sea with snow behind it. But you need to be patient with these birds. The harder you look, the more they withhold themselves. And just when you've given up and headed for the car, they're all around you with a splurge of laughter, a jangle of keys, conjured from the clotted snow clouds bearing down from Siberia.

So I'm in no hurry. I stroll down past the breakwater, the Gare itself, butting out into the river's mouth towards its twin on the southern side. They were built from iron and steel slag, thousands of tons of it from the foundries across the river, back in the old days. South Bank, Grangetown, Lackenby, Dormanstown. You can still pick up chunks of slag on the beach and see the gas bubbles frozen there.

And then I'm on the beach, strewn out towards Seaton and the dark stump of Hartlepool Headland. A couple of eider and a cormorant out on the water, common gull and yellowlegs. Ice at the sea's edge, crunching beneath my feet. You can look back along the river here, past the concrete hulk of the nuclear power station and Tioxide and the ghost ships at Able's, across the Seal Sands refineries to what remains of the Billingham site. And on the southern side there's Lackenby and Teesside Cast Products, some of it still running and some of it derelict, and beyond it more petrochemicals at Wilton. Wherever you are on the estuary there's a faint hum, the quiet respiration of all this industry. And when the last plant closes down even that will stop.

There's nobody else here. Colour drained from the river, the sea and the sky. Entropy. The sapping of energy. A universe staggering to a halt, unable to expand any more. And the cloud banks keep coming over the North Sea. Leaden and purple and swollen with new snow.

I've come way down the beach so I walk up into Seaton Carew and linger for a few minutes outside a sleeping pub. Jonah's local, when he was ashore. In summer he'd pad around Seaton with no shoes or socks on, just a tee-shirt and his crumpled tracksuit bottoms, wandering into the pubs and the amusements, frittering away his time. They never discovered what sank her. She just disappeared in heavy weather somewhere in the North Pacific. A freak wave probably, one of them giants thrown up by a trick of wind and water. I peer through the window, half expecting to see him in there, bent over a pint. But only the fruit machines stir in dreams of coloured light, gentle waves washing across the curtains.

When I come back along the beach there are one or two dogwalkers, faces swollen up with snow, pregnant with weather. And there's a figure on the foreshore between sea and land, where the shimmering tide moistens the sand. Sanderling are skittering almost to his feet, tiny and pale, legs a blur and bills dabbing.

I recognize the way he smokes. There's a thumb and forefinger raise to the mouth, then a quick sucking of breath, the cheeks concave. Pursed lips and a furtive look around like a schoolkid smoking in the bogs.

Snow buntings, he says, as I approach. Stands his ground, looks at me steady with them mobile grey eyes in the square face, skin sallow like parchment and the hair close-cropped and greying. He tugs the big donkey jacket around him, wings of the collar riding up round his ears.

I was thinking about Jonah, I say.

Oh aye?

An uncomfortable silence. Yan thrusts his hands deep into his pockets.

Did he ever tell you about the caul?

I nod.

What a chopper, believing in that cack. Didn't do him much good in the end like. I only hope it was quick. That he never went down inside her.

He smiles tightly.

Talismans don't work, he says. There's no magic.

Outside the river's mouth ships are waiting, lights blinking in a hesitant dawn, the shimmering lights of Teesmouth ahead like a winter city, on cooling towers and flare stacks, condensers and refineries. Yan turns and begins to walk away, along the beach. I stumble after him, and suddenly I'm a child again, struggling to keep up with those long legs. After a few steps he stoops and picks something up, brushes it with his fingertips, then rummages in a pocket and shows me a clutch of sea-smoothed glass in his palm. Clear, blue, green, the glass eyes of the sea, with cataracts of salt.

You used to collect these, he says. When you were a kid.

That was thirty year ago, I shrug.

But I take them anyway, from his outstretched palm.

We wander through the dunes, between the beach and golf course, snowclouds beetling above us. A couple of rock pipits, tails beating forlornly. I sit down on the flank of a dune where a fence of wire and staves is almost submerged beneath drifts of pale sand and marram grass bristles under the arctic hand of the wind.

What do you want Yan?

He looks taken aback. Squats down next to me, and spins a cigarette, while I inhale the warm aromas of stale tobacco and sweat drifting from his jacket. He sparks it up, wind buffeting the flame of his lighter.

I've been meaning to talk to you, he says.

Phone, e-mail, carrier pigeon, I drone ironically, raising my palms in supplication.

Chance is better, he says, eyes flashing mischievously. Anyways, I've been in Pattaya.

You've been in Pattaya most of the last twenty years.

And the rest. Kathmandu, Lombok, Sydney, Benares. But Pattaya's got it all. The beach, the beers, the boom boom. A bar takes a lot of running Dan. And the women are incredible, apart from the ones with dicks.

I hear there's no way of telling, some of them.

I can tell, he says, with a wink. And the opium is something else. Jesus Christ. Like raw cane sugar dripping over your brain. Have you ever?

He catches my glance.

No, he says. You wouldn't have.

He pulls hard on the little roll-up. Dust-devils of smoke scurry away on the wind.

What are you doing back here, then?

I've still got the house in Hartlepool. Tenants need a kick up the backside, every now and then.

He hesitates, licks his lips. Runs a hand over the stubble on his head. Look. He pauses. I wanted to see more of you. You've not made it easy for me Dan. You've kept me away, acted like you didn't need the old fella. Can't keep it up for ever man. You must be knocking on forty.

Thirty-eight. And you haven't been here most of the time. Pattaya and the rest.

Chicken and egg, he says. Squashes his dog end into the sand. What else was there to do, after Kate sacked me off?

I'm suddenly angry. I stand up.

You'd have gone anyway, I say. And I don't know what you've come back for.

I start to walk away, and he doesn't follow. When I look back he's still squatting there gazing out to sea, wind tugging at the loose skin of his face. And then snow buntings are whirling up from the ground, over the round dunes choked with gorse, along the runnels and hollow ways of the foreshore. I follow them, watch them feed among the thin stands of marram, Arctic sparrows in buff and white. And when I draw near the closest birds flick up and over the heads of the rest, and the whole flock flurries away like a rolling snow squall, tumbling over the next dune, coming to rest. Small contact calls, keeping the flock together. And then they're gone, lost among the tufts and scribbles of snow streaming across the sand and brawling through the dunes.

The house is enclosed, turned in upon itself like a seed case. Curtains drawn, blinds at the windows, no lights. Perhaps she's still asleep. I creep in, feeling like a burglar in my own house, wincing as the latch clicks. In the kitchen I stand at the fridge and pour a glass of cold milk. Neck it, feeling the cool liquid rise against my stubble. And then I take a step back and knock against one of the stools at the breakfast bar. It tumbles over, clatters across the tiled floor, comes to a stop. And everything is still. Kelly standing in the doorway, the cat rubbing at her calves.

I called you, she says, last night.

She's barefoot, long dirty blonde hair rumpled from sleep, curves hidden under the towelling dressing gown.

I know. Saw the missed calls. It's noisy in the pub, I don't hear it go off.

You know what alcohol does to sperm quality.

Yeah, and coffee, and sweeteners. And air.

She smiles, blue eyes bleary, that little curl, almost a sneer, tugging at her upper lip.

Anyways, I say. I wasn't on the beer.

She's rubbing at the side of her face insistently, letting me know I've still got milk smears in my stubble. I choose to ignore her for a moment.

She bends and rights the stool, perches on it.

You need to get yourselves some friends Dan. Some interests that aren't just for creeps and loners.

But I am a creep and a loner.

I close the fridge door crisply, and lean back against it. She puckers her mouth, sighs. I shrug, grab my work jacket down from the coat hook, start to thread myself into it.

Where are you going?

Got an installation booked.

It's Saturday.

Can't afford to turn work down.

I head for the door.

I'm ovulating.

Stop in my tracks, turn round and look at her.

The mucus, she says. It's just right. Wipe your mouth.

I wipe it.

Is there any point? I say. Thought we were going down the IVF route now. Perhaps I should be saving myself for that plastic cup.

She smiles, just for an instant. Just a tug at the corners of her mouth. Stops herself.

*

Stay there, she says, afterwards. Until you're flaccid.

I look down at her face and she smiles that little smile again and stops herself again. And I stay put. Like two dogs joined together, I think, despite myself.

Saw Yan today, I tell her. On the North Gare.

She looks up at me, that slight cast in her left eye. Struggles to focus.

Back in the country, is he? she says. What did he want?

Not sure. Wants to play happy families.

Bit late for that.

Mind, I had the feeling there was something he wasn't telling me.

Maybe he's lost his bar, got money troubles. Probably wants to tap you for a loan but couldn't spit it out.

That's not his style.

Hmmm, she says, unconvinced.

A bitter cold February morning, birdsong gusting like a shower of ice crystals from the mature trees in the High Street. Blackbird, chaffinch, wren, wind and sleet against the pane. I'm sitting in the office, a shabby underlit room on the first floor above the bookies and fast food joints. Lilac walls, a bad hangover from the eighties. Boot up the computer, the hard drive whining, lights blinking complicitly. But there's no mail, so I watch a blackbird in the horse chestnut outside the window, the song moving through his body like passing rain, pouring from his open throat.

It's wired in. He hasn't learned it.

I rest my head against the desk and the cold morning drifts through my bloodstream like a virus, those strings of gulls yelping over on their way inland, in search of turned fields dark and teeming with invertebrates.

Coffee. The jug has been steeping for a few minutes now. I pour a cup and let the black lava settle through my bones with a glow of fugitive pleasure. In a small business there's a slim margin between ticking over and stone dead. Before Christmas I was ticking over and now I'm dying on my arse. Had the usual January calls. Problems with machines bought in the sales, a few broadband set-ups. Then nothing. I look at the phone, small, squat and plastic, mocking me with its silence. And then it jolts unexpectedly into life with a sick metallic sound.

I snatch up the receiver. Always answer within four rings.

Heron Networks.

Is that what you're called now?

A faintly amused voice. It's a couple of weeks since I ran into him on the Gare.

That's what I've always been called. No reason why you should know. Imagine the heron of truth spearing the slimy fish of spyware and computer pandemonium. Anyway, what do you want? I've got a business to run.

Thought we could meet up, have a chat. Any cripplers about?

Dunno. There was a pectoral on Tidal Creek last week. Scopes were out in force for that. Think it's gone now but.

I'm going to cast an eye over Saltholme and Dormans. There's a burger van along the road there, does the best bacon buttie on Teesside. I could meet you there in an hour.

He sounds strangely insistent. I pause for a moment, then decide. I'll go along, just this once, and tell him he's wasting his time. He may as well go back to Pattaya. The beach, the beer, and the boom boom, as he so eloquently put it.

Okay, but I can't stay long. Snowed under with work here.

He's right about the bacon buttie. It's perfect. The bacon salty, fat perfectly crisped, and butter oozing into the ketchup. I bite in hungrily, realizing that it's the first time I've eaten this morning. Yan is blowing on his coffee, the steam hiding his face.

It's lung cancer, he says. Always knew the ciggies would catch up with me, so I'm not complaining. They kept me off the booze. When I started thinking about whisky I'd skin up a fag. One evil to chase out another.

I'm gaping at him, brain turning somersaults.

How's Kelly anyway? he says, matter-of-fact. Weren't you two trying for a bairn?

Yeah, well. Nothing happened there.

Wouldn't want a son of mine firing blanks.

There's a long pause.

It was a joke, he says. You know about jokes, right?

The cancer?

No. The firing blanks bit.

You don't look ill, I say, and it's almost true because he's still imposing, lean but well-muscled, firm grey eyes not wavering beneath the close-cropped hair. But the skin betrays him, looking a little tight and yellowed. Nicotine-stained, almost. We're standing against the roadside fence, saltmarshes crawling away on both sides, green and grey and wet. Flakes of snow still pirouette from the sky.

What's the prognosis?

Doctors are dysfunctional bastards who don't know how to communicate. And they're particularly shit at telling you you're dying. They're embarrassed somehow, can't wait to show you the door.

But he did tell you.

He give me a leaflet, he says. Can you believe that? I'm on the way to the knackers yard and they give me a leaflet. Options and Treatments.

Are you going to enlighten me?

The bacon buttie is finished now. I throw away the paper napkin and watch it bowl away down the road, carried by the wind. Birds on Saltholme Pool are going about their business quietly. Coot, dunlin, tufted duck, feeding across the silver water, rooting in the shallows.

Well, he says. I'm calling him Jim. Sounds friendlier than squamous cell carcinoma and we'll be living together for a while so we may as well be on first-name terms. Jim's a big lad. And he's going to get bigger. A right fat bastard, in fact. But at the moment he's not causing me any grief. Later on he might ring up his mates and get them squatting in other bits of me. Liver, bladder, brain, you name it. But for now they're going to give him some slimming pills – chemo, you know. They can't tell me how long – how much time. You know.

He grins.

I've always been lucky. Reckon me and Jimbo might spin it out for years.

I turn away for a moment.

When I came out here, I was going to tell you to forget it. Go back to Pattaya.

Can't. I've sold up over there. Nowhere to go back to. This is where – where I came from.

Yeah.

It's like the abos, he says. In Australia. Them dreamtime gadgies – you know, the ancestors and that. They came out of the ground and then they danced all over the continent naming things. Rocks, trees, mountains, birds. Naming things. But when it was finished, when their life was done, they had to find the same hole they came out of.

They went back in.

Aye, that's it. Look, there's plenty of life left in me. I'm going to push my luck as far as it goes. They're going to start pumping me full of drugs in a week or so. See if they can lick Jim into shape.

A fire engine roars past, lights blazing, from the station at Seal Sands.

Over-reacting again, says Yan. Anybody lights a fag on the Billingham site and they're out. They'll probably drown the poor bugger.

He pulls out a tobacco pouch and begins to twirl a skinny fag between finger and thumb.

Can't believe you, I splutter. Should be quitting them things.

He smiles, thin and tight.

Yeah, he says. They gave me a leaflet about that as well.

I have to laugh.

Have you told Kate?

No, you're the first. Apart from – I'm not sure what to do about Kate. Haven't seen her since she went out to Perth. How is she these days?

She's still got the bar, and Terry seems a decent enough bloke, I blurt out, catching a warning look in his eyes which brings me up short. He looks away across the marshes, sleet bristling into his face, inhales deeply from the cigarette. The tip glows brilliantly, then subsides into grey ash.

Nowt was the same, he says, when I came back. We had great sex, mind. Awesome sex. And afterwards we lay in bed and watched the light grow outside and I stroked the hair away from her forehead, over and over. And you lie there and think about the times to come. But when you look back you realize that *was* the time.

He pauses, rubs his stubble.

There's some time left, he says, for you and me at least. But I feel like we've become strangers, over the years.

You didn't move to Thailand because of me. There's no stopping you when you get the bit between your teeth.

How about we get on the grapevine again? he says. Maybes I could still add a couple to my life list.

He grins ironically and I laugh along with him.

I'll tell Kate, I say. Another fire engine bullets past towards Port Clarence, blue lights blazing under the darkening sky.

5. Wilson's Phalarope

(Phalaropus tricolor)

Good morning Vietnam, said Gary Hagan at the top of the stairs as he pushed me against the wall, a bulky hand either side of my head. The sound of a fire engine outside on Port Clarence Road, Doppler effect as it sped past.

I said nothing, watched his pudgy features swim in towards my face until his nose was almost touching mine. His jaws were working, chewing gum on his breath.

Vietnam, he breathed, the sharp smell of Juicy Fruit making me blink. Thailand. It's crazy shit over there son. Sodom and fucking Gomorrah. One day I'm going to take me a trip. Franco's been over. Got the snatch hair off a fourteen-year-old virgin, carries it around in his wallet. What do you think about that?

I shrugged, and Hagan sneered.

You're still a virgin, aren't you?

Kate was in the bathroom, one of her interminable soaks. And someone was climbing the stairs. I could hear the footsteps, boots reverberating in the stairwell.

Lasses don't want to go with people like you, said Hagan.

The large gold hoop in his left ear glinted. I imagined grasping it between my teeth and ripping it out through his flesh. The footsteps reached the top of the stairs and a figure passed through Gary Hagan, emerging again on the other side. At least I thought it was a figure, a shape created from interference in the air, like a snowstorm on the TV, popping and fizzing like an Alka Seltzer. It melted into the opposite wall and disappeared. Hagan didn't seem to notice.

Me, I've got nothing against you son, he said. It's just that you're so – he paused to search for the right word – so *hittable*. His face was so close it was blurred. I moved forward and kissed him full on the lips. He sprang back, rubbing his mouth.

You dirty little –

He raised his hand and I flinched away from the blow but he stopped and laughed.

Next time son, he said, and I ducked away down the empty stairs.

Later at Razia's house my eyes began to blur and swim, headache jolting into migraine. I slumped down wearily over the table, rested my head against a chemistry textbook.

You're not in the mood for this, she said.

I sat up and looked at her, deep brown eyes and sharp features, perky smile framed by the *hijab*.

Everyone's full of shit, I said.

She laughed at me.

Like what.

I dunno. Get your exams and go to university and be a suit. Jack it in and go on the pancrack. Raid the till and blow it on lighter fluid. Your mam needs you Dan, she's finding it hard to cope. Why don't you go and find out what happened to your dad? There's a million things.

A million?

Aye. A million. And you can only choose the one.

Raz leaned back on her chair, eyes twinkling, inwardly laughing.

It's more than a million, she said. And that's the beauty of it Danny boy. Any moment in time, there's a zillion different maybes, all hanging out there. Sometimes you never even see them brother. It's mad as biscuits.

Are you sure it's just a zillion like? Not a zillion and one, or nine hundred and ninety-nine trillion nine hundred and ninety-nine?

Actually, she said, very seriously, leaning back so far on her chair I thought she might tip over. It's a zillion and twelve. But I was rounding down for the simple-minded.

I wanted to kiss her. Instead I looked out of the window across the back garden. Over the saltmarsh a gull was levitating on the wind, perched at the apex of a blustery crystal-clear morning, half a mile above Port Clarence. I thought about the equations you need to fly – the hieroglyphic tangle of fluid dynamics, turbulence, chaos theory and the rest. The gull swayed, tilted, blew over with a raucous cry.

Well they can fuck off, I said. All zillion and twelve of them.

Shh, don't swear, Dad's upstairs. Puckered up her brown face into that expression, half laughing and half admonishing. Mr Shahid clattered down the stairs, on the way out for his shift on the minicabs.

Daniel, he said, by way of acknowledgement. His eyes glittered like Razia's above the thin moustache. The door clicked shut behind him and I heard his engine rev outside. We didn't speak much, just a word or two when he was going out to the taxi, or coming back in after a shift. He tolerated me in his house, at his kitchen table or on his sofa.

A ghost went through Gary Hagan, I said. Straight through him.

That means he's going to die, said Raz. No bones about it.

Ghosts don't have bones, I said. She wrinkled her nose at the lame joke. Seriously though, I asked her. Do you believe in them?

Aye, I reckon. Saw this old biddy once in Dhaka, going out to the well in the morning. Only she'd died the night before.

What do you think they are?

I don't reckon it's the dead coming back, rattling a chain. Maybe it's because time and space are all folded and wrinkled and scrunched up, so one place can rub against another. Leave a mark like pressing on carbon paper.

So a ghost is like a bad photocopy?

She laughed. Aye, maybe. Have you had any dinner? I think there are frozen pizzas – I could heat some up.

Better get back to the pub Raz, I said, I've got stuff to do.

I shuffled into my overcoat. I had to squeeze close past her at the front door. She sparkled at me,

Take care Dan, she said.

I pulled her towards me, but she squirmed away expertly.

Don't make things more complicated than you have to, she said.

Kate was in the living room with the TV blaring and the gas fire pumping out the heat on full whack and Trajan sprawled beside her toasting his bollocks. He was Yan's dog and I never worked out what breeds made him up but he was a big leathery bugger whatever.

She grabbed my jumper as I went past, nostrils flared like a horse.

Don't think, she said, her big brown eyes wandering aimlessly. Don't think you can fucking swan back in here without a word. After three years, you bastard.

Half drawl and half croak, with a blast of Coke and Jack Daniels on her breath. Sweet and sticky.

Mam, I said. It's Danny.

Looked down at her hand. Pastel-pink nails flaring against mahogany skin.

Don't think, she said. Gave my jumper a hard yank, almost overbalancing me. The heat was oppressive, sweat patches heavy under my arms.

Mam.

Aye, she said. Tried to focus on me. Danny.

She reached over the arm of the sofa and found her glass and took a good hit. Then she rummaged in her bag for tablets and shovelled a few down and chased them with more whisky and Coke.

It's *Randall and Hopkirk*, she said. I love this. Come and sit next to us and watch it like.

I sat.

Last night, she said. Did you notice anything?

Like what.

It got cold.

I didn't notice.

I woke up in me bed and it was cold. It was so cold I couldn't move and me breath was making crystals. I was frozen stiff as a board.

You were dreaming mam.

I was lying there paralysed. And there was someone standing at the foot of the bed. A man.

What did he look like?

You couldn't see him. He was just there. And you could feel him. Just a feeling of malice, like he meant me harm. It was steaming off him.

So what happened?

I dunno. I sat up and he was gone and the room was warm again.

You were dreaming.

I need to know what he wants.

Why?

Ghosts want something, don't they?

I dunno. I can't breathe with this fucking gas fire.

Gary Hagan wandered in with a bottle of Mexican lager in one hand and calfskin loafers on his feet. He sat down in Yan's chair.

What you watching Katie?

The way he was looking at her, seeing the long legs in tight stone-washed denim and the sunbed skin and blueblack hair like a fall of coaldust. Not seeing the nicotine stains on her teeth and the cracks in her skin, not smelling the raw panic on her breath. She was ten years older than him but she'd still pass for thirty.

Trajan padded over to him and sniffed at his groin and he looked worried but made a show of rubbing the dog's ears.

Who's behind the bar Gaz? said Kate.

Lads are looking after it.

You've got it under control, then.

Aye. Just leave it to me Katie.

She settled to watch the TV again. She flicked a sly look at Hagan.

You got big muscles Gaz.

Got to keep yourself in shape.

He was practically purring.

Aye. You're almost as big as my Yan.

Right.

He was – He is –

She burst out laughing.

Which is it?

Laughed again.

If he walked in now, right. I'd deck him. One hard punch. It was that bastard showed me how to throw a good punch. You know, not a lass's punch.

You're a tough cookie Katie.

And after I'd decked him, she whispered, breathily. I'd drag him down on the floor and fuck his brains out. Fuck them right out.

She was looking right at Hagan with her face wide open.

When Kate was asleep on the sofa I went into her bedroom and found the shoebox of Yan's stuff at the back of the bottom drawer in her dresser. There was an old paperweight and a wet shaver and a box of cufflinks, one of them old digital watches with the liquid crystal all faded away to nowt and a bunch of keys. I expected photos but there weren't any. Maybe nobody could afford a camera when they were growing up. And there was Yan's old diary for nineteen eighty-one.

I rifled through it in the green half-light seeping through bedroom curtains. There weren't many names and addresses in the back and most of these I didn't recognize. But a couple of them rang a bell. I jammed the little diary in my back pocket and closed the shoebox and buried it again at the back of Kate's drawer.

The curtains were closed in the saloon and the darkness was prickling with dust so thick you could taste it. I moved over to the bar, feet squeaking on the lino tiles, and when I got there I lifted the flap and ducked through. I had my finger in the dial of the phone and then I thought you don't just ring someone out of the blue and expect them to spill their guts. It has to be face to face.

Okay. I triggered the till and cushioned the noise when it opened. Plenty of notes in there. Hagan only cashed up once or twice a week. My breath was coming quick, spots swimming in my vision. But I stretched out a hand and brushed the pile of banknotes and then snatched it back when the front door banged and voices clattered in the hallway.

It's showtime, Magoo was yelling.

I slammed the till shut and got back into the mixer store. Got the cellar trapdoor open and tumbled inside and lowered the lid again. Boots in the saloon, dockers and dealers, on the boarded floor behind the bar. Resounding through my head, the world filling up with boots. Paul's boots in the cinder yard, Yan's boots coming up the stairs.

I was a kid, lying in bed in the dark.

There were voices up there, and the clatter and sigh of the beer pump as Hagan shelled out pints and the bump of the full glasses when he planted them on the bar.

You've got to do him Franco.

Get him on the ground and lace his head till it bounces.

Aye, but make sure you stop short of killing the bastard.

Not too far short, mind.

Remember when you had that pikey lad. Had to drag you off him like a radge dog.

Never liked that O'Rourke kid, intoned Gary Hagan. Some bad wiring inside his head. Loose connection somewhere.

Needs kicking back into circuit, like. Do the cunt a favour.

He must be doing summat right. Franco's lass is well tidy, like.

Was it his lass or his daughter?

It was both, I heard.

She's only fucking fifteen.

Well, if there's grass on the wicket.

Take the piss when he's been through your daughter, the fucking baghead, growled Franco.

What are you gonna say to him Franco?

Aye. Go on. Do the voice.

Do you feel lucky punk? creaked Franco in a strange high voice.
They erupted into laughter.

Sounds fuck all like Clint, that.

Well do yeh?

Down on the cellar steps I shivered. Dark and clammy in here, no light
at all, not even the smallest glint from the metal kegs. I leaned my head
against the brickwork and started to drift.

Rare birds drift off, sooner or later. When something tasty crashes
into Teesmouth and word gets around there can be a bit of a circus.
Twitchers come in from all over the gaff and you never need to ask
where the bird is. Just follow the scopes and the cagoules.

The bird itself – Siberian rubythroat, semi-palmated sandpiper,
whatever – is a wreck when it lands here. First landfall after the North
Sea, the Arctic Ocean, the Atlantic, and it crashes down on the brink
of death with its fat reserves empty. Needs to feed in a hurry so it stays
put for a while, resting and replenishing. But in the end, after a few
days or a few weeks, it disappears from the radar. No more sightings.

So what happens next? Some just die, of course. Exhaustion, starv-
ation, predation. And there are records of birds trying to get back to
where they should have been in the first place. What drives them I don't
know. Maybe the stars just look wrong here.

And some of them stay. Just get on with it. Immerse themselves in
flocks of similar species and hope nobody will notice.

In nineteen eighty-two there was a Wilson's phalarope on Reclamation Pond. It was a transatlantic vagrant, the first record for Teesmouth,
and it became a local celebrity for a couple of weeks. We didn't get
down there straight away because Yan was about to go back to the
regiment, the Task Force assembling for the Falklands. He knew he
was going, even when it wasn't clear how the government would respond or whether these remote sheep-encrusted rocks were even worth

fighting over. The day it started, when they reported the Argentine invasion on the news, he snapped off the TV.

Well, he said. I'm going for a little holiday. It's good birding down there Dan.

By the time we got out to Reclamation it was quiet. A vacant early Saturday morning, cold and blue. We parked up on the rise behind Dorman's and looked out over the open water and the tall reedbanks and the exoskeleton of the refinery beyond. Picked out the phalarope straight away, a small delicate wader swimming on the open water, head bowed in prayer with the needle-fine bill tucked down. It span slow in the water, white and grey and silver in the lucid dawn like a small apologetic ghost. Like a swimming moon.

We watched it from the window of the rusty Renault Twelve and I could smell Yan beside me in the donkey jacket which had absorbed years of his scent. Cigarette smoke and a raw tang of sweat. He had a few days' stubble on his chin.

Phalarope, he said, comes from the Greek, like. For 'coot-footed'.

You're making it up.

Nah, honest. They have these lobed feet. You know, like a coot or a moorhen. When they swim the feet stir up the sediment from the bottom, full of nice invertebrates, and then the bird spins round and snaps up the goodies from the water.

Right.

When your mam was pregnant with you I used to wash her feet. She couldn't reach round the bump. They swelled right up from the weight of the baby.

Why are you telling me this?

Dunno. Just came into my head.

The bird bobbed and span gently for a few seconds longer, and then it rose from the water and sprang into the sky like a pale swallow, dark wings and silver body. We tracked it in our bins, south over the reeds, a white punctuation mark in the blue sky. Eventually it became too small to see.

And that was it. The phalarope wasn't seen again on Teesmouth, and Yan left for the Falklands on the Tuesday.

Yan Thomas would have killed him, boomed Magoo, from above. Remember what happened to Jimmy Dillon?

And I was wide awake, questing into the darkness like a dog, heartbeat flaring. I heard Magoo subside heavily onto a bar stool which complained under his weight.

Jimmy Bananas? came Kurt's voice, muffled and indistinct.

Aye. The bloke came on to Kate, while Yan was on a tour in Belfast. She's a canny splitarse man. I cannot blame the gadge.

Well he was shiteing his duds when Yan came back and she told him about it. Now then Bananas, he said. You and me need to go for a drive. Jimmy was browning it but he went along anyway. They got into that rustbucket of his, that old white Renault, and drove off. No fucker ever saw Bananas again.

Pal, said Gary Hagan, you're talking out of your jug. Yan took him down the bus station in Boro, stuck him on a National Express to sheepshagger land and told him not to come back.

Tommy Hatton reckons Yan killed the gadge. Told him about it one night, when it was just the two of them in the bar. Somewhere lonely out on the brinefields, one of them places only birders go. Ripped his fucking throat out with a Stanley knife, let him bleed out on the mud so he wouldn't mess up the car seats. Told Tom he couldn't let it go, not even the once.

Ripped his balls off as well, I heard, said Franco, and fed them to his dog.

You're joking, aren't you? interrupted Kurt.

There was a pause and I heard him stifle a yawn. Pints clattered against the bar top.

Tommy Hatton talks out of his back door, he continued. He once tried to tell me his cousin was Muhammad fucking Ali, just so I'd buy him a pint.

A raw splurge of laughter. Hagan plonked his meaty forearms against the bar.

Local hardmen, he said, are ten-a-penny round here. No fucking shortage. Yan was mean enough, when he wanted to be. But when I was on the rigs I knew plenty of lads could have knocked seven shades off of him.

Fucking cable-pullers, laughed Franco. They're all meatheads. Every cable-puller you meet has a black eye, apart from the ones who've got two.

Nah, said Magoo, persisting. Yan's another one with some loose wiring. Fucking psycho on the sly, I reckon.

But he's not coming back, said Hagan. Is he?

The conversation drifted away, Hagan reminiscing about his years offshore. Chew. Women. Throwing up on the helicopter, watching *Debbie Does Dallas* on freezeframe. More chew. More women. My feet were cramped up beneath me on the cellar steps, toes becoming numb, my arm folded awkwardly against the wall. But I fell asleep anyway, descended into a place where boots reverberated in the sky like thunder, kicked and stomped at the wooden clouds until they split.

Can't believe it, said Paul, leaning back against the bus stop and necking the can I'd given him. You're doing a runner.

You want to watch Franco and them. They're after giving you a kicking.

I can handle meself.

Was it his daughter or his missus you went through?

He shrugged. The grey-green eyes looked bored.

I'm down to London next Saturday meself, he said. Crystal Palace. Always good for a barney like.

Thought you were working.

He shrugged again.

Day off, he said. If you're in that neck of the woods you could meet us at King's Cross after the game. Six o'clock, top of the main escalators.

How are you going to afford the train?

He looked at me like I was remedial.

I'm bunking the fucker, he said.

Later I lay on my bed in the box room and waited. Fully clothed, boots on, the red glow of the radio alarm on my bedside table. Numbers cycling painfully, time grinding to a halt. In my hand was Yan's diary, curled up into a tube. I wound it tighter.

There was something going on in Michelle's room next door. Bumping, shuffling, a sudden loud laugh and then a long female moan. She put it on a plate for just about anybody them days.

She was an odd one, Michelle. Always semi-bewildered, like you asked her a question and her eyes roved around in confusion before she hit on the right thing to say. I never worked out why Yan gave her the hours behind the bar, but fair play to him, she turned out to be a natural. Yan had this habit of adopting waifs and strays now and then. Paul O'Rourke was another one he helped out a couple of times when his mam had kicked him out. He was staying at ours when he first had the bonehead done but Yan didn't say owt, just looked at him funny.

You ever get that done, he said to me later, you'll be moving out.

No shit. I smiled as I plugged in the clippers and turned them on and then my hair began to fall across the pages of yesterday's *Gazette*, the soundless precipitation obscuring the newsprint. The blades ranged across my scalp, buzzing dispassionately. When it was finished I brushed stray hairs away and looked in the mirror at my own head gleaming nude like a pool ball. Ran a hand across the shorn scalp, felt it tickling like the new pink skin under a blister.

Downstairs in the bar it was pitch dark. I'd waited long after the last sound, long after the last arsehole had pitched out into the night. I counted out nine steps to the bar, hands stretched in front of me until I felt the pitted wood of the counter. Lifted the flap and sidled through, ran my fingers along the cold metal sides of the till, the drawer springing open and butting against my palm. Fingertips danced across the compartments inside, scooped up a wad of notes and smuggled it into my pocket. It felt like a lot. I stopped to listen. Nothing. Just the night-time breath of an old building. The bleating of water in copper pipes, the scratchy stubble of stale plaster, the insect legs of the clock crawling. I picked up the phone and dialled, flinching each time the dial clicked back against the stops.

I waited under the railway bridge, just a hundred yards down the road. I was nervous, skittering the sports bag against my ankles, fingering the notes in my pocket. There was no traffic here in the small hours. A street lamp flickered on and off, alive, dead, alive, and the air was cold. A minicab pulled up next to me, engine idling, and the driver wound his window down. It was Mr Shahid, eyes sharpened above the moustache.

Daniel, he said.

Darlo station, I said.

The train carriage was brightly lit and almost deserted. Flickering through the sleeping country like the calendar riffling past, the lighted windows of the year. Bright and rattling, and then gone, a memory. I leaned back in my seat and lit a cigarette. It gurgled as I did so, the flame searing into the paper and the dry tobacco. I unzipped the sports bag and looked over my supplies. Chocolate bars and crisps, a token apple. Some cans from the bar. I pulled out a can of McEwan's and ripped it open. It wasn't cold, but was rich and malty in the throat. I gulped at it.

Lightning crawled across the sky as the train ran south. I put my head back against the headrest and slowed my breathing. Emptied my conscious brain until the night country moved through me, the clay lands of the Vale of York, wide fields and ancient woodland, flat country and hill country, sleeping villages and dreaming farms. Hawthorn hedges knitting the land like sutures. A flock of sheep ghostly in the damp night. One or two of them coughing in their sleep, facing the east where the light was already beginning to mass. Wood beetles deep inside decaying trees, chewing at the timber, drumming with their hind legs. Birds roosting everywhere like fruit, half asleep and half awake, ever watchful for the death which comes in the night. Men and women and children asleep behind the blank windows of houses, in each other's arms, back to back like bookends, or alone. After sex, after arguments, after beatings, after bedtime stories, after full or empty lives, but mostly half full or half empty. And the sleepless were reading, masturbating, or just worrying, turning over and over to find a comfortable position, in the small cold hours of the night when dawn seemed an impossible solution.

6. Wandering Albatross

(Diomedia exulans)

You should try your colleagues' solution. Sarah laughs, gesturing with her golden head towards the far Nissen hut. It might help with the insomnia.

A solution of forty per cent ethanol in water? I throw back. Don't touch nothing stronger than beer, me. Not for fifteen years.

She looks quizzical.

It didn't agree with me, I say. Or rather, I didn't agree with it.

Our voices are stretched out like a flysheet over the constant noise. Imagine ten thousand claw hammers squeaking ten thousand nails out of ten thousand gobby bits of timber. Imagine all the demons in hell gabbling and cackling and speaking in tongues. Imagine it, but even then you won't come close.

Bird Island, South Georgia, is the biggest breeding colony I've ever seen, a sprawling shanty town of nesting seabirds. Gannets and skuas and five kinds of albatross, all camped on these untidy mounds of nest with scarcely enough room to turn round, reaching to jab with thuggish bills at anything that encroaches. They squawk incessantly, to maintain territory, to greet and threaten incomers and mates and chicks and parents. They gabble and bicker like biddies over the back fence. They squabble and fight like radge kids. They yelp and howl it seems for the sheer outrageous joy of the sound. I am here, they say, in a million clattering tongues. What are you going to do about it?

The nest mounds sprawl over every available surface, pebble beach and black rock and grassy slopes, streaked with guano and rotting seaweed. And the stench of the colonies comes as loud as the noise, a reek of ammonia that puckers the eyes and stings the inside spaces of the nose.

Away to the north stretches the open ocean, grey and restless with the white caps bristling across it like neurons firing in the lonely spaces of the brain. The boat sits at anchor in the shelter of the point, and we've pulled the inflatables up the steeply raked pebble beach towards the small complex of Nissen huts that's become our temporary home. To the south, behind us, rear the ranges of South Georgia, a long black fossil like the spine of a sea beast. Ice and snow on the peaks, white as the sun. Black rock matt and impenetrable, absorbing light, absorbing heat. The improbable green of tundra grasses on the lower slopes, spikes and globes rippling in the constant wind, each inflorescence a tiny world. White, black, green. And the incongruous scarlet and blue of our anoraks, as we stand above the colony and look back through the whirling melee of seabirds towards the huts at the head of the bay.

Sarah was sanguine when we turned up out of the storm, five castaways in a limping boat. Pointed a shotgun at us, told us that she was quite ready to radio the marines at Grytviken if we put a foot out of line, and then showed us the spare hut, chilly and damp from disuse. The others made themselves comfortable, lugged a gas canister and lit the heaters, and then, with the aid of a crate of whisky from the boat, wallowed in the pigpen of extreme drunkenness. But I couldn't sleep, even when the snorts and grunts and squeals of the others had subsided into slumber. Every time I perched on the edge of it and the circle of my thoughts threatened to fall into dream, I felt the rocks beneath us move, the island come adrift and begin to sink beneath the relentless ocean. I felt the water, breathtakingly cold, in my mouth and my nostrils, and I jerked awake, sitting upright and rubbing my eyes.

How do you deal with the loneliness, I ask. Here on your own?

She grimaces.

People never understand, but I'm not lonely. I find myself alone

in a dark house, late in the evening, and everything is deathly quiet –
then I'm lonely. But here there's always sound. The birds and the sea,
even in the middle of the night. The birds talk in their sleep. Dreams,
nightmares. You know.

Wonder what an albatross has nightmares about.

People, probably. Long-line trawlers, being hooked and dragged
under. Killer whales. Or perhaps the sea drying up, flying forever over
desert. Who knows.

So there were three of you here, monitoring the birds. What happened to the other two?

The other two went back when the island was liberated. We never
saw the Argentines, you know. Just a few ships moving out at sea. That
was the Falklands conflict for us.

Don't suppose seabirds give a toss about human wars. They just get
on with it. Sensible approach, if you ask me.

What about you Yan, she says, looking at me from behind a wing of
hair flapping on the wind. Do you just get on with it? Is that what's
brought you here?

I think, I say. That sometimes I just act on instinct.

Like an albatross, she says.

The wandering albatross is huge. The strange black triangular eyes of
the tubenose and a great bludgeon of a beak. Clumsy as a goose on the
ground, but in the air it soars beautiful and strange. An angel, or a
ghost. We stand close to a nest mound, blinking back the stench. One
of the adults is there with the giant brown chick, not fully fledged. And
out of the chaos of take-offs and landings comes a single bird, wingspan
held at just the angle to bring it through the rookery and down to this
nest, this one among thousands. It stands facing its mate, webbed feet
pawing the ground, and they greet each other with gurgling sounds
and clacking of bills. Then the newcomer yawns and regurgitates a
cropful of partly digested fish with an eyewatering wave of stink, the
chick gobbling the slime excitedly as it emerges from the throat of its

parent. All seem contented and companionable, a nuclear family within the metropolis of the colony.

They mate for life, says Sarah. Don't breed for a few years, but when they pair up, it's for good. They can live for forty, fifty years.

Raise the chick through the winter, don't they? I say. Must get chilly down here.

She's a good-looking woman, a few years younger than me, late twenties or early thirties. Golden hair cropped at the jawline, threshing around in the blustery wind. Through the all-weather clothing it's hard to distinguish her figure, but she has fascinating eyes, green like the tundra grass and always moving on the wind. A hint of sadness perhaps. Why did she stay here on her own?

No flies on you, she says. Chick stays on the nest all through the austral winter. The adults take turns to go fishing, even though there can be heavy snow, violent storms. We've monitored the distances they travel, with radio transmitters. If the weather's bad in the South Atlantic they head north, as far away as the waters off Brazil. Six hundred miles or more and back to this rock in the far south. They're incredible creatures.

The pair on the nest launch into another frenzy of head tossing and bill clacking.

Old mate of mine, worked the merchant navy. He used to reckon they were reincarnations – you know, of old sailors drowned, gone down with the ship. They would come alongside, inspect the radio masts and the rigging, check everything was shipshape.

We like to think everything revolves around us, she says. But they don't give a damn whether we float or drown. They inhabit their own world and we're not part of it.

Her eyes are tossing and she can't keep the anger out of her voice. Then she subsides, embarrassed by the outburst.

Sorry, she says, with a placatory smile. Just pisses me off that we expect the natural world to jump to our tune.

The colony howls and jabbers and vomits behind her.

Look at them, Sarah goes on. They deserve more than that.

Tears in her eyes. We stand in silence for some time, the sea and the sky toiling.

Penguins, you know, slurs Joe Fish, leery with alcohol, are a fantastic source of fuel. You know what they did here, in the old days, the sealers and the whalers? They had no raw material to power the furnaces for rendering the carcasses. No trees for timber, no coal. They used fucking penguins. Bashed their brains out and threw them on the fire, herded the stupid buggers straight into the flames.

He bangs his fist down on the edge of his bunk.

Never understood whaling, burrs Horse Boy sleepily, from above, where he's already under the blankets, whisky bottle in hand. They'd make rancid eating – all blubber and fat.

Oil boy, oil, shouts Joe impatiently. Whale oil and seal blubber, for streetlamps in Britain, in London and Edinburgh and even, god help us, in Sunderland. Bringing light to the masses. They were Titans, those men, raging out into the southern seas to bring back light, across half the world. Thousands of seals, thousands of whales, butchered in the factories here, boiled down for their oil. Men up to their knees in blood and filth. Heroes man.

He runs a hand over his slicked-back hair and the pockmarked face gleams in the light from the gas fire.

Not much left now as a monument to them, he goes on. A few rusting sheds and the whalers' graves. I wouldn't want to leave my bones down here, under the stones, with home on the other side of the world.

Those fellas were a rare breed all right, I say. But it was wholesale slaughter down here. Some of the whale stocks have never recovered.

I toast my hands in front of the stove, where a pot of beans is puttering slowly.

Charity, says Joe, starts at home. We need to feed and clothe and warm our own. The bosses aren't going to do it. We can start worrying about seals and dolphins when our kids have got food on the table. Me, I'd quite happily torch a penguin just to get me fag lit.

He winks at me. Do you want a plate of beans Yan?

I think I've just lost my appetite, I say. And I'm fucking sick of beans.

Mind if I come in? I say, standing in the doorway. They're talking about burning penguins in there.

Sarah wrinkles her nose, indicates the bench on the other side of the table. I sit. This cabin is far more comfortable than the other. A serviceable kitchen area with a built-in table, and beyond this the sleeping quarters with bunks, even a gas shower. Steam billows from the kettle with that soft smell that reminds me of early mornings in my grandparents' kitchen, boiling water chiming on the stove.

Cup of tea? she asks. I was just making one.

I nod. She busies herself and I study her from behind. Simple black leggings and a navy sweatshirt, the clothes emphasizing the curve of her body. Stray wisps of hair catch the light from the tiny window, flaring golden in the dying sun. We warm our hands around the mugs of tea. Feels uncomfortable, like a first date.

Tell me about yourself Yan, she says. What makes you tick?

Clockwork, I say. Same as anyone.

I shift uncomfortably.

All right. What I really want to know is what you're doing here?

Looks like I'm drinking tea.

You're married, yeah? Ring on your finger, guilty look on your coupon.

Aye.

Kids?

I've got a son, Danny. He's thirteen odd.

So. You could be sat on the troopship on the way back to them. Maybe they'd even have flown you back home. You could be there right now. But instead you did a runner and ended up here. With me.

A long pause while I wonder what to say. Her eyes are steady, holding mine.

Kate, I say. She's sound. We strike sparks off each other, you know.

We row and we make up. And Dan. Well sometimes he's just like me and then the next minute he's a space alien from another galaxy.

I pause. She waits.

I can't make it digestible for you, I say. It doesn't really make sense, not in ways you can explain.

You could try.

Well, people always want life to be like a detective story. You know, the killer has to have a motivation. Their dad was an abuser or their mam was an alcoholic. I once saw Frank Zappa live when I was an impressionable youth and that was enough to drive anyone to homicide.

I like Frank Zappa.

Nah. Way too much noodling.

Anyway, she says. Motivation.

Yeah. Well, it isn't like that for me. Sometimes it just wells up in me from nowhere and I just go with it. I jump. On instinct, you could say.

Like the albatross coming back six hundred miles to her nest.

Aye, I say. Like the arctic tern migrating to the other end of the world. When I was a kid I used to sit in me grandad's kitchen. He was a hewer up at Horden Colliery, working the seams that ran miles out under the North Sea. He used to sit there in his shirtsleeves with his elbows on the table and his back to the fire, and alls I remember is the coal grit under his nails that never washed out. Not his face.

She sips her tea and I glance at her and her eyes meet mine and then flick away sharpish.

Life is a seam of coal, he used to say. Black and glittering and snaking away deep under your feet, who knows where. And to make life happen you've got to hew it. The seam is already there under the ground from five hundred million years back, but you never know where it leads unless you put your back into it. Discover it.

Sounds wise, your grandad. What else did he say?

Drink your milk up son or I'll focken batter you.

She laughs.

So, she says. Life's already set in stone, like fate? The shape is there and you only have to discover it.

That's what he was saying but I don't completely buy it. I've got this mate who's a sculptor, eh? Now, he'll take a block of stone and look at it for hours like a heron stalking a fish. He'll walk round it, sniff it, tap it from all angles. He says there's a potential within each piece of stone, an inner shape waiting to get out, to be discovered by the blow of the hammer.

Just like the seam of coal.

Ah, but it's more than that. When you strike, you get a reaction – your active will comes up against the passive potential in the stone – and something completely new can come out of that shower of sparks, something you never saw before. See, you need that spark, that originality, to take you somewhere different. Me grandad never did that, just worked in the same job until it wore him out and he died, not far past fifty. The coal just led him deeper and deeper into the same place.

I sip my tea. It's getting dark outside with the peculiar speed of high latitudes, and the birds are still yammering but they'll soon quieten when the light dies. The gas heater purrs, blue flames shuffling like feathers.

See, I say. I'm a jumper. A chancer you could say. I don't want to die alone in a darkened studio, looking at an unworked piece of stone and wondering what I could have made. What excites me is the moment when the hammer comes down, when the dice are spinning, the cards coming to you across the table. That shower of sparks is a thousand different futures, all springing up and flaring for a moment and dying.

You want them all.

Yeah. I want to grab them and get my fingers burned. Before they die.

Is that what you're doing now?

It's what I've always done. I was engaged to Kate when I was eighteen, but then I met some squaddies in a bar and off I went. Dropped back in a few years later and married her – I don't know who was more surprised. But the chance of a few hands of poker or an inside tip on a horse, and I'm off again. To me and Joe it's like breathing. Joe's thermos flask, you know, that battered metal thing. Fifteen years of good luck and bad in there, fifteen years of risking everything on the turn of a card.

So, she says. What happened this time?

Ah, look. I've felt it coming for a while. Like a thundercloud, all them possibilities. We were in a firefight. Place called Mount Longdon.

I stop short, wonder what to say.

Afterwards I started walking. Couldn't help myself. Had to get some air into me lungs. Started walking and all the time I could smell it coming. A sharp smell, like windfall apples in autumn.

Sarah yawns. I realize it's getting late. She'll be up at dawn checking on the colonies. Photographs, leg rings, records. But then she transfixes me with her eyes.

What about people Yan? she says. The ones who get left behind when you change horses. Don't they get hurt?

She holds me with her eyes, and there's a long pause before I reply.

I'll be honest with you. I don't think about it. Not when the dice are moving.

And afterwards?

Well, that's different. You see, Kate and Dan are so much a part of me. But even when I'm with them, I'm still alone.

You don't really do relationships, she says. Do you? Not two-way ones, anyway. When people start getting too close, start getting right under your skin, you have to push them away.

You make me sound like a right bastard.

Maybe, she says, smiling. But I'm from exactly the same mould.

She holds my eyes.

Do you think you'll ever go home? she says.

Her face is smooth, slightly mocking. I want to cup it in my hands.

I don't know. I don't know how deep the seam runs.

Cheers Yan. Nice to see that your family went out of the window when there was a chance of a legover.

Danny. I was being honest. I'm trying to tell you the truth here.

But you did fuck her, right?

I wouldn't call it that.

Ah, look. It's too much information to be honest. There are some things I don't need to know.

I want you to know. I need to tell you.

Keep your voice down, the nurse is giving us dirty looks.

She's a battleaxe, that one.

So, we weren't in your head at all? Me and Kate.

Of course you were. It's just. The inside of a head, right? It's a lonely place. A lonely place to be.

Sarah shakes her head.

That lighter, she says. You play with it all the time, specially when you're being evasive.

I'm not being evasive.

She laughs. I test the weight of the lighter in my palm. Twitch the little lever to raise the cap.

Found it on the Falklands, I say. Upstairs in a derelict farmhouse. A bedroom with the sky poking through.

It's an odd design. Old-fashioned.

Doesn't work, but. Needs cleaning, refilling. New wick.

Do you mind if I have a drink? asks Sarah, moving across to the cupboards.

Feel free. Should get back to my own bed. Hopefully they haven't actually set fire to any wildlife in there.

The other cabin appears quiet, though there's a light still flickering. Probably Joe. It takes a lot of liquor to swamp him.

Stick around a while if you like, she says. I was enjoying the conversation. She smiles tentatively. You could have more tea, or a glass of milk.

Milk is fine. The juice of the cow.

She hands me a glass, sits down with a brandy.

Purely medicinal, she smiles. So how come you don't drink?

Ran with some wild lads when I was young. Drinking and fighting. Never had a drink problem, touch wood, but I've been on the edge a couple of times. Beer only, these days. No spirits.

I smile wryly at her.

So what made you stay out here on this rock, all alone? You could be sat at home watching Terry Wogan.

Reason enough, she says, quaffing the brandy. Well, for as long as I can remember I loathed my parents. Embodied everything I hated. Suburban dreariness. Betjeman to the power of a thousand. Dad pruning the roses, mum cleaning the house. They were bright people, they'd been to university, but somewhere down the line the lights went out and they settled for the routine and the little semi with the patch of lawn, changing the car every three years and gawping night after night at the stupid bloody telly gabbling away in the corner.

I sip at the milk. Thin longlife stuff.

I ran away from them, she says. Studied zoology, worked on reserves in New Zealand, the Galapagos. Sent them postcards from the corners of the world. They worried about my job security, about low pay. They worried about my boyfriends who, of course, were all scumbags.

Her voice is low and comforting, over the putter of the gas heater.

And then, just about a year ago, my mother died. I got a letter from my dad while I was working here, and I flew back home. He was trying to act normal, making tea and small talk, but you could tell that a light had gone out in him. He loved her. He missed her. An albatross without its mate. Did I tell you that they pair for life? Turned out she'd had cancer for four years and they hadn't told me. Didn't want to worry me.

Parents, eh?

It's final, you see. She's gone and I'll never have a chance to mend things. Say things. That's the problem Yan. You push people away, they don't always hang around until you want them again. They have this habit of dying, leaving the country, finding somebody else. They get on with their lives, and then it's too late.

She's crying soundlessly, shoulders quaking beneath the sweat-shirt. I move round the table and sit next to her, put my hands on her shoulders. A potential here, building, and I'm acting before my thoughts can catch up. Reach beneath her face and cup it in the palm of my hand, look into those green eyes that flicker like wind through the tundra grass.

What about you Yan, she says, very quietly. Do you pair for life?

By way of reply I kiss her, very softly. She tastes salty. The wind and the sea. Stands up and moves towards the sleeping quarters. Without an order from my brain, my body is straightening itself and standing up, following her into the coal-black glittering darkness.

The winter sun shrinks to the size of an egg and the day to a frozen puddle between two walls of dark. We see bergs out at sea. The nights are long, lit by gaslight and the wild stars. The boys emerge from their alcohol craziness, due mainly to the fact that supplies are running short and need to be rationed. They ration their craziness. I also sense that they feel bad about checking out, about being absent. The hut gets cleaned and swept, blankets are folded, rubbish and detritus are banished. We cook the everlasting diet of dried and reconstituted food together, curries, paellas, sausage and mash, and eat in companionable silence. We fantasize about fresh meat, fresh vegetables. Joe makes specific and bloodcurdling threats to the local wildlife. Butchery, flensing, rendering, à la carte menus. The unholy noise of the colony fades into the background. We no longer notice it. The albatross chicks are fed through the winter, thick down matted with frost, the parents wheeling stiff-winged out to sea and back. I sleep with Sarah, sometimes. Joe wonders too long and too loud about the best recipe for seal vindaloo. Sarah says she will be on the radio to Grytviken or Stanley if he so much as looks at a seal the wrong way. She will call down an air strike right on his bony arse. Joe looks at her with new respect. Seal is off the menu.

Months go by like this and it's hard to fill the time. I watch birds through the short hours of daylight. Horse Boy reads his endless paperback. Sarah is busy, monitoring, ringing, taking photographs, typing up reports on the typewriter, the keys purring through the long night. We all perfect the art of sleeping, long and deep. Almost hibernation. I no longer feel the island coming adrift. Solid ground, all the way down.

Evenings we sit in the cabin, if Sarah is busy. I'm stirring the rehydrating food, bubbles rising through the liquid, little orange jewels of reconstituted carrot and brown nuggets of reconstituted meat rising to the surface, dancing, sinking again. Horse Boy is reading, lips twitching. Fabián Rodriguez watches impassively, heavy lids over his eyes and a cigarette in his hand. Dave sleeps like a bear in winter. I'm worried about Joe. He doesn't seem to have the capacity to deal with the empty time. He fidgets, stands, walks over to the bunk, swears incoherently, lights a cigarette, mauls it until it's dead, sits down on the bunk, gets up again, goes to the door, comes back and sits down. A few minutes later it begins again. Like one of them polar bears kept in a pokey cage, going mad with the boredom, endlessly circling, repeating the same meaningless gestures. One morning I grab the opportunity to talk to him alone. The other three are outside, pissing about, throwing rocks at each other.

I'm fine son, he says, aggressively defensive. Don't need a counsellor. Go and play with your birdwoman.

Just asking Joe, I say, apologetically. Didn't mean to step on your male pride. I head for the door. Maybes I'll chuck some rocks too.

No, hang on. I'm not fine, he says. Sorry.

I turn and wait. There is a long pause.

Ever hit a blim when you're smoking? he says. One of those little rocks of seriously pure stuff?

I nod.

Happened to me once, he continues, and I started to hallucinate. Nothing crazy, just like a sine wave travelling down my body, my legs billowing out to one side and my head to the other. Bed, I thought. That'll sort it. But when I got there the room was tumbling, like being inside a rolling dice. So I made myself concentrate on a spot on the wall. There was a nail there and someone had drawn a little circle round it in biro. I just kept looking at this spot, and after a bit my consciousness started to shrink around it. Everything that I was, concentrated in a spot the size of a sixpence, with darkness outside. Then the spot shrank to a pinhead and I was gone.

There's a long pause while I wait for the punchline. I roll a skinny cigarette. There are shrieks from outside, a huge metallic clang as a rock hits the side of the hut.

Being here, says Joe, everything is shrinking down again. My brain isn't working enough. Just a small spot, a tiny spot the size of a pinhead. Get up, make the bed, look at the wall, make food, go to sleep.

His voice is rising aggressively. He stops and his head goes down in his hands. I spark up and suck tobacco smoke. Someone seems to be climbing onto the roof of the hut. Scrabbling, laughter, more scrabbling. I put my hands on Joe's shoulders.

We can get away soon Joe. As soon as the weather breaks. We'll get back to civilization. Chile, or somewhere.

He doesn't respond. Gaslight flickers over his pockmarks like the craters on the moon.

Look, I'll play you for it, I say.

His right hand comes up, clenched into a fist. I see it and bring up my hand, forefinger and middle finger extended.

Stone blunts scissors, I say, banging my fingers against his fist. You win. We'll leave as soon as we can.

I light his cigarette and he sucks pensively.

You let me win, he says. It doesn't count.

I'm considering an answer when there's a thunderous bang on the roof of the hut, then silence. After a few seconds I hear the voice of Fabián Rodriguez, shouting for help.

I don't think I can feel a pulse, says Sarah, standing up, rosy-cheeked from the exertion. I can't get him back.

She's tried resuscitation for twenty minutes now.

He threw a fucking rock, says Fabián Rodriguez, disbelieving. He was standing on the roof, threw a rock at me and then he slipped. Must be icy up there. Fell off the roof and hit his head.

The body of Horse Boy lies at our feet, a shocking wound just above the hairline, a slick of oily blood polluting the rabbit-fur of his head, moving slowly onto the shingle.

He threw a fucking rock, says Fabián again.

Up to their knees in blood, says Joe Fish.

We carry the body up to high ground, overlooking the colonies and the small cluster of huts. The sea is immense and troubled, the island shrinking. We lie him on his back on the frozen ground. Sarah tucks a woolly hat over the wound.

His poor head, she says.

We begin to pile stones around and over the body.

A burial cairn like a Bronze Age king, says Joe. Like Agamemnon.

Wait, I say, and run down to the huts, helter-skelter over the shingle, my boots skidding and sliding on the wet and silent stones. I return with the paperback, and lay it on his chest with what I hope is the appropriate degree of reverence.

What was his name? asks Sarah. I never heard you call him anything but Horse Boy. It seemed a bit rude.

Trevor, I say, Trevor Collins. He used to be in the Household Cavalry, something like that. Hence the nickname. He hated Trevor.

He was always reading that book, says Fabián Rodriguez. Never looked up, for hours and hours.

He couldn't read, says Joe.

We look at him.

He couldn't read, he repeats. Never really went to school much. He once asked me what the title of the book was, in case anybody asked. Swore me to secrecy.

I bend down and close one of the stiffening hands over the yellowed pages. We continue to add stones and rocks to the pile until the body is covered, no trace of the brightly coloured clothing visible from the outside. The wind is blowing, as always, tugging at the flaps on our waterproofs, tugging at the corners of our eyes and mouths. An albatross looms close over us, parachuting down to the familiar nest heap among thousands, snow white against the grey clouds and black rock. The immense bird doesn't register us at all. If, on its descent, it glances in our direction, it sees perhaps only a group of oddly coloured stones among millions of others.

7. Pallas' Warbler

(Phylloscopus proregulus)

Today I'm doing a webcam setup for the local archaeology unit – the only decent job I've got on at the moment. They want to film parts of a dig in realtime and link it back to their website. It's an Iron Age settlement, quite a juicy one apparently, and when Matt rang to offer me the contract I bit his fucking hand off.

For a start, I'm out of the office, away from that non-ringing phone. And it's good to be out on the gently rising clay lands north of the Tees, looking across the sprawl of Teesside to the Cleveland Hills, the contorted shapes of industry, the Transporter and the Newport Bridge all throwing back the insipid spring sun. They've stripped the ground back with an excavator and against that cheesy glacial clay you can see the scrawl of vanished ditches, houses, pits, blooming like black hieroglyphs. Matt bounds over to a trench, webcam in hand. It's a wireless one – saves them dragging cables in the mud.

I feel like Tony fucking Robinson, he yells, running about with this thing. Here we have the first Teessiders, looking out across the impenetrable forests of Stockton, dragging their knuckles on the floor.

Less of the cheek, I tell him.

I was born here as well, he says. I'm allowed to rip the piss.

He shows me round the site. The diggers are cleaning up where the machine's been working, shovelling and trowelling, wrapped up against a raw April day.

Good thing you brought wellies Dan, says Matt. The developer turned up in shiny shoes. Brogues, or something. Buffed to within an inch of their lives. Wanted a look round and fell right on his jacksy in the mud. I now have a degree in laughter suppression.

So what happens when you finish? I ask him.

Whole thing gets knackered. It's going to be new houses, an executive development, they call it. They'll probably name one of the roads Boudicca Crescent. You can't stand in the way of progress. Or should I say profit?

Crowds of jackdaws and rooks are massing in pylons, along the towers and even on the wires, almost ready to return en masse to their roosts. Turning over and over in a lengthy and garrulous public conversation. We adjourn to the site hut and I walk him through the basic functions on the webcam.

So does the site get written up somewhere? I ask him.

Yeah, we churn out a report for the developer. I don't suppose they ever read it. Just gets their planning permission sorted. Thing is, it's hard to say the things you want to say. Vanished people, vanished lives, what made them tick?

He sips on a cup of coffee, spilling steam into the air.

See, he says. Someone once told me that human skin is actually made from holes. It looks like a continuous surface but when you look through a microscope it's holes all the way.

I scan the inside of the portakabin. Strewn tabloids, polystyrene coffee cups heaped with ash and dog ends.

The past, he says, is like that as well. It's a landscape of holes. Think about your own memory. Your brain can't possibly store every single experience, every single sensation. It has to pick and choose. It just takes snapshots of the big stuff and sort of blurs it into what you think is a continuous surface. Your memory's like skin – it looks solid but when you get up close there's just holes. Think about yourself ten years ago, twenty years ago. What have you got in common with that person? Over that time every single cell in your body has died and been renewed. The only connection you have is this electricity in your head, these flashes of light and sound we call memory. It's a frightening thought.

He pauses, scratches at his stubble.

When you go beyond living memory, it's even worse. We don't even know our ancestors two or three generations back, what their names were, how they lived. History tells us about the rich and powerful but the average Joe has vanished from the record.

So why do you bother?

He thinks for a moment, blowing more steam from his coffee.

Well, it pays the rent, just about, he grins. But it's more than that. These scatters of pottery, the voids left behind where wooden posts have rotted – they prove that there were people here once, real people with beating hearts and brains full up with experience.

Touching vanished lives, I say.

Yeah, sort of. Or rather, not quite touching. Overlapping. You can't ever quite touch.

Outside, a huge cloud of black birds begins to stream from the power lines, heading back towards Teesside in the evening gloom, whirling and chattering. We step outside the hut to watch them.

It's like that Hitchcock film, says Matt. At least I've got me hard hat if they come a-pecking.

The diggers stop to watch the stream of birds.

Back to work, scum, yells Matt, cracking an imaginary whip.

She's lying on the sofa when I come in, knees tucked up towards her chest, one hand neatly under her cheek. At first I think she's asleep. She doesn't stir when the latch clicks shut behind me. But when I come into the living room I see that her eyes are open.

Tried to call you, she says, her voice passive, drained of colour. The eyes don't look at me. She's gazing into space, not really focusing on anything in particular. I go over to her, try to brush aside a tendril of blonde hair which has flopped over her face, but she flinches away.

No reception out there, I tell her, retreating back to the armchair and perching on the edge.

It hasn't worked, she says, baldly. I did the test today. It's negative.

I try to think of the appropriate platitude.

I'm as gutted as you are, I tell her. It's not the end of the world, though. We could have another cycle. Or we could think about adoption.

We'd have to go private to get another cycle. And we don't have the money.

Her voice betrays no emotion. Like she's rehearsed this conversation a dozen times, lying here waiting for me.

I go over to the sofa and squash onto the opposite end, lift her feet up and place them on my lap, bare and cold with blunt toes and rough skin at the heels. I start to rub them with my hands, massaging with my thumbs up into the instep the way she likes it. And some of the tension melts out of her.

It *is* the end of the world, she says, quietly.

It feels like that, I say. You just have to take it easy. Just look after yourself for a few days. Don't do too much thinking.

Yeah, she says, uncertainly.

I was thinking Kel. Why don't I take a day off work tomorrow. We could drive down to Whitby, you know, like the old days. Walk on the beach, fish and chips on the pier, lob a week's wages in the fruities.

She smiles, reluctantly. Don't think I've got the energy, she says.

Do you good to get away. Change the scenery, blow some cobwebs away. Remember that hotel we used to stay at?

She giggles.

Fucking hell, that squeaky bed. Didn't get much sleep, did we?

We're both quiet for a moment but it doesn't feel uncomfortable.

Aye, she says, eventually. Let's go. Maybe you're right.

I'll put a brew on, I say, levering myself up from the sofa. Then I remember.

Shit. Said I'd meet Yan tomorrow, up the Headland.

I hover in the doorway waiting for her response.

Thick as thieves, you two, is all she says.

She sits up, and her voice is flat again, and weary.

I don't know, I say, shrugging.

You always made him out to be a bit of an ogre. Self-obsessed, short fuse, wanderlust.

That's all true. But he's growing on me. I spent all those years resisting the *idea* of him, I'd forgotten how likeable he is in reality. Even though he's dying, it doesn't feel uncomfortable.

He's working the charm on you, she says. That's what it is. The blarney.

I know. But I can handle it.

What do you talk about?

Nothing important. Just banter, really.

You don't talk about us. The fertility stuff.

Of course not.

Because that's private.

She crosses her legs under the dressing gown, purses her lips.

Dan. Flip him off tomorrow. Let's do Whitby anyway.

I hesitate.

Can't stand up a dying man, I say, my voice wheedling. We can go Sunday instead.

She breathes out, long and slow, deflating like a balloon.

No, she says. You can't stand up a dying man.

So the next day me and Yan and more than a dozen others are peering over a back garden wall close to the church on Hartlepool Headland. The doctor's garden, they call it, though who the doctor was or what he thought about the army of anoraks at the bottom of his garden is not recorded. After October storms and spring gales the Headland can be teeming with migrants blown off course from Siberia, Scandinavia, the Arctic. It's the first landfall after the North Sea.

Pallas' warbler, says Yan. And she's a beauty.

On the other side of the garden there's a tiny bird, pirouetting like a leaf among the tendrils of a bedraggled climber. Yellow stripes through the eyes and across the crown of the head, yellow wing bars and rump flashing whenever it flutters to a new perch. It's not a life tick for either of us, but enough to get us out here on a raw Saturday morning.

There's a chippie just across the road with a crowd of kids hanging around outside. Lads in baseball hats and baggy sportswear, lasses with bare and blotchy legs. They smoke, swear raucously to impress. But the crowd of birders doesn't merit comment. Just part of the scenery here. Saturday morning cars drone past bound for out-of-town superstores.

All the way from Siberia, says Yan.

The bird is deftly picking small insects from the leaves and bark, intent and exhaustive.

No wonder she needs to feed up, he says. She's not much bigger than a mouse, blown right across from the far side of Europe. Pound for pound that's like you or me trying to hitch-hike to the moon.

I don't answer him because his words barely register. I'm thinking about Kelly, the failed IVF cycle.

What's eating you, anyway? he asks.

Have I missed something and you've turned into Jeremy Kyle overnight?

He laughs.

Fair dos, he says. I know we haven't talked much over the years. But sometimes it helps to blurt it out, kick it around.

I'll bear that in mind.

We watch the bird again for a while in silence, following its delicate movements, the green and yellow plumage like spring sun dripping through new leaves, a splinter of stained glass in the dour October day.

She's intent on surviving, he says. Isn't she? Totally single-minded. The chances of that tiny thing making it here must be a million to one against.

But she's here, I say.

Aye. She's still here.

*

After, we head to the chippie. Yan's still not looking too bad if you consider the radical therapy he's getting. Red rims around his eyes and a flush at his cheekbones, but otherwise fine. I follow him into the shop. It's warm inside, the air heavy with grease. The girl at the counter looks at him blearily, crusts of pea mush on her apron and a short denim skirt underneath.

Small chips and mushies, he says. Salt and vinegar.

She goes for the scoop, sweat on her forehead, frayed ends of hair stuck to it.

Had a long day, he says.

Tell us about it.

What time do you finish?

Don't be nosey.

She plonks a scoop of chips onto the paper, sprays salt and vinegar on top. Grabs a plastic cup and ladles mushies into it, thick and vivid green.

Industrial relations, he says. Got to make sure you're not being exploited. Long hours and that.

Righto, she says. Rolls up the paper over the tray.

Three o'clock, she says.

That's not so bad.

He hands over the money.

Might have to sit outside in the car, he says. Just to check.

You do that, she says.

She hands him the change, looks down and flushes, trying to push her hair out of the way.

Still got it, he says, when we're out of the door.

We walk past St Hilda's church, named for the abbess who planted a monastery on this rock fourteen hundred years ago, and continue through streets of terraces to the sea. Cast-iron railings along the front and jumbled flat rocks below where waders dart and skim at low tide. Turnstone and purple sandpiper, the smell of rotting seaweed. We lean on the railings and look out into the distance, into the mist. Yan grazes on his chips. Then we turn and walk along the front, past big Victorian townhouses three and four storeys high with attic windows towering over the sea. Dirty wood and paint decaying in the constant salt wind, falling away. Televisions flicker behind replacement plastic windows.

How's Jim? I ask.

Getting on like a house on fire, says Yan. Apart from his taste in music. He's a modern jazz kind of carcinoma, and you know I'm strictly rock and blues.

We had a cycle of IVF, I tell him, surprising myself. It didn't work.

He takes this on board, worries at the buttons of his donkey jacket.

I feel the cold more since the chemo, he says. You ever think about adoption?

I shake my head, feeling the words tickle inside me, but leaving them unspoken. Blood's thicker than water.

And then I change the subject, tell him about the archaeologists and the webcam.

Always wondered about being an archaeologist, says Yan, sucking on a cigarette. But then I never stayed on at school. Taught meself everything I know. Must be fascinating, digging in the ground. You never know what you're going to find. I bet that's a thrill, when the blade of the excavator bites into the soil.

You're more educated than anybody I know.

That's because I decided what I was going to read. Never let the schoolteachers decide for me.

We're walking down the Heugh breakwater. Silent grey waves rush down the seaward side in the mist. The other side, towards the docks, is calmer. In the mist there is no view towards Teesside. The world is blanked out. The moment, now, shrinks to two people, perhaps a father and son, walking along a breakwater.

At the time it didn't feel like there was an option, he says. Leave school, get a job. Everybody was doing it. Billingham site and the ship-yards. I just drifted into it. Worked out later that I wanted something else. You fucking get a sniff of the world and you want more. You want it all. Sat on St Helena watching the sun rise out of the Atlantic. Sweating your balls off in an armoured car in West Belfast with cunts busting petrol bombs against your hide. Down on the Falklands with the wind straight off the Antarctic and the tundra grass rippling like catfur. Tagteaming some sweaty tart in Famagusta.

Don't.

It's the truth. The army gave me all that, but in the end even that wasn't enough. I needed more.

We reach the end of the breakwater, watch the visible patch of sea heaving restlessly in the mist.

I always wondered Dan, why you came back here after university. You had a degree in computers. The world was your lobster in the nineties. You could have gone anywhere. Silicon Valley, Europe, the Far East.

He sounds almost starry-eyed as he rattles off the list of places.

But you came back here to this dump, and set up your own business. You're scratching a living and you could have been raking it in.

Don't know, I say. Was it me who made them decisions? It doesn't feel like me. More like I've just inherited them. I don't share an atom in common with him, whoever he was.

There's a cormorant fishing on the misty sea. Every now and then it resolves into view, low and black on the surface of the water, diving and resurfacing, fading out like white noise on the television.

Perhaps I'm not like you, I say. This is the place I know, where I grew up. I know people. It feels comfortable. I've travelled around and seen stuff, but I don't need to keep pushing at the boundaries.

I don't know, he says. Where did you and me drift apart? We're made of the same piss and wind boy. The same blood. Only a whisker between us but sometimes it's like we don't even speak the same fucking language.

Matt said that today. You can never really touch another person, just kind of overlap for a bit.

Ha. Wise fella.

He stops, and the mist closes down around us. Globes of moisture in his stubble, in the tufts of his hair.

Dan, he says. I don't know where to start.

Start with Mount Longdon, and carry on from there.

Christ. Why would you want to know about all that?

Because you never told me, like all the times you went walkabout. Just left us joining the dots for ourselves. Like there's this whole side of you I never saw. Not Danny's dad and Kate's fella. Someone else.

The dark side of the moon, he says.

Don't.

Okay. You want to know everything, I'll tell you everything. But it's a long time ago now.

I know.

Where did you get Longdon from anyway? It wasn't from me.

When I was sixteen I robbed the till and went to see some of your old mates. George Barlow and Charlie Fraser. They opened my eyes a bit.

He looks surprised.

Never knew you had it in you Dan, he says. But Christ knows what they told you. You need it from the horse's mouth, I reckon.

I'll tell you all about it, I say. It's only fair. A story for a story, eh?

Maybe, he says. Maybe you're more like me than you care to admit.

Am I fuck.

You're in denial, he says. It's understandable.

Then he spins away, laughing, fighting back a cough, laughing again. Thumps me on the back so I almost choke. And we continue walking back towards dry land. The mist thickens, the visible world shrinks to nothing, and the two people on the breakwater disappear from view.

8. Nightjar

(Caprimulgus europaeus)

It was Barlow I went to see first. He had a caravan park down on the Isle of Purbeck somewhere round Wareham. I remembered him faintly, a florid barrel of a man who stayed at the Cape once when I was small. He tied up the arms of my cardigan so I couldn't get my hands out and then he laughed and I cried.

It was a long night, chainsmoking on trains until my throat was sore, lying sleepless on the platform at Temple Meads like a corpse on a slab and watching dawn precipitate slowly through the glass roof. I checked Barlow's address in a street atlas in the station bookshop and the girl on the till had a face on her like a bulldog licking piss off a nettle.

And then more trains through a hot early summer day, stuffy and rattling and painfully slow, stopping in sidings and fagsmoke swarming in sunlight. Body and brain at fever pitch, bitter with adrenaline.

I walked out of Wareham station into the late afternoon, the sky fresh and blue as a clean sheet and the unwashed smell rising as the sun dried out the sweat from my shirt. Holiday traffic on the roads and the fishtank looks of other kids behind the safety glass. Beyond the town the road was quiet and when I crested a hill there was heathland stretching away. Heather, gorse and furze scrabbling down towards the sea, the heather buds just showing a pale lilac which shimmered in the distance like a field of stars. And on this moonscape gorse and broom spattered their yellow blossom like a chipfat fire roaring in the late sun and the scratching songs of warblers dribbled from thorn scrub. The sea in the distance, a blue strip beginning to smoke and merge with the sky.

A mile or two further on I turned onto an unsurfaced track signposted to the caravan park, straggling pine trees on either side. A horse was coming slowly towards me, ridden by a girl about my age. She looked down at me disdainfully and when we'd passed I glanced back a couple of times but she never turned round. Inside the park I wandered between the vans, statics and a few tourers set in an ocean of clipped grass stretching downhill towards the sea. And there he was, loading gobs of water with a hosepipe into troughs of gaudy summer annuals. He moved patiently, stealthily even, from trough to trough.

Watched you coming up the road, he said. That was my girl you went past. Polly. Fucking bitch.

He went back to splashing water, moved on to some hanging baskets around the steps of a static van. The eyepatch was the first thing I'd noticed. I tried not to stare. He was a stocky man, built like a barrel, a beige flannel shirt buttoned tightly over the paunch. A florid face topped with crisp greying hair and the black patch stretched tight across it on elastic.

What do you want? he said. Ent got no casual work this time of year. Me and the wife do that, and Pol. When I can get the cow to lift a finger. Who told you we was hiring? Were it that slut at MSC again?

No pal, I wasn't after work. You're Georgie Barlow, aren't you?

And he came right at me and knocked me off my feet and down to the floor on my stomach. Face pressed against the grass, right arm dragged up behind my back ready to pop out of the socket.

Who are you, you little turd, eh? a voice hissed in my ear.

He jammed the side of my head down harder, grass stems pressing an imprint into my cheek.

What you're thinking is, that was pretty nifty for a fat one-eyed fucker. Aren't you? See, the training never leaves you. I'd fucking crush your windpipe soon as look at you. Who sent you?

I struggled but he held me firm. I was starting to black out.

Yan, I croaked. He slackened the grip on my throat. Yan Thomas. I'm Danny, his son.

Let's look at you, he said. Rolled me over on my back like a prize trout.

I met you, he said. Up at the pub. It's no joke, that place – so far fucking north I nearly got a nosebleed. You were a humourless little bugger.

He stood up.

Yan Thomas, he said, shaking his head. That lunatic. You know where the word lunatic comes from, don't you?

Nah.

The moon son. Lunar. They used to reckon she'd send you mad if you spent too much time under her belly. Your old man was a moonstruck bastard if ever I met one.

He put his hands on his hips.

Sorry I kicked off back there, he said. But I can't be too careful, you know. There's all sorts after me. Inland Revenue, loan sharks, the bank.

He lowered his voice, tapped the side of his nose.

And they're just the civilized ones, he said. There's others I can't even tell you about.

I got to my feet gingerly, brushed the grass off.

So what can I do you for son? Don't tell me they've finally found the body.

No, I faltered. I just wanted to talk to you. About what happened when he went missing. I need to understand it.

I don't tell them stories any more, he said. Like a little kid shutting up shop. He retrieved the hose from the hanging basket which was now dripping like a sponge, and dropped it onto the ground. Silver snakes of water looping through the grass.

It was a mess, he said. It was all a mess. Best forgotten. Best left alone.

He stomped over to the standpipe tap, looked at it, tapped at his eyepatch. The girl on the horse was coming slowly back up the drive, sitting absolutely erect. Black hair coursing down her back.

Look, he said. I'll give you a van for the night. On the house, like.

The hose was still on the ground, water pissing away into the grass. The horse passed behind the pine trees and disappeared. Barlow shifted on his feet, pulled some keys from his pocket and tossed them at me.

Number twelve. She's a leaky bitch but if it rains you can stick a saucepan under it. Tomorrow I'll run you down to the station.

He turned and stalked away towards the house at the top of the site. I watched his rolling gait and broad back retreating up the site. The hosepipe at my feet, still hissing, the silver slick of water swelling and spreading, punctured by the sharp stems of grass, starting to gather momentum and flow downhill. I walked to the standpipe and turned off the tap. The hissing stopped and Barlow turned to look at me and his face was startled.

In the caravan I sat down at the table, breathed that indefinable caravan smell of furniture polish, spent matches, propane fumes. Always tricky to work out exactly what you're feeling, what you're supposed to be feeling. You've come all this way for a sniff of a story, so why do you feel half relieved when he won't spill? Can't fathom yourself Danny, never could.

If in doubt, there are two solutions. Brew up or skin up. I was trying to light the gas hob when there was a knock on the door of the van. She came in before I could answer.

You didn't bring the horse, I said, stupidly. She looked at me.

Dad sent me over with towels and stuff, she said, dumping them on the table. At least you can have a shower.

She wrinkled her nose and I flushed. She was shorter than me, slim, with dark hair falling over her eyes. Kept trying to flick it out of the way with her hand.

Thanks, I said. Got some clean clothes in the bag.

Not a flicker of interest.

I'm Polly, she said. Don't call me Pol cos I fucking hate it. Dad always does.

There was an awkward pause.

Anyways, she said. I sometimes go and sit on the beach in the evening, watch the stars come out. Might nick a bottle of something if Dad ent looking. You can come if you want.

Yeah, maybe, I said, flushing.

Well don't bite my hand off, she said. About nine o'clock. You have to click the ignition to light the gas.

She swept out of the van without waiting for an answer.

I did what I was told and had a shower. Clean water carrying away the sweat and dirt and clearing my head. And then I lit the gas hob and brewed up and the stovetop kettle spat steam through a broken whistle and a cup of scalding tea nibbled at my stomach.

Later I sat at the base of the dunes above the high-tide line and watched the evening sky darken. It was half past nine. Polly wasn't coming. She probably never even meant to come. It didn't matter. The sky at the rim of the world faded to the purest, most luminous blue, and then began to fall gracefully into the sea. And the first pale stars appeared, newly emerged insects flapping nervously at the horizon. Small waves ran against the beach, breath of the sleeping world, and when they broke the runnels of foam were ghost white in the gathering dark. The world wiping itself clean and beginning again.

I jumped when she slipped down beside me.

Thought you weren't coming, I said.

Like to keep a bloke waiting, she said, brandishing a bottle of Pernod. She'd changed into a denim skirt and a black jumper, a faint rim of eyeliner at her eyes. Her skin clear and pale as the twilit sky. Behind us a nightjar began its churring note in the darkness, the sound of an exotic insect vibrating in the night.

*

Is that a northern accent or something? she laughed. When you say may it sounds like *mare* – and you say *craw* instead of *crow*.

It's the way people talk, I said. (*Tark*, she giggled.) Anyway you say *loike* instead of like. Not exactly the fucking queen.

Shut up and have a drink, she said, thrusting the bottle of Pernod at me. It smelled sickly and overpowering, the liquid oily and golden. She'd already downed a good third of it.

You don't drink Pernod on its own, I said. Got to let it down with something. People drink it with water. It goes cloudy. Cloudy like when you light a coal fire and the smoke froths out of the damp rocks. Or you can drink it with black – blackcurrant that is. Goes kind of cloudy and pink.

Listen to you, she said. Do you run a pub or summat?

Lived in one almost all my life, I said. You pick up stuff, biting ankles behind the bar.

She looked at me, halfway interested.

Me mam – Kate – she's been in the trade all her life. Grew up in a pub and never felt at home nowhere else. She did a couple of year on the army camps with me dad like, but then she got homesick and made him buy the Cape. He got it for tuppence I reckon cos it was a fuckin dive with strippers and lads selling billy in the bogs. Yan – that's me dad – he cleaned it up a bit, but Kate kept it going. Sounds daft but she's like a queen behind that bar. Half the customers are in love with her. The rest of them – it's lust. Keeps the trade rolling in, mind. Or it did.

I took the bottle and swigged, taking a jolt of the liquid straight down my oesophagus. Ice crawling through my scalp. My stomach heaved. I knew why Yan steered clear of anything strong.

The full sweep of night was slowly descending, more stars beginning to blink in the eastern sky but the western horizon still pale. The sea coughed gently, small waves flickering towards us. A lighthouse flaring and subsiding somewhere off to the west. Four slow white beats and then quiet. The nightjar buzzing in the dunes.

Portland Bill, she said, as if reading my thoughts.

She was reduced to two circles of eyeliner in the near dark, her face a pale blur.

Four flashes every twenty seconds, she said. Like the heartbeat of the sea.

We watched the cycle again, in silence, light calling out over the empty sea.

It helps, she said. Proves the world's carrying on. Time is still moving. I need that. Over the other way, you can sometimes see the Needles. That low red light there. On for fourteen, off for two, on for two, off for two. Then it starts over again.

We watched the two lights sleeptalking in the Channel. Sometimes it seemed they were falling into a rhythm, the flashes becoming habitual, approaching synchronization. But then they dropped apart, the rhythm becoming disjointed, trying to communicate in mutually incomprehensible dialects.

Like two people, I said. You try to communicate but you can't reach. Not really. In the end, you're on your own.

She didn't answer.

You were going to tell me about your mum, she said.

Was I?

Yeah mate. You was.

So I told her the whole story. Yan missing on the Falklands, Kate dropping into paralysis and valium and Gary Hagan steaming in there with his loafers and his pecs. I told her about Jonah and Yan's diary and that dumb fucking cat in the box. I told her what her dad said to me up at the park. She drank long and hard.

Got any snout? she asked. I popped a couple out of the crumpled pack and lit them and two red coals danced in the dark, hissing like dragons when one of us took a drag.

Dad, she said, lives in a fantasy world. I catch him hiding in the bushes sometimes, and he won't use the phone cos he reckons it's tapped. He's got MI5 trying to waste him and the Inland Revenue trying to take him to the cleaners and the banks trying to repossess the house. It's like he's on the edge of a volcano man.

She took a long pull on the cigarette and exhaled, smoke milky in the night.

But I'll tell you the truth, she said. He owns the park and he ent got a mortgage and he pays his tax on time to the penny. Got a nice army pension as well, keeps him topped up. The whole fucking thing is made up.

What's he so paranoid about?

Dunno. He was just different. You know, when he came back.

She stubbed the cigarette into the sand.

Parents, she said. It's like looking after fuckin kids, innit? What's the point, tying ourselves in knots trying to please them or tying ourselves in knots trying to shock them. In the end, I reckon, you just got to escape.

The lighthouses continued their disjointed conversation. Polly's voice dropped to a whisper, a night insect buzzing close to my ear.

When he come back from the Falklands, she said. Of course I was chuffed to see him. We all was. But he was different. He is different. I somehow felt cheated, like they'd taken my dad and given back someone else. Sometimes he just looks at me and I feel a cold chill go through me.

I took the bottle from her hand and glugged hard. Thought about that feeling of relief when Barlow clammed up on me.

Don't you want to know why he's like that?

Nah. There's some stuff I can live without. He put himself in that situation and now he can deal with it. It's not my shit.

Yeah.

Maybe Danny, she said. You don't really want to find him at all.

Her breath tickled my ear and the hairs stood up on end.

I'll tell you summat else, she whispered, conspiratorially. He's still got both his fuckin eyes, yeah? Started wearing that patch a couple of years back and he tells people all sorts of bullshit about how he lost it.

Car crash, tumour, whatever. But there's still an eye behind there. Pull it off and take a look if you don't believe me.

On the way back through the dunes she leaned on me for support, alcohol going to her legs. I felt the cool length of her body against me and it weighed almost nothing. We steadied ourselves. There was a pale ribbon of sand snaking away from the sea between dark humps of gorse, and flickering along this channel in complete silence came a bird, sharp-winged and slender, a falcon sculpted from shadow. It passed close to my face, a moth paddling in darkness, and skimmed away into the dunes. Moments later I heard the long, churring sound start again, an antique motorcycle mining the night.

It's a nightjar, I said. People used to think they sucked the tits of nanny goats at night and dried 'em all up.

You're full of shit, she whispered.

We sat in the van with the curtains drawn and the lampshade cast a pumpkin glow over everything and then her tongue was in my mouth like a small flame fiery with aniseed. I moved my palm up to cup her chin and the edge of her jaw, the fusion of cheek and neck, and it fitted perfectly. She weighed almost nothing. And thirty minutes later I held her hair out of the way while she knelt and hawked her stomach contents into the caravan toilet. I looked at the whorl of her ear, that strange bud of flesh. And afterwards she stumbled to one of the sofa beds and fell asleep with strands of bile at the corners of her mouth. I watched her, chest rising and falling like the incidental murmuring of a lighthouse.

Hours later when she woke up I saw her back across the park towards the house and my legs were numb and then jumping with pins and needles. Well-worn stars hung in the summer sky, weathered by solar storms till they were smooth as river cobbles. I picked out the summer triangle. Arcturus. Deneb. Vega.

Penny for them, she said, croakily.

I was just thinking. Plenty of lads would have nailed you when you were passed out back there.

Missed your chance Danny, she said, sleepily. Too much of a gent.

I left her at the fence and she hurried towards the darkened house. I looked towards the sea, hoping to catch a glimpse of the Portland light, but it was hidden behind the row of pines.

Cold fusion, said Barlow, his eyepatch a glossy black comma in the red expanse of his face. That's the answer to all our problems.

We were sat in a curry house near the station in Wareham, filling the hour until my train. Barlow scooped up lime pickle with a scrap of poppadom and crammed it into his mouth.

Imagine it, he went on, spitting a small spray of food. You've got unlimited clean power and it'll never run out. It will set us free son. No need to worry about buttering up the ragheads just because we want their oil.

He picked up his pint of lager in a heavy fist.

Look, he said. It's simple, really. You meld together the nuclei of two atoms and bang! Unimaginable amounts of energy. It goes on in the sun all the time. But the scientist who reproduces that in the lab is going to be as powerful as God himself.

He snapped another piece of poppadom.

Only problem is, as soon as someone cracks it, they'll be after him. They'll be after him because they need to control it. They can't afford to let it get out.

What about Calvin Howard? I asked, changing the subject. He's in Yan's book. Wasn't he in the platoon?

You can't be too careful son, he said. They keep an eye on me because they can't afford to let me go too far. His voice dropped to a hiss. They think I won't let on but maybe one day I'll get carried away and tell somebody, and they'll have me snuffed out, just like that. He snapped his fingers. It'll look like an accident, a car smash, even a fatal illness. They know how to do that.

I studied the flock wallpaper over his head.

Calvin's dead, he said. Not much use to you.

The waiter arrived to clear the pickle tray and Barlow waited until he'd gone. His forehead gleamed with sweat.

Listen son, he said. I felt bad last night, that I didn't give you more help. See, I owe Yan. He's into me for a couple of grand. Fucking cards. Thing is, it's impossible to say no to him. Do you want a few hands Georgie? Just for monopoly money like.

He ordered a couple more lagers. My head was beginning to swim.

What happened to Calvin?

Mount Longdon happened, he said. It was one of their last positions on the approach to Stanley and they told us we had to take it.

Was my dad there?

Yeah. Your dad and those sidekicks of his. An ugly old bastard called Joe – I forget his surname. He only had a couple more years to serve. Stuck to Yan like glue and no-one else could get a word out of him. And this young lad they called Horse Boy on account of his time in the Blues and Royals. He was all right, was Horse Boy, but once in a while he'd lose it and hurt someone. They were misfits, really, the two of them. But Yan liked misfits. It was like he adopted them.

I know, I said, thinking of Michelle and Paul.

Yan and Joe used to play this game. Paper scissors stone, you know the one. Whatever decision had to be made, big or small. As if to say we don't give a toss.

The waiter arrived with the main courses, manoeuvring the trolley broadside to the table and loading the steaming dishes in front of us. I scraped rice onto my plate, added a couple of spoonfuls of Madras. The sauce was red, volcanic-looking. Barlow took two naan breads, tore them up and began using them to shovel curry sauce towards his mouth.

They were dug in on Longdon, he said, and it was high country. Peat bogs and fearsome rock runs. Grass that looks dead even when it's growing. We were on the extreme left of the attack, using a gully to work up to the high ground. But there was a group of dagoes dug in at the top with a fifty cal machine gun. It was a good position. Kept us pinned down all night, streams of red tracer fire sweeping down the mountain. And then it was early in the morning, fresh and cold, and the ground was damp with dew. A beautiful day, the sky swept clean by rain in the night. You'd think the world was starting afresh. But all we could think about was wriggling on our bellies, soaked through, winning a few yards here, a few yards there.

He paused to take a deep slurp of lager. The Madras was too hot for me. Sweat prickled my forehead and my lips felt swollen.

We was working up the base of the gully and Yan was taking his lads along the left side, above. There was no cover. When they opened up with the gun we lay down on our bellies like worms. Lads who got hit ended up just lying in the open, moaning and calling out, and no-one could get forward to them. That was when Calvin got one, right in the stomach. It bleeds a lot, when you ship one in the guts. We had to listen to him dying for four hours and you don't want to know what that sounds like. Only when he's quiet, you feel glad.

He piled another dollop of blood red curry onto his naan and crammed it into his mouth.

He was a dad, Calvin. Two kids, I think, maybe three. The youngest only just born. He liked his job, though. Maybe he liked it too much.

How do you mean?

When it goes hand to hand it's all about who wants to live most and sometimes you can't be choosy about weapons. In the action at Goose Green I seen Calvin batter a spic's head in with a trenching spade and when he grinned at me afterwards I never seen him more alive.

Jesus.

Jesus weren't there boy. Not down in the South Atlantic. We all done stuff like Calvin.

He belched. I'd given up on the Madras by now and was gulping at a glass of chilled water from the jug.

Right, he said. In the end we got round behind them. Nice and quiet, nice and slow. Just crawling on the ground like cockroaches. And then we started to get them pinned down. And some time before midday one of them stands up, hands above his head and we shout for them to stand up and show themselves and four more of the buggers get up. So me and a couple of others go up there, and Yan's wandering up from behind with his lads. Thank God, I'm thinking, we are being sensible. We can all enjoy a few more hours under the sun. And when we get to the dugout we see they're just skinny kids, not much older than you. Pale faces with grey circles under the eyes from lack of sleep, wearing those rain capes they all had, dark and slicked with water. We was eyeing up their boots.

Why?

They always had decent issue boots, the spics. Ours were fucking shoddy – there were lads ended up with trench foot. Yan started to offer them cigarettes. He always liked a smoke. Cupped his hands round as he tried to get them lit, sharing a joke with these young lads. And he's trying to barter for a pair of boots with this one kid. Keeps pointing at his feet and going how much. A packet of ciggies, he says. I'll give you a packet for your boots. The kid shakes his head, backs off, laughing nervously. Yan sort of pursues him, half laughing, half serious. Because you don't say no to Yan, do you? Ow dago, he says. Give us your boots. Two packets, eh? And he catches hold of this lad by the rain cape and he won't let go and the others start laughing.

Barlow stopped for a moment, breathing heavily, sweat starting out on his face and neck. He tapped with a finger at his eyepatch.

And I see this lad put his hand inside the rain cape. Kind of remember it in slow motion. The hand goes in. Three packs, Yan says. That's me final offer. The kid looks scared shitless. And then the hand starts to come out again, only there's something in it. You stupid bastard, I thought. You stupid little cunt. See, he's got this Beretta pistol in his hand, and all the time my rifle's been rising up to my cheek and now it's in position. And it's a beautiful blue morning like cold milk. And I squeeze the trigger and the boy turns his head towards me. Stays upright for a sec and I clock the early morning stubble on his chin and this fine gold chain round his neck and I think about the girlfriend or sister who put it there. And his hair's thick and black and glossy and his mouth is slacking open in surprise. One of his brown eyes is looking straight at me but the other one's been replaced by a bloody screaming hole the size of the fucking universe.

He reached across the table and seized my forearm. I looked down at his swollen fingers on my sleeve, then up at his face where the other hand was tapping at the eyepatch.

You don't want to know this stuff, he said. You don't need to.

What happened to him?

Your dad?

Aye.

Barlow slowed his breathing. Took a big gulp of lager.

He disappeared.

What, like a magic trick?

We was dealing with the aftermath. Processing prisoners and trying to get the wounded shipped out of there. And then one of his lads comes up to me and says where's the corp? Well, we look but there's no sign of them.

Them?

Yan, Joe, Horse Boy. Like someone's reached down out of the sky and smudged them out.

Was there like a search for them? You know, like mountain rescue, helicopters and that?

He laughed.

Yeah, he said. We stopped the war and combed the islands for three wasters.

But they were your mates.

Look, I did me best, but the orders were to keep moving. You've got to do your job, blank everything else out of your mind. I thought I was doing them a favour not reporting it straight away. Give them a chance to turn up again.

But they didn't.

Nah.

So what do you reckon happened?

He banged his fist violently on the table, face engorged with blood, and cutlery bounced into the air before clattering back onto the table-cloth. He steadied himself, breathing slow and heavy.

Your train'll be here any minute, he said through gritted teeth. You better go.

I stood up, scared. Slung the holdall across my shoulder. He stayed there, frozen. Deflated now, his colour greyer and his belly flatter.

Charlie Fraser, he said. You go see him. He was our CO. Always kept an ear to the ground, did Charlie.

He held out his hand and I gave him the diary and he scribbled the address down and handed it back. Then he shook his head like he was shaking out a bad dream.

I better get going myself, he muttered. They might think I'm spilling the beans to someone.

9. **Magellanic Penguin**

(Spheniscus magellanicus)

I spilled the beans to Sarah, pretty much, them months on South Geor-gia. She dipped into me, unpicked my brain with her light fingers. And when I said goodbye I never heard what she said in return. The words were torn out of her mouth by the wind and thrown away and the sea was scudding and the wind was jostling. And I was going to embrace her but she offered me a hand and I shook it. Very British. Then she walked back to the huts and never give me a backward glance. Left me thinking about her eyes, fields of tundra grass dancing and rippling in the sunlight. And Horse Boy, up there. What was left of him, under the stones.

But now South Georgia's an ocean away and Cape Horn island hovers like a thumbprint on the horizon and the radio bellows and spurges and lapses. Fabián sings along with the music gusting from the little speaker and his singing is tuneless, but at least he fills the silence.

Dave leans against the bulkhead, his big head resting on the wall. He bangs the back of his skull against the metal in time to the beat. His eyes are low slung, with big grey bags. A shapeless tee-shirt draped over his ample form.

Bad weather coming Joe *hermanita*, sings Fabián.

Joe wrinkles his pockmarked nose deeper into the oilskins, runs a hand over the oilslick grey hair. Says nothing.

We swing into the coast west of the Horn, seeking shelter as the weather thickens up on us, the swell growing glutinous and grey like a sago pudding. We left South Georgia in spring with the wind behind us, aiming for a landfall in Chile. We'll need fuel soon, and supplies. Argentina is out of the question. Pinochet's Chile isn't much better, says Fabián. Military rule, disappearances, death squads. We'd better not draw attention to ourselves.

Islands loom in the closing visibility, some flat and stony with drifts of windswept tussac grass, others mountainous with blue glaciers high up and dark mossy forests below the tree line. There are sinuous channels branching between their shoulders and here the water is calm and desolate, sheltered from the sea. The place is crepuscular, forgotten by the sun.

Dave idles the engine as we drift close to the mountainous walls, the boat bucking like a wanton horse. Penguin colonies on the shore, acres of guano streaked across the slopes, the distant shimmering of countless bodies in motion. Joe is quiet. He looks out at the shore with a cigarette clamped between his lips. Thrusts his lower jaw out and strokes the growth of grey beard.

You know why they call this place Tierra del Fuego? says Fabián.

Volcanoes, says Joe.

Wrong.

Dave yawns, his big elephant seal yawn. The tendons in his jaw crack.

Come on Fabián, he says. I can't stand not knowing.

Yagán people, says Fabián. Used to live here. More or less lived in their canoes, boats of skin stretched on a frame. Men, women, children, a family in each boat. Travelling the waters, a thousand islands and a thousand channels.

Uh-huh, yawns Dave.

See, the women kept the embers of the fire in the bottom of the canoe, from place to place. The fire moving through the world. Moving through the darkness. And when the Spanish came they saw the Yagán fires rising into the sky everywhere, and they called it Tierra del Fuego, land of fire.

Today's factoid, says Dave, with a slow handclap.

These days, says Fabián, there's no-one here to see our smoke rising.

Just as well, says Joe. Someone's pissed on my campfire and it's just about fucking sputtered out.

He taps out his cigarette against the bulkhead and sends the butt arcing into the sea.

What happened to the Yagán? I ask, knowing the answer already.

Epidemics, suicides, low birth rate, he says. Native people were surprisingly resigned to extinction, almost like they chose not to carry on. Smelled the modern world coming, far off, and saw there was no part in it for them.

Collective suicide, says Dave, shuffling a layer of blubber. Now that's a new one on me. Personally I like the modern world. It has whisky and pizza and fat whores. No suicide for me.

Sea spray is beaded in his floppy hair, dampening it and pulling the fringe down over his eyes.

Fabián grins.

You'd never make a Yagán anyway, he says. They would harpoon you and eat you.

We find a channel running north between islands and follow it, the bucking of the boat becoming calmer away from the open sea. Come about beyond a rocky headland and make anchor, chain clattering down to the seabed. And mist descends over us with soft chewed fingertips, wet and insistent, and the islands become a dark bulk, sensed rather than seen, like great whales calling just beyond the limits of the ear. We cluster in the wheelhouse and drink hot coffee, fountains of steam grazing the windows.

There's a man in a canoe, says Joe Fish, matter-of-fact. He's paddling north. We look out and see nothing. An expanse of dark sea shifting listlessly, shreds of mist lifting and falling like litter on the wind.

Your mind is playing tricks Joe *hermanita*, says Fabián. It's the mist, shapes in the mist.

I saw him, says Joe.

Dave is asleep on the bench seat, mouth sagging open.

Somebody stick a sweaty sock in that fucker's gob, says Joe.

I put my finger under Dave's chin and gently raise the lower jaw. He sucks and swallows without waking. Joe gets up slowly and stumps out of the wheelhouse, the door clanging behind him. The coffee works in the pit of my stomach, brutally hot. I get up and walk outside, the deck beneath me performing the constant tilting, shuffling, realignment that becomes part of life at sea, however calm the water. Eventually you don't even notice, but the body is always adjusting to allow for the fidgeting of the boat, some primal part of the brain always awake, calculating the mathematics of balance. I move over to Joe, hunched over the gunwale, looking into the mist.

There he is, says Joe.

I peer into the shapelessness and at the limit of vision there is something. Something darker than the mist but paler than the water. The mist has clamped down on the world of sound. Everything muffled, as if beneath a heavy blanket of snow. But I hear something that could be a paddle dipping into the water.

You there, shouts Joe. Ahoy!

A slight thinning of the mist passes over us and I see the man. Paddling away from us, maybe a quarter of a mile away. Joe shouts again. No reaction. The paddle continues dipping into the water in unhurried rhythm. The canoe rises and falls gently on the swell. He is heading north, along the channel, away from the sea. The mist falls again and he's gone. Joe squints hard, willing him to reappear. Nothing.

We could go after him in the inflatable, says Joe. Who the hell is he?

We'll go nowhere in this mist, I say. We'd be lost in minutes. Might never find our way back.

He knows I'm right. Back in the wheelhouse we tell Fabián.

The ghost of a Yagán, he says. Nobody lives down here. Stay in the wheelhouse. Keep your minds in the twentieth century.

Do you believe in ghosts? I ask him. Missus thinks she sees them, sometimes. Round the pub, like. They never help her with the hoovering, mind.

Perhaps, says Fabián, perhaps not. The church teaches us about limbo. The in-between place, not heaven and not hell. A grey place, without shape or substance.

A bit like here, says Dave.

It's where you end up, says Fabián, if you never had the chance to convert. Say you died before the birth of Christ, or you came from some remote tribe. You get stuck in this misty nothingness for ever. I always wondered whether anyone escaped from limbo.

Decided to go a-journeying, I say.

Exactly, says Fabián.

So ghosts are men who are just too bloody-minded to die, I say. Who find a way to come back without anyone really noticing.

Bollocks, says Joe. You live, and then you die. Meat for worms. They tell us all that shit to make us behave ourselves. Meanwhile they're busy robbing us blind. There are no ghosts. The man was real.

Some time later the mist lifts as suddenly as it fell, and it's late afternoon. The sky is muscular, clouds clenching and unclenching. Shafts of pale sunlight stab through from time to time, animating a patch of sea or a distant mountainside. Joe stands in the stern, peering through binoculars.

Got him, he says. Do you want a look?

I take the binoculars and scan the sea. The man is a speck now, almost out of sight. Mountains rise either side of him, dwarfing the tiny boat.

We could get after him, says Joe.

Something glittering in his colourless eyes, something that has been absent.

What are you thinking? I ask him.

He shrugs.

You think it's Horse Boy, don't you?

He says nothing. Eventually he shows me a clenched fist, looks at my two extended fingers.

Stone blunts scissors, I say. You win. Let's go.

That was for real, he says. You didn't let me win.

For real, I say. Can't be lucky all the time.

Now the deadening mist has gone, sound in this landscape is somehow purer. Perhaps it's the absence of background noise. Perhaps the mountains and the channels amplify the slightest whisper like a Roman theatre. The sound of the outboard and the inflatable running through the water like a long, satisfying drink, rattling the throat as it goes down. Joe is in the bow like a Labrador, sniffing the air. I sit at the stern and guide the outboard. We continue along the channel, rocky shores and dense low forests to either side, vertiginous green slopes rearing above. It's cold on the open water, my face reddening, feeling pinched. We round a headland, a tongue of shiny black rocks and forbidding trees, find a larger expanse of open water before us and the shorelines of the two islands dropping away to left and right. The shore in front of us is high and craggy and drained by distance. It must be several miles away.

We've lost him, says Joe.

He lifts the binoculars and scans the black water ahead, towards the far shore. The light is fading and I'm anxious to get back to the others. A mug of tomato soup, the agreeable warm fug of the galley.

Perhaps he was a ghost after all, I say.

We'll check five or ten minutes along each shore, says Joe. He must have gone one way or the other. He isn't out in the open water.

Then we'll go back.

He nods assent. I roll a cigarette between damp and numbed fingers, spark it up with a sear of flame from the lighter. The smoke feels dense and gloomy. The bright coal bobs and nods in the growing dusk.

Fire moving through the darkness, says Joe, grimly, as the inflatable chugs along the blank shore.

We check to the left for ten minutes. Headlands and coves, empty and echoing. Return to the channel and continue in the other direction, the outboard puttering into the loneliness. Ten minutes, and nothing. I touch Joe on the shoulder. The dusk is indigo and dense. We should go back.

One more headland, he says.

We round a low line of rocks bobbing in the surf like a grin. A cove opens up before us and we see a small knot of fire ahead, bubbling in the half light at the head of a pebble beach, between tide line and forest. Someone is standing by the fire, scanning the sea. I kill the engine and we sweep in towards the beach.

You speak very good English Matteo, I say.

He guffaws through the grizzled beard.

You are too kind, he says. It is my Oxford education and my extensive library of classics, of course.

There's a strong smell gusting from him, of smoke and sweat and the goatish tang of unwashed body. He's a small man, dainty beside the gangling frame of Joe. He wears the remains of a tattered set of oilskins, weathered almost into oblivion, and his hair is long and black and gathered at the nape of his neck with a knot of elastic. His features are small and delicate, much obscured by the vegetation of beard. A pair of large dark eyes loom above the foliage, intelligent and intensely watchful.

Joe thinks he's a loony but we squat down by his fire anyway, warming our numbed fingers while the night thickens around us in Tierra del Fuego.

You live down here all year round?

There are camps where I stay, says Matteo with a charming smile. Sometimes all winter, sometimes just two or three sleeps. You see, I'm always on the move. The canoe knows the roads, roads defined by the wind. I eat shellfish and roots and fruits and seabirds from the colonies.

You eat seabirds? says Joe, lugubrious.

Only what I need, says Matteo. I only take what I need. No more.

You didn't seem surprised to see us, says Joe, matter-of-fact.

Matteo bursts into a peal of delighted laughter.

No. Never surprised at anythings, he says. Because anythings can happen in this world.

Joe seems bemused and Matteo lets the words hang. Besides, he says, I heard and smelled you coming some time ago. The senses are sharp with no TV and no traffics.

Why do you live down here, I ask him, tentatively. Problems with the law? It must be lonely and hard.

He bubbles with laughter.

He-hey, yes my friend. Matteo is dangerous criminal. Worse than paedophile, worse than nincompoop.

Come on then, says Joe. Spill the beans.

I am a back-to-front man. A man who wears his arsehole on his chest and his dick in his backpockets.

Joe looks at me pointedly. I ignore him.

Most people, says Matteo, are happy in the city. It is the parliament of fools, like the penguins in their colonies. They crowd together because it protects them from the predators. It gives each individual citizen penguin a smaller chance of being eaten up. See?

He smiles and laughs, looks to us for affirmation.

Okay, I say.

And, says Matteo, most people would go crazy out here alone. The quietness would turn them into stark raving maniacs.

Aye, fair enough, says Joe.

Well, gentlemen, says Matteo, I am back-to-front because I defy the logics. In the city I am lonely. I have wife and children there, but I am still lonely. Every one of us living in a bubble, all alone. I try to touch other people, even my family, but the bubble is too strong. I would die alone, inside my bubble, and nobody would see. They would only see the bubble walking and talking and never know that I was dead inside.

He spits succinctly onto the beach, then he gets to his feet and pulls the oilskins around himself. I stay squatting by the fire, warming myself, and the night begins to precipitate around us, a solid wall of blue darkness.

I heard the call, he says. Just very quiet, in my head. Get up and follow me, like our Lord said. So I walked out of the house where my wife and children were asleep, I got on a train and I came to Tierra del Fuego and then I walked into these islands. And I have never been lonely since. This is why I am back-to-front.

When was this?

Since ten years.

How do you square that, in your head? I ask him. Leaving them. Not being there.

Matteo is here, he says. Tussac grass here, and pigvine. Fish also here, and penguin. We are connected. Wife and babies are not here.

You can't tell me you don't miss civilization sometimes, growls Joe.

Of course. Matteo laughs crisply, like a handbell. What is it like to have a woman? Or drink espresso or cold beer, take a warm bath? You tell me my friend, because I cannot remember. Most people, they would go mad alone out here.

But not you?

He laughs again, more gently this time, fingering his beard.

You see, he says. Modern man, he thinks he is separate from the outside world. An individual, yeah? Like he has a wrapper round the self. Like a chocolate bar. If he was out here and he tried to keep the wrapper safe, with the sea and the sky and the beasts and the birds all pressing on, tearing at it, then he would go mad.

What about you?

I had a wrapper, once. But now it's gone. It's blown away. And when your wrapper goes the chocolate starts to melt. Where does Matteo stop and where does the world begin? I become part of the world and the world becomes a part of me. Water and rocks and animals and vegetations. When I kill a penguin for food I am killing myself but I am also sustaining myself. When I eat shellfish I am eating my own flesh but I am becoming stronger. When I die I will melt into all of this, the tussac grass and forests and the shellfish singing in the sea and the birds crying in the air. This *Signor* Yan, *Signor* Joe, this is why Matteo is never lonely.

He stops talking. The small waves flicker at the edge of the shingle beach and the fire laps at our feet.

Why did you follow me? asks Matteo.

I open my mouth to say something but Joe is already talking.

We lost somebody, down on South Georgia. A friend. More than that. Fuck it, you could say he was like family. A brother.

He stops, passes a hand over the greasy mane. Blinks a couple of times as a gust of woodsmoke splashes over him.

When I saw you in the canoe, he carries on. I don't know, I didn't think you were him, that's too simplistic. But I was somehow reminded of him. I smelled him. You know that cheap spray deodorant he used to wear Yan, that fucking stuff that used to make your eyes water like a flamethrower the amount of it he put on? Well, I smelled that, when I saw you. I smell it now.

You were following the smell of a dead man, says Matteo.

Yeah, says Joe. Stupid, isn't it. I realize that now. He's gone and we have to accept it.

No, says Matteo. Not stupid. The dead are here, and they outnumber the living. Yagán people, animals and birds, countless generations. Here at the end of the world. I don't know why. Perhaps the entrance to the underworld is close by.

But death is final, says Joe. Anything else is delusion.

Ha ha, says Matteo. Religion is the opiate of the masses, okay. But Matteo sees the dead. They walk and run and fly and swim around him. We have many worlds to pass through and perhaps there is only a heartbeat between one world and the next and perhaps we do not notice when we pass from one place into another. Who knows, you may be dead already. Perhaps we are all dead.

There is a strong and thick silence. The forest behind us is bubbling with darkness.

*

Matteo moves over to his canoe, which is pulled up beyond the tide line alongside our inflatable. He pulls out two bundles, and carries them over to us.

See, he says. Food for three dangerous nincompoops. I get them from the colony today. Immature adults, not the chicks or the breeding adults. Nice and fat.

He puts the bundles down on the shingle, and the firelight washes over them. Small black-and-white penguins, trussed motionless with cord. A single eye looks up at me. I watch the eye, and it watches me. It seems quite calm.

Magellanic penguins, I say. You can tell by the markings.

Uh-huh, says Matteo. You write the name on the wrapper, *Signor* Yan. They are ourselves. They are your friend.

There's a shallow pit scooped into the shingle, some way beyond the fire, and he carries the bundles there and lies them gently down. He smoothes the feathers of the first penguin and whispers to it so quietly that we cannot hear the words. A knife appears from inside his oilskins and he draws it across the bird's throat. A small hiss as air escapes from the lungs through the severed windpipe. Thick blood bubbles onto the pebbles, black in the dying light.

Now the dead will come, says Matteo. They are drawn to the blood. Your friend will come back. Their blood for his life.

And then the smell of it is in my throat, dark blue, smoky and wistful like semen. The smell of Mount Longdon.

Matteo dispatches the second penguin the same way, black blood draining into the pebbles.

They are curious, but shy, he says. They will gather at the edges of the forest, for they do not know what we are. Later when you sleep, you will see them.

He sets to plucking the birds, throwing clouds of feathers into the air.

I'm lying on the shingle, close to the embers of the fire. Woodsmoke tickles my nostrils, wood ash tinkling as it gradually subsides. The uncomfortable shape of Joe is humped close against me, Matteo asleep on the other side of the fire. My stomach shifts alarmingly. It's the penguin meat, greasy and with a pungent aroma of fish. Swallow hard and turn onto my back, trying to get comfortable on the uneven shingle. The sky is largely clear with shreds of cloud ripping across on the wind. And behind them, unmoving and unmoved, are the stars of a strange hemisphere. They don't offer me the comfort of picking out the familiar patterns I've seen on a thousand other nights, when I've looked up and been glad to see them like old friends. They remind me that I'm in another place altogether. A windscreen has shattered into a million sherds of glass and they've been smeared across the glacial sky. They drip, here and there, from the edges. I am astigmatic. I am old.

Turn again onto my side, questing for sleep. Movement in the heavy darkness at the edges of the forest. Perhaps the dead are indeed gathered there, scenting the black blood in the pit, bubbling between the stones.

Perhaps he is there.

I hover on the edges of sleep. Men and women and children, silent among the trees. Pale faces turn, hands rest on the shoulders of impatient children. Thousands of them, rippling like a wheatfield in the wind. I strain towards them, looking for a boy with a rabbit-fur scalp and a paperback in his hands. But they shift and the faces change, mocking me. Animals and invertebrates crawl beneath their feet and the trees are encrusted with birds like overripe fruit, and the sea is crammed with fish, fat silver bodies seething at the shore.

I know that I'm dreaming, and in the dream I'm sitting at that kitchen table, rough-hewn and rounded by time and use, and there are cards in my hand. But I get a strange feeling, sitting there. A bubble of darkness, of blind horror, somewhere down deep inside of me. Every so often I feel it start to rise to the surface, draggled with weed.

I've been here before, I think inside the dream. Four jacks in my hand. I look at Dave's heart flush, already turned up on the table, and feel the glow of triumph.

I drain my glass of beer. It is astringent, medicine for the heart. Their eyes are on me, shining. The deep mahogany sheen of the tabletop. I begin to lay my cards down, one by one, looking at the pillar of ash teetering at the tip of Dave's cigarette, notched into the edge of the ashtray.

A pair of jacks, Matthew and Mark. And then nothing. Three, seven, ten. No Luke, and no John.

Softly and soundlessly the pillar of ash drops into the ashtray and the cigarette dies. A moth still presses at the window, patiently and persistently, looking for the moon.

This is the poker game you're dreaming about, right? Back on East Falkland?
Correct.
But you're dreaming it the other way — you lost that hand. Like you were saying to Joe, perhaps there's another world where things turned out different.
No flies on you Dan.
It was on your mind, though. It's natural that you'd dream about it.
I've dreamed this dream almost every night for the last twenty-five years. I've come to thinking this is how things were meant to be.
Meant to be?

Dave guffaws, wipes sweat from his brow on a grubby shirtsleeve. Begins scooping up the money from the table.

Now that, he crows, is magic.

He flashes a little wanker sign at me, grinning from ear to ear.

Joe is standing behind me and I feel his hand on my shoulder.

We'll leave it till first light, he says. Then we'll head out. A couple of hours to get your head together.

When I was here before, after I won that hand, I went for a wander around upstairs. Remembering it, the bubble gives a little lurch and my heart jumps. I hear the others talking, but their voices in the dream are thick and impenetrable like moss. I stand up and walk, shine my torch up the wooden tunnel of the stairwell, start to climb. On the stairs the bubble rises and the reflexes of fear work on my body. Heartbeat audible, sweat leaking out, a tightness in the stomach.

I stop here, in the dream, and remind myself what happens. There's nothing to worry about. You go upstairs and poke around in those empty rooms. You find that old lighter, lying on the floor among the debris. It's one of them old-school Heath Robinson things where a little cap on a lever comes down and snuffs the flame. You pick it up and dust it off and decide to clean it up later and make it work again. And then you come back downstairs to the others.

This thought steadies my heart and I carry on up to the landing. It's a long corridor with a single window looking out to the east, glass long gone from the panes and a green wind loping through straight from the South Atlantic, charged with salt and moisture. Strips of wallpaper have slumped from the walls, and the torch beam moves over their tortured bodies on the floor, raddled with damp and mould. I step carefully over them and try a door. The bubble lurches and I feel sick to the stomach. I'm looking at a bathroom, the bath and toilet a grim shade of avocado, offcuts of faded green carpet on the floor. A mirror above the sink. Look at my face for the first time in weeks and I don't recognize myself. I know it's me, that the grey eyes, receding hairline, thick stubble and broad nose belong to Yan Thomas. But there's no sense of recognition. It reminds me of looking at the stars and seeing no constellations, only chaos.

Later, when you sleep, you will see them, I hear Matteo say, as I stare at my own strange face in the mirror.

Back on the landing, footfall dampened by the thick pile carpet. Open another door, the bubble still rising, in my chest now like pleurisy. I'm in what used to be a bedroom. I feel relieved. I have been here before. Everything just as I remember it. Collapsed rafters lying across the bed, clothes strewn across the floor, crumbs of ceiling plaster across everything like icing sugar. It's important now for the dream to follow what I remember. So I sweep the torch beam carefully across the floor, and there it is, glittering with reassurance. I bend and fold it into my hand like a metal egg, let my body heat leach into it, incubate it. The bubble rises and I taste bile. The penguin meat, my dreaming brain says. You're going to be sick.

Back on the landing. Now it's time to go down to the others. But there's a feeling of incompleteness. I shine my torch down the landing and there's a door at the far end. Planks and cross-braces, the brass doorknob shimmering, and when I look at it my head swims and my heart hammers. The bubble climbing my throat, hard and pneumatic like a ball of undigested food.

Go downstairs, I tell myself. That's what you did. Go downstairs to the others. But my body's beyond control now, moving towards the door, one step and then another. Go downstairs, my mind screams, but my hand reaches for the doorknob. It turns and I hear the latch click and the bubble has almost reached the surface where it will burst and whisper small words of oblivion wriggling like worms into the emptiness.

The door swings towards me and I step back and there's a stairwell, leading upwards, wooden steps painted white. An attic up there under the bones of the roof. A wave of nausea sweeps over me but my feet are on the stairs and the sound of my boots swelling out, filling the world. The bubble of horror at the back of my throat, burning in the nasal cavity and behind the eyes. Stomach acid crawls into my mouth. The lighter still in my hand, warm now. Hot.

And then I reach the top and see the two dago conscripts crouched there where they've been hiding from us all along, and there's no sound because they've already fired their rifles and the last thing I see is the two ragged muzzle flashes like the last pale stars nuzzling at the belly of morning.

I wake up and the first pale and unhealthy light is creeping into the eastern sky and I'm retching gobbets of half-digested meat into the pebbles of a lonely beach on Tierra del Fuego. The forest is full of ghosts and the sea is full of fish and beside me Matteo and Joe are sleeping the sleep of the dead.

10. **Spotted Redshank**

(Tringa erythropus)

Thought you were dead this morning, he says.

I was asleep.

Bet Kelly gave you a hard time, the old man banging at the front door at five o'clock.

No, she didn't.

The sound of our boots crunching through cinder, each footfall like a dry cough. When I was a kid he woke me with a cup of coffee, bitter and outrageously hot, and it was still night outside when I tumbled out of bed and pulled jeans on over my pyjama bottoms. I remember the handbrake creaking off on the battered Renault Twelve as he willed it out of the yard on those perishing mornings, and the pear drop smell of the upholstery as we headed down the Seaton road to Saltholme and Dormans, the reedbeds by Reclamation, the Long Drag. My feet already pulsing with cold inside the wellingtons and that coffee still burning inside.

You were up early, I say. You had that dream again? The one where you die.

Aye, he says. It's always the same dream.

We're tramping down Long Drag towards the Seal Sands hide. It's a rough cinder track running alongside a low bank which used to be the sea wall, before reclamation. Tidal pools beyond there now, fringed with reeds. They dumped thousands of tons of slag to drive out the sea – the excreta of steel creating the land on which the chemical industry grew, back in the thirties and forties. Like tomato plants springing from undigested seed in the beds of a sewage farm.

My nan had the same dream every night, he says. When she was dying from stomach cancer. She dreamed of pork pies.

That's cruel.

There's an early haze over the marshland, the rough grass and thorn scrub. Refineries and distillation columns and gas flares looming with their feet in the mist, the strange fruit of industry sprouting from quiet earth. Pipelines rearing into pipe-bridges and burrowing beneath our feet. Brinefield valves like rusting root crops in flat green fields.

They use them for storage these days, says Yan. Inert gases and that. Nitrogen.

Where?

Under the ground man. That's what brinefields are. They used high-pressure water to scour out the salt deposits, and left these immense voids underground.

Right.

When I wake up, he says, three, four in the morning, I think to meself I should have died back there. If I'd gone up them stairs. See, I cheated it somehow.

Aye, well. That time in the morning, it's hard to keep those thoughts away.

I cheated it then but it's catching up with me now. I feel smaller Dan. Like I'm shrinking. Do I look smaller?

No. You're all right.

Maybe one day I'll just disappear, and the next thing you hear will be that they've found my bones in the Falklands. In some old tumble-down house. And that I was there all along. And that I never came back at all.

Is that right?

Something as small as a hand of cards. Or which way you fall off a roof. Which stone you hit. It can change everything. It can put things on a different track.

We walk on. The wide silver pools hold the compass of the sky within their placid surface. The low pervasive hum of the refineries like a quiet respiration.

When you get to the end of the Drag you see the Seal Sands hide stark against the sky and beyond it the tidal flats sweeping out towards the river's mouth. It's a new hide – arsonists got the last one back in the late eighties. The creosote catches beautifully and the whole thing goes up like a hayrick.

We approach it with careful feet and slow breath blooming in clouds, and nobody else is awake and the sky is a deep milky-blue just creeping into life. Mount the steps, shudder the door open and breathe the dry and pent-up air inside, heady with creosote. We wait in the darkness for a few minutes to let things settle, light chinking in shyly through cracks and knot-holes. Wormholes of light tunnelling through wooden planks. Plenty of room for both of us.

Yan lights a fag and the lighter flame splashes from his face.

Is that it?

Yes, he says, handing it to me. Still warm from his hands.

Funny to think you picked it up on the other side of the world.

Mmm. Didn't need much cleaning up, really. Just a new wick and a dab of Brasso.

I try the mechanism, relishing the warm, oily smell of petrol, the big sprawling dab of flame. And then I lower the little cap to dowse it.

We could have another shot at IVF, I tell him. But we'd have to fund it ourselves. And there's still only a one-in-four chance of a viable pregnancy at the end of it. Reading between the lines, they think we're too old anyway. They keep dropping hints about fostering.

One in four, that's not bad, you know, he says, quietly, shifting on the bench. In my poker-playing days I'd have taken them odds. One card to a flush, say. If you gave me those odds of seeing the next couple of years out, I'd bite your fucking hand off.

Do they give you the numbers? You know. Percentages.

Sometimes, if you push hard enough.

He sounds weary, suddenly. Clears his throat.

They're pretty confident I'll get into next year. That's only a couple of month, mind, so I'd have to go downhill pretty snappish not to make it. Five to ten per cent chance of getting to the end of next year.

It's still a chance.

Aye.

It's true, he says, about your horizons shrinking. Used to think, if I was given a death sentence like this, that I'd just make a quick clean end. Under a train, off a block of flats. What's the point in spinning it out?

But now?

Well, the end of next year is an eternity away. If I can get a few more months, a few more weeks. Days even. It would be worth it.

He pauses to cough. Not a particularly alarming or sinister cough. Just persistent.

Your life list, I say. How many?

Britain?

I nod.

Three nine eight. I'd like to get four hundred.

We lapse into silence, absorbing the still darkness of the hide. Neither of us wants to open the shutters, breaking the moment open with light. The rapidfire calls of redshank outside, jabbing urgently into the dawn sky like the bleep of an electronic alarm.

They're nervous buggers, says Yan. Keep going off like a dicky trip-switch.

Aye.

In the darkness I sense him smiling, and I feel close to him.

Yan slips the shutters open and secures them and the vast mudflats of Seal Sands are spread before us. There are thousands of waders feeding across the mud, crawling over the glutinous surface, and loose parties of duck further out in open water – wigeon, merganser, shelduck. In winter there are whooper swans on the ice-encrusted flats, visitors from the Arctic. And in the distance you can make out the bulky forms of seals hauled out on the more remote banks.

We scan with bins, and Yan sets the scope up between us. I like to watch waders feeding. Tiny white sanderling skittering over the mud like clockwork mice in perpetual motion. A couple of piebald oyster-catchers winkling shellfish from the ground with those garish plastic orange bills, using the prehensile tips to unlock the shells. Pale dunlin everywhere, nagging insistently at the mud. Groups of redshank moving through the shallows with their high-stepping walk and orange legs.

Greenshank, over there, says Yan. See the three refraction columns on the horizon? Follow the middle one down until you get to a group of knot. Count in three from the left and you're there.

Got him. There's a whimbrel in there as well.

Yeah?

You've got the twitcher gene, I say.

Meaning?

You're always looking for the odd one out. If it was just dunlin you'd be off home.

He grunts.

Aye, he says. Always been one of them birders. You can keep the common stuff.

Been there, done that, I say.

There's something about a rare bird, he says. It's a survivor. Come over them uncharted seas from fuck knows where.

We're opposites, me and you. I could look at the common stuff all day.

He snorts, goes back to the scope.

What have you got anyway?

Couple of little stint over there, in among the dunlin. Couple of bar-tailed godwit out there. Elegant buggers, dipping their beaks right in to the hilt.

Yeah, got them.

And let's have a blast through these redshank, see if we can get us a spotted.

He starts to scan through the mixed flock, and I focus in on them too.

Got it. Spotted redshank. Left-hand end of the flock. Paler than the rest, stripe through the eye.

I can't see a stripe at this distance man. But yeah, there is a paler one. See how it's feeding different to the rest? Sweeping its bill through the water, like. Side to side.

Like your missus doing the vacuuming, he laughs.

Careful now, she'll have your guts. Mind, she doesn't do much of that these days.

What, the vacuuming or having your guts?

Either. Both.

I bet this fertility business has hit her hard Dan.

Aye. It's like we circle round each other but never really meet. She goes out with her mates, comes back mashed.

Nowt wrong with a bender now and then, he says, calmly.

I know. But sometimes she doesn't come back till the morning. Says she slept over at a mate's house. That's why you never woke her up this morning.

She wasn't there.

Right. Look, I shouldn't be telling you this. You've got enough on your plate.

What you mean is I never earned your confidence. You feel disloyal, spilling your guts to me.

Yeah, that's what I mean.

You've got to talk to someone.

Did you ever regret blowing it with Kate? You could have come back from the Falklands and made a go of it. You could have been a stay-at-home husband and dad.

Pipe and slippers, he says.

Garden centre on a weekend.

Nah, he says. Life's too short for regrets. You can't look back.

I look at him but he's got the bins up to his eyes.

Me and Kelly, I say. It used to feel like we were a unit. We'd do stuff together. Nowt special, like – the pub, the flicks, club on a weekend. We had a sex life. But none of it's happening any more. We haven't got anything in common except childlessness. It's like we remind each other of the problem.

Sounds like you need to ship out, he says. It's making you unhappy.

It's not that simple.

It is from where I'm standing.

He coughs, softly.

The sun rises beyond the flats, beginning as a small red disk nudging at the horizon. The flat surfaces of mud and water become gilded, subtly at first but then flaring into life like fields of molten copper, like the surface of the sun. And a collective dread begins to pass through the waders. They shrug and shuffle their feathers, looking around more often, concentrating less on feeding. I can't see any possible cause for this. No bird of prey visible, no other birders around, no dogwalkers. Sometimes it just happens. Fear gusts unbridled through the flock like a virus.

And there's only ever one outcome. Thousands of waders rise into the air, the vast flock turning and wheeling as one, a huge double helix twisting itself inside out. The spotted redshank disappears among the others, among the telegraphy of white rumps and wing edges. They raise their voices now and the empty air fills with the urgent message carried from ten thousand feathered throats.

We used to roll back to the Cape around nine o'clock and fry up bacon and eggs for breakfast, scorching and salty. You felt glad that you'd sat in that wooden icebox, that you'd been outside in the cold for hours when everyone else was only just swimming into consciousness. And there wasn't any time or space beyond this, at all.

*

The door to the hide clatters behind us and I look at Yan and appreci-ate for the first time how much weight he's lost. He's a skeleton, with the donkey jacket dwarfing him, flapping up around his scrawny neck. And he's struggling to keep up. I can see his chest working, red spots flaring in his cheeks. I slow down appreciably, and he fires me a hard glance, keeps striding ahead.

That fucking eyepatch of Barlow's, he barks. I never knew about that. He always played it by the book, did Geordie. Regulations man, all the way. And it turns out he's got a screw loose all along.

Aye, well. It must have been pretty traumatic. That young lad shot through the eye.

It was a war, he says. We were professional soldiers.

He coughs deep, expectorates noisily, and voids an oyster of phlegm onto the ground. Keeps walking hard, pushing himself, and now I'm struggling to keep pace with him.

The lighter, he says. It's still in your pocket.

I grope for it and test its weight in my hand. It's turned fiercely cold in the minutes since he handed it to me. I toss it to him and he fields it in both hands.

So, he says. The girl. Molly, was it?

Polly.

You missed your chance there, didn't you?

I suppose you'd have got stuck in.

Nah. I never needed to rely on booze or rohypnol son. Never had to beg for it or play tricks.

We carry on walking. Huntsman Tioxide and the Seal Sands refiner-ies are shooting giant and knotty middle fingers into the sky and our conversation fades out behind the hum of the estuary, the deep respi-ration of the place, long and slow like the tidal breathing of a sleeper.

11. **Long-Tailed Tit**

(Aegithalos caudatus)

Paul was fast asleep, breath coming slow and the headphones still buzzing away at his ears. The train rattled through North London, sunless cuttings and sidings frothing with buddleia and spray can graffiti, the backs of industrial units. Paul licked his lips, swallowed, snuffled. His eyelids twitched, pupils in motion beneath. Asleep, he looked like a little boy.

When you think about birdsong you probably call to mind the spectacular ones. A nightingale trickling into a summer night like a girl's breath on your neck. Or the black treacle drizzling from a blackbird's throat, infused with the essence of dusk. Fiercely alive and at the same time weary of life, a blackbird can make your heart swell to busting without ever knowing why.

But most bird calls are mundane stuff. Little fragments, little ticks and chinks of sound. Contact calls, like social glue, keeping the flock together. Like sonar. You fire out a pulse of sound. I'm here, it says. What about you?

And it's reassuring to hear the answer come back. Yes, I'm here.

He was standing where he said he'd be, top of the escalators at King's Cross, and I was absurdly glad to see him. Bruising on one side of his face and a split lip.

Did Franco catch up with you?

Nah, just the footie – a few boots in the napper like. I've had worse from me dad. Lucky me brains are in me dick, eh?

How did we get on?

We were shite.

He stood there like a rock, brown skin and the facets of his shaved head. Commuters streamed either side and some of them ignored him and some of them glanced at him shyly, with fear and disgust and desire, because he was ugly and beautiful and contemptuous and unapologetic.

Paul glanced down at the holdall in my hand. A commuter barrelled against his shoulder as he did so and Paul swivelled aggressively, giving the evil eye to the man's broad back as he beetled away up the stairs, daring him to turn round.

You did it, eh? he said.

Aye.

He erupted into hoarse laughter and his eyes flared sea-green and brilliant.

Danny Thomas, he said. Tealeaf and absconder. London Rent Boy of the Year, nineteen eighty-five.

Fuck off.

Tell us, he said. Go on.

So I told him about Barlow. People frothed around us, the world turned.

What a fruitcake, said Paul. Wearing a patch when you got both eyes. Two or three short of a six-pack and no mistake. Where you headed now like?

Somewhere near Peterborough. It's a junkyard.

I'll pal you up there.

What about your job?

I'm on an extended sabbatical Danny.

He turned and started yomping down towards the platforms and I followed him.

How do you mean, sabbatical?

Me boss, he said. Jimmy Kelly. Thinks he's the king of shit. He says no you can't have Saturday off to travel for the match. In the wonderful world of landfill, Saturday is the big day. People been doing the garden, clearing out the shed, and down they come in their little cars itching to throw it all in a big hole in the ground. You listen to it on the radio like every other cunt, says Jimmy.

But he changed his mind in the end, eh?

Nah. Stuck the nut on him and walked off the job. That'll learn him. He'll have to cover the shift hisself instead of wanking in the office.

The train from King's Cross was crowded. By the doors the space was crammed with backpackers, sitting or lying on humongous rucksacks. Paul pushed through and stormed down the corridors, dispensing the evil eye to all sides, barely waiting for the sliding doors between carriages to open. I streamed behind in his wake. All the seats were full, passengers already crouching behind newspapers, paperbacks, personal stereos, guarding their hard-won territories. We came to the smoking carriage, a thick topiary of smoke already blooming. There were no seats. Paul scowled, then lighted on two pairs of seats facing each other, occupied by four kids not much younger than ourselves. Paul stood in front of them.

'Scuse me lads and lasses. I can't help noticing that you're not smoking. And I believe I'm right in thinking this is a smoking carriage.

A silence while the kids looked at Paul and wondered what was coming. They were two couples, the boys in jeans and pinstriped shirts, one blue and white, one pink and white.

Well, Paul continued affably. Me and my mate here are both smokers, and we'd like to enjoy the facilities British Rail has placed at our disposal. So I'll have to ask you to vacate these seats immediately.

The kids exchanged nervous glances. Judging by their bags they had been on a shopping trip to London and were now on the way home.

You can't make us move, said one of the girls, the one sitting next to Blue-and-White.

She was blonde, horsey, a string of pearls quivering with indignation at her throat.

We were here first, weren't we Harry, she added, looking to her boyfriend for support. Harry was bricking it.

Look mate, he said. We don't want any trouble. But you can't just take our seats. Possession is nine tenths of the law, isn't it? Why don't you just try further down the train?

I stood behind Paul, saw other passengers notice what was going on. They shrank away, embarrassed. Nobody was going to help the four kids. Paul breathed a deep sigh of frustration and fixed his glare on Harry. Pink-and-White was looking out of the window, willing himself elsewhere. The lights of suburban London blinked past in the drab twilight.

Now listen here, Paul said. Old chap.

A meaty hand shot out and grabbed Harry by the throat, blurred blue spots at the knuckles. The other kids were frozen, petrified. He dragged the younger boy up off the seat to eye level. He had floppy hair, combed back into a wet-look with gel. With his other hand Paul retrieved a lighter from the pocket of his combat jacket, and brought it up close to Harry's face.

These seats are ours, said Paul, amiably. If you want to argue about it, I'm going to burn your fucking face off.

He flipped the lighter and a blue flame roared at least a foot into the air.

I hear hair gel burns a treat, he added.

Come on, said the other girl, the one with Pink-and-White. Let's just go.

She hustled out of her seat and down the carriage, boyfriend scurrying after her. Paul threw Harry after them. He stumbled and sprawled in the aisle. Passengers glanced at him in annoyance.

You can stay if you want, gorgeous, Paul said to the blonde horsey one. She pushed past him, shaking with disgust. The carriage settled down to normality, people burrowing back into the comfort of magazines and paperbacks. Paul beamed and settled back, contentedly planted his boots on the seat opposite. He lit a cigarette and began exhaling smoke rings that billowed into the air and burst against the cool surface of the window.

Possession is nine tenths of the law, he said. I like that.

Ten minutes later he'd rummaged through my holdall and found my Walkman and now he was screwing the earpieces in and twiddling with the volume.

Do you want one or what? he said, waving a packet of chews towards me. I fumbled for a couple of the squashy green lumps, compressed them into my mouth. Paul put both feet up on the seat opposite, lit up ostentatiously and cracked a can of Tennants Super. He sipped on it, eyes closed, and I looked at the home-made tattoos on his knuckles. A blue point on each one, faded into an amorphous blob. His hair was beginning to grow out. It was an inch long now, just enough to hint at parting and curling and lying flat like catfur. Blue veins at his temples.

Dan. Paul jogged my elbow so that I suddenly spilled forward, waking in confusion. I shook my head, hard.

Sleeping like a baby, he said. We're nearly there pal.

He balled up the Walkman with its speakers and tossed it back to me and I fielded it. The train was beginning to slow towards the station.

What do you think you're going to find, anyway? he said.

People don't just disappear, I said.

Aye they do. My dad did one when I was six, and I never seen the bastard since.

Maybe they're two peas in a pod, your old man and mine.

Maybe.

He tucked both hands behind his head and yawned. Stubbed his cigarette down onto the seat cushion. I watched it scorch a hole through the tartan cover and into the foam rubber.

So, he said. Did your dad ever beat fuck out of you with a belt buckle when he was mashed up?

Nah.

Did he ever like stub fags out on the backs of yer legs?

He wasn't like that. You should know.

Did he ever knee you in the bollocks and then laugh his cods off because he loved that little squeak you made when he knocked all the air out of you?

No. He didn't.

Right, he said. Just checking.

We got as far as Whittlesey before we ran out of trains and decided to bed down on the platform for the night. Paul was talking to some lasses and I watched how they leaned against the fence and arched their backs like cats and laughed too hard at his jokes.

I went for a walk.

Down the road I found a farm track and cut down among fields with the sinking sun clenched hard like a lump in the throat, still warm on my back and the top of my head. Climbed a hedge bank and vaulted the fence and walked along a hawthorn hedge where luxuriant growth had exploded from the trimmed-back bones of last winter in wild and sprawling locks of thorn. And the hedges were bubbling with white blossom, etched across the green contours like crisp snowbanks.

A flock of feeding tits came gusting along the hedgerow, one of those loose alliances of small birds swirling like smoke through the early summer fields. They were all around me, blue, great and long-tailed, pinging small contact calls like neurons firing in the forest of the brain.

I'm here. Are you there?

I came to a halt where grassland rolled downhill towards a stream, bristling with introvert trees like a furred artery in the base of the shallow valley. The sun strengthened and the light was flooding through stained glass, the bitter deep blue of the southern sea and the tart nose-wrinkling green of an early apple. I listened to the wind moving through foliage, the quiet rippling of grasses, the shuffling of hawthorn leaves like a soft insistent rain, the polite applause of mature trees. The flock had raced on across the landscape, just a solitary long-tailed tit still coasting the hedge above me, pricking the foliage with little thorns of sound. But now there were no answering calls. I imagined a sink emptying, water spiralling down a plughole. Emptying the world, emptying my body. There was only a hillside, impossible blue and green. The wind moved in the hedges and high up a tiny bird was ticking.

Dark when I got back to the station, a wind whipping through from the Fens. There wasn't much shelter on the open platforms so we hunched down in the lee of a gaggle of baggage trolleys and waited for dawn, when we could get our connection. A full moon blazing, and while the orange glow of Peterborough eroded the western fringe of the sky, the centre was deep and unruffled. I thumbed a paperback I'd bought at King's Cross. *Crime and Punishment.* It was one of my set books.

Don't know how you can read all that stuff, said Paul. I never got into it at school. Too busy driving teachers over the edge. Remember that Mr Hunter we had for physics? I think I give him a nervous breakdown. He used to run out the classroom and stand outside in the yard smoking a fag with his hand shaking. We'd all be sitting there waiting for him to come back.

Waiting to have another crack at him, you mean, I said.

Aye, he agreed, with a grin. It was a blood sport. Like that bear baiting they used to do. What's it about, anyway?

Bloke kills an old woman with an axe. And her sister. Just to prove that he can. That he's got the power to act, to do something.

That sounds good, said Paul. Bit of mindless bloodshed like.

It's more the psychology of it. You know, what's going on inside his head. What makes him do it.

You know Dan, he said. Forget what I was saying to you before. About quitting school. I reckon you got the brains for it, all these books you read. You could go to university, be one of them yuppies on the stock market.

I'll do what I want pal, I said. Thanks all the same.

Steady on daft cunt. What's got into you?

Careers advice from a landfill operative (retired), I said. I can do without it.

Fair enough like.

He lit up a straight and blew smoke at me.

Away Paul, I said. Lighten the mood. What about them three lasses?

Prickteasers, he said.

Do you reckon we're going to get any sleep on here?

Cold concrete was already leaching into my bones, bruising the joints.

Going to be a long night, said Paul. Endless. Plenty of fags to see us through.

I jolted awake on the platform. Tendrils of cloud drifted across the face of the moon and the light spilled along them in shallow mercury rivers, braiding across the lush water meadows of space. It was cold, earth's heat spilling into space.

Did I ever tell you about the mercury? said Paul.

What mercury?

It was one of me grandad's scams. At least they said that's who he was. Gadgie called Jed Wallace. I think he just had a ride off of our nan once upon a time.

He pulled a face.

Jed used to work as a pipefitter on LP Ammonia. Always thieving, the little cunt. See, he went to work on this little pushbike every day, cycled in past the security on the North Gate. And at the end of his shift he cycled out again, only he was weaving all over the road like he was either pissed or giving Giant Haystacks a croggy uphill. These security charvers used to stop him and search him, but they never found owt. Even had the bobbies down once to give him a breath test, but he come out clean.

He paused and lit a fag, shielding it from the wind. Flame between his fingers.

There you go, he said. Fill your boots. Handed it to me and lit another for himself.

They never worked it out, he said. Jed had a little tap-hole in his bike frame, with a rubber bung. Used to fill the frame up with mercury off the site. Weighed a fuck of a lot, sloshing around in there fit to bust. He used to come round to our back door and wheel his bike right into the bathroom and empty it out into our bath. It's amazing stuff, liquid metal.

Quicksilver, they used to call it.

He only took a day or two to sell it on, but while it was there we couldn't go in the bath. Mam said not to touch because it was poisonous.

I bet you did though.

I was fascinated by it. Couldn't leave it alone. Just sat and watched the light play off the surface of it. It was always quivering, like it couldn't sit still, and it used to bounce the light all over the walls and the ceiling. Sometimes I couldn't resist touching it. I had to know what liquid metal felt like. I'd scoop some up in me hands and let it drop into the bath. When it hit the bathtub it split up into hundreds of tiny globes and they flew apart, like a shoal of little silver fish swimming away. Then they'd slide back into the middle and start to join back together, the big fish gulping up the minnows.

What happened to Jed? Is he still around?

Nah, he said. It was weird.

What was weird?

He was working in a vessel on the site – one of them ones with the inert atmosphere inside, no oxygen so you can't get a fire or explosion.

Full of nitrogen, aren't they? It doesn't react but you can't breathe it.

Paul shrugged.

Jed was wearing breathing apparatus, he said. But when he got to the middle of the tank he stripped the mask off.

Why?

They reckoned he might have puked in his mask. The rubber does that to you sometimes. Pulled it off to clear it. But his mate reckoned he never even tried to get it back on again. Stood there like he was waiting for something, with this look on his face and his eyes glittering. He was dead before anybody could get to him. No oxygen, you see.

Sorry.

Paul ground his cigarette out on the platform. The nub wasn't properly extinguished, and continued to leak stale, sour smoke.

Good way to go, he said. Quick and clean. Better than cancer or something like that.

We sat in silence and watched the moon crash-land in slow motion into the plain of the Fens. As her belly sagged into the ground the light rippled out along the horizon, like a shoal of little silver fish swimming away. And then the floor of the wetland swallowed her whole. Her silver tail waved pitifully from the black maw, and vanished.

12. **Southern Lapwing**

(Vanellus chilensis)

Count them off.

Yan is the pylon, close by us, soaring into the clean spring sky. The tracery of steel superstructure, high voltage lines loping across this flat country wrenched from the sea. And the next pylon and the next, the giants becoming smaller and more delicate with distance. I can smell her. Her hand is on my chest.

Tean is Kate. Kate Murphy as she was. The two of us. Dark and slender, smooth and acrid as seacoal, a black mole beneath one breast where the globe of flesh rejoins the taut drumskin of her belly. She was with her boyfriend in the pub, her dad's pub in Greatham, and I couldn't stop looking at her. I was embarrassing myself. Too much to drink. I could barely stand up. She came over, something in her eyes taunting me. Salt and seaweed on her tongue.

Tether is the boyfriend. Motorcycle boots and black leather. We were outside, the moon swimming at the bottom of a deep deep glass. He was saying something. Angry, dismissive words, buzzing like night moths around my head. He punched me in the face but I didn't feel nothing, just sat down gently on the floor. It was a soft cushion made from the silver sand of stars. He was astride the bike, the engine blaring like a foghorn. He beckoned Kate to sit behind him but she didn't move. She was so still I mistook her for a shaft of moonlight.

Mether is the river. The Romans called it *Dunum Sinus*. Kate turned away and looked out over the breakwater and the wind caught her hair and whipped it away from her face. I was looking at the curve of her cheek, at the saltglaze of downy hairs and Hartlepool Headland brooding to the north. The wind is amazing, she said. It goes right through me. I am made of oxygen. Pure oxygen.

Pip is the towers. Refraction columns, flare stacks, cooling towers. The waste gases are burning with blue and orange flame, tropical fish flashing in the night. At night you would think it was a city, like New York, with a million lights blinking from the soaring tower blocks. But it's an empty city, humming to itself. A few lonely men in control rooms turn dials, sit and watch the panels.

If you count off every lump of time that dribbles past you, it makes them all the same. Give it a number, assign it to the past. Charlie Fraser told us this is what you should do under torture. You withdraw your mind from the body and take it somewhere else. Deep inside. So now I'm eighteen years old and she's moving on top of me in the corner of a field at Back Saltholme between the feet of a giant pylon. Danger Of Death, read the signs, and there's a stick man being struck down by a thunderbolt. I'm counting to stave off the inevitable and her back arches like a flying buttress and her bony shoulders are flashing in the weak sun and her breath is coming fast.

See, it was a beautiful morning today, sailing into Puerto Angelmo, with sunlight hovering over the sea, trailing its fingers in the salt water. A long trek from Tierra del Fuego, up the west coast past the glaciers and the mountains dribbling down to the Pacific. We drew into the harbour with its wooden staithes and fishing boats tied up and crates stacked up bulging with the silver bodies of salmon. The islands low and green around us, iridescent like plovers, and the old men squatting on the dockside appraising us through narrowed eyes. And when the boat nudged the quay Fabián jumped down with an easy confidence and began making the lines fast. And we walked into town, board-built houses two and three storeys high, bristling streets, brightly coloured roofs ripped along the river.

After months at sea, everything assaults the senses. Colours and smells of the town, not salt and wind but sweat and woodsmoke and rancid fat. The girls on the street, impossibly beautiful. The incredulous joy of being clean and showered, free from the sting of salt in every crease. The softness of the bed in our hotel room, where I decided to remain, cocooned for ever. But then the rumbling of my stomach became imperative, and we went out to a bar, hungry for real food, real beer. And it was pure pleasure to taste fresh seafood, great brimming bowls of *caldillo* steaming with heat. The beer was cold and citrus and beautiful. And Fabián was talking to a girl who sucked on a long cigarette and fixed him with her black eyes. During the meal they got up and left and I drank a silent toast to him. My glass was still raised, foolishly, when I felt cold metal at the back of my neck. The muzzle of a sub-machine gun.

Gentlemen, would you please to come with us, said a voice in imperfect English.

We stood and they herded us outside. Nobody in the bar batted an eyelid. I took a last, longing look at my unfinished *caldillo*, still steaming in the bowl. You can do whatever you like to me, I thought, if only I could stay and finish that bowl of *caldillo*. No matter what darkness comes after.

Yan, the pylon. *Tean*, Kate Murphy. *Tether*, the boyfriend. *Mether*, the river. *Pip*, the towers. The numbers are the old language, right back before the Romans. Before every bugger. Old men still use them to count sheep, up in Teesdale. And I use them to count away the time in a windowless cellar below a detention centre in a medium-sized Chilean town.

Lezar is the old man. Never misses a day on the chemicals, not one. Six proud walkers, silhouettes in the icy dawn, striding out towards the North Gate, snap tins in hand. Work, drinking, the football. A cyclical world. I don't want cyclical. I want linear. The long downstream with backswamps and oxbow lakes, eyots and wharves and the slow sea.

Azar is death. Seven-footed and seven-handed. She always called it women's troubles, and we didn't ask. Polite words were spoken. Complications. Passed away quietly. Bone stone fucking dead, I want to shout. But instead I look out of the window where the Pleiades are rising, quiet and icy.

Catrah is the cards. Five to deal and three to change. Branigan showed me in the pub, smoke and Guinness and April rain fat and soft and lovely. I was a quick learner. Played the dunce, the jack of fools, and lost and lost and lost. And then I cleaned them out. Three aces, said Branigan, slamming his cards down on the table. What about that then son, what about that? His jowls were round and slobbery with stout, soft and vegetated with his whiskers. Four eights Mr Branigan, I said. Laid them down nice and slow. Matteo, Marco, Luca, Giovanni. You fucking little cheat, he snarled. Don't come back again or I'll purloin your gonads, so help me.

Borna is the magpies. Nine of them on the high-voltage line. Kate quivers, lips drawn back from her teeth in a grimace, nails clawing my chest. They never get electrocuted, never touch both lines. How does it feel, a river of blue power screaming between your toes?

Dick is the army. Ten men to a tent, ten *contubernia* to a century, ten centuries to a cohort, ten cohorts to a legion. Twenty-five years coming, long and hard. The northern frontier. It's fucking scratched with a stick, a line in the dirt. On one side it's the empire. On the other side it's chaos, hills straining at the leash, sniffing with brutal noses, giving tongue.

A shout erupts from Kate's throat. Not yet. There's a burst of blue sparks from the high-voltage wires, like a heart stopping. I watch, deaf and dumb and paralysed. The cable breaks and comes dancing down onto us like a charmed snake. Kate fries in an electrified dance and the cable burrows into the base of my spine, into my coccyx. And sends a billion volts of blue power, gruelling as the sun, slamming up my nerve pathways and into the base of my skull. It's seeking out the one part of the brain, that tiny hazelnut where the essence of me is resident. It finds it, squeezes it, and everything is black.

It was kind of unfortunate that you came here, says a voice. It's quiet, resigned, gentle. I open my mouth but no sound comes out.

You lost your voice a while back, he says. After you had been screaming for the first twelve hours.

I'm lying on my stomach. My eyes don't seem to work at the moment. Either that or there's no light. Ghost lights are firing off in the field of my vision. Reminds me of a firework display. A shower of blue sparks. I'm lying in wetness. It has a bitter, acrid smell. A balloon of pain erupts in my head.

Who am I?

I am Yan. One is one and all alone and evermore shall be so.

You can do anything you like, says the voice. Piss, shit, swear, blubber like a child, spit at God. But you can't go to sleep. Get up.

Another bubble of pain, this time in my kidneys. I am being kicked. *Yan*, the pylon. My arms are grabbed from behind. There must be two or three people present, because they lift me off the ground, off my feet, until I think the arms will come out of the sockets. I imagine my tendons tearing like the pages of a book flipping out of the spine. They set me upright on my feet and surprisingly I remain upright. I can feel liquids dribbling down my thighs, my calves, pooling on the floor.

It was rather unfortunate that you came here, he says. Because now we're obliged to make you disappear.

Why did I leave Kate? Not once but twice. This is the stark question that pops into my head. The two of us.

Why don't you have something to eat? It must be two days since we brought you in.

I'm ravenously hungry. I open my mouth but only dribble comes out. Laughter. I nod my head.

Excellent, he says. Gentlemen, perhaps you could bring Mr Thomas a spot of supper.

I hear suppressed giggling behind me. The voice isn't English. A good accent but a trace of something else behind it.

You might be wondering how I know your name. Your friend told us, you see. The fat one, the one who doesn't like pain. He told me all your names. Ah, here is your food.

Somebody standing in front of me. A rich, thick, sickening smell hits me in the face. More laughter.

I don't think he can see it Juan, says the voice. You might have to feed him.

An explosion of mirth, just behind me and to the right. I try to pinpoint the position of his face in my head. The smell becomes stronger and I start to gag. I recognize the heady aroma of shit and understand what I was lying in, what's now running down my legs. Something brushes against my lips. I clamp my jaws shut.

Come now, he says. You really must eat. Especially after Juan has gone to all the trouble of producing your meal for you.

Without warning I'm slammed down onto the concrete floor on my back. I'm gaping like a fish slapped on the dockside, my spine bruised. Can't move.

Open your mouth, he says, gently.

Something else begins pushing at my lips, nudging towards my teeth, something hard and metallic. A star explodes inside my head, goes supernova, swallows the world in blue fire, and just as suddenly shrinks to a cold walnut. He has a cattle prod in my mouth.

Eat him up, he says. There's a good boy.

Another burst of energy, colder than the moon, and my jaw bounces around in rictus, in spasm after spasm. I can no longer close my mouth. It sags open like a burst stomach.

That's better. Feed him Juan.

The one called Juan mashes his shit into my idiotic, paralysed, sagging mouth, sniggering as he does it. Must be the best entertainment he's had in years. My tongue lolls as my mouth fills up, and when the glutinous material touches the back of my throat the reflex kicks in and I swallow. And then I'm vomiting, hot and sharp like desert sand being ripped from my body in waves. I could puke the Sahara desert. Lie there doubled up, jack-knifing.

I'm starting to drift, like one of them sand dunes. *Yan*, the pylon. It comes from Hartlepool now, the power. The nuclear facility squatting like a concrete gnome on the estuary. They think the pylons are frying the kids, giving them brain cancer. *Tean*, Kate Murphy. That was it. These numbers have an end, you see. They don't wank on for ever like the integers. They only go up to *jiggit*, twenty. If you get to *jiggit* there are no more.

There's another squeal of electricity, this time in the side of my neck. My vision comes back and the room flashes into negative. I see black faces and ghostly white darkness. A man holding a white wand. Black sparks of power dribble from it.

Get up, he says, the inside of his mouth glowing white like a phosphorescent cave.

I wait for the hands to haul me up again to my feet.

Deserters, he says.

Dave has really spilled the beans. Console myself with the fact that he doesn't know where I hid the thermos.

Really, you should have gone home, the voice continues. Why did you have to come here?

I hear Juan clear his throat, and try to pinpoint him. Behind me, to the right again. Close. The other one is to the left. He's much quieter, much harder to find.

You know, now we are into the endgame, he says.

I look at him, for the first time. Moderate height, snowy white hair and grey skin. His eyes are large, with jet-black irises and white pupils. Wormholes of light pour from his nostrils. He takes something from his breast pocket with a dark grey hand. A cream-coloured cylinder. He snips one end off, then takes a lighter from his pocket. He puts the cigar in his mouth.

Just tell me who your contact is, he says. One name. Who were you going to buy the drugs from? You can do it now and die painlessly, or we can stretch it out for an unbelievable long time, and we can pump you full of antibiotics to keep you alive while we do it.

What drugs? I try to say. My voice formless in the dark.

He retrieves a lighter from his pocket and clicks it. There's a black spark and a black flame appears, wavering, liquid like ink. He snaps the lighter and the flame disappears. The end of the cigar is a black hole. He sucks on it contentedly and the black hole crackles, growing stronger. I feel its gravity.

Charlie, he says. Colombian snow. Bogotá marching powder.

I choose this moment to slam my knee into his groin as hard as I can. A satisfying thud and as he starts to go down, groaning, I turn and pound my right fist into the face of Juan. A squelching sound as his nose flattens and white blood jets into the air and across my face. I turn for the other one but he's already pulled a revolver and he rams the muzzle into my face. Yelling. He wants me to kneel on the floor. Kicks my legs from under me, shoves the gun against my forehead and cocks it. The other two are righting themselves, coming up from the floor. The third man still shouting. He's going to shoot me. I lie very still and wait for the supernova, for the black hole. It doesn't come. Instead, they start kicking. I draw myself up into the foetal position to protect my internal organs. They work me over, kidneys, face, knees and ankles. I notice somewhere here that my vision has righted itself, that dark is dark and light is light. Dull pain, mounting like a tide that comes over the sea wall and rushes towards the houses, sweeping away the cars, sweeping away houses, people clinging to flotsam. I'm tired of clinging. I discharge myself into the water.

And Kate spills from my chest and I'm on top of her, lips and tongue miraculously springing to life and racing across her breasts. I ram her into the tired grass. Her heels against my buttocks, teeth in my shoulder.

*

Yan-a-dick, the town. A stamp collection wrecked on the estuary, sherds of brightly coloured roofs ripped along the river, pages rifling in the constant wind, green fields in a thousand colours smeared across the sky. Matted flames of the sea. Coal, iron, steel, chemicals, shipyards. People springing from the stubble fields where their fathers were sown and cut down and burned.

Tean-a-dick, the demolition. The houses where we were born, the nests we lined with black trinkets. Ripped down in piles of rubble. Twelve weeks. The Cape of Good Hope standing like a sentinel on the corner, almost alone. Concrete, rubble, brick, cinder, bulldozed away like crumbs. Oh god oh god oh god, she shouts.

Tether-dick, the sky, in thirteen shades of steel and glass and iron and concrete and chemicals and rain. And rain. The biggest thing I ever saw, heavily muscled and kneading like a pair of buttocks. The sand and the sea and the fields and the roads glistening in the wet weather, all bleeding into the sky. Blood dripping from my head and down to the clouds where it splashes in clots.

Mether-dick, blood dripping from my head and down to the sky where it splashes in clots. No, that's already happened. What is *mether-dick*?

Blood dripping from my head and down to the stars where it splashes in clots. I smell cigar smoke. Another lash of cold water across my body. I start to shiver uncontrollably. Get him up again, says the voice. The oily aromas of cigar smoke and shit mingle. I need a cigarette. That's it. Cigarettes.

Mether-dick, cigarettes. Fourteen left in the crumpled packet when I offered one to Kate. We were in her bed upstairs in the pub while her dad lugged barrels in the cellar. She flicked ash at me, playfully. I looked at it, grey and dusty on my pale skin. Dabbed some onto a fingertip and smeared it on her forehead. A star drawn from ash, against her brown skin.

A star drawn from ash, against her brown skin. She had a funny cloak thing, dark green and rounded. I suppose it was some sort of sixties poncho. I put it around her naked shoulders. You look like a lapwing, I said, a green plover. Unlike most girls, she knew what I was talking about. Plover is an old nickname for a whore, she said. Did you know that? But I like them, I said. The wings are so round and soft, they hardly make a sound. Like green owls in the daytime.

She reaches over and jabs the raw end of her cigarette into the side of my neck. Somebody else is pinning my arms behind me. Pain rises up like the snout of a mole. My flesh is burning, like a tallow candle.

So, says Kate, in her sexiest voice. Are you going to tell me that name, or am I going to play some more join-the-dots?

I want to tell her that there isn't any name. And I want to tell her that I'm sorry. About leaving her, not once but twice. But the cigarette sears into my cheek. She keeps it pressed there while I scream.

Why do we have to play this game Yan? she says. You're always the same. You have to follow your nose. I went through hell when you left me, when we were eighteen. It took me three years to work you out, and when I'd finally done it, you came galloping back from Belfast and I fell for you again.

She drags on the cigarette and blows the smoke into my face. I feel the caress across my eyeballs.

Shall we burn off your eyelashes? she says. I feel them scorching and shrivelling. Shame if we slipped. We could burn a hole in your eyelid.

She stands there, framed in the stark light which pours from a single electric bulb above our heads. No doors or windows. The floor is concrete, slippery with my own ordure. My blood and my piss.

Kate, I manage to say, imploring. And then I can't say any more, because I don't know the answer.

You have this streak of piss through you Yan, she says, laughing. Everyone thinks you're the big man, because you've got the brains and the looks and the reputation and the fucking blarney, and you've read all them books until they're coming out your jacksy. You're everybody's mate and nobody's, aren't you? But it all counts for nowt when you disappear, like some migrating bird, with this electricity in your head that no-one else can hear. You can't help it. It's just faulty wiring.

She kicks me, hard, in the groin and I double up with pain.

You're going bald, by the way, she says. The thing is big man, you're a fucking coward. You play at being married, you play at being a father, but it's not enough for you, is it? You probably think it takes courage to take off on a wing and a prayer. But maybe it would have been braver to stay put. Sticking at our marriage, being there for Dan. Saying no to the wiring in your head. That would have been real courage, and we could have done all that together, the three of us. But it's okay. Me and Danny are moving on without you now.

Tears are running down my face. I tell myself it's because she's burned my eyelids.

Anyway, a side issue, she smirks. Those drugs Yan, darling. Four foreigners turn up in an unregistered boat. You and Horsey and Fat Dave and Stupid Joe. The four stooges. What are we supposed to think? Just tell us who your contact is?

It takes a moment for me to realize. Four of us.

Juan, give him a caning, she says.

Four of us. She steps back and another woman takes her place. I'll be buggered if it isn't big Janet from the Red Lion. She's wearing a cotton dress and a pastel cardigan.

You're looking bonny Janet, I say.

She smiles, then takes a rubber truncheon from behind her back and smashes it into the side of my head. My eyes explode and the room stretches sideways like an elastic band. I'm on the floor, shaking violently. She stands astride me, legs encased in beige tights. She carries on whaling me with the truncheon. The room becomes still more attenuated.

Four of us. She doesn't know about Fabián. They haven't got Fabián.

Yan, the pylon, walking out with a kit-bag on his shoulder.

Tean, Kate Murphy, sitting alone in her room. Many-paned windows, light flooding in from the enormous sky.

Tether, the boyfriend, dead on the road with his face burned off.

Mether, the river, jammed with silver fish, gaping for breath.

Pip, the towers, falling in one graceful curve.

Lezar, my father, kicking the legs out from under me and cocking a cigar against my head. My father, on the bed, gasping for breath.

Azar, death. White wormholes from a man's nostrils. Black flame from a lighter.

Catrah, the cards. I'll turn them over now love, she says. You have a gypsy look about you son. If I was a few years younger. She flips them over, one by one. The hanged man. The hanged man. The hanged man. The hanged man. That looks fairly conclusive then, you say.

Borna, the magpies. They like to collect black things. Black jewellery in the nest. Whitby jet, like Queen Victoria. Hopping through the hedgerows in spring flipping the naked chicks from the nests and swallowing them in one.

Dick, the army. They like to collect black things. Rifles glittering in the black sun.

Yan-a-dick, the town, sinking into the marshes. *Tean-a-dick*, the houses of Haverton Hill, sinking to their knees. *Tether-dick*, the sky, with thirteen ripped holes in its face. *Mether-dick*, the cigarette, burning a hole in my eyelid.

Bumfit, the sheep. Straggling over the marshes with dirty shaggy fleeces hanging off them. Wild yellow eyes with a black slit at the centre. They browse on the salty grass, on the mounds of rubble and nettles, on the angular towers and flare stacks and refraction columns, on the bright river and the metallic sky, on the crumbling houses blasted by the breath of the North Sea, on the metal flowers of the pylons and the high-voltage brambles coiling across the country. I imagine grabbing the greasy wool of the belly, hoisting myself into the forest of fleece, white wires springing from the pink and bulging abdomen, ticks and lice as big as birds, bulging with blood. I notice my hand grabbing a tussock of nettles and wrenching it from the ground and feeling nothing. Kate is banging the back of her skull against the ground.

Mr Thomas, my name is Colonel Barriga.

It's the same mild-mannered voice as before. He sits on a chair in front of me. Look, he says. There is nothing extraordinary about me. I'm just doing my job. I'll go home in an hour and play with the children and bathe them and put them to bed. When I was younger I excelled in swimming, so much so that my teacher once called me a true son of Poseidon. But I was never quite good enough to reach the national team.

He chuckles with pleasure at the memory.

I look at Barriga. He is indeed, average. Average height and build, podgy around the stomach and thighs. Black hair, cut short with a side parting. A round face with full lips, clean-shaven. Cigar smoke swirls around us, harsh and guttural.

Look, he says again. Nothing extraordinary about me, and nothing extraordinary about your situation. Don't take the fall for the big guy. He is the one we want. Not insects like you. Help me out with some information and I can spare you a great deal of torment. Otherwise, I will turn you over to Juan again. I understand he finds particular enjoyment in feeding people their own genitals.

I begin to weep because everything is clear. I feel the burns on my chest and neck and face beginning to blister and suppurate. Every inch of my body is livid with purple bruising. Fingers on my left hand are black and obscenely swollen. They must be broken. I work my dry tongue into holes where the stumps of teeth have been wrenched out. The stench of my sweat and excrement is terrible, lacerating. I begin to weep, copious and unashamed. I cannot even raise a hand to my face. The tears crawl down my cheeks like slugs.

Bumfit, the sheep. The flock has gone and I can't get any further. There's no more hope. I'll just lie down on the ground and let the sand settle over me, grain by grain, until I'm buried and forgotten about. I will sleep. Yes, I will sleep.

But now comes a piping call in my head, that nobody else can hear. Brimming from numberless throats, high and fluty with that husky quality, that sweet tang of seaweed like a bourbon whiskey. I open my eyes and see them flopping above the fields on rounded wings, black and white wings, stroking the air like eiderdown. They begin to alight all around us, sunlight fizzing from the bottle-green backs and white-furred bellies, bobbing crests expressing curiosity. Lapwings. Green plovers. As restless as the sea, furrowing as they feed, like the dark earth turning under the plough. And every few seconds one will flip into the air, owl wings jerking randomly, at once spastic and masterful, scrawling a fool's parabola with that whiskey-bitter cry. How many of them? I begin to count, Kate jerking beneath me. *Yan, tean, tether, mether, pip. Lezar, azar, catrah, borna, dick. Yan-a-dick, tean-a-dick, tether-dick, mether-dick, bumfit. Yan-a-bum, tean-a-bum, tethera-bum, methera-bum.* I feel my balls clench and know what's coming.

Jiggit. Kate springs a leak and the air rushes out of her as she shrivels up like a dying balloon and thick fluid roars from my cock in pulse after pulse. And the lapwings take to the air as one, sherds of green glass in a thousand colours smeared across the sky, the sun leaping from their throats. And I'm lifted up with them, above the green field where a naked girl lies, above the brown river and the bright and tattered roofs, above the towers and the pylons and the ragged powerlines. There's a cumulus cloud like the belly of a great sheep. I have only one chance. I grab the white fleece as it passes and climb into the foetid darkness.

The tears crawl down my face like slugs. I'm lying on the floor again. The furniture has gone. I wonder whether I imagined the conversation with Barriga. Juan is above me, pissing into my face. His cock like a rubber truncheon.

Okay, I say, I'll talk. Get Barriga.

*

I've been thinking. About your dream. The one where –

The one where I die.

Aye.

What have you been thinking?

You said the smallest thing can put you on a different track. Well, how would you know if your destiny switched tracks like that? You could be alive one moment and dead the next.

Or vice versa.

Yeah, obviously.

You don't know. When you are dead you have always been dead. When you are alive you have always been alive. The box opens. Daylight floods in.

It's a week since any of us have seen daylight. I blink at Joe Fish and Horse Boy, the rips in their faces, cigar burns weeping liquid from the angry centres. Dave looks suspiciously unharmed. I scowl at him and he flinches. We're in the yard of the detention centre, high blank walls all around. Barriga cuffs our bruised wrists and opens the back of an unmarked van. There are no windows. We pile into the stuffy darkness and the door slams and then we're driving, the suspension tormenting our bruised joints.

Yan, says Horse Boy.

He's just a voice in the dark. Like a kid calling out for its dad.

Aye.

How did you get through? he says.

Counting.

Counting what?

Sheep, I say. Lapwings. How about you?

I thought about South Georgia. When I fell off the roof and stopped breathing and then Sarah brought me back. I was dead, wasn't I? Dead for two minutes. And then I opened my eyes and saw you all against the sky, looking down. Like I was born again.

Alleluia, drones Joe. The lad's found God.

That got me through, says Horse Boy. The thought of being reborn.

Come forth Lazarus, says Joe. Crackles with bitter laughter.

We bounce around in the back of the van and the air gets hard and close and sour with petrol. It goes to your head.

Where are we going? says Horse Boy.

Somewhere quiet, says Joe. Where they can put us against a wall and then bury us in a lime pit.

No, I say. We're going to the hotel.

When we get up to the room Barriga takes the key and locks the door behind us.

So, he says. We'll wait for your contact. This is where we find out whether you've been a truthful boy or not.

What did you tell him Yan? hisses Joe, and I don't reply.

We wait, and down below us the city crawls with life and cloud shadows move across the buildings. The room is panelled in orange varnished pine boards, garish and tasteless. I'm breathing heavily and sweating and every part of my body is grumbling with pain. It would be heaven to lie down, here and now, on this bed, and go to sleep. Let Barriga shoot the lot of us. Sleep. Instead I look down at his patent leather shoes nestling into the electric blue shagpile like a pair of scarab beetles.

You're running out of time, says Barriga. He glances at his watch and I see that he's sweating too. Takes that little Mauser machine pistol out of his jacket and cradles it in his arms, like a new baby. Time dribbles away down the plughole. When you're in the southern hemisphere, Decko said in the pub one night, water swirls down the plughole in the opposite direction. Been here all this time and I never took the trouble to check it out.

Okay, says Barriga. No more time. He's not coming, is he?

He brings the Mauser down and runs his fingers along the top of the barrel.

Look, I say. You want money? I sit on the bed and open the bedside drawer, rummage for the screwdriver. Barriga levels the gun at me and clicks the safety off. I raise my palms to reassure him. Then I insert the screwdriver between two pine panels above the bed and pop one of them out and reach behind it into the hole we scraped into the wall plaster. Slowly I bring out Joe's thermos flask. I look at Joe. His hand is flat and mine is forked.

Scissors cut paper, I say. He shakes his head and laughs silently.

I slowly twist open the cap and place it on the bed, followed by the inner seal. Barriga looks bored. I reach inside and find the bankroll of notes and toss it onto the floor by his feet. He looks down, then one of his shoes comes down on the roll like he was crushing a snail.

You have no respect, he says. He bends and picks up the roll, holds it between thumb and forefinger. Pulls out his lighter and sparks up the end of the bankroll like it was a Havana. Tosses it onto the bed. Then he levels the Mauser at me and swings it round to cover the other three.

I'm afraid I am going to have to kill you now, he says. Be so kind as to move over there against the wall.

His voice is mocking, fleshy mouth twisting. I swallow, hard.

You didn't think I was really going to let you go, did you?

He smiles, apologetically.

We're herded together in the corner of the room, the four of us. The bankroll smoulders on the bed, black smoke frothing from the counterpane. I can't look into their faces. Instead I stare pointedly out of the window, at the sprawling town, the changeable sky rolling towards the Pacific. Think of my unfinished bowl of *caldillo*, down at the Canta Luna. I would give anything to finish that bowl, those few mouthfuls of steaming food. Time moves like a key turning quietly in a lock and a door breathing open. My attention is taken by a flock of birds, spiralling over the streets. For a moment I could swear they are lapwings, shifting points of iridescence loping over the unfamiliar streets. Are there lapwings in Chile? The cry comes, like the hand of a small child slipping into mine, tears springing to my eyes.

*

I wonder why we are not dead yet. Perhaps we're dead and haven't noticed, like Matteo said, simply wandered into the next world like beggars. But no, Barriga hasn't pulled the trigger. He is frozen. I glance at the others and their eyes are fixed not on Barriga, but on a point behind him and just to the left, where the barrel of a Walther pistol is pressed into the back of his skull like the wet snout of a dog. The pistol is held in a hand, which is connected to the body of Fabián Rodriguez. He cocks the pistol, lazily tilts his face with its hooded eyes.

Put the gun down *pajero*, he says calmly.

Barriga appears to be thinking. A cloud passes over his pudgy face. The bankroll still guttering on the bed. Then Barriga engages the safety catch and drops the Mauser to the floor where it nestles into the shagpile.

Kneel down, says Fabián, levelling the pistol at Barriga's head. The colonel drops to his knees in front of us. Fabián retrieves the keys from his pockets and tosses them over to us and we wrestle out of the cuffs. Fabián snaps a pair onto Barriga, locking him to the foot of the bed.

You fucking took your time, I say to Fabián.

He laughs. I nearly stayed for an extra beer, he says. Then you would have been fucked, *chabón*.

That was your plan? snarls Joe, incredulous. Bring him back here and hope Fabián turns up? We were nearly dead men.

Aye, I say. But I knew something would turn up.

A torrent of flame belches from the bed as the foam mattress ignites, acrid black smoke bubbling up to the ceiling and hanging there in sheets. Fire seethes up the panelling, pine boards weeping great tears of sap and lacquer.

Let's make like a tree, says Joe. We can take this bugger's van.

Aye, I say. North to Bolivia. I always fancied seeing the Andes.

Barriga is kneeling there, chained to the bed with the room burning behind him. He looks at me. *Yan*, the pylon.

Well, I say. You didn't think I was really going to let you go, did you?

I tell you what, says Horse Boy, his face a mass of scabs, I want one of them cigars.

Let's go, says Dave. Before we're toast.

Fire howls across the ceiling tiles, molten plastic dripping onto the carpet. But Horse Boy reaches into the colonel's top pocket and pulls out a slim box of panatellas, a cigar knife and a lighter. He cuts and lights a slender dark cigar and sucks contentedly for a second, right back into his lungs without gagging. Then he grips the back of Barriga's skull and forces the burning tip into his right eye. He holds it there while Barriga bucks and squeals like a rabbit with a broken back, holds it there until it sizzles through the eyelid and into the eyeball with a hideous stench of burning seaweed, holds it there until it burns through to the vitreous humour and is extinguished with a sound like a hot saucepan going into the sink. Horse Boy releases Barriga and lets him slump unconscious to the carpet, the dead cigar still protruding from his eye socket.

Enjoy your cigar Colonel, says Horse Boy. Then we walk from the burning room, stiffly, limping, dragging our broken wings. Down the stairs to the lobby and out into the sunshine, measuring our steps in the bright world.

13. Long-Toed Stint

(Calidris subminuta)

It isn't difficult to find Paul. His old woman still lives at the same house, behind Port Clarence Social Club. I ring the doorbell and a large dog batters itself against the frosted glass. She's frail when she opens the door, the sweet smell of overflowing bins behind her.

I don't want double glazing like, she says. Windows are already done.

I'm not selling anything Mrs O'Rourke. I don't know if you remember me. It's Danny Thomas. I used to live up at the Cape.

She eyes me up and down before replying. Her face is narrow and pointed, bobbing in the doorway. Tucks a lifeless strand of grey hair away behind an ear.

They knocked it down, she says. Druggies kept getting in, setting it ablaze.

Aye, I know.

The wind is cold, a steely rain lashing in from the west.

I can't let you in son. The dog'll have your bollocks. He doesn't like men.

I was looking for your Paul. We used to be mates.

She sighs, shifts her feet in the slippers. I try not to stare at the swollen ankles, varicose veins bulging under the tights.

That waster, she says. He's nigh on fucked hisself with drink and drugs. You want to stay away. Well away.

Inside the house the dog pounds at a closed door.

Do you know where he lives?

Aye, he's sponging off the social. It's some kind of hostel for junkies and loonies. When they can't look after themselves no more. Hang on and I'll write it down for you.

I pull the van up outside and sit for a moment, idling the engine, watching cold clear raindrops collect on the windscreen, crawl across the glass, coalesce. And then I sweep them away with the wipers. Across the road there's a young girl, back arched precociously against the car park railings, short skirt and high boots, her long hair strong and sodden. She's wondering whether I have the look of a punter.

Paul lives in a halfway house in St Hilda's. The original town of Middlesbrough was here, but now it's cut off from the modern town centre by the railway line and the flyover. Over the border, they call it. Bleak blocks of new houses with tiny windows and razor wire, in among the old buildings falling apart and the open stretches of brownfield nobody wants to build on.

I decide to leave it. It's years since I've seen him – he may not even remember me. But I don't drive away, just sit for a minute or two and tap my foot at the accelerator pedal. Think about that station platform in the Fens and the moon going down. And then I swing myself out of the car and into the rain and that girl watches me impassively from across the street.

Have you got any chews on you Danny? says Paul, wheedling. Them green ones are the best.

I don't think you can get those any more mate, I say. Not for years.

The warden has let me in and I'm sitting with Paul in a communal kitchen. Cooking facilities, two rough wooden tables with benches, and white light spilling in through windows high up. He slurps at his cup of tea.

Aye, I'm not bad Danny marra, not bad at all.

He grins idiotically at me, a little old man in a baseball cap, a jumper and jeans many sizes too big. He hobbles slowly and painfully across to the kettle. A knotted quality to his limbs, sinews in his neck grinding against each other like cables. He breathes out, heavily, to recuperate. Then he lifts the jug kettle unsteadily towards the tap and fills it. Replaces it carefully on its base and flicks the switch with a trembling finger. I notice how his fingernails are clubbed, turning over the tips of his fingers. He turns and leans against the edge of the sink.

Do you remember the time we went up Pally Park to monkey with that lass? Dirty bitch, she was. Had to hospitalize her in the end. What was her name?

That wasn't me Paul. I'm Danny, remember, from the pub? Yan's lad.

Yan Thomas, he shouts, fucking murderer that gadge. He laughs. Complete fucking psycho.

What do you mean?

He looks confused. Erm, I don't know. His face crumples. Don't take any notice of me. Sometimes I don't know what I'm talking about. Booze, drugs, Holme House, it takes it out of you.

He pours water into the mugs, the full kettle shaking alarmingly.

Have you got any of them green chews? he asks, brightening suddenly.

Paul, do you remember that time I bumped into you down south? We went up to that junkyard near Peterborough.

He looks blank, mouth sagging open.

We were sat on the platform in the middle of the night, I persist. You told me about your grandad nicking mercury and pouring it into the bath.

He beams.

Aye, mercury. I used to scoop it up with me hands, watch it running about like a flock of chickens. It was beautiful stuff, that. Beautiful. You know, I had a job once. It was on the bins.

It was the landfill Paul. Cowpen Bewley.

Aye, the landfill. I had a run in with the foreman. Little radge bastard, always on my back.

He dumps the teabags in the bin and slops milk into the mugs.

There you go, he says, handing me one. I can look after myself, you see. Well, one day I told him to fuck off, and I walked off the job.

Thought you stuck the nut on him.

Probably, he says.

Then he looks thoughtful.

If I hadn't done that, I wouldn't be here with these loonies. It's the small stuff that can mash up your life. Should've carried on smiling, carried on doing the job. Thought fuck off to him inside me head.

You can't think like that, I say. You'll send yourself mental.

He looks confused. A long pause while I slurp my tea. Somewhere in the building a fire door flaps open and shut.

What happened in that book? he asks suddenly.

I look blank.

The axe murderer, he says. Did he get away with it?

That was twenty years ago, I say, gently.

He looks at me expectantly.

Well, I say, no he didn't. It wasn't that he really left any clues, it was more the weight of the murders pressing on his mind. In the end, he incriminated himself. He admitted to it.

What a twat, he says. Should have fucking kept shtum, eh? What happens in the end? Does he die?

No. It's odd really. He's in prison for years. He becomes a human being again. And in the end he just walks out of the book and disappears from view. As if a door opens into another world and he simply steps through it.

I pause.

Paul, I say. Do you remember Gary Hagan? Used to work behind the bar at the pub. Weights and steroids. Big gold hoop in his ear.

Oh aye, I remember him. He was slipping it to your old woman.

I want to know what happened to him, after Yan came back. He disappeared from the scene.

He wasn't a mate of mine. How should I know?

Because you helped him. You were there, and I wasn't. People used to reckon you'd staved his head in, the two of you. Put the body in the landfill.

He looks as if he's concentrating hard, screwing up his eyes and staring into space. He opens his mouth to speak, but nothing comes out. He closes it again. Then he sighs.

I'm sorry Dan.

Tears brimming at the corners of his eyes.

There are these big black holes, he says. When I can't remember nothing. Like someone's torn a page out of the book. I was drinking too much, too many year.

He slumps back in his seat. The fire door opens and the warden comes in. He's bearded and well-built, with wiry black hair.

Everything all right Paul? he asks breezily, looking pointedly at me.

I'm dandy thanks Dunk, he says. I'm thinking about going out soon, find a sweet shop.

Yan is sitting up in bed, leaning against a pile of ghastly pink pillows.

The colour scheme in this hospital is shambolic, he says, I'm going to phone that nancy boy, get him to do a makeover.

He's looking grey, his face pale and a little shrunken, the skin sagging more than usual. He coughs, reaches for an oxygen mask from over his shoulder, sucks deeply.

Oxygen, he says, fucking lovely. Every home should have one. What have you got for me then boy? Flowers, bunch of grapes?

I brought you a chocolate bar, I say, slipping it from my pocket and under the covers next to him. I'm not sure if it's legal. It's one of them chunky ones, the ones you like.

Better eat it quick before the Gestapo get here, he says, tearing the wrapper and squashing a chunk into his mouth. You want some?

He tosses the next chunk over to me, and I cram the greasy chocolate into my mouth.

I've got fluid on the lungs, he mumbles through a mouthful of chocolate. Jim's a dribbly bastard. And they've told me to pack in the smokes.

They've actually told you that?

Erm, well. They gave me a leaflet about quitting.

I laugh out loud.

Are you going to quit?

He thinks for a minute, chewing.

I'll give it some thought. Might be worth it if I can get a few more months on the shanks. Few more ticks on the list, you know.

He starts coughing, reaches for the oxygen, and sucks it in. A sinister wheezing noise as he inhales.

Remember Frank Dowson from the bird club? Well, he was in this afternoon. Said there's a long-toed stint up at Greatham Creek. That's a new tick for me.

Not for me, I say. I saw the one in eighty-three. On my own.

I missed out on a lot, he says, indistinctly. Not just birds.

He falls silent. I walk over to the window and look out, high above Stockton. In the gathering darkness the land is becoming indistinct, its shimmering contours picked out by pinpricks of restless light. Orange streetlights, white headlights and red taillights, rectangles of colour spilling through curtains, the raw blaze of security lighting. And the monotonous grey estates unfolding like a Mandelbrot set in concentric circles and grids and triangles, wave upon wave rippling away into the distance like phosphorescent plankton, over the river, across Middlesbrough. Beyond, there is a deep, still blackness, where the hills are. Whalesong in the sky.

I went to see Paul today, I say. Paul O'Rourke.

I turn round, my back against the window ledge.

You remember, I was telling you about when we were down in the Fens together, looking for Charlie Fraser.

He looks surprised and a bit discomfited.

Right, he says. Why did you do that?

I don't know. Felt like Paul and me might have been friends, if things had worked out different.

You felt guilty, he says. That you'd lost touch. That you hadn't been to see him before.

Aye, I say. That as well. He's in a bad way. Looks about seventy-five. He's only my age, you know. We were in the same year at school.

Well he's got the virus, hasn't he? What did you expect?

How did you know that?

Dunno Dan.

He reaches for the oxygen and inhales deeply. His face narrows alarmingly when he sucks in his cheeks. It's like seeing someone without their false teeth, when the face becomes a collapsed bag of skin.

You must have told me, he says. He was your mate, after all.

There's something guarded about his answer. Something unconvincing.

I didn't. He never told me anything about it.

I look at him hard and he seems to shrink.

So, I push him. How do you know?

Must have just heard it through the grapevine, then. Still keep in touch with a few from down that way. You remember Cleo, the old witch who used to clean at the pub?

I nod.

She's in a home now, in Hartlepool. I went out to see her the other week and we had a good natter. Maybe she told me about Paul.

He's quiet for a moment.

Were you really tortured? I ask him. In Chile, I mean. I'm never sure whether to take you as gospel.

He points at the side of his neck, where there's a small puckered scar like a silver coin.

Pinch of salt, he says. They tortured me, I tortured myself.

Call it quits, I say.

He grins.

I think I'm starting to understand, I tell him.

You'd better tell me quick, then. Sixty-three years and I still haven't got a scooby.

About you, I mean.

He flops back against the pillows, spreads his arms in resignation.

See, I always thought you chose not to come back. Chose to leave Kate and me. Because of who you were. Who you are.

I can't sidestep it, he says. I was clear-minded enough.

No, I say. But you weren't. This is what I'm starting to see. Something happened, didn't it? Something sent you off the rails up on Mount Longdon. When you tried to walk out of there, you'd have walked into the Atlantic if you hadn't bumped into Fabián and Dave camped out in that farmhouse. You hear about it on the telly. This post-traumatic stress disorder thing.

It's psychobabble Dan, he says.

But you weren't in control.

I've always been in control.

Maybe that was an illusion.

You sound like Joe Fish. There's no such thing as chance, he used to say. Everything is predetermined. But doesn't a man have free will? If I can't knit my own fate then I might as well just lie down and wait for death.

Have some more chocolate, I say, breaking him off a chunk.

Nah, you finish it off.

There's a long silence while Yan sucks at the oxygen mask. I cram two chunks into my mouth together, half sucking, half chewing until the glutinous mass slides down my throat.

What did you talk about with Paul? he says.

The eyes look weary, that's the difference. They used to be big pools, wide and full of movement, leaping with the wind or rippling in the rain. Now they look tight and brackish, no light brimming from the surface.

Just chewing the fat over the old days. His memory's shot, mind.

Oh aye?

Booze and the rest.

Right.

He sighs deeply, as if a balloon has sprung a leak. I look at his left hand, laid out on the pink bedcover. The broad fingers and blunt nails. I used to think Yan had the hands of a sailor, an adventurer. Hands for doing, not for lying still.

The past, he says. I haven't got time for that no more.

No?

No.

He starts to cough and his body shudders. He reaches for the oxygen mask again. I hover helplessly at the end of the bed while he composes himself.

A woman breezes round the corner into the bay, slender like a tall candle, a sheen of black hair bristling with grey and a long coat falling to her ankles. She bends over the bed and kisses Yan plumb on the lips. Long and slow and lingering.

You must be Danny, she says, straightening up. I'm Jean. I live round the corner from your old feller.

We kiss awkwardly on the cheek. I look at Yan and he gives me a shrug and a wink.

Is this man bothering you? says Jean, pointing to the bed.

No, I say, he hasn't suggested we play cards yet.

You watch him if he does, she laughs. He doesn't take any prisoners. Is it hereditary?

No, I shrug. I'm colossally lousy at cards. I think I'm being clever, but I'm so crap at bluffing that nobody falls for it.

I gave up on making a poker player of him, says Yan. Used to try teaching him fancy shuffles, card tricks, when he was nine or ten. He was fascinated at first, but he didn't want to put the graft in. Got bored when he couldn't do it after five minutes.

No staying power, I mimic, rolling my eyes at Jean. Listen, I'm going to leave you to it. You've got my mobile. Give me a ring if you need anything.

If I'm out soon we'll go and get that long-toed stint, says Yan. Make up for lost time.

Thought I'd stay a bit and read to you, says Jean.

I walk down the ward and look back at them, gilded in the reading light like figures in a Caravaggio. The nurse at the desk looks at me as I walk past. I try to smile. She has hard eyes, like knucklebones.

As I drive up to the house I can hear the stereo grinding out dance music. The whole street shakes with it. Fight my way into the living room and kill the volume, rub sweat from my scalp.

Hiya Danny, says Miriam, from the corner sofa.

I jump, because I hadn't seen her there. She's slimmer than Kelly, dark, with a decent pair of legs shown off by the leather miniskirt. She catches me looking and tosses her head, and then Kelly sways into the room.

Dan, she says, unsteadily. You know Miriam, don't you? From the salon.

Raises a half-sucked bottle of vodka to her lips and closes her eyes. She's in full war paint, curves bubbling from a slinky black number.

You've got too much blusher on, I tell her.

It's daubed across her cheekbones, bright orange and brown.

Like you're the expert, she says. Hands the bottle to me.

I look at the lipstick smears around the rim, pass it on to Miriam.

You going out?

Kelly fumbles in her bag and lights a cigarette. Sucks on it hard.

Aye, says Miriam from the corner. Girlies misbehaving. I'm busting for a shite here Kel. Can I use your bog?

She meanders out of the room, up the stairs.

No need to ask where you've been, says Kelly.

He's in hospital. I feel guilty.

You poor bleeding heart.

I pushed him away for years Kel. You know, everything's black and white when you're sixteen.

Kelly slumps into the sofa, giggling, feet in the air. She draws hard on the cigarette, flecks of ash dropping down the front of her dress.

Isn't it? she says.

I don't know. He's just a man who things have happened to. As much a victim as anybody else. All the shit that kicked off over there – it sent him off the rails.

You're the only victim here Dan, she says. He's got you right where he wants you. Running over to the hospital, hanging on his stories like a gormless kid. All you do is talk about him.

Bollocks. I don't even like him much.

Yeah you do. You *are* him.

When they've gone out I drive over to Norton village, stop in at the Unicorn. Waiting at the bar, I recognize Matt's broad back and mop of curly hair.

You want the Cask Magnet, he says. It's like brown treacle, make you all warm and fuzzy. None of that creamflow shit.

I watch the beer rush into the pint glass, turbulence like a stubble field burning, gradually resolving itself. Chestnut like the glistening flank of a horse, the head thick and white. Back at their table I drink, a creamy moustache of foam drifting over my upper lip.

You look like you needed that, says Andy.

It's a warren of a pub with three small rooms and low ceilings, full to the brim and bright with voices and brash laughter.

I like this place, says Matt. Decent night out in Norton, these days. In town every fucker's coked-up and looking for chew.

How's the webcam going? I ask.

It's dynamite mate, laughs Matt. You're a genius. We've had thousands of hits on the website, from all over the world. Even had an e-mail from some bird wanting a date.

Thought it was just your mam watched it, laughs Andy. It's a bit weird though, digging away knowing that people are watching your arse sticking up in the air from all over the world. You should come out to site again, see some prehistoric goodies.

Andy and Julie are a couple, both skinny and swathed in too-large overcoats. Andy's hair is dreadlocked, Julie's is short and dyed pink. They skin and smoke roll-ups almost constantly, the rich smell of the tobacco drifting across us.

Can't believe they're going to ban smoking in pubs, I say. It'll wreck the atmosphere.

You a smoker Dan?

This is Clare, grinning lazily. Dark unkempt hair and grey smudges beneath her eyes.

Lapsed, I say. But with many happy memories. I smoke vicariously by sitting next to people like you.

Aye, it's a bit of a bugger, says Andy. Some of the sites you work on, the away jobs. You're out in the middle of nowhere all day, some quarry full of freezing mud. Bastard of a supervisor, present company excepted of course. And you get back to the digs in the dark only to find that the heating doesn't work, or that there's a coin meter and you don't have any fifty pees. So the pub's the only bright spot in the day, warm and fuggy and you can make a couple of pints last all night.

Andy's a genius at spinning out pints, says Matt. Puts us all to shame. I drink three to his one.

That's because they pay you too much, laughs Julie.

Matt pulls a face.

I've got a frigging divorce to pay for, woman, he says. No wonder I drink too much. She'll be after the beer money next.

Anyway, says Andy, the last place you want to go is back out in the cold to have a smoke. Mind you, some of the places we drink, they'll probably ignore the law anyway.

Talking of lawless, says Matt, Danny here used to live out at Haverton Hill. You know that pub standing on the corner, all on its own?

I know the one, says Clare. It's gone now, hasn't it? Always thought it looked impressively rough. Last pub before the sea.

I stay for another pint before I head home. On the way out I notice something behind the bar, alongside the golden cuboids full of cigarettes, the rolling papers and matchboxes, the quivering packets of peanuts pinned to a cardboard backing like so many butterfly specimens. I fumble for change in my pocket.

Leave the chews alone, I say to Yan, slapping his hand away. They're for Paul.

Those take me back, he says, stretching in the passenger seat of the van. I didn't think you could get them any more. That artificial chemical flavour pretending to be spearmint. Sugar dragging the enamel off your teeth.

Saw them in the pub the other night, I say. Thought it'd make a nice surprise for him, next time I'm down there. I haven't seen these for years. Maybe they're a lost batch, the batch that time forgot. You could be like the man who shot the last great auk, paddling the islands for ever and never finding another one.

He laughs.

Sure you're well enough to do this? I ask tentatively.

Fuck off, he groans. I'm fit as a fiddle. Listen Dan, living without fags is doing my nut in. Are you sure I can't have one of those chews, take my mind off it?

No, I say. Paul's.

I take the packet from the dashboard and put it in my pocket.

I didn't know you had a van, he says. Is it for work?

Aye, well, it's for everything since I sold the car.

Only a two-seater, mind. Won't be big enough when you've got bairns.

I don't reply. Yan leans back again, blunt hands stroking the stubble at the back of his head. He coughs, brings it under control. I make a show of concentrating on the road, the van skimming through reclaimed land, the creeks and pools, the pylons bristling and reedbeds holding up the sky. We pull the car up on the verge just before Greatham Creek. The bird's been seen further away from the road, in a group of small pools lying beyond flat, wet fields. The van shudders each time another car speeds past. I open my door just enough to squeeze out, run round the front, open the passenger door. Yan gives me a hard look, says nothing. He folds himself out of the car and grabs his bins. His skull is greyer, smaller than I remember. A shrinking nut.

We walk across the field. He's wheezing with the effort.

Shite, he says. You get. Short of breath. Quickly. Hang on. A minute.

He stands still for a minute or two, breathing beginning to ease. Grimaces at me. Gulls blowing over, loud and harsh, buffeted by the wind. We stamp down the rambling foliage of a barbed-wire fence and step over, careful not to snag our trousers. The pool is on the other side, flat and unruffled, throwing back the white expanse of the sky.

Got it, says Yan, quietly. Long-toed stint. All the way from East Siberia.

A tiny wader moving mouse-like at the pool margins, shallow water almost to the belly, picking its way slow and patient. The nervous energy of the thing, trembling with alertness. It holds its neck extended, peering intently down into the water as if contemplating its own reflection, the white belly like a slice of freshly minted moon, the scalloped wings whittled from tortoiseshell and autumn. Bird and reflection feed in tandem along the pool margins, slender bill tapping the water like the needle of a sewing machine and the mirror bird shimmering below, worrying at this world of air and light with its own slender proboscis.

One more tick for the list, gloats Yan on the way back to the car. I wonder if it'll be the last. I'll move. Mountains to make sure. It isn't. You know you were saying. About the great auk. The hunter who shot it. Didn't know it was the last one. So he kept on looking. On his deathbed he still hadn't. Given up hope.

We are back at the car, Yan breathing heavily again.

They're talking about putting oxygen in. At home, he says. So I can get a fix any time. They try to keep you. At home as long as possible.

He folds himself back into the passenger seat of the van. I start the engine and move off towards Seaton.

Fancy a bag of chips? I say. I'm fucking starving. A big bag of chips with sparkling salt and dark vinegar, smelling of the winter stars. Can of shandy too.

Does a one-legged duck. Swim in circles, grins Yan. We speed towards Seaton.

There are going to be more ticks, I say, as we approach the Seal Sands roundabout. This is Teesmouth. You never know what's going to turn up.

Hey, he says. I'm the last great auk. When they shoot me, there won't ever be another one along.

14. **Grey Heron**

(*Ardea cinerea*)

Fraser wasn't at the scrapyard. There was a bored young lad behind the counter in the site office, looked me and Paul up and down and shrugged.

It's his daughter's wedding, he said. Mr Fraser's daughter, that is.

There was a half-eaten bag of chips on the counter, soft and floury and filling the room with the sharp smell of vinegar.

I'll give you directions if you like, he said. To the house.

So we walked for hours in the glaring heat of the day and stuck our thumbs out to cars but nobody stopped. Straight roads, black soil, prairie fields of wilting root crops yawning away to the horizon, peaty water glowering undrinkably from the ditch bottoms. I felt like the skeleton of a seagull curdling in the sun, delicate fronds clotting into filth.

I wanted that bastard's chips, said Paul.

We were crouched in the shade of a rhododendron thicket outside Fraser's house. It was a big place with the look of an old rectory, a four-storey building in muddy red brick with them fisheye Georgian windows.

He was picking at them like an old biddy with no teeth, said Paul. Me, I'd have lobbed them straight down the hatch. Wouldn't have touched the sides like.

Should have swiped them. What could he have done?

Thought about it, he said. But you were giving me that look.

We were quiet. The sky became translucent with the arrival of evening. We watched cars arrive for the reception, sleek forms in glistening black, navy, silver. Driven carefully, gingerly, like yachts manoeuvring in harbour. Men and women emerged, equally sleek, the women in plunging dresses showing their shoulders and backs, the men like seals in black tie, pastel dress shirts fluttering in the evening breeze. Doors were crisply shut behind them and gravel crunched as they moved away across the drive.

My feet are knacking, moaned Paul. Don't think I've ever walked that far. You've caught the sun Dan the man.

It's the bonehead, I said. Not used to it.

I ran my hand over the top of my bare skull, where the scalp was beginning to feel tight and raw. Hoped it wouldn't blister.

Away, said Paul. He must be here by now. We may as well get in there.

I held back.

When you've picked a scab halfway, said Paul. You may as well rip the rest of the fucker off.

I looked at him, surprised.

Anyway, I'm fucking starving here, he went on. I'm wasting away. There's got to be scran in there, tons of it.

He grabbed me by the arm and we broke cover, crunching across the gravel, the weakened sun spilling across us once more.

We followed the trickles of wedding guests around to the rear, down a narrow path winding between drifts of cottage garden plants and through an opening in a high wall flanked by yew trees. People looked sidelong at us, said nothing. Then we were in a walled garden, lined with vines and fruit cordons, and on the clipped grass stood a marquee, white canvas flapping gently. We stepped over ropes and ducked into the entrance.

At the far end on a raised stage a string quartet was playing. The scratching of summer insects. There were long trestle tables set for eating and starched waiters and waitresses, some of them no older than us, bustling about with trays of champagne glasses. In front of us a gaggle of guests was trickling slowly into the marquee. A reception line. There were the bride and groom lined up with their parents, and the arriving guests filing past. Handshakes, greetings, guffaws and air kisses. My scalp throbbed. Paul was next to me, tall and rangy, tanned and confident, with those deep, calm green eyes.

The bride was voluptuous, red hair swept up from her face and a simple white dress. The groom next to her with dark oilslicked hair and pale unnerving blue eyes. As we edged our way towards the front of the line I was trying to pick out Charlie Fraser, all the time aware of the smell of my own body, goatish and insistent.

We shook hands with an older couple, the man with a prominent chin and a jutting greyish white beard he kept thrusting down into his collar. The woman was tall and airy and as she peered towards us I recognized the birdlike face and questing blue eyes of the groom. I shook hands awkwardly, Paul behind me, and moved on to her husband, who crushed my hand in a strong grip. They had no idea who we were. We moved on to the bride and groom. I pecked the proffered cheek politely and moved away quickly. Paul was pumping the hand of the groom, grinning broadly.

Congratulations mate, he boomed. Making an honest woman of her at last, eh? Good luck anyways. You'll need it with her track record like.

He winked, released the hand, and we stood in front of the last couple. The man was stocky and pale-skinned with crisply curled hair like copper wire. I grasped a moist and pudgy hand.

Mr Fraser, I'm sorry to bother you today.

He looked alarmed.

I'm Danny, I persisted. Yan Thomas' lad. I wanted to talk to you.

I trailed off. A long silence while he studied my face and slowly released my hand. The burnt skin on my scalp tightening. Guests behind us began to shift uncomfortably, waiting for us to move on.

This isn't the time, he said. Or the place. Come to the yard tomorrow.

I lowered my eyes.

Darling, he said. You remember Yan Thomas. Of course you do. Well these are his boys. Daniel and his brother. Lads, this is my wife, Helena.

There's a lot of Yan in you, she said. The eyes are just the same. Deep and mysterious.

She was looking at Paul. He grinned, sheepishly.

Erm, no, Danny's the son, he muttered. I'm just a mate.

She turned to me. Shoulders turned from smooth rosewood, gold circlets about her upper arms. The peacock-blue dress plunged at the back where coltish muscles jumped beneath the golden skin right down to the first swell of her buttocks. Her face a bitter almond, short blonde hair cropped at the jawline. She looked disappointed.

You don't look as much like him, she said.

It was a calm voice, public school but not harsh. The unhurried contours of southern England.

Perhaps around the mouth, she conceded. Out of the two of you I would have sworn it was him.

She looked Paul up and down again, as if appraising horseflesh. Fraser noticed.

Daniel and Paul were just leaving, he said.

Surely you won't turn them away. The honeyed voice. You can see they've come a long way.

They aren't dressed for a wedding, he said, crisply.

Poppycock. I won't hear of it. They'll behave themselves, I'll make sure of that.

A smile materialized on Fraser's face. Emotions seemed to dawn on him slowly, his features taking a moment or two to arrange themselves as required.

Of course, he said. Silly of me. You must stay boys. Help yourselves to food. Enjoy yourselves.

He stretched his arms out towards the interior of the marquee. We moved off, drawing curious glances.

Did you see her looking at me? muttered Paul, a slow smile creeping across his face.

He was flushed when he stood to speak, but the small intent eyes were hard and concentrated. The room subsided into a hush. His wife was seated beside him, long viscous neck tilted towards him, chin resting on one hand. The picture of attention.

Perhaps some of you may be aware that I spent some time in the paras, he began. You'd be forgiven if you weren't aware, because I tend not to talk about it. There was an explosion of laughter here. He acknowledged his audience with raised palms and they quietened. But at the risk of boring you still further, I want to tell you what I learned in the army.

This could go on all night, muttered Paul, next to me. We were right at the back, among the distant relatives and hangers-on, small children bored and running noisily between the tables.

Because I only learned one thing in the army.

Hurrah, shouted somebody.

In fact I only learned one small, simple word.

Even better, came the shout. There was a gentle frisson of laughter. Fraser paused. He knew how to work a crowd. They were silent, attentive, champagne glasses forgotten on the tables in front of them.

Respect, he said, quietly. Respect. That's all. Not much for twenty-five years' service. But actually, it's all I've ever needed. It's a code for life. And since I learned that, I have striven every day to show respect to my wife, respect to my beautiful, clever daughter. Ah, sighed the audience. And respect to my friends and comrades.

Respect my arse, smirked Paul. He was going to chuck us out of here.

He drained his toast glass without waiting for the speech to finish, and sloped off towards the bar. I was growing sleepy, full of buffet food and without much shut-eye in days. Plus I'd been tucking the booze away since we arrived. I steadied myself on the table with an elbow, and the marquee lurched.

What do I mean by respect? he continued. Well, I mean accepting another person, entire and whole. Accepting the good points and the bad. I mean generosity, and I mean hospitality. Because we're all connected, aren't we? No man is an island, as the poet said. What goes around comes around, eh? – as the lager commercial said.

A splurge of laughter. I watched Helena's occluded eyes circle the room, until they came to rest. Not on her respectful husband, but on Paul, leaning against the bar and quaffing a pint of lager. She blinked like a buzzard.

Bile rose in my throat and I swallowed back hard. I wanted to sleep, to lie down and sleep. I would do it anywhere, with my arms wrapped around a toilet bowl and my cheek resting against the cold tiles, in a shrubbery with a holdall scrunched beneath my head, on another cold station with the moon melting into the world like an aspirin. My chin slipped from my hand and I pitched forward, before shaking myself awake. Fraser was winding up.

So you see, he said, respect breeds respect. That's what I learned from my daughter. And from that day onwards I swore that I wouldn't let any man marry her.

He stopped, abruptly. There was bemused giggling. Helena lifted a canapé and popped it into her mouth like an owl swallowing a chick.

Until, he carried on, to cheering. Until she found a man who would show her the same respect that I always have. And in Jonathan –

He was slowing towards his conclusion now.

– in Jonathan, she has found that man, and I wish them the greatest of happiness.

He raised his glass.

To Selena and Jonathan, he boomed. Selena and Jonathan, echoed the room.

The string quartet had been replaced by a four-piece band playing cheesy covers from the sixties and seventies, and many of the guests were dancing as evening fell away into night. I looked at the pint of lager in front of me and couldn't remember how it got there. Bubbles rising insistently through the yeasty liquid.

What's the matter, boomed Paul. Can't take your drink?

He raised another pint to his lips and tilted his head back and necked it in seconds. Plonked it down aggressively on the table, where there was already quite a collection of empties.

I'm fine, I said. Tired.

The turf floor of the marquee was beginning to look inviting. I could just crawl away under the tables, into a dark corner.

Have you enjoyed your evening boys? Helena Fraser was sitting at our table.

Grand, said Paul. Free bar, he added. Grand.

Then he looked at her.

How does it feel? he said. Your daughter getting married.

She laughed.

She's not mine. I'm just the trophy wife. Number one had the child-bearing hips.

I swayed on my seat, trying to bring her into focus. Small, perfect white teeth like beach pebbles, her tongue flicking between them. She looked at me but her body was turned towards Paul.

Yan, she said. Your dad. He was an unusual specimen. One in a million.

She looked sidelong at Paul.

He could charm the knickers off just about anything, from what I remember. She touched my arm with her hand, long turquoise nails immaculately manicured, matching her dress.

Including me, she said, very quietly.

Her skin shimmered, the tip of her tongue between her teeth.

I haven't shocked you, she said. How old are you Danny?

Sixteen, I slurred.

Sixteen, she purred. Sixteen and legal.

Then she turned to Paul like I didn't exist. Conversation over.

You must be older, she said. Do you work out?

Nah, he said. It's all natural.

Me too, she said, tongue between her teeth.

So if Selena's not your daughter, he said. I reckon you must be feeling like a bit of a spare part at this bash.

Perceptive, she said. I don't like all this upper-class backslapping. I prefer my entertainments to be a little more diverse.

I was just saying exactly the same thing to Danny.

She laughed.

May I have the pleasure of a dance?

The pleasure, he said, is all mine.

He stood up, tall and tanned, his eyes flashing, and the two of them disappeared onto the dance floor. Like a stricken Zeppelin my head descended towards the table and burst across my forearms, and I waded in and out of a shallow sleep.

I thought I saw them dancing together to something slow. Her blonde head was on his shoulder, eyes closed, and coloured lights swept across them like the onrushing sea. They turned and I saw how his hand rested in the deep V-shaped plunge of her dress at the back. It was proprietorial, the way it hung there in the fabric, with every right and intention to move down across those glossy buttocks, but choosing not to, for the moment.

I slipped back into sleep, down into the depths and then rising slowly again to the surface with bubbles crawling from my mouth. Glanced over and they were gone. My clothes, my boots, were soaked with cold sleep, weighing a ton, pulling me under. I let myself go down, into the depths, felt salty sleep rush into my nostrils and my throat, filling up my stomach to the brim.

Ow Danny.

I was being shaken by the shoulders, none too gently. I opened my eyes. The marquee was almost empty, the band beginning to pack up their instruments, sharing a smoke and a few drinks from the bar. Some of the young waiters were still around, collecting up empty glasses and litter, light beginning to grow outside.

Danny, you awake?

It was Paul. I looked at him and strained to focus. He sat down opposite, plonking a glass on the table in front of me.

There you go, he grunted. Sort yourself out.

I ogled the oily turquoise liquid.

Looks like toothpaste, I mumbled. I'm not drinking that shit.

Crème de menthe, he said. Minty taste, kind of fresh. Really sorts your head after too much beer.

I snatched up the shot glass and drained it. He was right. It was cold and sharp, sending a shiver through me. I felt marginally more awake. I looked at Paul.

What happened to you?

He winked.

Kicked her back doors in, he beamed. Outside in the fucking rhodies.

I collapsed into gasps of laughter, which I struggled to suppress.

You Paul, I slurred, you are a fucking Titan mate. You're something else.

What's that? He looked embarrassed.

A giant of the ancient world. You've got the life force man, you're a colossus.

That's just the booze talking Danny. If it makes you feel better, you're me best mate an' all.

Next morning at the scrapyard we picked our way through fields where the beached hulks of cars were spread out to the horizon. Early-morning sun shimmered across the rows of bonnets and roofs frosted with globes of dew. It was wet underfoot and we splashed through furrows and runnels of mud.

Never thought I'd be a scrap merchant, mused Fraser. A crisp voice, deep and insistent. It doesn't exactly run in the family. Winchester School, Sandhurst, a commission. But this place, it's far more lucrative than you'd ever imagine. The profits from here are putting my youngest through school. *Ex paedore aurum*, you could say.

I looked confused.

Gold from shite, he grinned. Ran a pale hand through the deep red of his hair. I looked at the gold watch glinting at his wrist beneath the waxed jacket and flannel shirt. Paul was loitering at a distance, opening bonnets and rooting about, not wanting to intrude. We continued almost to the edge of the field until we came to the end of the cars, looked out over a wetland bristling with reedmace and stands of dense alder and thorn. A stretch of open water, black and inscrutable, tufts of morning mist caught in the vegetation.

Beautiful, no? said Fraser. The whole of the Fens was like this, once. One vast wetland running away to the sky, millions of wildfowl rising with the wind thrumming in their feathers. Imagine it.

Then he slapped the roof of a car.

Take a seat, he said.

It was a brown Cortina, lacking tyres and side windows. We could still see the fen through the windscreen, streaks of polarized light smeared across it. A heron stood stock-still at the edge of the reeds, its head cocked. The morning was blue and cold, like the edge of space.

Fraser slapped the steering wheel, let his hand rest there.

Of course it's all been drained. Farmland now, the richest in the world.

He smiled.

Shall I tell you a secret Danno?

I never said anything but he carried on anyway.

You'd think that landscape is pretty permanent, wouldn't you? he said. The shape of the land, the contours. We die but the land remains, the hills and the valleys, durable as stone. Well, this land is blowing away. On the wind.

He paused for effect. I recalled how he'd done this a number of times during his speech last night.

Peat, you see. The fenlands left behind a peat soil when they were drained. The richest soil. But when peat dries out it crumbles to dust. One breath of wind and it's gone. There's been too much drainage. The soil just blows away off the fields. It's light as a feather.

He continued looking pensively out of the windscreen, then seemed to gather himself.

Sorry, he said, you didn't come here for one of my lectures. Did you hear my speech last night?

I nodded.

Respect, he said. It's like karma. Give and take. You give kindness today and tomorrow you receive it back. Because we're all connected Daniel. We're all in the same boat.

He looked into the distance, tapped the steering wheel with a thumb. I jumped into the silence.

Do you know what happened at Mount Longdon?

Fraser was quiet. I fidgeted nervously with the plastic knob of the gear lever between us. Out on the fen the heron waited, stock-still.

I saw George Barlow, I said. He told me about this kid getting shot through the eye – an Argie, like. And then Yan and his mates just disappeared into thin air. I got the idea there was something he wasn't telling me, mind –

Silence, said Fraser, cutting me dead. Silence doesn't always need filling. You should remember that.

I waited.

War is war, he said. People get shot. That doesn't really interest me. He stopped, exhaling pensively.

What does interest me is people. Human connection. It's what knits us together into the fabric of a society. It's what stops us blowing away in the wind, just like fen peat. The army's like that – like a big family. You're connected to these people whether you like them or not. You rely on them and they rely on you.

Fraser didn't look at me, carried on gazing out of the windscreen at the distant fen. Ghosts of polarized light swam across the toughened glass.

That's what your dad didn't get, he said. In the final analysis, he was just a fucking waster.

He turned to look at me.

You look shocked, he said. But you need to know the truth. When you're a little kid your parents seem as permanent as the landscape. Solid, like hills. But then you're a man, and you find out that they're only people. And sometimes you find out that they're worthless. Those hills are light as a feather. One breath of wind and they're gone.

He gripped the steering wheel with white knuckles, smudged with faint freckles.

Yan always had something faulty inside him, like a broken spring. Don't get me wrong, he was great company – most people thought he was the life and soul, men and women alike. But I know the type. People got close to him but they didn't touch him inside, and when he got bored he'd cut them loose and ship out.

He sniffed, and pinched his nostrils closed.

The type of man who'd sit at your table and drink your beer and laugh at your jokes, and then help himself to a little of whatever it was he wanted, without a care.

Your wife, I said. Helena –

He swivelled quickly and his thumb was pressed against my carotid and his eyes were cold and dark like collapsed stars. I shivered, felt my blood beating against his hand.

You don't talk about her, he said. If you talk about her again I'll cut your fucking throat.

Okay. I won't.

Good lad.

He relaxed his grip and gazed determinedly out of the windscreen. I looked at the side of his face, framed in delicate sunlight.

You asked about Longdon, he said. I don't know any more than Barlow, not for sure. He disappeared, two others with him. Never seen again. But if I had to guess I'd say that he got bored, and he cut the threads, and he pissed off.

He smiled, ruefully.

People like Yan, he said. They don't see it. The ties that bind you to other people, that sometimes feel like shackles and halters and trusses constricting the life out of you. Those ties are also your veins and arteries, your life blood. If you cut them, what are you?

There was a long silence. I pushed my hands under the backs of my thighs, warming my fingers between car seat and denim. Looked up into the blue of space, felt the planet buck and lurch beneath me like a scarce broken horse plunging wildly through the universe.

But what happened to them? I said. I still don't know.

He turned to me. That rueful smile again, and his watery blue eyes. He rapped his fingertips against the steering wheel.

Go home Danny, he said. Go home, wherever that is. You seem like a nice enough lad. Too nice to be wasting your energy on Yan Thomas. He's damaged goods, take it from me. Even if he's alive, he's in no hurry to find you, is he? Your position's simple. Go home and get on with your life. Let him go.

I looked out of the windscreen across the fen and felt tired and dirty and a long ways from home. Weightless tears rose to the corners of my eyes and I tried to blink them back. I could hear metallic taps and crunches as Paul pottered his way back towards us among the dying cars. And then the heron rose from the fen like a huge soft smut from a fire, great rounded wings billowing up above the reedbeds and into a painless blue sky. And with it a huge weight was lifted from the world. The bird flapped lazily and drifted away on the wind, in search of another island of water among the arable prairies.

15. Chilean Flamingo

(Phoenicopterus chilensis)

Becalmed here with no wind and pitiless sun and the frozen surface of the sea. All the tiny ripples and dreams which are the ocean's constant conversation with itself – all them little tics and furrows and wrinkles – have solidified and come to a stop like a kettle furring itself dry.

Islands and mountains float above the horizon in dizzy blueness. Reality and mirage are the same thing. There is South Georgia out to the east with Bird Island at its tip, but when the sun licks the black chain of mountains I remember that South Georgia is a lifetime away. The mountains sizzle and melt into the low blue cones of a drifting volcano.

Eyes and mouth crusting up with salt, more than a day now since we had fresh water and my tongue a wrinkled lump inside my own head. Lips like blistered wood, eyeballs pickled by the constant flare of light. They wept liquid for days but now they're dry, as if the outer layers have shed. Keep them downcast beneath the wide-brimmed hat but the glare reflects up and slides a flat-bladed knife inside my skull.

If I were a sailor I'd whistle for a wind, says Joe Fish. But I'm too dry. Can't make a sound.

He blows a few dry notes and grimaces.

Is that an island on the horizon?

I squint into the sun and the blade slides further, the tip of it between my frontal lobes. Pull the hat down and cower in its shade. But there is an island, and it's getting closer as we trudge across the solidified surface of the sea. Why the hell did we need the boat before when we're making such good headway on foot?

Fabián, how far is it to La Paz? asks Horse Boy gruffly, with the tone of an impatient child.

Once we are on the other side of this, says Fabián, it is still some way. But at least there are roads. We can try to find a lift.

La Paz. Landlocked capital of a landlocked country. I shake my head and remember straight. This is no sea but a vast salt pan. There was a lake here once, but sun and time have congealed the water into a vast flow of sparkling white mineral, shimmering to the horizon where the blue peaks of the Andes hover. Rippling geometric patterns etched into the surface of the salt, running away into painful distance.

When I look back I can no longer see Barriga's van. For a long time her carcass was still visible back there where she boiled dry and died, a still black point in waves of salt, the origin of our slow hoofprints. I think about the boneshaking months coming out of Chile and into the south of Bolivia, and I'm almost glad to see the back of her.

You tell each other stories, about quenched thirst, about swimming in highland rivers. There's me and Kate in York on a chilly spring morning, walking on the old city wall behind the Minster and stopping every few paces to tongue each other silly. And there's this garden down below, running from the back of an elegant Georgian house. A grace and favour pad for some cathedral bigwig, I'd hazard a guess. An expanse of clipped lawn, turquoise like a submerged forest of seaweed, the surfaces shimmering with dew, with a billion tiny globes of moisture. You could dive into that lawn and submerge beneath the wet grass. You could drink those lucid worlds of dew.

Now I can't forgive myself. I saw the jewelled lawn but I didn't dive in. We continue plodding towards the cone of the island.

Okay, says Horse Boy. When I was seventeen or eighteen.

His Wiltshire burr is growing stronger. He pauses to gather enough moisture in his mouth.

We drove up to the Ridgeway. One of them late summer evenings when you think it's never going to get dark. A harvest moon, massive and orange and hanging like a pregnant belly and the sky blue like smoke. You could see the White Horse on Uffington Hill. Looks like its leaping, that horse, from one hill to the next. Made out of chalk, dry as a bone and thousands of years old.

He licks his lips and the sun bludgeons us about heads and shoulders. I look at Dave, huge patches of sweat burgeoning on his back and under his arms, dried to a white crust around the edges. Dry as a bone.

We went down to Wayland's Smithy. It's a prehistoric tomb, right, just off the path in a grove of trees. This long low mound of grass and at one end there's a facade of big flat standing stones like a row of teeth. We looked out across the fields, acres of wheat moving in the wind. And I thought, this is how it's been, for five thousand years. The quiet tomb and the trees whispering and the wheatfield stirring. And then I thought, maybe five thousand years ent really that long at all. Just the blink of an eye.

We march on across the salt pan, the dead sound of our feet mopped up by the soft mineral. Tramp tramp. Horse Boy looks like he's lost the plot. Tilts his head from side to side, as if considering.

We got off our tits down there, brew and cans and blow. Me and Emma ended up doing it. I'd been wanting to for so long that it was over in a few minutes.

Shot his bolt, roars Joe. You should wait for the starting pistol son. Next time you give her my number.

Horse Boy winces, but continues.

And then we passed out too. I woke up in the middle of the night and I've never been so thirsty. That's what made me think of it just now.

Tramp tramp tramp. I stumble and almost drop but Joe grabs me under the armpits and sets me upright. The island isn't far now, shimmering in unbearable light.

In the end I got to sleep again, says Horse Boy. And I heard this drumming sound. Like the hardest rain bouncing from the pavements.

Apples, hard and bitter, raining from the trees and buffeting the ground. Hooves, coming across the downland. The white horse, careering across the sky, just cresting the hills. I could see froth brimming up out of its mouth, and running down its neck and sides. The front hooves were over me like crescent moons and the spit was dripping from them, down into my mouth while I was asleep. It was like opium, like sherbet. White and sweet and bitter and tender. And I weren't thirsty any more. He was in the field with me and I was standing up, holding out my hand. He nuzzled it and it became a green apple, huge, like a cooking apple. I held it out and he bit into it with these clean white teeth.

You forgot to tell us about the magic mushrooms, Joe guffaws. Or was it an acid trip son? Can you conjure up a white horse out here?

I don't think so, says Horse Boy.

We reach the island and the day's long-drawn-out scream of heat is dwindling into a cold Altiplano night. It's a shallow conical hill of rock, rising only a few metres above the salt pan and studded with bulbous cacti clinging to crevices in the rock. Fabián takes out a machete and butchers one and a milky fluid begins to drip out.

It'll be salty, says Horse Boy, don't get excited. Can't be no fresh water round here.

Perhaps the cacti drink rainwater, says Fabián. There's only one way to find out.

He raises a slice of cactus flesh and squeezes it so that the milk dribbles into his open mouth. Stands like this for some time before closing his mouth and gasping.

It may not have dripped from the hooves of a white horse, he says, but it is fresh.

So we take turns to guzzle milk from the cactus flesh, ignoring the spines which puncture our skin. It's bitter but refreshing, like a thin coconut milk. And when we're sated we sit, shivering as the temperature plunges. There's a thin crust of salt across our skins, stinging the sore corners of mouths and eyes, and our boots and trousers are white. The stars come out like clumsy fists and beneath them the salt pans glitter.

Joe wets his lips and whistles a few bars and I lift my voice and join in with the words. *We're a bunch of fucking animals, we're the airborne infantry.*

When I dropped off that roof, says Horse Boy. If I'd fallen a few inches to one side, I'd have caved my skull in. I'd never have come back.

Bollocks, says Joe. And I'll tell you for why.

Go on then.

Because it's all predetermined boy. From the day the universe set rolling. There is no such thing as *what if*. You were always going to come back.

I reckon, I say. There's a parallel universe where Joe is a right looker and he has the gift of the blarney and has the ladies eating out of his pants.

Horse Boy laughs. Now you're stretching credibility Yan.

When I started walking, that day at Mount Longdon, I say, I thought I'd walk down the hill, into the belly of the ocean. Look where I've ended up.

So why did you start? says Horse Boy.

Dunno. Why did you come after me?

Dunno.

Horse Boy laughs and shakes his head, hunkers back down on his rock. Night thickens.

Tongues of rock begin to appear among the salt flats, and we realize we're nearing the far side. The sun swamps the entire sky in floodwaters of sulphurous heat, and dark bare hills begin to loom. We scramble up and over a low ridge encrusted with garish minerals, and look down on a lake of blood, many miles across and encircled by pure snow. Bare rounded hills float behind it, hazy in the heat. We scramble down closer to the shoreline and find, not virgin snow, but a white crystalline precipitate. Fabián crumbles some of the mineral and dabs it with his tongue.

Borax, he says. And the lake is blooming not with blood but with red algae. This is Lago Colorado.

There are thousands of flamingos feeding across the lake. Chilean flamingos, a vivid salmon pink, legs crooked at improbable angles as they wade, their dark bills inverted, sweeping through the water to strain out algae.

The algae give them the colour, says Fabián. Otherwise they turn white.

More birds stream in from the sky, legs trailing, and the blood-red lake is alive with movement and chatter. We watch the garish pink birds skimming the algae out of the water, squabbling and flirting, sleeping with one foot tucked up and bill smuggled among the back feathers. They are at home here, on a lake of rusty blood, lying in a bed of congealed minerals and salts, high above sea level in the Altiplano of Bolivia.

I sit down on a rock, shade my eyes. As Fabián passes in front of me his skull blots out the disk of the sun, like the knurled fist of the moon making an eclipse. The sun's corona spills out around him, straggling in his long hair, making an improbable halo.

And seven days later in La Paz, the man sitting opposite me also has a halo. Sunlight pours from the thin blue sky and streams, ghostly, from behind his crisp black shape. The air is attenuated, low in oxygen. Even sitting motionless I can feel my lungs working, wringing the meagre gas from each breath. Across the table his face remains in shadow, thrown into eclipse, but there are flames around it where shafts of light ignite his wispy golden hair and solar flares leap out into space, cold and giddy. He sips at a short dark coffee and one sleeve of his black suit rides up to show a shirt cuff so sharp and white it's almost blue.

So, he says, you have decided.

I'm not sure if this is statement or question. His voice is flat, but resonates with the heat of coffee and tobacco. I swallow a mouthful of coffee and it drips from my vocal cords like golden lava. I look away, beyond the billowing corona of gold, beyond the pavement café in

Plaza San Francisco and up towards the Altiplano and the bleached horizon, the three peaks of Illimani floating in the sky like jagged sherds of moon, cupping La Paz like a day-old chick nestling in the hand. Small houses jostle down the steep sides of the canyon, and below them the encircled city thrusts up buildings of concrete and glass into the emptiness like jewelled stems of summer grass.

The man with the halo is waiting for an answer, his manicured fingertips drumming against the white porcelain of his coffee cup.

I'll do it, said Dave, earlier in the hotel room. Don Hernán is my contact after all.

Don Hernán is my contact after all, scoffed Joe Fish unkindly. Listen to you. You think you're a big-shot drugs baron. You smuggled a bit of snout, end of story. He lolled back in the armchair.

I'm in, said Horse Boy, pacing across the room. I'm sick of this, since the money ran out. He ent offering us much, but at least we can get back to Europe. I'm ready to go home lads.

I looked around the little hotel room, the metal shutters still closed, pinpricks of light clattering around the room like small change. Delved into my tobacco pouch and found it almost empty. Just enough bum-fluff in the bottom to fashion a loose cigarette. I lit it and it burned quickly and the smoke was harsh and sallow.

I'm against this, said Fabián, sitting on the bed and running a hand over his straggling hair. There's too much risk. I'd rather be penniless in La Paz than in jail. Drug mules can get twenty years.

He paused and exhaled.

I'm against it, he said again. But you've drowned me in the Southern Ocean and burned me in that hotel room in Chile and if you are all for it then I will go.

I have to say it's tempting, said Joe, gruffly. Passports, good forgeries. Tickets to Europe. And money. Just to take one suitcase each, and hand it over to somebody at the other end.

I was lying on the bed, hands behind my head. There was a ceiling fan above me which didn't work. Flies were buzzing round it, alighting on the blades.

But your man has seen us coming Dave, said Joe. He knows we're desperate and that's why the wedge is shite.

The sun was pawing at the shutters, desperate to come in. I couldn't work out why we were sitting in the dark.

It's up to me and you, then, Joe, I said. If we're in, we can tell the man yes. If we're out, then it's no deal.

He cleared his throat and tugged at a pendulous earlobe. Raised one eyebrow, and slapped a closed fist on the arm of his chair. He looked at my hand, flat as a pancake, and rolled his eyes.

Paper wraps stone, I said. We'll tell him yes.

I walked over to the shutters and lifted the metal bar. Then I threw them back and the sunlight roared across the room like a breaker, motes of dust and cigarette smoke sparkling and twirling.

Solar flares continue to erupt from the golden mane of Don Hernán. He has finished his coffee now and the bustle of the market moves around us in Plaza San Francisco, but we sit still like chess players, like boulders in an upland stream. I drain my coffee and his corona shimmers.

The answer is yes, I say, putting my coffee cup carefully down in its saucer.

I'd normally smoke a cig here but I'm out of tobacco and the money's finished. I feel restless, rub a finger against my thumbnail, tracing the same pattern over and over again.

Good, he says.

He picks up his briefcase and gets to his feet. A respectable businessman.

Go back to your hotel, he says. My associates will be in touch about your travel arrangements.

He moves away through the market, starkly black and white among the colourful Indian shawls, his golden head burning like a field of summer wheat.

So we wait for two days and then Dave is handed a brown envelope in a pavement café. Back at the hotel we rip it open and empty the contents onto the bed. Five passports and five tickets. Somebody will meet us at the airport with our luggage. We examine the tickets. All flying into Köln–Bonn, but on different days and by different routes. I look at my passport and see that they've done a sound job – a British passport in the name of Michael Cornelius, place of birth Wakefield. How do these people know about Wakefield?

In with the tickets there's a small advance of cash, just to tide us over. We walk out of the hotel feeling buoyant, looking for a bar and some smokes. We look at women on the street and Horse Boy barks like a dog and draws some bemused smiles. The sun is warm on our faces.

Late at night, in the hotel room, Fabián shells a photograph out of his wallet.

Your kids?

Yes.

He lays the photo down on the table. A boy and a girl.

He has your eyes, I say.

Carlos. He will be twelve this year. Wants to be a footballer. Amazes me, sometimes, what he can do with the ball. You have a boy also Yan.

Danny. Aye, he'd be older now. Fourteen, fifteen.

Bet he's a card sharp, like the old man.

You bet. All the fancy shuffles. Bluffs like an old-timer. Thirteen years old he was breaking hearts.

I grin.

Nice kids Fabián, I say. So why don't you go home?

He tosses his head like a spooked horse.

Why don't you?

I shrug.

I'm light as a feather, I say. Life is light as a feather.

*

All the fancy shuffles. Bluffs like an old-timer. Why did you tell him that?
I don't know why I told him that Dan.

Maybes you were ashamed of the real me. The lad who was all thumbs at cards and turned puce whenever a lass spoke to him.

I wasn't ashamed. It was just – I wanted to make this image for Fabián. To make it a good story, that was all. Maybe I just wanted to impress him.

That's pretty sad Yan.

Aye. I suppose it was.

You couldn't even remember how old I was.

And we play cards for small change, the few pesos and bolivianos we still have rattling around in our pockets. Fabián opts out, falls asleep on the bed, hands tucked behind his head. Light splashes across the mahogany sheen of the table.

I'm out, says Horse Boy, grey circles around his tired eyes. He lays his hand face down on the table and the light flutters over a series of faint notches in the edge of one of the cards.

I'll see you Dave, I say, clattering a handful of pesos onto the table. I run my fingers down the edges of the cards in my hand. This one has a little notch in, just below the corner. And this one. Both of them are kings.

Thou shalt have a fishy, on a little dishy, sings Joe, thick smoke guttering from his filterless cigarette. I smell you Dave.

He lets a handful of little coins fall onto the table, shimmering like a waterfall in sunlight.

Okay, says Dave, taking a sip of whisky from his glass. Now for the draw. How many Yan?

Three.

Thou shalt have a fishy, when the boat comes in.

He slides them across the table to me, and I notice for the first time how he runs a finger down the edge of each card as it comes. How he does the same thing when dealing out two cards to Joe, one card to himself. I take a suck of beer, cold and clear and constant. Keep watching Dave's hands, not his face.

I'll stand pat, I say.

Raise you ten, says Joe.

Another shower of clattering coins.

Ten, and raise you twenty, chirps Dave, shovelling more in.

Dance for tha' daddy, sing for tha' mammy.

And then I see him do it. Flips a thumbnail across the corner of a card, making a little notch.

I'm out. Slap my cards down, sick to the stomach.

Aye, says Joe, with a wink. Too rich for me, as well.

Come on, crows Dave, reaching out both his arms to sweep up the drift of coins from the centre of the table.

I grab one of his forearms hard, and twist. Suddenly Joe and Horse Boy are deadly serious, looking at me. Dave wriggles like a fish on the hook.

Marking the fucking cards Dave, I say. I've just seen you. What is it, a notch on the court cards? One for a king, two for an ace?

He twists free, puts both his hands flat on the table. A sheen of sweat across his face.

It's not on, he blurts. You're questioning my integrity. What –

And his voice rises to a squeal as I go for his throat and the table goes over, little pesos and bolivianos exploding everywhere, glinting like fish scales. Glasses smash, whisky slicks the floor. Dave backs against the wall, knocking down a flimsy shelf as he does so, chipboard splintering and rawlplugs ripping out. I press him against the plaster with my forearm at his throat.

Fucking your mates up the arse for loose change, I say. What kind of a cunt are you?

He backs along the wall. Joe and Horse Boy are on the floor, patiently picking up the spilled money, and Fabián is reclining on one elbow, watching.

Come on, Dave stammers. Don't have to ruin our friendship over it.

I pick up the Walther and smash the butt into one side of his head and he squeals again and goes down on all fours. Then I grab him by the hair and hoist him back up.

Get out, I say.

He hovers, incredulous. I watch a gob of dark blood come adrift from his hairline and sway down the side of his face, making a neat detour round the eye socket and the corner of the mouth, disappearing below the neckline of his shirt.

But we've got a deal with Don Hernán, he stammers, face a ghostly white.

We've got a deal. But you just counted yourself out.

His jaw quivers. I'm sorry lads, he says. It won't happen again.

Just go Dave, says Joe.

Aye, before I kick you up and down the fucking street. Look at him Joe. He'll be blubbering in a minute.

Dave looks from one of us to the other, his eyes flickering and uncertain and hurt. Then he walks unsteadily out of the door.

I'm the last one to fly out and when the others have gone the time hangs heavy. I'm lonely, I guess. I walk through the city looking for Dave. We could patch things up, crack a few beers, check out the lowlife. But I can't find him, so I just sit in a pavement café and watch the world go by. Street kids beg for money and collapse into gales of laughter when I make small change appear from their ears. Men in severe suits stride past with briefcases swinging, their faces obscured behind dark glasses. Every other car here seems to be a Volkswagen Beetle, the city filled with the drone of aircooled engines. I think of the others, flying into Europe by different routes. Like the wise men, each bearing a suitcase full of snow. I think of that shimmering explosion of little pesos and bolivianos. But most of all, I think of Don Hernán, his golden head flaming like the sun.

16. **Whooper Swan**

(Cygnus cygnus)

Danny, I can tell when you're avoiding me, says Kate, from the other side of the world. You're a coward with bad news. Always have been. The longer I don't hear from you, the more I know something's wrong.

What time is it there? I croak, blearily, rubbing the sleep out of my eyes. It's the graveyard shift here.

Sorry love, she says. Never can work out the time difference.

The echo as her voice bounces from satellite to satellite. I sit up in bed and pull the duvet around me. Kelly's side empty, not slept in. I stare into the darkness of the bedroom. Liquid green numerals on the radio alarm and the tired blue glow of my phone display.

So how are you? How's Terry? Still working on the handicap?

I stifle back a yawn, but my jaw insists on unhinging itself silently.

We had a pool put in. I'm trying to persuade him to spend more time at home, less in the clubhouse. But you're changing the subject. Come on, spill.

I take a deep breath.

Yan's dying, I say. Lung cancer. A year at most. Probably much less.

There's a long silence in Western Australia, while satellites poised over the Indian Ocean wait for a response. Then a snuffle over the line and I can tell she's crying. I wait.

Thanks for being upfront, she says. That man, he's hopeless. How is he at the moment?

Still getting around fine. There's more shortness of breath now. He needs oxygen sometimes. Think he's due for another round of chemo soon.

I still love him, you know.

Come back then.

I can't. I like him best when he's on the other side of the world.

How do you do it?

What?

Stay so detached.

He gave me plenty of time to practise Dan.

Yan lives in a small Victorian terrace in Hartlepool, the house he bought after the pub was sold. It seemed easy at the time, the way him and Kate divvied up their assets and turned their backs on each other. The detritus of a marriage. We linger in the back yard, strewn with binbags and loose rubbish.

Who's turned your bins over?

Kids, he grumbles. There are some right ones around here. I'd give 'em a tap if I could catch one.

You'd have the dads round here offering you on, cancer or no cancer.

I right the dustbin and start to pile stuff back into it and a blustery wind elbows down the back alley and across the yards, lifting waste paper into the air and over the neighbouring fences. Next door a net curtain is slipped aside and a sharp face watches from the back kitchen.

Is Mrs Rusniak twitching the curtains? calls Yan from inside.

Yep.

Always swore I'd show her my arse one day, he yells. Never did. Too much of a gent.

Too scared she'd set that little Westie on you, you mean, I shout back. Vicious little tyke. I've always wanted to boot it over the wall.

He laughs.

You sound better, I say. Not so breathless.

Aye, he says. I'm winning young James over to my way of thinking.

I finish stuffing the bags back and wedge the plastic lid on.

Any chance of a mash?

The house has been rented out most of the last twenty years and it's showing the wear and tear. Fag burns in the carpets and sofas, mould erupting in the bathroom. We sit in the back kitchen drinking tea, strong and scalding.

You've got your travelling photos up, I say.

A collage of photographs stuck to the wall above the kitchen table. Palm trees, mountains, jungles, beaches, temples. In front of the views is Yan. Smiling at the camera. Flicking a middle finger, raising a can. Grinning in the middle of a gaggle of young backpackers. Arm round a woman, young and nubile. Never the same one.

Yeah, he says. I miss it. Specially Pattaya.

Never did much travelling, I say, wistful. Bali, Lombok, Kathmandu, Macchu Picchu. Just a dream to me.

He taps the side of his nose infuriatingly. Grins.

Never were the gambling type, were you?

Stifles a slight cough. I slurp at the hot tea determinedly.

And the fags?

It's getting easier. Chocolate's the answer. Every time I have a craving I eat a chocolate bar. Can't put weight on at the moment, so it's a win–win situation. Want to share one now?

He reaches into one of the top cupboards, splits a bar and passes two fingers to me, stuffing the other two into his mouth.

So, the Christmas decs, I say. Sure you want me to put them up for you? You've never bothered before.

Thing is, he says, through the chocolate. Probably the last one I'll have. Seems daft, but I want to do it properly.

Thought you were a cynic.

But it's been so long, I can't really remember how to do it. It was always Kate who decorated the pub, and you when you were a kid. Wasn't really my department.

Leave it to me, I say. Cross my palm with cash, and I'll buy the decs. Back round here tomorrow to put them up.

Perfect. He shoves a wad of crisp twenties at me. That do?

Bloody hell Yan. I only need a couple of darwins.

Old men playing cribbage at the pub Dan. Small fry. If there's any change, get yourself a few beers.

I push my chair back and stand up.

Dan, he says. I was meaning to ask.

He stops, and I wait.

Charlie painted you a picture, didn't he? A bit of a bleak assessment. A complete fucking waster or whatever it was he said.

Damaged goods.

Aye.

Well, you did nail his missus.

Aye, I did that.

So what was it you wanted to ask?

He runs fingertips across his stubble.

Is that how you feel about me too? he says.

I slide a chair out, feet squeaking across quarry tiles. Sit.

Maybe, I say. At the time.

How about now?

Now I'm not so sure.

Right.

If I could understand what happened, up on Mount Longdon. What it was that set you off. You always skate over it, don't you? Barlow shoots this lad through the eye, but then what? Something must have happened to start you walking. Everything else came from that.

The expression on his face is half laugh and half frown. Half irritation, too. Whites of his eyes flashing as the light fades.

You feel drunk, you know, he says. In an action like Longdon, you've not had any sleep for days. I'm not even sure I know what happened meself.

I don't buy that.

I'm still trying to fit it together Dan.

He looks at me and he's suddenly a confused old man and I feel this surge of tenderness towards him and put my hand on his shoulder, but later I wonder whether he was just playing for sympathy.

Kate rang the other night, I tell him.

How did she take it?

Cried. Said you were incorrigible. Said she couldn't come over. Still loves you. Prefers you on the other side of the world, though. That was it really.

Sounds about right, he muses.

As I close the back door behind me he's hunched over the table, staring into his untouched mug of tea.

When I get home, there's a man in the kitchen with Kelly, helping her empty the dishwasher.

This is Martin, she says. I told you he was staying the weekend.

Yeah. I'd forgotten.

We shake hands and Martin smiles, wagging his shock of dark hair. He's stick-thin and tanned. Tight denim and a black tee-shirt. Teeth glitter in the leathery face.

You must be Danny, he says. Looks at my rumpled work suit with amusement. Martin and Kelly went out when they were at school, and they've kept in touch. My partner in crime, she calls him.

Thought you could cook us your moussaka Dan, says Kelly. Always reminds me of Mykonos.

Yeah man, says Martin. Party island.

We were in the quiet bit, I tell him. Beach, taverna, a stack of good books.

I struggle with the moussaka while Kelly and Martin drink wine and giggle in the front room.

How's Brighton, then? I ask him, after dinner. Never feel home-sick?

Wouldn't be seen dead. Brighton is one happening place. Clubs are banging, disco biccies coming out of your ears man. Never get bored.

You want to hear about all the nurses he's been through, says Kelly.

The NHS is a considerate employer, he quips. Slumps back in the armchair, crossing one slender leg over the other, crooked like a daddy-long-legs.

So what floats your boat Dan? he asks, turning his eyes on me. They're dark, like burnished silver.

I shrug.

He's a birder, says Kelly.

I try to keep it quiet, I say.

The long winter evenings must just fly by, says Martin.

Anyway, I say. I'm going to turn in. Can't keep me eyes open these days.

Dan, says Kelly. Don't be boring.

She turns to face me from the opposite end of the sofa. Not made up, her skin is like fresh dough, a soft flour-dusted loaf. I want to bite her.

Don't worry about it babe, says Martin. Let Dan catch some zeds if he wants to.

Upstairs, I lie awake and listen to the splurge of their conversation. Shouts, giggles and laughs, rising and falling. I strain to catch their words but they wriggle away into the dark.

The next day, Jean opens the door before I can knock. Wrapped in that long coat, sleek and pencil-slim.

Oh, hiya Danny. I was just going.

She eyes the plastic bags in my hand.

Lads' night in, is it?

Something like that. Bloody hell it's cold. Feet went numb on the way over. Jean grimaces at the darkening sky. A smoky smell in the air, and a stillness. One or two stray flakes of snow spiralling down.

Winter coming on, she says. I'd better get going.

*

What's the story with Jean? I ask, when we're sitting in his front room. The gas fire creaks and hisses, a warm orange glow starting to build.

She's lived down the road for years. Nice place, too. Set up just how she wants it since the divorce. Dipped her a few times, over the years, when I've been back. Both like our own space is what's good about it. Bears and their lairs. And when we meet up, well it's more exciting, more like a date. I guess we're trying to string out the excitement. The excitement you get when you first meet someone. Heart still jumps when the phone rings and it's her. Bet you don't feel like that when Kelly rings up. Get some frozen peas on the way home love.

Anyway, I say, changing the subject. You want to see these decorations?

He nods without much enthusiasm. I unpack the bags one by one. A string of bulbous lights, each hand-painted like a Chinese lantern. Another string in the shape of golden stars. One of them candle bridges everybody seems to have these days. And a fibre-optic tree, small enough to sit on a tabletop.

No flashing reindeer, he says. You've gone upmarket.

And the fairy on the top, I say, pulling a floppy raft of cans out of a bag. Something to toast them with.

He looks at the six-pack with satisfaction.

McEwan's Best Scotch, he says. Now you're talking.

Doesn't take long to hang the decorations. Yan helps but he's out of breath when he has to reach up above his head. We put the plugs in and switch off the room lights. The Chinese lanterns glow peacefully above the fireplace like faraway planets, the stars are strung across the sash window with the candle bridge beneath, and the fibre-optic tree sits on the sideboard, shuffling gently through its sequence of colours which slowly wash over the room in turn. Red, magenta, green, yellow and ice blue. Relaxing, like the edge of the sea, each colour washing over the sand, slowing, stopping, retreating. I go to the kitchen and clatter about in the fridge, returning with two almost frozen cans.

Crack them both, enjoying the crisp sound, hand one to Yan.

Cheers, he says. Here's to. He pauses and thinks. To winter. To mid-winter. May she freeze our pipes and bugger up the central heating.

He sips, mischievously.

Something's fallen out of your pocket, he says.

I grasp around on the sofa cushion, find the tube of sweets I bought for Paul.

Shit. Keep meaning to go and see him. But.

You keep putting it off. Because he's in a bad way.

He's hard work, it's true.

I take a gulp of the malty liquid.

I love this stuff, I say. You can feel the darkness in the lining of your nose, before you even take a drink. And then when you hold it in your mouth it's like a toffee apple, round and brown like a conker. Rolls right up into the roof of your mouth.

Sound like a connoisseur, he says.

The smell of it, the taste of it. It brings back the past.

I smile, suddenly almost tearful.

Brings back fierce memories, I say.

Smells and tastes, he says. Far more powerful than pictures in your head. Your memory's shot with holes like an old dishrag, but a few molecules of a particular smell, and you're right back there.

He smiles, the crow's feet at the corners of his eyes crinkling up like parchment.

Powerful medicine, he says.

We sup the beers in silence, watching the surf of colour creep over the room time and time again.

Go and see him, says Yan, suddenly. You don't know how much time he has left. I'm sure he'd like to see you. He's not a bad lad, really.

Why the interest? I ask. You never had much time for Paul, when we were kids.

He makes a steeple with his fingers and taps them together, not speaking.

There's a Chinese just down the road, he says, finally. Fancy some chow?

Dark outside, snow beginning to fall insistently from the smoky sky, animated by the orange flare of streetlighting. I look up and watch the flakes rushing towards me like a field of stars. We wait in the Chinese while a large television babbles in the corner and gloomy fish hang in an aquarium. The girl smiles as she hands over the bags of food. I look at her over my shoulder as we walk out of the shop.

Back in the kitchen I find plates and start to portion out the food. Mounds of rice, a bowl of prawn crackers. I pour glossy red sauce over battered balls of chicken, spoon out the pink-tinged char siu pork with bamboo shoots and water chestnuts. Yan is still out in the yard, freezing air pouring in through the open door.

Shut the door, I call.

Shush, he replies. Listen.

I join him at the door, but hear nothing. The slow rumble of traffic in the town, the quiet buzz of next door's TV.

There, he says.

I strain to listen. A faint blare of noise, like a distant car horn or the yell of an excited dog.

Whooper swans, he says. Arriving from the Arctic. I bet they're on their way to Seal Sands. Like a pack of hounds giving tongue, hunting across the sky.

Or a brass band warming up, I say.

He smiles. The sound gets louder, nearer, more urgent.

The winter swans, he says. A sure sign the cold weather's coming.

We strain our eyes upwards into the sky. Snow whirls towards us. The honking is very close. And suddenly we see them, almost brushing the rooftops, in a tight V formation with stumpy wings working tirelessly and long necks stretched out before the squat bodies. Sodium light splashes back from their white bellies, illuminating them a ghostly orange against the blackness of space. We squint upwards and they pass almost overhead. The discordant baying echoes and booms in the yard, clatters off the stone setts, and we hear the singing of cold air through the stiff primaries. And then they're over the house and out of sight and we're holding on to the sound as it recedes towards the cold black estuary.

The plates of food are stacked in the sink. I'll do the washing-up before I go. Kelly insists on a dishwasher, even though it takes the two of us almost a week to fill it. We butcher more cans and Yan puts some music on the turntable.

Still think vinyl's better, he says, as the needle crackles through some static. Of course the sound quality suffers a bit, but vinyl records are so much purer, deeper, more organic. Digital music always sounds tinny to me.

Luddite, I say. I get plenty of business out of helping people with MP3 players. They buy them and then they realize they don't know how to download the tunes.

Don't start getting techno-geeky on me. This is Dylan, by the way. *Planet Waves.* Recorded in nineteen seventy-three and not a digital thingy in sight.

We sit and listen to the music for a while. The fibre-optic light circles and circles.

He's your brother, says Yan.

I stare at him.

Or, technically, your half-brother.

You mean Paul, I say, after a brief stunned silence.

He nods slowly.

I've kept in touch with him, over the years. Not often, just the odd phone call. That's how I knew about the virus.

Who knows about this? I ask angrily. Does Paul know? Does Kate know?

A long pause.

Nobody knows, he says, finally, with a resigned look. Just me, and Deb – that's his mam – and now you. She didn't want me to tell him anything about it. She was married to Anth at the time and he thought the kid was his. I would have liked to tell him, to be more of a father to him, but I had to respect what she wanted. And I couldn't tell Kate. No way.

How did it happen? Paul and I are almost the same age. You must have – when you and Kate were trying for me.

He takes a deep breath.

I'm not proud of it. It just happened the once. It was getting on top of me, trying for a kid. Took the spontaneity out of things. Out of sex. I had to perform to order when Kate's cycle was right. And at other times she'd lost interest. Deb used to work the odd shift in the bar, just to tide her over. She wasn't bad-looking in them days. Average coupon but a decent body. And one time she stayed late to clear up. It was pouring with rain outside and I offered her a lift home. Don't know how it happened, maybe I was just looking for kicks. Pulled the car off the road by the Synthonia ground and then her knickers were round her ankles, skirt round her ears. Quick and ugly and the rain hammering on the roof, and that was all it took.

I stare at the fireplace for a moment, at the warm glow of Chinese lanterns.

Didn't realize you'd been shitting in your own kennel. Right under Kate's nose.

You wanted the truth, he says. All of it.

Aye.

I never felt like I was unfaithful, not really. It was just a physical thing, like a cow needs milking now and again. I was never unfaithful to Kate in my head.

He pauses and sighs.

But you're right, it was a mistake. Regret it, now.

Still couldn't stop yourself though.

You know me Dan. Too late to change. Relationships always turn stale on me, sooner or later. You ever learn about the Magdeburg hemispheres, when you were at school?

Nah. It was the eighties. They didn't believe in formal learning.

It was an early physics experiment – air pressure and vacuums. They locked together two brass hemispheres and pumped the air away from inside. More or less creates a vacuum. Even when they hitched a horse to each side they couldn't pull the damn things apart. See, that's what it feels like to me. Two people glued so tight together, they use up all the oxygen. I can't breathe. I have to pull things apart and let the air back in.

So why now? Do you want me to tell Paul?

He ponders before answering. Bob Dylan chimes away in the background, forgotten.

Up to you, he says. Tell him if you want. Just wanted you to know about him, really. It was in the back of me mind, all when you were both growing up. That there was somebody missing. Just go and see him. Make contact. Why are you laughing?

I shake my head.

I was just remembering Fraser's wife, all them years ago. She thought Paul was your son and not me. And it was the truth all along.

It's easy to be unfaithful, he says. The easiest thing in the world. You just have to jump on when it comes past, like. I'm proud of you Dan. You haven't done that. You've carried on working at it with Kelly, even when I told you to jump ship. You've stayed centred, son.

I don't feel centred, I say. I feel like you said. Like there's no air.

Snow falls quietly down in orange flurries, corroding on contact with the wet car bonnets and the tarmac. A few miles away Whooper swans are settling on the dark mudflats. Winter is coming.

I don't want to go home, don't want to cook another meal for Kelly and Martin while they rip the piss out of me. So I stop into the Unicorn on the off chance. It's Friday evening, the last before Christmas, and Matt and the gang are there drinking steadily in the packed side room and smoke is blooming above their heads.

Danny boy, shouts Matt, clearly the worse for wear. Fancy meeting you in a place like this. It's Black Eye Friday son. Happy holidays. He launches into song, school's – out – for – ever, before collapsing into raucous laughter.

Last day on site, explains Clare as I squeeze into a seat, her pale face intent. No more work till after New Year's. Mind you, no more pay till after New Year's either.

Don't you get holiday pay? I ask.

They smirk.

That's shit, I say. Mind you, I'm self-employed. Same deal, really. So is the site finished now?

Nah, says Clare, pushing her hair back under a woolly hat. Still some bits and pieces to do. Matt's coming back with a couple of others in January, to polish it off, but the three of us are going. Big Roman site near Hull.

Hull, scowls Matt. Rather you than me. Pint Danny? They've called last orders.

He weaves off towards the bar.

Must be cold, digging in this weather, I say. Been snowing on and off for a while.

It's not too bad when you're working, says Julie, sucking on a thin cigarette.

There is a group of girls, an office party, squealing happily at the table behind her. They wear Santa hats, tinsel twisted into their hair.

And the snow never seems to stick around here, she says. Hits the ground, turns brown, and melts.

Teesside microclimate, I say.

It's when you stop working, she goes on. Filling in sheets or doing a drawing. Then it really starts to bite. Clare never gets cold, do you Clare?

What?

She comes to with a start.

Sorry, miles away.

She has a pinched pale face, like a street urchin, and deep grey eyes which remind me unaccountably of Yan. She's squashed against me on the bench and I can feel the warmth of her against my side. Matt returns with a tray full of drinks, contents slopping lightly down the sides. He passes them out. My phone rings. I look at the display and recognize my home number. Reject the call.

Putting off going home? says Clare, lightly.

Something like that. So where are you going for Christmas?

Well, spending it on my own in the flat didn't seem too attractive, so I decided to foist myself on the parents. Going up there on the train tomorrow, in fact.

Whereabouts? Scottish borders, I'd say, from the accent. Jedburgh? She smiles.

Not far away. Selkirk.

Nice part of the world.

Aye. It's a bit of a depressing experience though. There's my brothers and sisters, all grown up with proper jobs and mortgages, all married, starting to have kids. And there's Clare, thirty-three, unmarried, hasn't even got a steady boyfriend, you know. Persists in doing archaeology, like a student. But doesn't she know there are no prospects? Living in these awful rented flats, like a gypsy. When's she going to settle down?

Sounds like fun.

It's not too bad, really. Mum always puts on a good spread.

She lifts her pint up and knocks back a good third of it.

So what are you doing for Christmas Dan?

I'm momentarily stumped. Kelly and me haven't talked about it.

Do you know what? I haven't got a clue, I say, bursting into embarrassed laughter. Supping beers with my terminally ill father, maybe. At least he's got some decs up.

People are beginning to drift away from the pub now. The bar shutters have come down and the staff are winkling the stragglers away from their tables.

Chucking-out time, says Andy. You getting the bus back Matt?

I'm starving, says Clare, anyone up for chips? There's one just up the High Street.

I realize I haven't eaten since breakfast, beer rapidly rising to my head. I feel flushed.

I'm in, I say.

Hugs, kisses, Happy Christmases, and the other three head to the bus stop.

Looks like it's just you and me kid, says Clare.

The chips are mealy and pungent. We stroll back along the High Street, browsing on them, towards where I left the car, trying to avoid slicks of black ice across the pavement.

Need a lift? I ask her.

Nah, I'm just round the corner. You know the flats over behind the church there.

I'm about to answer but my heel slips on a patch of ice and I'm suddenly sitting on the pavement. I've banged my coccyx and for a moment I can't speak, but sit there gaping like a fish. Clare bursts into ringing laughter, and then I'm laughing too. She holds out both hands and pulls me to my feet. Small, warm hands. We carry on until we arrive at the car.

You know, she says, if you still want to put off going home, I've got a bottle of sloe gin back at the flat. It's good stuff. Antifreeze for the soul. Some friends of mine make it every year.

Sounds right up my street.

We walk along Norton Green and into the churchyard. Completely dark, trees looming either side of the drive.

It's a good short cut through to the flats, she says. But you get all sorts in here at night. One time there was this couple over there, lying on a sleeping bag. The moon was out and all you could see was his white arse going up and down.

I like the way you say arse, I grin. Sounds sharp and Scottish. Say it again.

She looks at me inquisitively.

Arse, she says.

We've passed through the lych gate, and now we're walking alongside the church itself, past a war memorial with stone steps.

Another time, she says, conspiratorially, grabbing my forearm with her hand, I was walking up here and there was a figure standing right there, on the steps, all dressed in white. Like a ghost. A young man, tall, with blond hair. As I walked past he said something. The time of test is at hand. Something like that. Asked him who he was and he said I am the Christ. He was agitated, you know. Fidgeting. I just hurried on. That's care in the community for you. The time of test is at hand. Later on I realized it was Easter.

We walk through the cemetery to the rear of the church, the dark hulks of churchyard yews and the pale headstones. Her arm is still through mine. At the churchyard wall there's a gate through to the street on the other side. We slow and stop and then she's in front of me, still holding on to my forearm, and I fall towards her white face and kiss her. Gentle at first, tentative, but then our tongues are sliding together, turning over and over, my hands holding her waist and her arms around my neck.

That was nice, she says quietly, when it ends, her dark eyes peering into mine.

You know I'm married, I say.

I'm not a bunny boiler Dan, she says. I'm going away tomorrow. You just look like you need some company. And I happen to fancy you, quite a lot. It's simple, really. Easy.

Cut to the chase, I say. Don't beat around the bush.

She laughs and we kiss again. Then we walk through towards the flats. I retrieve the phone from my pocket and turn it off.

Do you want a lift to the station tomorrow? I ask, knocking back half a glass of the magenta liquid. It's stronger than I imagined, thick and heady with a melancholy aftertaste of autumn.

Aye, if you're offering. Got to be away early, mind.

No bother. I'm heading over that way anyway. Going to visit some-body.

What, your other girlfriend? she murmurs, snuggling against me on the sofa.

Half-brother. Only just found out tonight. And he doesn't know it yet.

Bloody hell, she says. You do lead an eventful life. And I thought you were just a boring computer geek. Refill?

She glugs more into the glass without waiting for an answer. My cheeks already burning with the alcohol.

Heating's crap in here, so you'll need a few glasses.

I tell her about Paul as we drink. The flat small and cold, the furniture shabby. Dirty yellow foam rubber spills out of the sofa. Sirens echoing across Stockton.

I'm going to bed, she says, yawning. Coming?

I follow her into the bedroom. A sleeping bag rumpled across the bare mattress and a smell of damp.

Not exactly the Hilton, I'm afraid, she says, sitting down on the edge of the bed and stripping off her jumper and bra over her head in one swift movement. Her long wayward hair bounces darkly down over her smooth shoulders and full breasts, her white belly and hips. I stand in front of her, alcohol pounding in my head.

It's easy Danny, she says, taking my hands. You just have to let your-self fall.

I lower myself on top of her and she rolls backwards into the bed, pulling me after her, quick and nimble fingers flipping open buttons and pushing down trousers until I slide into her, her fingers running up my spine, her breath of bitter autumn berries in my face. The easiest thing in the world.

Next morning I pull up outside the hostel. This is him. The way he thinks, the way he experiences life. The simplicity of last night. Perfect and inevitable. Why should I feel guilty?

Me and Clare were reserved this morning, polite small talk in the car, a kiss on the cheek as she got onto the train. Self-loathing like stale cigarette smoke clinging to my clothes. I look at myself in the driver's mirror. Slight bags beneath the eyes but otherwise the same lived-in face. Tell myself that nothing's changed.

The warden, Duncan, is busy with paperwork behind the reception desk. I finger the packet of sweets in my pocket.

Hi, I say.

He looks up abruptly.

I'm here to see Paul. Paul O'Rourke. I was here a couple of months ago?

Duncan looks uncomfortable.

Perhaps you'd better step into my office. We can talk more private in there.

A chill passes over me and my heart pounds. It's too late. I sit down in the proffered chair and Duncan wedges himself behind the desk. A tiny office, piles of paperwork and correspondence on the desk. Shelves with box files cover nearly all the wall space.

Paperwork, he says. Bane of the public services these days. Supposed to be a Labour government.

He's going to tell me that Paul is dead. I prepare myself.

Sorry to have to tell you this, he says. We'd have got in touch with you, but you didn't leave any contact details. Paul's not here. He checked out.

You don't have to beat around the bush, I say. You mean he's dead.

He stares at me.

God, I'm really sorry. No – of course, you must have thought – he really has checked out. As in left. A couple of weeks ago. The real worry is that he left all his medication here. Anti-retrovirals, everything. Could be in some danger without it.

He rubs the bridge of his nose between finger and thumb.

Anybody know where he is? Did he say where he was going?

Talking about Whitby, according to a couple of the regulars. No guarantee of course, but I've alerted the social services and police down there just in case he turns up.

He liked Whitby when he was a kid. Used to go down there with his mam. A week in the summer. But why leave the medication?

Perhaps he wasn't expecting to be gone long. Although I wonder whether he was thinking of –

His voice trails off and I finish his sentence.

Going there to die.

17. **Curlew**

(Numenius arquata)

It was getting dark when we pulled into Darlington. We stumbled into the echoing station, pigeons flapping high up against the glass roof with fathoms of night mounting above. Walked past the idling engine of the locomotive, the death-defying thrum of the diesel.

It was already a dream. The caravan park, the wedding, the scrapyard. Bright splinters of memory – stars dipping into the sea, circles of eyeliner in the dark, a shot glass of crème de menthe.

And out into the taxi rank, sloping downward towards the railway bridge. I made straight for a taxi and got in the back.

Haverton Hill mate, I said. The Cape of Good Hope.

He started the meter running, luminous red figures beginning to cycle. Paul was still outside, finishing a cigarette. I craned my neck backwards and saw him crush it beneath a boot, then he was jumping into the seat beside me.

Wagons roll, he shouted, extracting a beer can from his jacket pocket, popping it, slurping greedily.

The driver looked unimpressed. Reversed slowly out of the space, drove down the ramp and out onto the main road. He took Darlington Back Lane, through Norton and across the Billingham Beck valley on the new flyover. Tanks and towers and columns bristling above Billingham itself, above the squat tower of the Saxon church and the houses clustered like battlements along the ridge. We ran up Central Avenue and on out of town, the vast expanse of the Billingham site burning to the right, fields of shimmering light leaping into the black sky. And beyond the site was Haverton Hill and the Cape of Good Hope on the corner.

Paul began to stump off down the road, jacket pulled tight around his shoulders. He turned.

Don't do nothing I wouldn't do, he called.

Something clicked inside.

You never did it, did you? She prickteased you all night but you never got nowhere.

She likes a bit of rough, he said. She likes to rub Charlie's nose in it. Like she did with your old man.

All your stories are made up, aren't they?

Son, he said. I done stuff you never even imagined.

Then he marched off and left me standing there looking after him. I pushed open the front door and went in. Stairs in front of me, up to the flat. Swing doors to the bar on my right. Quiet in there, a few low voices droning like flies. The stairs shimmered drunkenly, somebody whispering at the top. I flipped the lightswitch and the bare bulb flared into life. Nobody there. The electricity buzzed.

I climbed the stairs, hand on the smooth wood of the banister, reached the top and went into the flat. The living room was empty and dark. That buzzing on the cusp of awareness.

Kate was at the kitchen table, bent over some paperwork. She got up and hugged me until I broke away, embarrassed.

What happened to your hair?

Oh, I said. Low maintenance.

Trajan loomed up at me, blunt face questing, paws on my shoulders. I pushed him down and he began scrabbling at the lino with his claws. The blinds at the windows weren't drawn and the blackness outside was pressing on the glass. I could feel it mounting. The pub was at the bottom of the sea.

Where have you been? she asked.

Nowhere really. What are you up to?

I'm filling in the form, she said. For the insurance.

Oh. Expected you to be bugging in front of the telly.

Yeah, I know. I'm cutting down on the happy pills. Still feel drunk all the time, mind. Hazy.

She sat back down and looked at the form.

It's his life insurance, she said. I'm making a claim.

Right.

Draw a line under it. Then we can sell this place. I can't carry on here.

It's not so bad.

It's haunted Dan.

The man at the end of your bed, I said.

Somebody got into bed with Michelle, she said.

I laughed.

That's most of Teesside mam.

Kate pursed her lips.

She was on her own. She heard the springs creak and the mattress give, and then someone pulled her by the ankles, down under the covers.

I'm knackered, I said. I could do with a shower.

Yeah, she said. You could.

I was halfway to the door when she spoke again.

You went to look for him, didn't you?

Aye. Sort of.

Did you find him?

No.

She smiled. Nicotine stains on her teeth, lines gathering at the corners of mouth and eyes.

He was a waster, I said.

She shrugged.

I was in the box room, showered for the first time since the caravan park. Pulled on a clean black shirt and jeans. Darkness pressed its nose to the window and I shivered. A tap at the door and I opened it and there was Hagan, larger than I remembered him, the muscles more pumped and the skin darker.

You'll get cancer on them sunbeds, I said.

He smiled. Even white teeth in the pudgy face, gold earring glinting against the tan.

Danny, he said. I like the bonehead. It suits you, kind of. Can I have a word?

Have as many as you like.

Listen, he said. We haven't got off on the right foot, like. Can we start again? Fresh start and all that.

He held out a hand, gold bracelets at the wrist beneath the designer shirt. I thought for a moment and then I shook it. Looked into the face, at the expressionless blue eyes. He was smiling, but they were cold.

Nice one, he said. Listen, why don't you nip down the bar for a pint later? There's something I want to ask you.

He looked at me appraisingly, well-trimmed eyebrows raised beneath the gelled blond mane.

Aye, I said. Later.

He turned and trotted down the stairs and the air was shimmering around him.

Hagan held a pint glass aslant under the beer tap and let the foamy lager rise, the head overflowing time and again until it was displaced by clear liquid.

On the house, he said, holding the glass out to me. I took it and sipped, putting the dripping glass down on a beer towel.

It's about territory, he said.

The glasses on the shelves were glinting, reflections multiplied in the rank of mirrors behind the bar.

Got to piss in the corners of your life, he continued. Mark it, like. With your scent.

Like a dog.

Aye. Like a hound dog swinging his dick. Like a boss wolf on his patch.

A knot of them around the pool table. Franco, Magoo and a few younger lads not much older than me. Hagan started slopping lagers and stouts into pint glasses, lining them up on the bar.

Anyone sniffs your piss and keeps on coming, he said. That's when you need to show your fucking teeth.

Pulled a tenner out of his pocket and shoved it at me. I shifted uncertainly on the bar stool.

Have a look, he said. Whose mug shot is it?

I looked.

Darwin, I said.

Aye. Charlie fucking Darwin. Why's he on the money?

I shrugged.

Because he knew the score, said Hagan. Survival of the fittest, eh? The strongest. Not just strong in the arm. Anyone can be a meat axe these days. Strong up here as well.

He tapped the side of his temple with a broad forefinger.

Got to be in tune with the times, he said. Maggie Thatcher. Aye, she's a woman, but she's going to fuck the lot of them. Dole wallahs, bedwetters, coal miners and puffs. Shove 'em in the gutter and tread on their fucking faces.

His enormous upper arms swelled and glistened.

Natural selection, he said. The strong get selected and the weak get lost.

He took a sip from a bottle of lager, frosted with condensation. I gulped at the gassy pint he'd given me. Magoo was threading coins into the jukebox. They clattered down and the machinery whirred.

Do you like the new George Michael? asked Hagan. He's a pussy magnet that charver.

I shrugged.

You sniffed my piss and kept on coming, he said. Didn't expect that.

He sucked thoughtfully at his lower lip, put both elbows on the bar and looked at me.

You got big *cojones* Danny, eh?

There was a roar from the pool table and one of the young lads was picking up a bundle of wedge from the rail.

Pleasure doing business with you Mr Frankland, he crowed, cigarette dangling from his gob and gold chains at his wrists. There was this smudged blue tattoo on the side of his neck next to a livid purple lovebite.

Winner stays on, said Hagan. I'm next up.

He rounded the bar and moved over to the table. I stayed perched on a bar stool.

I'm next pal, said one of Lovebite's mates, a skinny feral kid with cropped ginger hair. That's my cash on the side there.

Hagan stood in front of him, muscles bunching like thunderclouds beneath the tight tee-shirt.

Did you hear something Franco? he asked.

Franco shook his head with mock seriousness.

Thought I heard something squeaking, said Hagan. Like a little high-pitched mouse.

He fixed the gaggle of younger lads with a hard stare, one after the other. None of them said owt.

Must have been imagining things, said Hagan. I was wondering where I'd put me cash down, and there it is.

He picked up the coins from the rail and slotted them in, releasing the balls with a low rumble. Looked over at me and winked.

See what I mean Danny? Natural selection. Fuck off son, you're barred, he said to the skinny ginger kid. Go and sniff glue in the park.

The kid looked at his mates.

The rest of you can stay, said Hagan. It's just that ginger cunt.

The kid thought for a moment, turned and walked slowly out of the bar. None of his mates glanced after him.

I watched Hagan win Franco's money back from Lovebite. He raped the table, hard and fast and powerful. Buried the black and held his hand out for the cash. Lovebite and his mates sidled out of the front door, left the bar almost empty. On their way past one of them gobbed a great slick of curdled phlegm at the front window and then we heard them sprinting away. The gob hung there like a raw egg before sliding down the glass, and the walls bowed under the pressure of night.

This is our territory Dan, said Hagan, back behind the bar, polishing a pint glass with a towel. Our patch. The lads wanted to take you apart for robbing the till, but yer mam doesn't want you hurt and they'll do what I say. They're my dogs.

He put the glass down on the bar.

She said she'd give me an answer. Once she's got your dad's insurance money.

An answer?

Aye. You know what I mean. We're all grown-ups, right? I need you to make sure she's filled out that form and sent it mate. I need to know she's not just playing me.

I saw her filling it in tonight. Upstairs in the kitchen.

Good lad. You let me know when she's posted it.

Razia ran into my arms and hugged me fiercely. Then she dropped away, embarrassed.

Dan Thomas, she said. Back in town and twice as ugly. Did you find what you were looking for?

We walked through to the living room, where the TV chirruped innocently in a corner.

No, I said. Not really.

You're back, anyways.

She flounced down onto the threadbare sofa. I perched on the arm.

He's a waster, I said. Not worth the effort. I don't know why I bothered.

Yeah, you do. He read you bedtime stories, wiped your little arse for you. He took you out birding on Saturdays.

Yeah, he did all that. Until he got bored and went somewhere else.

Whatever he did or didn't do, he's still your old man. Blood's thicker than water, I reckon.

Not me Raz, I said. I've got thin blood, me.

And in the night I wake up and can't get back to sleep because of that buzzing in my ears and I pad through to the kitchen and there she is sat at the table with her back to me and a bottle of Napoleon at her elbow. Barefoot in her towelling robe and she's shredding that insurance form into the pedal bin and the sobs she's making sound like an animal and blue night pissing from the pipes like gas.

I want to reach out and touch her but I can't.

And Hagan sat at the same kitchen table in the morning in his boxers and a tight tee-shirt drinking a protein shake and sunlight hissing from his blond highlights. Turns to me and winks and says, she's posted it, hasn't she Dan? Tell me she's posted the form. And I look at him.

Aye, I say. Took it to the postbox meself.

And a summer went by, dribbled by like a gas leak only nobody made a spark. After exams I helped around the pub, bottling up, shifting barrels down in the cellar, with Hagan to the cash'n'carry. A hot summer, curdling in the bowl of Teesside, trapped between the North York Moors and the Durham coalfield. Haze over the estuary, a lush topiary of steam hanging heavy over chemical plants. My hair grew and I shaved it off again. Exam results dropped through the front door, good but unspectacular. Time slowed.

I thought about Yan. I had it in my head that I was going to let him go, like one of them birds you trap in a mist net and let off with a ring round its leg. Had it in my head too that he wouldn't be as obedient or go as quiet as a ringed bird. Not yet, anyway. I was waiting for September, for the cool and blustery winds you get from the sea, for the wide blue sky swept clean with a yardbrush. When autumn was here and passage migrants were finding a desperate landfall along the coast, then it would be time.

Going to check out the new supplier in Hartlepool, yelled Hagan up the stairs. Are you coming?

The van sped along the Seaton Carew road, heat squatting on us like a truculent frog, flat expanses of reclaimed land scorched from green to yellow. Petrochemical plants no longer bristled but drooped like a Dalí wristwatch. Outside the fire station there were two figures waiting and Hagan slowed and pulled up. Kurt and Magoo. They loped to the back of the van and jumped into the cargo bay. One of them thumped the plywood partition and Hagan moved off again. I looked at him with raised eyebrows. He was totally relaxed, designer sunglasses pushed up onto his forehead and a matchstick twirling between his lips. Drummed a rhythm against the wheel with his thumbs. He saw me studying him.

They're going to help us load some gear, he said.

But at the roundabout we turned right, and pulled up at the security gate of the nuclear power station. The guard came out, sweltering in a military style navy jumper. Flashed a thumbs-up sign at Hagan, and I recognized Franco. He raised the barrier and then jumped into the back of the van with the others. Hagan sped off down the approach road.

Quick detour, he said, but his mouth was becoming tense, teeth squeaking on the matchstick. The great concrete stump of the power station brooded over us. No vegetation around it, just a vast spread of recycled slag where the odd dusty thistle had gained a footprint. Beyond this were tall mesh fences topped with razor wire. We skirted the power station and continued behind, the ground becoming scrubby with mounds of overgrown rubble. Butterflies beating lazily from plant to plant, revelling in the heat. A red admiral flopped onto a thistlehead, angling velvet wings to the sun.

We came to a halt at the end of the road. Beyond us was the estuary, dark grey and unconscious where the river limped into the sea. A bare bank of shingle leading down to the water, and across the river the vast sheds and elevators of British Steel shimmering in heat haze.

Help us unload, said Hagan breezily, slipping out of the driver's door. I wondered what was going on. Fly tipping, maybe. Jumped out and slammed the passenger door. Crickets were lazily creaking in the spoil heaps. Round to the back of the van. Hagan flung the doors open and the three of them jumped out. Magoo, blubbery and sweating. Franco, lean and knotted. Kurt, tall and athletic. Each holding a hollow steel pole six foot long, the sort they use in metal fence panels. Spines of mesh still attached, where they'd been twisted away. They formed a triangle around me.

What's going on lads?

A sharp sick feeling in my stomach. I tried to push out of the encirclement but Franco rapped me hard on the kneecap with his pole. A hard hot flare of pain and I knelt down clutching the knee. Hagan spoke from outside the circle.

Stand up.

His voice was calm, empty. I stood, my knee throbbing.

On the beach lads, he said.

They began to walk forward, herding me in the middle with the steel poles. We walked down onto the shingle bank, towards the water's edge. The beach had a steep rake and soon we were hidden from the approach road. Eventually, they stopped. My heart was racing.

Just do it, I said. Whatever you're going to do. Just do it.

Hagan smiled. He stepped inside the circle.

I'm in control, he said. Not you.

Grabbed my face in a huge hand, squashing my cheeks and lips together.

Smelt the piss, he said. But you kept on coming. Look at me.

I looked.

The tanned, handsome, pudgy face, sparkling blue eyes and white teeth, the single gold earring and streaked blond hair. He had thick black eyebrows. I wondered what his natural hair colour was.

*

Raz was right about the bedtime stories, you see. He told me this one once about the seven whistlers, six curlews searching for their lost companion. They searched through the ages of the world but they haven't found him yet. And if they ever do, then the world will end. I thought that was a bit odd, when I was a kid. I could imagine the world ending in fire or flood or a fuckoff big earthquake, but I couldn't imagine the world ending in curlews.

You got big *cojones* Danny, eh? said Hagan.

There was some sniggering from the others.

The lad's got exams, shouted Hagan. He's supposed to be brainy. He thinks he's better than the rest of us.

He delved in his pocket and pulled out a fistful of paper and threw it up so that little snowflakes of it drifted down on me like tickertape.

I found it in the dustbin, he said. Tell me what it is.

I didn't need to look.

You know what it is, I said.

Aye, I do. It's a fucking claim form for the insurance, that some panda-eyed bitch kept me hanging around for and never had any intention of sending. And Santa's little helper here told me he'd put it in the post himself.

He smashed a meaty fist, studded with rings, into my face with the full force of his pumped-up body. There was an explosion in the front of my head, and I found myself splattered across the shingle, my nose pulped and blood pouring from it.

Get up, he said.

I stayed down.

Stay down and you're dead.

He kicked the side of my head like a football and it bounced on the ground. There was a flash and my hearing had gone. I groped around in silence and clawed my way back to my feet and they looked at me, laughing. Hagan was saying something but I only heard a high-pitched whine. He walked away down to the water's edge and picked up a handful of flat round pebbles. Tested one in his hand and skimmed it out across the river and I watched it bounce up six or seven times before nuzzling finally down. The sun, hammering at my bare skull.

I asked Yan about the end of the world and he said bollocks to it son, it's only a tall story. If you ask me the world will just run out of juice and go dark and cold until there's nowt left. Curlews are just doing their own thing – I daresay they're either hungry or horny or both. Birds are in a world of their own, Dan, unconnected to us. That's what I like about them.

So I watched Kurt and Magoo and Franco close on me, and Magoo swung his pole up above his head and thrashed it down across my left shoulder and dislocated it. The pain jumped like a salmon screaming in the unbearable air with its tail beating. Kurt took a run-up and got me full in the ribs and I was down on the ground struggling for breath and my skin was shredded where spines of mesh had ripped it.

They stepped back and waited and I saw Franco mouth the words get up.

I got up.

Franco smiled.

Then he lashed me across the mouth and I tasted the raw metal as I spat teeth and blood and my lips and tongue were beginning to swell. Hagan span another pebble out into the Tees. It undulated across the calm water, five bounces, and was gone. Magoo smashed his pole into the small of my back and I flipped over and slammed back into the ground.

They stepped back and waited.

I struggled to my feet.

Another pebble jumping out across the water, skimming in silence.

It wasn't so much the stories, though they were good. It was his voice, dark and smooth and strong as coffee. He always said the same thing when he came in, in this mock stern voice.

You should be asleep.

The bedside lamp had a yellow glow like a small planet and there was darkness beyond the curtains all the way across the sea to Denmark.

I wanted to sleep, that blinding day on the estuary. Lie down and sleep. A few minutes of backbreaking pain and then nothingness ebbing out to the sea. But instead I did what I was told. Got to my feet, got knocked back down. I was drenched in my own blood, dark splashes of it dripping silently onto the pebbles. It poured from my nose and gums and ran thick and salty down my throat The stones drank it up and there were container ships and a power station and steelworks and chemical plants all humming away oblivious in the roaring summer heat. Hagan kept flicking his wrist, sending a new pebble bouncing across the surface of the river.

And then I was kneeling on the shingle with a heavy steel pole bouncing off the top of my skull, watching a pebble crawl from Gary Hagan's hand and saunter in an elegant loop towards the surface of the river, when a curlew alighted a little further along the beach, right by the water's edge. They'll be coming off the moors this time of year, off the breeding grounds and back to the coast. Brown plumage, speckled like an egg, and the long bill drooping moist and black like an anteater's tongue. Another blow across my shoulders forced tears from my eyes and the pebble rotated on its axis and bounced on the water. I watched the breeze stir the freckled neck feathers as I began to leak away into the shingle. Vertebrae bouncing on the water, running out of energy, almost skimming the surface, and beach pebbles alighting at the water's edge, fresh from the moors and freckled with salt and chiming sweetly together and curlews hammering at my spine.

And then the bird opens its beak and that call bubbles up like ether into my silence, breaking in the middle and lifting like the absence of pain. The sound of loneliness. Casual, everyday loneliness, sharp and lovely enough to end the world.

And then the bird was up and Hagan's boots were tramping back across the beach. He grabbed a handful of my hair and pulled my head up.

You look amazing, he said. Listen, here's the deal. You go now, and you don't come back. Ring Kate and make up an excuse. I don't want to see you in my pub again.

My pub.

He dropped my head back onto the ground. I tried to focus on the salt-encrusted stones in front of me. I heard their footsteps crunching away, the van engine coughing and receding into the distance and the world ending in curlews.

18. **Jackdaw**

(*Corvus monedula*)

I'm still in the air but I can smell Europe already. The musk of petrol engines, people who stop at red lights, policemen without guns. And them old cities built on boneyards. The layers going down, medieval and Frankish and Roman right down to the black mud.

We've begun the descent into Köln–Bonn, engines treading water and the nose inclined down. Look out of the window where the sky is darkening, a livid blaze of light at the horizon like a splash of mercury. And below us the wrinkled surface of a cloudbank ripples away to the edge of the world. In two days I'll be home, with Kate and Danny. My heart skips a beat and I don't know whether it's anticipation or terror.

At the airport taxi rank I glance at my reflection in the glass partition. Rumpled and mundane as fuck in a dark suit and scuffed brogues. And this taxi pulls up and the parking light glowers above the driver's head. He's dark-skinned with these meaty forearms resting on the wheel and they're carpeted with thick grey hair. Some untipped cancer stick clamped between two fingers with thick smoke pouring steadily from the tip, up past the evil eye charm in blue glass which dangles from the mirror. He sits and takes a long phlegmatic suck on his cigarette and lets me load my own suitcase into his boot, and when I'm inside he moves off, blowing smoke through a small crack of open window. The meter and the fascia of the radio glow a ghostly red and green in the darkness. With hairy fingers he punches buttons on the radio, and Middle Eastern music wails into the Rhineland night. The taxi turns out of the airport and towards the city and the black heart of Europe swallows us.

An hour later I'm in a petrified forest of tenement buildings, squat and rectangular and cast from crumbling concrete. A raw winter night, smelling of snow. There's an open space in front of me, bleary sodium light shimmering from damp pavers, and in the centre of it there's a sculpture – a concrete human forearm sprouting from the ground and topped with a clenched fist like a defiant flower. I follow the driver's directions, along a walkway diving like a canyon between two walls of apartments, and my footsteps punctuate the night with metallic pockmarks. And here's the apartment block, a pair of swing doors with panels of security glass. I stub out my cigarette underfoot and push through the doors into the stairwell.

Leck mich am Arsch, says somebody loud and insistent inside one of the flats. *Leck mich am Arsch*. A wave of cold air bursts over the parapet like stale vomit. I hurry on, until I find the right flat. No light visible inside. Blue paint on the door, cracked by the weather, and brass numbers nailed on aslant. I knock. Silence and darkness. I wait a minute or two and pound my fist against the door again. There's somebody moving inside. I cram my mouth to the letterbox and yell.

Is anybody there? It's Yan.

Bitte warten, comes a creaky, muffled voice from inside the flat. Wait. Slow footsteps pad towards the door, the latch scrapes, and the door opens.

That was classic, laughs Joe Fish, sprawling back in the armchair. Yan, you really are a tool. Stood there clutching your suitcase like one of them evacuees in the war. Thought you were going to pee yerself.

You snidey gets, I grin. Pause and look at the three of them. It's good to see you.

The flat is ugly but warm, electric fires pumping out heat. The furniture is shabby and the place is carpeted with hideous orange shagpile, much the worse for wear. Horse Boy slumps on the sofa, chugging a can of cheap lager. The trouserlegs of his suit are too short and ride up, exposing six inches of white calf. He raises the can.

Good to see you Yan. Fancy a game of cards?

Any time you like son. Any time at all.

Joe sits in the armchair, chainsmoking cheap German straights and tapping the ash into his empty can where it sizzles broodily.

Got to get out of this penguin suit, I say. Not my scene at all.

Shit, grumbles Joe, stamping at a cigarette nub which has leapt onto the carpet, searing a hole through the synthetic material.

Don't worry Joe, says Fabián, shoulder-length hair falling over his eyes. The carpet is evil and deserves to be punished.

He laughs, bright and clear. I wander through to the kitchen at the back of the flat, black and white chessboard tiles on the floor and a rickety formica table. There's also an antique fridge, buzzing with the effort. I liberate a chilled can of beer. Back in the living room I crack it open and gulp greedily.

All the suitcases are still here, I say. What do we do with them?

I light one of Joe's cigarettes and inhale deeply. The cheap tobacco is stale and dry but my head is soon buzzing with the hit.

I asked the taxi driver, drawls Horse Boy, crossing his legs. He said we do nothing. Wait. They will come to us.

He looks over at Joe, but Joe looks away.

They better hurry up, I say. I'm just about ready to go home. A little bit of hellraising here first, naturally. Anybody been into the city centre?

Nah, coughs Joe. Thought we'd better lie low.

He seems on edge. I watch him while he fidgets and lights another cigarette, skin grey and rumpled in the harsh overhead light.

Yan, here's to you, says Fabián, raising his beer can high above his head. The last of a bad bunch.

He comes in the morning with the new light spreading like a puddle of cold milk. Dogs bark sporadically somewhere outside. I wake to a polite knocking on the outside door, scramble up from the sofa to flip the latch open. And he steps through, pepper-and-salt hair and a rumpled leather jacket like somebody's paunchy and jocular uncle. Closes the door carefully behind him.

Guten Tag gentlemen, says the uncle.

He goes through into the living room and stands, tapping his foot. Joe goes back into the bedroom and returns with the cases. The uncle produces a carpet knife from his pocket and bends over the first one, sliding the knife into the lining and gutting the case in one easy movement. Small plump bags of pure white powder spill from the hidden cavities like the roe squeezed from a gutted fish. He repeats the process with all the cases, then packs all the fisheggs back into the first one, checking carefully he's left none behind.

Fünf Mensch, he says, looking at the suitcases with a little concern. *Oder vier Mensch*. Five of you?

No, I tell him. He didn't come. Bottle job.

You went over the top, says Joe.

The uncle shrugs. Then he smiles again, producing a bundle of notes from his pocket. Joe holds out his hand and takes the money.

You can stay here, says the uncle. Two days, maybe three. To make arrangements. Then you go.

He hoists the full suitcase into one hand, breezes into the hall and then out through the front door. The door, left open, swings gently on its hinges.

Close the door, says Joe, it's starting to snow.

Fabián emerges from the innards of the flat, hair still tangled from sleep.

Starting to snow, he says with a slow smile, in more ways than one. He looks sideways at Joe Fish, who closes the door with a gentle click.

Am I missing something gents? I ask.

Joe beams a thunderous look at Fabián, his face clotted. Horse Boy appears, blinking away sleep.

I think we should show Yan our nest, says Fabián, gently, and leads the way into the living room. Without artificial light the room is cold and bare. Blots of dark mildew bloom in the corners of the ceiling like sweat patches. Fabián pads over in his socks to the sofa and lifts the foam seat. There, in the base, is a cluster of snow-white eggs. Horse Boy was incubating them last night, when he was sprawled across the sofa. Fabián picks a couple up and prods them.

Pure nose candy, he says, then replaces them in the nest. Good street value.

Joe and Horse Boy are quiet, waiting for my reaction.

These are serious people, I say. Not a great idea to take the piss.

Fuck sake, growls Joe. How many bags were in those cases. Two hundred? Three? They aren't going to miss these few. I didn't see him counting. We're home and dry. The cattle drovers in the old days – they got paid handsomely, but they always took a few fine fat cattle on the sly. We're just keeping up the tradition. These little snow-white cows will fetch a good price at market.

Would have been nice to be asked, I say. Seems like the decision was made before I got here.

Joe glowers, opens his mouth, closes it again. Then he speaks.

Well Yan. We made the decision in time-honoured fashion, best of three. And you lost all three. Paper wrapped stone. Stone blunted scissors. Scissors cut paper.

Seems like my luck ran out, I say. I'm going to blow away some cobwebs. Might go for a poke around the city. Anyone coming?

They all look at their hands.

I'm going to butcher a little cow, says Fabián.

He delves into the sofa and emerges with one of the fat little bundles. Then he slits its belly with a carpet knife. Horse Boy takes down a picture from the wall and hands it to him. It's an uninspiring little print in a glass frame, the sun shining over a woodland scene. Deer scampering through the trees. Fabián lays the picture across his knees, glass upwards. Uses the knife to scoop out a wisp of powder and dumps it on the glass in a little mound. Then he dabs a finger in it and rubs it against his gums.

Virgin snow, he says, and crosses himself, grinning lackadaisically. With the knife he marshals the powder into a zigzag line.

Money Joe, he says.

Joe hands him a wrap of notes and he bundles them up into a tube and hoovers up the line in one go. Tendrils of his black hair buzz against the glass. He looks up, tears in his eyes, white powder and mucus round his nostrils, and gives a thumbs-up sign. I hover at the door.

I'm off then.

Get some firewater in while you're at it, says Horse Boy. Whisky whisky whisky. Whisky.

I take the U-Bahn down towards the city centre, come out into Roncalliplatz with the Christmas market in full swing. The place is a coral reef of colour in the damp December city, music trickling into the cold and smoky air, stalls encrusted with light. People sprawl past in large groups, mummified in padded layers of clothing. I'm still wearing that cheap shiny suit and my hands and feet are feeling the cold. To warm up I buy a glass of *Glühwein* from a stall. A large swollen-faced woman hands me the drink.

Vielen Dank, I say. She beams back.

Fröhliche Weihnachten.

I warm my hands on the glass and sip at the *Glühwein*, deep red fruit with a raw kick of alcohol. Cloves and nutmeg and cinnamon. Steam blooms from the surface. I'll buy the lads some cheap whisky later, but I'll have to go careful. Me and Johnnie Walker are old pals.

See, I could just go home now. Take my share of the cash and split. Could be there today, in fact. Two-hour flight to London and then the train home. Could be touching Kate's skin tonight, that unbearable smoothness like coal ash.

Christ.

Why didn't you?

Eh?

Why didn't you just come home? This must have been December eighty-three,
right?

Aye, I suppose so.

So it took you another two years, near enough.

Yeah.

You didn't actually want to come back, did you? Not then. Like you said, it was
easy. Could have been here the same day.

I blame Cologne Cathedral.

You what?

It's like a huge black gothic beast squatting on the city. Like somebody's plucked an ordinary cathedral by the shoulderblades and
stretched it upwards into the sky – exaggerated the vertical dimension
until the two spires are brushing the winter cloudbase and the hackles
of the nave are bristling far above the city. And there I am sitting in the
square beneath it and a great bell starts tolling somewhere high beyond
imagining, a deep sonorous boom born from the crags of fog and
blackened stone. It's the same note as the Southern Ocean, the oracle
of despair. And I stand up and thrust my hands in the pockets of that
thin jacket and there's only one place I'm going. They can wait for their
cheap whisky and you can wait for your old man.

Dark and still inside, lit by the faint glow of great windows where
winter berries of stained glass spill in plump clusters. My hollow footfall on the stone floor, and the deep bell baying from above.

I find myself before the Shrine of the Magi, where a golden reliquary
hides some shabby-arse bones they claim are the three kings. Yeah,
those three kings – the real deal. Light spills across the intricate golden
surface and it shifts and furrows like a brow clenching and relaxing.
There are jewels and intaglios set into the gold. A noseless face, a medusa in turquoise and white, a carved garnet showing Theseus slaying the
Minotaur. Somebody's bones in there at any rate, mute and crumbling
in the quiet dark.

I climb the tower right up to the parapet above the bell chamber and stand in the wire cage which stops people jumping. The mesh is rusting in the mist, bleeding droplets of moisture, and snow spins across blackened stone in tiny scribbles of interference. Down below, the city fades away into whiteness and that broad three-humped railway bridge loops across the Rhine like a sea beast and disappears.

Out of the whiteness comes a high clear barking, an ill-tuned chatter of handbells, a clatter of black wings, and I'm surrounded by jackdaws perched on the massive stone tracery with the blank drop beneath, perched on the blistered mesh of the cage itself. Sleek black bodies glittering like coal and grey heads soft as spent ash.

Soft as Kate's skin.

They cock their heads with these quizzical eyes, bright as brushed steel with a pinpoint of night, and they bounce from perch to perch. And all the while they fling out metallic droplets of sound. A collective conversation, a vast mind churning over, each bird a mischievous neuron firing its own crisp signal. They tolerate me while I stay still, those mobile eyes kind of weighing me up for who I am. And just for a moment I am part of this covenant and it feels good. The yapping of a thousand others on the thresholds of my soul.

Below us the bell begins to boom out the hour and the low frequency grates in my spine and the stones sing out in their bass voices like an orthodox choir. And now the jackdaws fall away from the parapet and into snow-whirling whiteness, the beating wings winding an acrid smoke trail down across the dim city and the dim Rhine and away into nothing.

And I want to go with them but the cage stops me, and now I'm alone again.

Later, I climb the stairwell towards the flat and think of the Magi. Dervishes of snow lash through the wooden slats, spin and die. A full plastic bag wallows from my hand, the attenuated handle cutting into my fingers. Gold for the whisky. Cheap and cheerful stuff for Horse Boy and Joe. Frankincense for *Glühwein*, spiced and heady. I can smell it on my breath still. And myrrh? A bitter herb for anointing the dead. Well, two out of three ain't bad.

The door of the flat is ajar, swinging off the latch. I can smell Middle Eastern cooking from the flat next door, cumin and coriander.

Honey, I'm home, I shout, shouldering through the doorway. Beware geeks bearing gifts. I rattle the bag of bottles.

And then I bend and vomit a purple slick onto the greasy orange carpet. Because they're in there. The noseless man, Medusa, and the Minotaur. They've escaped from the shrine. And when I've seen what's in the flat I run, and the bag of bottles is shouting in my hand and in the stairwell there's a sharp stink of urine, my own urine, where I have pissed myself with fear. Snow still rattles in machinegun bursts through the wooden slats and there are wet footprints blooming behind me down the stairs, following me as I run, in diminishing hoofmarks of black, and then in ghostly form all the way down to the U-Bahn and along the tracks to the ancient city.

So I'm back on the edge of the fountain on Roncalliplatz and the icy water plays behind me. The cathedral is floodlit in winter dark, twin spires looping into the giddy heavens. The bag of bottles is nestling against my legs and I reach down for one. Twist off the cap and the sweet sickly fiery smell hits me.

Yes,

Raise it to my lips and drink, long, hard and deep.

Yes.

The level of the amber spirit descends the bottle and I come up for air. Strange how the floodlit cathedral is bending down towards me. I drink again, feeling the chemical taste of the Scotch burn in my gullet. Water rising about my ankles, cold and black and peaty. Must be coming from the river, from the black mud below the earliest levels of the city, below the U-Bahn. Creeping up my calves, soaking simply through the cheap shiny fabric of the suit. Shudder as it climbs around my midriff, my shoulders. Take a last suck of whisky. And then it swallows me in blackness, and I'm drifting into the green depths, a plastic bag of bottles still knotted in my hand.

19. **Guillemot**

(Uria aalge)

Whitby is a shitmagnet of a town, attracts more than its fair share of human flotsam. Maybe it's the geography of the place, stuck out on that far eastern bulge of Yorkshire behind miles of empty moorland. They used to exile people here, before they invented Australia.

In summer it's packed with trippers, cramming the narrow streets on the East Cliff, swarming up the steps to the abbey on the headland. But at dusk they stream away to the car parks and the courtyards and alleys are bare and empty. It's quiet in winter too, wooden staithes looming above the harbour, gulls reverberating in the empty town.

I walk past the rampart of Victorian hotels on the West Cliff, shabby whitewashed hulks with pensioner deals and tea dances. At the top of the slope I look down over the harbour, the Esk crawling between shale cliffs and slipping through the embrace of sandstone piers to the troubled North Sea. Then I pick my way down the steps and through the tunnel to the fish quay.

Where do you look for someone like Paul? In summer he'd be chugging cans on the beach, sprawled out in the warm sand. But this is raw winter. Luminous blue sky, a low insipid sun casting long and sullen shadows, and a buffeting northeaster bringing a deep swell racing against the coast.

I start with a trawl of pubs and arcades, the indoor spaces of the town. The amusements on the west side of the harbour are almost dead, fruities chirruping and pulsing in the warm darkness. No Paul. I move on over the swing bridge where gulls perch on the rotted stumps of old staithes, grown sleek and fat on the leavings of tourists. In the pubs of the East Cliff there are few drinkers, a couple of low-season tourists and a few hardened regulars, faces battered by drink and weather. In the Duke of York the girl behind the bar looks bored as she restocks the fridge.

Could be any number of people, she says, yawning. Skinny bloke with home-made tats and a baseball cap. Doesn't narrow it down any. You get all sorts in here, specially on a night when it gets rammed. I'll keep an eye out anyway. What's his name?

Paul. Paul O'Rourke.

She looks directly at me for the first time, eyes rimmed heavily with black. Long windows behind her, snow and sleet scribbling over the harbour.

I'll give you my card, I say. Call me if he comes in.

Fumble in my wallet and hand her a work card. She takes it and grunts.

You need a photo, she says, suddenly. If you're going to ask around the pubs. It'd be better than your description.

Haven't got one.

He's your brother and you don't have a photo?

Nothing on the East Cliff. I head over the swing bridge again and down towards the station. Check tourist information and wander through the elegant Victorian station building, two sets of cold, dank public toilets. Then I walk away from the harbour, up the main shopping street with its scant cluster of chainstores. More people here, pensioners doing the weekday shop, gangs of sullen kids leaning against shop fronts, mothers with gaggles of toddlers in outsize buggies. I need something to eat, and stop at a cashpoint. As the machine whirs a voice speaks from the pavement next to me.

Spare some change for a cup of tea pal?

I look down and recognize Paul. Cross-legged on the pavement with a soiled yellow blanket spread over his knees and pulled up to chest height. Still wearing the duckbill hat I last saw him in, face unshaven with raw cheeks and bloodhound eyes.

Paul, it's me, Danny, I say.

Muttering from behind me. I take my cash and vacate the cashpoint, squatting down on the other side of Paul. He looks at me in confusion, trying to work out how I've moved from one side of his vision to the other. No recognition in his face.

Do us a ciggie charver, he says. Go on.

I don't smoke, I say, not any more. I've got something to tell you. Something important.

Have you got a fat penny then? Go on son, cross my palm with cash. It's good karma.

Grope in my pocket and find the battered tube of sweets. He's shivering beneath the blanket.

Look, I say, them green chews you used to like. Found some in a pub.

He looks at the packet quizzically, a blackbird eyeing up a worm.

Nah mate, I don't use 'em. Cheers anyway. Spare some change for a cup of tea pal?

He's addressing an elderly man in a dark overcoat, using the cashpoint and steadfastly ignoring him. He smells bad, a sweet smell of decay. A bunch of kids on the opposite side of the street, staring malevolently at the two of us. I stare back.

Is there a problem lads? I say.

Eh?

Just wondered what you were staring at.

It's a free fucking country isn't it? shoots back a lad in a snow-white tracksuit. We can look at who we like. What's it got to do with you anyway baldy?

The others laugh, and I feel the anger shooting up into my face, blood roaring. But then they move away, posturing and muttering to themselves.

I'll burn your fucking faces off, yells Paul, suddenly.

Passers-by turn to stare, give him an even wider berth than before. The lads turn round and flick middle fingers, but keep moving away.

Just like the old days Danny, he says. Thought we might get us a barney there, eh?

I look at him curiously.

Do you know who I am?

Aye, you're Danny Thomas. Used to run together when we were bairns. You've lost a bit of hair recently son.

When I was at the cashpoint. You didn't recognize me at all. Unless you were winding me up.

Paul thumps the side of his head with the heel of his hand, like he's shaking ketchup loose from a bottle.

Couple short of a six-pack, he says. One minute I know what I'm doing, the next I haven't got a scooby. One side of my brain doesn't know what the other side's doing.

I buy a packet of cigarettes from the newsagent's and we sit in a nearby caff, order a pot of tea and two full English. Paul attracts some sidelong glances and the stench rises from him in the heat. When the food arrives he wolfs it down and then eyes my toast hungrily. A sudden shiver of sleet lashes the window.

Aye, go on then, I say.

He crams the toast into his mouth, chewing noisily.

Me dad went loony, he says, through his mouthful of food. In the end. That's where I'm going Dan.

I'm wondering how to break the news to him, but he continues.

One time, must have been seventeen, eighteen, I was on the bus to Stockton, back seat of the bottom deck. Gadgie got on in Thornaby, forties, fifties, one of them purple heart attack faces with the blue lips. Decent shell suit and trainers, like, but no socks. Shambles down the bus and plonks himself next to this young lass. Starts muttering to himself, rummaging in this plastic bag, and then he pulls out a joint of meat. Fucking great thing like a leg of lamb, wrapped in brown paper. Raw – you could see the blood soaking through. Starts gnawing at it through the paper, smacking his fucking lips, and there's grease and blood smeared all round his mouth. Lass next to him was nearly bubbling, her mates behind cackling like crows.

He leans forward over the table, quick green eyes latching on to mine.

You know them clockwork toys. Wind it up, time after time. Keeps moving, eh? Going through the motions.

I nod.

One time, he says. You wind it up and the spring snaps. Not a loud noise, just a little pop. After that it's fucked for good.

He pauses and looks out at the damp street.

That gadgie on the bus, he says. The spring had snapped.

I take a sip of tea. Paul lights a cigarette, shoots smoke through his nostrils like a dragon.

When he got off the bus, he turned round and stared at me. Slack jaw, nobody fucking home. Fat and blood on his chops. Hadn't recognized him up till then. But it was our dad. Anth O'Rourke. Didn't know me from Adam, just went weaving off into Stockton market.

Paul, I say. That doesn't have to happen to you. I need to tell you something. He looks sharply at me and his eyes are glazed.

Mate, I've got to keep moving, he says. Cross my palm with cash, will you? It's good karma.

I pull a fiver from my pocket and press it into his reddened hand, watching the bluestained knuckles close over it. He jumps up suddenly from the table, out of the door before I can react, spinning between clumps of shoppers. I rise to follow, but a pointed glance from behind the counter reminds me I haven't paid for our breakfasts. Try to juggle change from my wallet as quickly as I can, but awkward fingers spill an explosion of coins onto the floor and I crawl under tables and chairs to retrieve them, cheeks burning. I hurry down the street and catch up with him down by the harbour where he's leaning against the railing by the payphone.

You remember that game we used to play, he says. When we were bairns.

What game?

With the phone book.

Aye, I say. I remember.

You ring up somebody at random. Someone on the other side of the world.

Yeah. If anyone picked up we used to piss ourselves laughing and slam the receiver down.

Let's do it now, he says.

He backs into a phone box and lifts the receiver. Dials a long and random number.

I don't even know what country it is, he says. Could be like Outer Mongolia or somewhere.

You'll probably just get number unobtainable, like.

He listens intently, brow furrowing and lips moving silently. Then he motions urgently at me.

Away, give us some cash.

I shovel change into the slot and Paul's face lights up.

It's ringing.

We wait a full minute with his ear pressed to the receiver.

There's no-one there Paul.

There is. He'll be along in a minute. Away man, I need more cash.

I feed the machine again and Paul waits while his credit ticks away towards zero.

Give it up mate. No-one's going to answer.

He'll be along in a minute Danny. I just need a bit more cash.

I'm out of change.

Please Dan. Just another fifty pee.

You've spent it all.

It's fucking gone dead now.

Paul looks around wildly, then he tries to yank the receiver off its metal tether. It stays fast and he slams it down instead and pins me against the side of the kiosk with shocking strength, his hot sweet breath across my face.

He was just coming, he shouts, eyes bloodshot.

Who?

I don't know.

He lets go of my jacket and storms off and I stand there in the kiosk shaking while sleet rattles against the safety glass.

I wander aimless for a bit, find myself on the West Pier. Waves whump the seawall with a deep percussion, sending splurges of freezing foam across the promenade. I walk along the pier towards the sandstone lighthouse, turn my collar up to the shellbursts and the icy water lashing across. And halfway down I stop and lean on the railings and crane my neck down the coast towards Sandsend and the tall shelving headland of Kettleness. Ranges of wrinkled water rush towards the coast and dissolve into ferocious turbulence before walloping the pier.

I feel sick.

Right down below me there's a guillemot in the water, wallowing like a small penguin and too waterlogged to fly. It paddles gamely to keep away from the stone wall of the pier, but the waves are brawling in at an angle and slapping it down, cutting off any escape. Sleek head and pointed bill held just above water, dark as a little scroll of ink. A serif of life.

A fresh breaker roars in and the sea splinters into chaos and the bird dives to avoid being dashed against the pier. I scan the surface in the wake of the wave and there's nothing for a long minute. I give the bird up for drowned, but then it creeps back to the surface like an apology, a moth mired in puddleskin.

And with each new bellow of turbulence, each howling tumult of whitewater, the guillemot dives again and I wait while the webbed feet are kicking back up towards that lungbursting silver skin of air and life. Spinning out your last breath in struggle until the sea strangles you.

If I was in that water I wouldn't keep kicking.

And now I don't want to watch any more. I turn away and walk by the lighthouse, where the warm golden sandstone has been knit by the weather into an intricate landscape of whirlpools and sinkholes and runnels. But the outer arm of the pier is closed by the weather, a barrier across the walkway, and I'm forced to return towards the town. Despite myself I stop and crane my neck over the side of the pier and now there's no guillemot, just the exultant pandemonium of the sea.

Back in my hotel room I sit down heavily on the bed. Stayed here with Kelly, the best part of three years ago. Not the same room, but the same smell of ancient woodsmoke infused into the bones of the building, the same eventful firelight exploring the darkened surfaces of panelled wood.

Do you like this place? I said.

She lounged across the bed, dumping her shopping bag on the floor.

It's very you Danny.

Flashed me that wan smile of hers, the one that wasn't really smiling. I sat down on the bed next to her.

You mean like old and venerable but ultimately pretty fucking fantastic?

Now she smiled genuinely, her broad face illuminated. I stood up and lit the gas fire. Flames twirled up through the basket of imitation coal, sending a sinuous play of orange light over the panelling.

Well, she said. I'd have preferred something a bit more plush. You know, like one of them boutique hotels, maybe an infinity pool.

An infinity pool in Whitby, I snorted. It's called the North Sea.

She reclined onto her side, curving in a contented feline way. Flames caressed the rim of her nostrils. It was getting dark outside.

You can laugh, she said. Anyway, I wouldn't have expected you to take me anywhere like that. This is more your style. Hundreds of years of woodsmoke and kippers. They've made a good job of restoring it, but it's not quite finished, is it? Still a bit poky in places. The panelling stripped but not varnished. The paintwork blistering on the bathroom ceiling. And worst of all, this bed creaks like a bastard.

Ah, I said. You can wonder whether it's me creaking or the bed.

She laughed silently, the corners of her mouth drawing up.

I need a child, she said. I want to be a mother.

I looked startled.

She grinned. That put the cat among the pigeons.

Put a finger to my lips before I could speak.

You know we've talked about it in the past. But it's always been a theory, something we were going to do one day. She paused. Well now I want to make it a reality.

I looked at her as she sprawled across the bed like an earth mother.

Okay, I said.

There was a brief silence while flames roared in the grate.

Is that all you have to say?

Yes. It's simple. I'm ready too – I think.

She reached a hand round to the nape of my neck and began to pull me down towards her.

We can start now, she said.

The bed gave an admonitory squeak, but I continued moving down towards the veins of fire lashing across her body.

It was a good weekend, that one. As good as it got. The bed carried on squeaking and we carried on regardless, quaking with laughter when we heard voices and footsteps in the corridor outside. We were happy, then. Even talked about buying a boat down here. Nowt fancy, just enough for a bit of day fishing offshore. Never got round to it mind.

I lie back on the bed, feeling sick from self-loathing, and there's no creaking, just a soft sigh from the mattress.

Next morning the sea has calmed to a brisk surf and I find Paul again at the far end of the West Pier. On the footbridge across to the outer arm I pause and look down at the sea crawling between my feet. Crests clash in the narrow space and spew foam up towards me, troughs suck the water away from weed-draggled stone almost down to the seabed. I steady myself and continue onto the wooden walkway towards the figure at the far end, hunched over the railings. He stands out from the early-morning fishermen wrapped up in all-weather gear, flinging out their near-invisible lines into turbulent water. As I approach he raises a can to his lips and drinks deeply.

I edge past the metal struts and ladders of the harbour beacon, breathing in the faint tang of rust and urine. He swivels towards me and grins, drinks from the can again, turns back and leans against the railing facing out to sea where the water is shredded by a raw wind. I lean on the railings next to him, feeling the slight warmth of his shoulder through my jacket. He offers me the can and I shake my head. He drains it, crushes it like a moth in his fist, sends it spiralling down into the water. I think of the guillemot. Paul lights one of the fags I bought for him yesterday, shielding the lighter flame from the bruising wind. His hands are like lumps of meat.

I decide to blurt it out, no preamble.

Yan's your dad, I say. You're my brother. Half-brother.

He brings the cigarette up between the fingers of a flat hand, sucks lazily, and lets the smoke sprawl out of his mouth before it's torn away by the wind. A long pause, while herring gulls echo across the harbour and the sea continues a destructive conversation with itself. I feel obliged to carry on, to fill the vacuum.

He told me the other night. Slept with her, just the once. When she used to work in the pub.

A fishing boat wallowing towards the harbour mouth, tilting one way and then the other in the heavy swell. I can hear the engine working above the sound of the sea. Gulls whirl behind it, glittering in the early sun.

No, says Paul. Turns towards me and shakes his head. No.

The cigarette spins down into the sea, still smoking until the moment it hits the cold water and dies. Paul turns away again and hunches over the railings. I wait a moment, then I touch his upper arm.

She went with anyone Danny, he says. Anyone. Used to hear her through the wall when I was a bairn. On that logic, I'd have a hundred dads.

The boat approaches the harbour, steadying itself to pass crisply midway between the two outer piers. Figures inside the wheelhouse, dark jerseys and pale faces. Voices raised in laughter, cigarette smoke.

You remember Helena? Fraser's missus? She thought you were Yan's lad, didn't she? Ahead of me.

He's not my dad. He would of told me. When he saw what I was doing to meself. Where me life was headed. He would of fucking stepped in Dan. Wouldn't he? He would of put me back on the rails.

I don't know.

He shakes his head.

Anth was my dad, he said. Like two peas in a pod. I saw meself in his eyes, that day on the bus.

The boat passes below us, into the placid and oilslicked water of the harbour, the engine rattling comfortably. There are five crew, one of whom has come out of the wheelhouse to prepare for mooring. He looks up at us haughtily and dispassionately with hooded eyes, a young man with a sallow complexion and shoulder-length black hair gathered in a ponytail. As the boat moves on his eyes flick away to some other detail of the harbourside. I take Paul by the shoulders and gently turn him round to face me.

Let me help you, I say. You need your medication. You need a safe place to stop.

A derisive curl to his lip which grows as I speak. He grips my wrists with his raw hands, which burn like molten iron.

Get your hands off, he says, angrily. I don't want it.

Don't want what?

Pity. There's no pity in the world. Look at it.

He gestures around him at the bleak sea and sky, at the bleary port in the winter morning.

It's cold, he says. Got to keep swimming or you get bashed against the rocks. In the end it's always the same. You're too weak. You have to give in.

Paul.

No. I don't need a dad, or a brother. Not now.

Firmly, with surprising strength, he disengages my hands from his shoulders, holds my wrists for a moment, anger welling in his face as if he would snap me. Then he lets go with a shrug, turns back to the railings.

Paul, I say, imploringly.

He ignores me. I pull one of the business cards out of my wallet, push it towards him.

Look, my number's on there. Home and mobile. If you ever change your mind. Just reverse the charges.

He makes no attempt to take the card. I slip it into the top pocket of his jacket and begin to walk away down the pier. A long walk, hoping that Paul will turn and shout, or come running down after me, knowing at the same time that he won't. When I reach the lighthouse I look back at the distant hunched figure, one foot resting on the lowest railing, and fancy I see a small white card spiral down like a sycamore seed into the restless sea.

20. **Herring Gull**

(Larus argentatus)

I lay stranded on the shingle until the pain was no longer a sky of sharp stars like ground glass, until it became a dull but insistent dawn overcast with cloud. And then I got up and stumbled towards Seaton with the breaking summer weather and the cloud boiling up out of the hazy estuary and the thunder beginning a low throat-clearing grumble somewhere far off. It was hot. Too hot. All the frustrations and nonevents of the summer precipitating out and taking solid form in the sweat on my neck and the blood crusting my clothes and the bruises swelling like clumsy purple fists in my flesh. Going to rain soon, and hard.

Charlie said Yan was damaged goods and now I was damaged to match. Broken nose and a couple of teeth gone and when I tried to move my left shoulder there was a twang like a snapped elastic band and a bright shaft of pain. When a dislocated shoulder jumps back into its socket there's a sudden agony like a star imploding and then bliss, but it had left something torn in there – muscle, ligament, tendon. My ribs were the worst, a hot blade of it every time I breathed or jigged an arm, a rusty saw quartering my chest cavity.

Seaton Carew, shambling and downtrodden in the heat. Boneheads in the crumbling art deco bus station, drinking from cans and stomping them down into the concrete. I thought of Paul. Every time I'd seen him over the summer he was bagged off his head.

The beach sprawled out towards a leaden North Sea, shabby gift shops and chippies along the road. A herring gull perched on top of a waste bin and the cowl of its head was aspirin white and painless but the beady yellow eye connived in the world with a fullstop at the centre. I stared back and the gull cracked the snowy head open like a snap-dragon and showed me its gape all slick and sharp-tongued like a spread vulva.

Hissed. Tossed its head back and ululated somewhere in between alleycat and pterodactyl.

Down the road a man came out of a chippie and chucked a bag of scraps across the pavement and there was a mugging of wings and beaks and howling, yelling, ripping.

They'll fucking eat anything these, he said as I passed. Bog roll, johnnies, turds off the sewage outfall. Rats of the sea, I call them.

Aye, I said, smiling at him. He was short and bald, a film of sweat on his scalp.

When you think what it eats, he said. Where it sticks its head. How can it stay so fucking white? Crystal white. That's what I don't get.

I pressed on. People were hurrying now as clouds bulked up like bruises. A sudden wind revved up from the sea, squalls of dry sand scampering across the road. And then the rain, vertical and vindictive, gouts of water bursting on the hot concrete and the tarmac. I was drenched in seconds, rain hammering at me like pebbles. The shingle beach.

I knocked on the door of a pebbledashed grey house in one of the bleak streets behind the sea front. Small windows to keep out the North Sea. The rain was unabated, rivulets of water gathering and beginning to hurry down the roadway. The door opened and a man stood there in a rumpled tee-shirt and tracksuit bottoms, no socks. His dark skin was wrinkled and his hair was cut close like grey ash. Jonah. He had a can in his hand, regarded me for a moment as if weighing things up.

Danny, he said. Come in man.

He ushered me into the doorway and I stumbled through into a front room littered with bulging ashtrays and empty beer cans.

I'd give up the boxing if I was you, he said. Looks like you're not much cop. I started out on a smile but my face knacked so I stopped.

You should see the other bloke, I said.

He grinned.

I can't go back to the pub, I said. Wondered if I could stop here. Just for a day or two.

Lowered myself into an armchair, which bulged lazily under my weight. No lights on in the house. Livid stormlight slopped through the windows, through broadfingered fronds of rain.

Temporary problem, said Jonah apologetically. Had a slight disagreement with the electric. A few modifications I made to the meter.

He winked at me. I knew better than to try a smile.

We're still cookin' on gas though, he quipped.

He sat down opposite me, glanced at the doorway through to the back kitchen. A slow arc of lightning flapped across the sky, and we waited a second or two for the bellow of rage to reach us. The window frames rattled. I didn't think the rain could get any louder, any harder. And then it did. A small pool began to well under the front door.

All the time I've been in the merchant navy, it's been me biggest fear, boomed Jonah, over the noise. Trapped inside a ship that's going down. In a bubble of steel and air with miles of water closing over your head. I never thought it'd happen to me in my own house.

The lightning crawled again and the shell burst, closer this time. Jonah looked pensive.

Let's have a look over you son, he said. I got some medical training at sea, years ago. We need to work out what's what. You might have to go to hospital.

I nodded acquiescence, wearily.

Jonah swam over and perched on the edge of the armchair. He commenced measuring me with his nimble, quiet fingers moving like a draughtsman's compasses, pinching here, appraising there.

Heard you'd been away, he said. Does that hurt?

I shook my head through gritted teeth.

Should have come and told me how you got on. How about that?

I bellowed in affirmation as pain shot through me, synchronized with another lightning bolt, another explosion.

Still, he said. It's your funeral.

With a flick of the wrist he twisted my nose straight, and I almost passed out.

Sorry about that, he said. Diversionary tactics. You've been lucky, I'd say. Nose. Ribs. A bit of ripped muscle. The rest of it's just bruising. Nothing medical science can do to help you there. Rest and healing, that's all. So how did you get on then?

He was a waster, I said. Wasn't he? A right feckless bastard. Didn't connect right with anyone – just thought of himself.

That doesn't sound like you talking, said Jonah. Who's been working on you?

Never mind that. It's true, isn't it?

It's easy to be swayed, said Jonah. Easy to paint a caricature of the man. But sometimes the real thing isn't black and white and you got to make your own mind up about that. Weigh things up for yerself. Nobody's whiter than white.

He looked appraisingly at my face.

Looks like you've been getting into some chew yourself, he said. Maybe you're not the one to point the finger.

I looked down at the floor. Jonah stood up and shifted from foot to foot.

Do you want to see it? he said, almost shy. He slid a drawer open in the dresser and passed me a slim package wrapped in tissue paper. I opened it, curious. There was some kind of transparent membrane folded in there, crisp and weightless like the husk left behind when a reptile slips its skin.

It's your caul, he said. Part of you, once. Like you were part of your dad. Do you want it back?

No. I don't want it.

I thrust it back at him with a fierceness I didn't understand. He took it, sort of reverently.

Hope it brings you luck, I said.

He winked at me.

You should go and get some kip, he said, but there's someone here you ought to meet first.

He glanced round again. Then he led the way through the rain-streaked room to the kitchen door.

In the grate a young fire was fledging, trying out new feathers. It mewed and bawled and puked gently, knitting the darkness into a dense knot of red coals and flame. The room gravitated around it, a twilit solar system leaning towards an infant sun, and the distant rumbling of rain and thunder were forgotten, in another galaxy altogether. A couple of shabby armchairs were pulled up close to the fireguard, and in one of them an old man sat gazing into the fire's heart and into his own thoughts. His hair was long and straggling and dirty and the bald patch at his crown glowed a deep red in the firelight. He raised a hand to his lips and sucked on a skinny hand-rolled cigarette. The nub glowed brightly in the draught of oxygen and then it subsided. Jonah cleared his throat and the old man turned to look at the two of us framed in the doorway. His eyes were grey and crinkled at the corners and as limitless as the sea. They seemed to frame a question, eyebrows slightly raised. These disparate features blurred and swam and finally knit together into a familiar grin. It was Yan.

Nice weather for ducks Danny, he said.

21. **Black Redstart**

(Phoenicopterus ochruros)

A flake of light spirals down like a sycamore seed into the husk of a man floating upon the water. The rise and fall of the ocean, inbreath and outbreath. The gentle applause of water in the eardrums and the wind riffling through wavetops. Herds of cumulus mass above him miles up in the clean sky, moving and migrating according to the rules of their kind. Black voices rumbling in the void beneath him, blind fish groping for their prey.

I was once a man, walking on the earth.

Cornelius, says Johann. How did you come to be on the streets? You would like us the story to tell, yes?

The fire splutters, threatens to subside. A thick rime of frost on the ground, on the piles of rubble and the sprawling brambles. Michael Cornelius – the name's in my passport. It was in my jacket pocket, along with a heavy brass lighter, when Johann and Franz Josef pulled me out of the Rhine that night. The night I was born.

I don't remember me, I tell him. I don't have a story.

Desperation, he says. Yourself in the river to throw.

I was running, I say. Down the stairs, away from a flat. I don't know why.

Johann shrugs.

Look, he says. The little pigdog. He steals the fire. I follow his pointing finger to where a small ash-grey bird is hopping away, tail and rump blazing russet like sycamore leaves in autumn.

In his tail, Johann roars. Like a red-hot poker.

He laughs and I can smell his rotten breath crackling with alcohol. In agreement, the fire begins to choke and collapse inward, flames dwindling and shrinking.

Be damned, Johann spits, and throws a stone at the little bird.

It simply hops away, head on one side, regarding us quizzically, and then carries on feeding.

Since fifteen years, since I here came, have they my fire stolen, he says. But one day, one day soon, I will him catch, and I will him slit and his tiny heart out-pull. No bigger than my little fingernail, he croons, raising a pitted nail crusted with filth. And I will it in my mouth pop like a bonbon, sweet and pure. And no more will this bird our fire steal. From now on, every wino, in every concrete city, will warm feet have, until the end of the world.

I look at him, plastered blond hair around his red and lumpen face, a stinking overcoat tied with string. Raise the half-empty bottle of raw spirit to my lips and drink. Small grey birds hop across the surface of my brain with scratchy claws. I look around at the graffiti and the rubble, the railway tracks over to our left and the tenements beyond. It could be any city, any corner of the earth.

What is this place Johann? I say,

Behind him the old man, Franz Josef, chokes with laughter behind that big white tobacco beard.

It is a watchmaker's factory, he rambles. I many times told him. Straight up and no mistake. But he declined to listen. Lick me on the arse. Lick me on the arse I tell you.

Johann rolls his eyes at me.

Cologne, he says. In the Federal Republic of Germany. Although you should yourself remember.

Cologne, I say. But why speak we all English?

Johann roars with laughter, flashing big yellow teeth like a horse, deposits of calculus stuck to them.

Cornelius my friend, we speak not English, he says. We speak German. You have it quite well picked up, since you on the streets were. But your accent is shocking.

He holds out a hand for the bottle and I reluctantly pass it to him. The U-Bahn rattles past on the tracks, raddled with graffiti. The old man climbs unsteadily to his feet. He is wearing a padded jacket as an extra pair of trousers, with his skeletal legs thrust into the arms. The hood flaps obscenely down in front of his groin. He begins to sing.

I am, from head to foot, wrapped around with love.

Yes, that is my world, and otherwise nothing.

Later, when Johann is unconscious, the old man sits down next to me.

The little bird, he says. He doesn't steal the fire. That one, that Johann.

He makes a gesture indicating a screw loose, rolls his eyes.

It was after the war, you see. There were great open spaces like this, from the bombing and the firestorms. It was a terrible thing, I heard. All the oxygen out of the air by the flames sucked. Women and children in the houses trapped, screaming.

He pauses and shakes his head.

Many of us came into the city then. Vagrants and broken men. And the grey bird with the burning tail came too. He was a bird of the villages and the farms, but after the war came he to the broken cities, and he liked what he found. So he stayed here, nearby the rubble and the railway tracks. He is one of us.

His face balloons in the firelight.

But, he splutters, his voice rising, I tell him to come back to the watchmaker's factory and he does not listen. He does not listen.

At dusk we wander into the city centre, find a department store with a deep entranceway making a sheltered pocket from the cold. The old man is soon asleep under several layers of cardboard. Me and Johann squat in the darkness, out of the wind. We have cigarettes, but no matches. I finger the brass lighter in my pocket, but I know it doesn't work. Needs a new wick, a refill of fluid. Johann goes out onto the street, starts asking people for a light. I don't see them, mushrooming out of the dark, but when I look up he's surrounded by boneheads.

Do you want a light junkie? Do you?

They crowd in, young and excited, spray-on jeans and knee-high boots and the shaved heads shimmering like pale moons on a sea of streetlight. One of them clicks a lighter open and sends a flame shooting a foot in the air and they shrill with laughter.

Burn him, shrieks one of them. Do it Hank.

Listen, gentlemen, we only for a light asked, says Johann, hands raised in placatory manner. I have cigarettes. You are very welcome.

He holds the crumpled packet out towards them. The sheltered entranceway now a trap, in which we are cornered.

Filthy habit, says one of the lads, casually smashing the packet out of Johann's hand and stamping on the cigarettes until they are pulped.

You look cold, says one of them. Poor things, out here all night. Perhaps can we you up-warm.

He has a bottle of spirits in his hand, schnapps or cheap brandy. Walks over to the pile of cardboard where Franz Josef slumbers, unscrews the bottletop and splashes the contents all over the makeshift shelter. The others are giggling nervously.

Give me the lighter Hank, says the boy.

He only looks sixteen or seventeen. A puppy's face, with big plaintive eyes below the shorn skull. Hank throws the lighter over. The puppy looks at us.

Run junkies, run, he says. Unless you want in our bonfire to join.

We run as he lights the cardboard and leaps back, and there's a roar of blue flame and splintering glass. The boneheads are already sprinting away as the alarm system begins to wail, and Johann and I run helter-skelter in the opposite direction, not stopping until we've covered several blocks. We stop on the apron of a busy road, cars teeming by into the night.

What about the old man? I say. Shall we go back for him? Johann shakes his head.

He's dead. Sure as shit. It's an occupational hazard Cornelius.

His haggard face is lit sporadically by the headlights of passing traffic.

He was on the Russian front, during the war, says Johann. Saw some terrible things. That's what a wino of him made, right back in forty-five. He was before that a watchmaker.

I was once a man, walking on the earth. When I stretch my feet out, down into the water, there is nothing. A yawning depth beneath me. Sleep is no longer sleep, just an endless, wakeful treading of water. I long for a pillow of sand beneath my cheek, moulding itself to the contours of my face. I long to lie on solid ground, on the fringes of some island.

Cornelius, says Johann. You are a golem. Not a man.

We are sitting on the U-Bahn platform at Ebertplatz, waiting for the transport police to throw us off for the night.

What is a golem? I know I have somewhere of it heard, but I don't remember me exactly.

He snorts, slumps against the wall, momentarily losing consciousness. I shift my buttocks impatiently, where I'm starting to get pressure sores from cold concrete.

Johann, I say, shaking him.

What? Oh right. Well, a golem is an empty shell, a man without the soul. A magician in the Prague ghetto made the golem out of clay, and breathed life into it. He used it his bidding to do, secretly, for it would always its master obey, always to him return.

I can see two policemen on the opposite platform, eyeing us up. It won't be long now. Johann is looking at them too, his story in abeyance. They head up a stairway and he continues.

You are an empty shell Cornelius. A man without a soul. A man without a story.

You're just jealous, I say. You drink your soul to kill. You drink your story to drown. I have it already done.

You are my golem Cornelius, he says. I sculpted you from river mud. From the Rhine. And you will my bidding do.

Come on gents. The two policemen are in front of us. You know the score. The fat one with the moustache shells a couple of cigarettes towards us, which Johann palms and pockets with practised ease. We haul ourselves to our feet and shamble towards the stairs, Johann stumbling and leaning heavily against me.

Cornelius, he says. You know, I am sick and tired of cold feet. Perhaps I will you command the tiny bird to kill.

I sigh, thinking only of the cheap schnapps we have bought and the too-short oblivion it will bring.

In the morning we shuffle past the department store where Franz Josef was incinerated. There are blue lights flashing, a police line taped across the store entrance. Staff and customers are huddled outside the barrier and we shamble over to join them, noticing how they edge away from the miasma of our stench. Johann bares his teeth at a group of young shop girls and they stare, revolted. After a few minutes, medics come out with a prone figure on a stretcher, red blanket drawn over the face and head. The crowd shudders. The back doors of the ambulance close behind the stretcher but the vehicle stays put, engine idling, blue lights firing limpidly. I recognize the two cops who regularly kick us off Ebertplatz.

Hey boys, I croak. Have they another poor wino immolated?

The fat one with the moustache looks at me. Disgust mingled with pity.

Nah, he drawls, then lowers his voice. A skinhead bought it. Young lad.

The other one is wiry and blond, face blotched maroon by the cold. He leans conspiratorially towards me and Johann.

Ripped open from stem to stern, he murmurs with relish. Inside out turned, pretty much. The scary thing is, it looks like somebody with their bare hands did it. No sign that a weapon was used. Who would the strength have, to do such a thing?

He shudders delightedly. The fat one looks more pensive.

I won't his face in a hurry forget, he says. Reminded me of my little ones at home. Just a little boy, big eyes like a puppy.

He shakes his head slowly, the pale blue eyes moist. Johann and I shamble away, winding through the morning crowds. I look at Johann but he's avoiding eye contact. Then he says it.

You did it, golem.

What?

I look at him again, confused.

Only a golem would have the strength to rip a man open with his bare hands. You, Cornelius, killed him. In retribution for Franz Josef.

How could I have killed him? Been with you the whole time.

You wander in the night Cornelius. When I fall asleep, you are wakeful. An empty shell.

And you are full of shit, I tell him.

The sun against my face like the hot muzzle of a shotgun, bullying me into consciousness.

Cornelius, look. Cornelius. I've found him, shouts Johann excitedly. He is bouncing like a big stupid dog with a dark patch of piss at his groin. He shakes me by the arm.

Lick me on the arse Johann, I say. I need to sleep.

I turn over. The weather is warmer now and sleep more comfortable. He shakes me again, this time angrily.

Golem, he booms. Awake. Your master commands you.

I stand abruptly and grab him by the mouth.

Enough of this golem shit, I snap, looking into his big stupid blue eyes. He shakes himself free, grins crookedly.

Come and look, he says.

We push between the big buddleia bushes which are scribbling purple prose all over the wasteland, shooting out these long and rampant spires of doggerel. The other side of the bushes, down a little slope, a burnt-out lorry is slowly rusting. Looks like it has been here for years, everything of value – wheels, upholstery, engine – stripped away. A slowly subsiding island in a ragged sea of brambles.

Shhh. Johann has his finger to his lips. Through a tunnel of thorn we can see the back end of the lorry. I follow his pointing finger and squint into the darkness underneath. A bird flits up and perches on the back axle, silhouetted against green vegetation. It gives a twitch of the head, a flick of the tail, and there's a high-pitched churring like a matchbox full of crickets. The bird jumps to one end of the axle and I realize there must be a nest there against the corroded wheel arch, the adult stuffing insects into the lurid gapes of the young.

It's them, Johann breathes, excitedly. The fire-stealers.

The adult bird hops out from the darkness onto a pile of breeze-blocks and his body blends in with the soft greys of the rubble but his russet tail is flaming like a Japanese maple with the light blazing through. The little black eye darts around and the bird flickers away in search of insects. Johann touches my arm.

I'm going to do it. The chicks are there. The new year's birds. I will them stop, now, before they grow and my fire next winter thieve away. I will them in my mouth pop, one by one, and the bones crunch.

His large, slug-like tongue crawls slowly across his lips and a candle of slobber dangles from his chin. He starts to move forward and I grab his arm.

Johann, you cannot eat them, I say, urgently. You are not a magpie, or Königin Victoria in black mourning.

His face twists into an ugly snarl.

Get you filthy hands off me *Engländer*.

He pushes me back and I slump into a confusion of brambles which clutch at my clothes and hair. Johann bounds towards the back of the lorry and suddenly there's magma rising to my throat. I thrash myself clear of the brambles, globes of blood like tiny red chillies at my forearms and on my face. He's stooping like a crane beneath the back bumper and I run at him, pulling him away so that he turns, arms flailing and his face purple and engorged.

You are with them in league, he roars, slamming a knee expertly into my groin. I collapse, winded, in front of him.

First I have with you to deal, he whines. You fucking firescreen, you sapsucker.

He pulls a full bottle of Canadian rotgut whisky from the inside pocket of his overcoat and tears off the top and wrenches my head back by the hair so that I fear being scalped. Instead he turns me over and plunges the bottle into my mouth.

Have a drink Herr Cornelius, he shouts.

The neck of the bottle almost down my throat, Johann on my chest, pinning my upper arms with his knees. I'm forced to swallow, and swallow, and swallow, bubbles of my life wriggling upwards through the golden fluid, until half of it's gone and replaced by my breath. Queen Victoria puts the bottle down carefully on the ground, her jowls quivering. She reaches inside her black organza cleavage and a huge knife like a flatfish jumps into her hand.

You killed Albert you whore, she spits, the piggy eyes incandescent with rage, raises the glittering flatfish into the air above my throat.

I'm going to rip you, she murmurs, with some relish. And then I'm going to gobble them fledglings.

As she says this, jet earrings a-quiver, one of her dumpy knees lifts just a little from my bruised upper arm. Just enough for me to wrench the arm free with a brutal effort and smash my fist into her face. She topples backwards and spits broken teeth, black blood dribbling onto the ground. Twist myself to my feet just as she flies at me with the giant blade, catching me on the chin and tearing off a flap of skin.

By royal commission, this, she laughs, waving the knife above her head, black skirts billowing and hair coming astray. She points to the royal crest on the blade.

That's me sonny. VR. Read 'em and weep motherfucker.

She comes at me again with a Miss Piggy squeal, but this time I manage to sidestep and grab the chunky gold chain holding the pendant round her neck. She jerks back like a hanged man reaching the end of the rope and I force her to the ground while she slashes at me behind her back with the knife. Little mouths open and gape in my flesh, and I begin to leak onto the floor, but I twist the gold chain tight and hold on, praying it doesn't break. I twist the gold chain while her quaking dewlaps turn purple and then blue, tongue protruding from the twisted mouth. I hold on until she is finished, and the knife stops dipping its beak into me and falls to the ground. Then I sit down and watch the adult redstarts shyly observing me, alarm calls ticking and autumn tails nervously beating. They come closer, among the glowing buddleia leaves and flakes of blue sky, and I can see the bundles of tiny insects clamped in the needle-sharp beaks. Then, courage restored, they flit back beneath the lorry and I hear the rasping cries of the brood.

Evening is growing and the air-raid sirens beginning to wail by the time I drag the old woman's body deep under cover, at the centre of a thicket. I take her velvet cloak to cover my bloodstains. Bombers are beginning to drone overhead as I hurry back to the rusting lorry. The bottle is there, where she left it, perched primly on the ground, the raw gold beckoning within. Searchlights are clutching at the night sky over the city, revealing flocks of bombers like black bats hanging upside down from heaven. Guano begins to drip from the blunt bodies. I tilt the bottle where a small sun has been left brewing, and swallow it down whole, hydrogen and helium and sunspots and solar flares and all. The crump of high explosive echoes from the edges of the city and I lie down in the middle of the wasteland and wait for it to come.

So, you're healed now, she says, from the other side of her desk. At least, your body is healed. The knife wounds, you know.

Her English is good, the voice calm and assured. Antiseptic, like the hospital smell of her little white office.

How long? I stammer, uncomfortable on the plastic chair.

You've been in hospital five weeks, she says. Lucky to be here. You lost a lot of blood.

I reach a hand up to my scalp. It's naked, brutally shaved.

Sorry, she says. The locks had to go. You were quite badly infested.

And then I look at her. A white face with a long clean jawline, a lascivious turn to the upper lip. Coarse black hair swept away and gathered at the back. She's wearing a sleeveless top and I can't help staring at her arms which are thin and bare and white as a pelagic bird. And bluegreen snakes coiling around from wrist to shoulder in whorls and vertices like a double helix.

Caroline Baumann, she says. Everybody calls me Cally. I'm the alcohol project worker. There's no compulsion, of course. You can go back on the streets if you wish. But we can offer counselling and support —

Her voice tails off. My eyes rove over her white skin, the elaborate tattoos, then snap, embarrassed, back to her face.

I got them done in Kreuzberg, she says. After a colossal acid trip.

She stretches a thumb and middle finger round the broadest extent of her slender bicep, slides it down towards the elbow.

So why the snakes? I ask her.

I don't know. I've always been fascinated by them. I love their skin, the patterns on it are so intricate. Like an engraving by Escher.

She pulls herself upright. So Mr Cornelius, shall we begin?

It's not Cornelius, I tell her. The passport, it's fake.

So what is your name?

I try to rub the creases out of my forehead with my palms.

That's the thing. It's gone. I need to get it back.

Your memory will come back, eventually. That's what happens in almost every case. Let's start at the beginning.

I sigh deeply, lean back in the chair, put my hands behind my head. Fix her with my eyes.

To be honest Miss Baumann. Cally. I'd rather talk about snakes.

*

Four days later I wake up in her apartment, bathed in sweat. The tenor bell of the cathedral has a deep penetrative note which vibrates through the building each time it sounds the hour. She's next to me, twisted in the bed.

It's okay, she says. You must have been dreaming.

Yeah. I grin uncertainly. Dreaming about the sea.

You have to rest, she says. Get some of that strength back. No time for worrying.

You know, I... I think I had a kid. A wife. Years since I saw them. How many? I don't even know what year it is now.

Perhaps, she says. But you can't go looking now. You've been through a lot. Got to eat, like John Wayne said, get off your horse and drink your milk. Good for the bones.

She pads through the small flat in the half-light, to the kitchen. I hear the fridge pop open, see the flood of light. Back to the bedroom with a glass of milk and a slice of black bread. Ghostly light outside, not quite dawn, the city still asleep. I drink hungrily, thick milk smeared across my stubble. Cally giggles.

Du Ferkel! You need a – *Lätzchen* – I don't know the word in English – for a baby.

A nappy, I offer, smirking.

I know a lot of English men like that sort of thing, but no, I know a nappy is for shit, huh? This thing goes around your neck.

You, I say, smiling.

And she twists her head from side to side on the pillow as I move above her, in the bed in the half-lit room beneath the deep tenor bell of the cathedral, in the lost room deep in the dark heart of Europe. Her arms with the snake tattoos are around me, raking my back, cupping my buttocks, rubbing at the stubble on the back of my head. Her thin legs are moving around my thighs, knees jutting out an angle like bent coathangers. She imprisons me with the thin bars of her limbs, limiting me to this one simple movement of the buttocks, ploughing backwards and forwards. When she comes and cries out harshly she clasps me fiercely with her arms, the white arms with the coiled tattoos, constricting my chest so that I can hardly breathe, holding me fast so that I can't escape, so that I'm pouring out my life into her.

And days go by. Weeks. When Cally is at work I sit slumped on the sofa. There's a fog outside, soft and absorbent, the gothic bulk of the cathedral sensed rather than seen. The television is beginning to occupy more and more of my days, as I get fitter and more mobile, bright moving pictures and sounds occupying the front part of my brain. Like a group of vacuous and noisy squatters, chatty but ultimately pointless. But they stop the real heavies moving in, the ones I don't want to meet.

The key turns in the outer door. Has she been locking me in? I've never checked, never yet felt strong enough to venture outside. But the thought of being locked in troubles me. It's like a pond, this apartment. Comfortable and warm, but too murky. I think of going across Roncalliplatz to the cathedral, climbing up into that tower until my knees are jelly. Climbing up above the fog, above the booming of great bells in the murk.

Where have you been? I missed you.

Have to earn us some bread, she says. I have clients who need me. Not just you.

Plenty of alcoholics in the world, I say. You know, I used to have these migraines – a blur would move slowly across my vision, like a sunspot swimming across the sun. Eventually it would drop over the rim and I could see again. But right then I'd get a blinding headache, like I'd been hit with a hammer. It's like that now. Everything's blurred, but I can feel the blur moving. I want to see again.

When that happens you might have to put up with a big headache, she says.

A few days later she gives me a key. It winks on the string like a fish.

Had this cut today, she said. For you. You can go explore when I'm at work. I take the key and put it in my pocket. It feels light, almost weightless.

Fresh air, she says. You need to build up the strength in your muscles.

Yes, I tell her. Walking is good. Walking is fine.

We're sitting in the living room of the flat, bars of sunlight jutting through the diaphanous curtains. The television is babbling. When she's gone out, I close the flat door behind me, lean against the outside. Sweat prickling on my scalp, dark patches welling like tears in my armpits. Look down the dark stairwell. It reminds me of others. Wooden banisters worn smooth by the passage of hands. Whitewashed steps leading up. Snow blowing through slats.

Take a step down, heart accelerating wildly, knocking in your ears. Both hands braced against the walls. Focus on the street door at the bottom, mail lying haphazard on the floor, flyers for restaurants and bars. Focus on the bright flags of paper and make yourself walk. The sweat patches have swollen, become dark moons. Walk to the bottom.

I grasp the brass latch of the street door, open it a crack. A sliver of sunlight, with a hot breath of coffee and pastries and dusty pavements. I open the door a little more, scrutinize the passers-by. A tall man, slightly stooped, wearing a black leather jacket. Greying hair, slicked back. I'm straining to see his face, but he ducks into an alleyway. And then there's a younger man, well-muscled, hair close-cropped like suede and a sleeveless tee showing off his upper arms. Their names are on the tip of my tongue.

And then there's a hand on my shoulder, and I turn in surprise. That gentle pressure.

That was classic, he says. Yan, you really are a tool.

Joe.

He hovers in front of me for the moment it takes me to realize that it isn't Joe, but the tenant from the upstairs flat, and that he's put a hand on my shoulder because he wants me to move out of his way.

Entschuldigung, he repeats softly, spectacles like moons. I move to make way, click the door shut after him. Slide down to the floor, back against the closed door.

Joe, Horse Boy, Fabián. I'm walking down the stairwell of a block of flats. The stench of piss, graffiti on the walls. A plastic bag in my hand, bottles clinking. Whisky. I can smell it. When I look up I can see my own footprints coming down the stairs, the tread of my brogues.

Stairs and stairwells. Over the months I linger a little longer, each time I leave the flat, feeling my heart palpitate and my gullet tighten. At the bottom, sunlight bristles through the panel of the street door. Smooth wooden banisters on the stairs at home, where Kate thought there were ghosts.

Kate. Her name in my mouth like a sugared almond.

And there were whitewashed stairs in an old farmhouse, back on the Falklands. I dreamed an attic and muzzle flashes and then nothing, like I cheated death there without even knowing. Or perhaps I really died there and now I'm a ghost, dwindling in the bright world.

I finger the brass lighter in my pocket and it turns cold.

There's a third stairwell, somewhere close in a block of flats, and my shoes leaving great damp stains on the concrete.

At first I linger in the square by the cathedral, soaking up the sun and feeding the pigeons. Birds crowd and tumble about my feet like jugglers, perch on my hands with those scaly feet, pink and crabbed. And then onto the U-Bahn, rattling through the city and suburbs, riding the different lines to places I've never heard of, enjoying the anonymity, the sense of ease. But underneath this lazy convalescence I'm looking for a scent. Narrowing down the options.

And then I find it. That line north to Chorweiler with the stations like a poem learned many years ago and then forgotten. Altonaer Platz, Mollwitzstraße, Breslauer Platz. And one day I ride out to the end of the line and I recognize the buildings, the mazy concrete tenements blistered by the weather. Walking around with my collar turned up against the spluttering rain and the flowers of damp graffiti, walking past these Turkish kids playing football in an underpass and they look at me like I'm in a specimen bottle and I say *merhaba* and they shrill with laughter and the ball thuds into the wall close to my shoulder and they laugh again.

I come out of the underpass and there's an open space, and in the centre is a human fist cast from concrete. As if this form could vegetate under the ground, lie dormant for years under the skin of slab and hardcore and rebar and then casually break through and flower like a tulip with the blood drumming in its face. And now I know exactly where I am. I move like a dog on the scent, twisting and turning through the warren of buildings. Swing doors and piss in the lobby and kids yapping up and down the corridors, a woman's voice tearing strips off somebody who never answers back, and the open stairwell rising up the corner of the building, damp light and cool air entering between wooden slats. Streetlights flick on with sodium glare and deep shadow, my feet leaving deep stains of dark.

Blood.

Now I get it. I stepped in blood. I tracked it down the stairs, slopping great wet stains across the concrete. I crouch down foetal against the slats and press my face deep into coatsleeve. Run a finger across concrete and raise it to my lips, cold and damp but no blood there now. Are they still there, inside the flat? Brace myself against the wall and haul upright and force myself to climb to the fourth-floor landing and to the door. Brass numbers on blistered blue paint. One five two.

Knock and wait. The smell of cooking, onion and garlic. Joe could cook a mean chilli.

Ja? There's a slender, dark-skinned man standing there, buzz of small children behind.

Meine Freunde waren hier, I say. *Drei Mensch. Ausländer.*

He looks blank.

Nein, he says flatly, breaking eye contact. Not here. We live here six years.

But I was here. Only a few months ago.

Entschuldigung, he says, eyes averted downward. Begins to close the door. I throw my bodyweight against it and slam the little man into the internal wall and rampage into the flat.

In the kitchen there's a woman cooking on the electric stove. Bright clothes and headscarf, terror in her eyes. I remember the stainless steel sink and the drip from the cold tap and the chessboard tiles on the floor. The formica-topped table with the wonky leg.

Where are they? I shout at her.

She gabbles with fear and backs against the stove. Into the living room and the same worn leather sofas and ghastly orange carpet and the same smell of damp and the same black mildew patches on the ceiling. A small cigarette burn on the carpet, just inside the door. The television babbles and three small children stare at me in fear. Toys all over the carpet, plastic cars, building bricks, naked dolls.

Joe made that burn, I tell them, gesturing idiotically. He dropped ash. Who cleaned up the blood?

The little girl screams and begins to cry noisily, and then I'm seized from behind and turned round. Several men in the hallway, including the small man who opened the door. He's been to round up the neighbours.

Du, says one of them. Time to go. *Abhauen.*

Jerks a thumb towards the front door, a kitchen blade flashing in his hand like a silver fish. I raise both hands in a gesture of appeasement.

Nicht schießen. I'm going.

Edge through the pack of men towards the door. A final glance into the living room. There's a small imperfection in the wall, at head height above a shabby armchair. Somebody's filled in a hole in the plaster, painted over the top without sanding down the filler. The repair shows as a rough patch of fresh paint.

My fingers close around the lighter, deep in my pocket. No question that this was the flat. They grab my arms, try to propel me out, and the lighter spills onto the floor with a thud, brass glinting like cheap whisky. I go down on all fours to retrieve it.

In the cathedral there was the shrine of the Magi and the jewels on its golden skin. A noseless face. Medusa in turquoise and white. A garnet carved with Theseus slaying the Minotaur. And then I was standing right here. Right here. And brass shellcases glittered where they'd fallen like sloughed skins and *Glühwein* on my breath and the smell of cordite, bitter and green.

See, they must have shouldered the door because the latch is splintered. Into the living room where Joe was sitting in the armchair and the first shot missed above his head and left that raw wound in the plaster, now patched. But the second was point blank to the face and the entry wound took away his nose and the exit took his brains and the back of his skull into the headrest of the chair. There's still one of them Rote Händle cancer sticks in his hand, burned right down to the knuckle with a long column of ash clinging on.

The noseless man.

Fabián was sat on the sofa marshalling a line on that picture frame when they pumped three rounds into his chest and he sat slumped with the black blood draining like tar from mouth and nose. It's drying in his long locks now and they're snaking at improbable angles like a gorgon's head.

Medusa, in turquoise and white.

And in the shower room Horse Boy was coming out of the cubicle naked and steaming and they emptied a gun into his unprotected belly and he collapsed like a slaughtered bull on the threshold with offal spilling from his burst abdomen.

The Minotaur.

This is the flat, but every trace of the three of them has been carefully rubbed out. They lived, and now they have never lived.

Night in the centre of Europe. Dustbins upended across the city and stars strewn like trash across the backyard of the universe. In Cally's apartment a small fire breathes in the woodburner, tiny flakes of wood ash tinkling like glass.

Cally, I say. She angles her chin towards me, firelight brindling her flesh. What happened in the flat. To Joe and the others. I caused it. I brought them here.

She smiles sleepily.

It's complicated, she says. How things come to be. Perhaps there is no cause. No why and wherefore. We are where we are, right now. No cause leading up to us, and no effect running away from us. Me, you, that old brass lighter of yours. We're all present in this moment and how we got here doesn't figure.

And where we go now?

Doesn't figure either.

I like that thought.

Draw myself up close to her on the sofa, feel the warmth of her through the dressing gown.

Yan, she yawns. I like your name. Glad you remembered it. But I'm sad too, because now you will want to go home.

Why does that make you sad?

Because I love you.

We sit for a minute in silence.

You've gone tense, she says. Why?

Love, I say.

What about it?

Well, it kind of springs up unexpected – like a sword with that point sheer against your breastbone. And the invitation is to push yourself right on, like a Japanese samurai or one of them old Roman senators, yeah? Transfix yourself right through the chest until the tip comes out at the back, underneath your shoulderblade where you can't even see it no more.

That's about right, she says. And once you're on, you can't back off. Not without making a mess.

Every time someone makes me that offer, I say. Well, I'm honoured and I'm perplexed in just about equal parts, but I just got to make my excuses.

Then I'm a little bit sorry for you, she says.

I sigh.

Crazy, really. I've come this far. War and tempest, desert and darkness, flood and madness. And I've learned nothing. Just my own name.

Who wants to learn? You have a story, that's what matters.

She picks up the lighter from the coffee table and rattles it.

You're not an empty shell any more.

She runs her fingertips over the bare skin of my arms.

Silver, she says. Your scars, where that guy stabbed you all those times. They were red and angry. But now they're silver. Like little fish.

She rests her chin on updrawn knees.

Tell me the whole story. Beginning to end.

It can wait until the morning. We both need some sleep.

Her hand strokes my forearm slowly, raising the hairs.

Yan, darling. The night is without end, and sleep is not for the likes of us. I can prop my eyelids open until dawn, if necessary. Just tell the story.

I smile and sigh. Then I begin.

I was once a man, walking on the earth.

22. **Thrush Nightingale**

(Luscinia luscinia)

Two lads framed in the empty gaze of the streetlights, eleven or twelve years old and skinny as cobras, faces hidden from above by the peaks of their baseball caps. From Yan's bedroom window I watch one of them twirl out into the street on a little silver scooter. The other stands quiet with his body slouched into a nonchalant question mark. Something dangles casually from his hand, a stave from a wooden fence. He tests it for strength, thwacks it into the opposite palm, and the other boy spirals round him on the scooter like a moth.

Did you. Go to the Heugh?

There's a metallic edge to his voice you could cut yourself on, like the ragged rim of a tin can. You can hear his lung volume shrinking day by day. I turn away from the window into the darkened room, letting sodium light billow through the gap in the curtains.

Aye, I say. I went.

A hiss as he takes a suck from the oxygen mask, the inside of it beading with his moisture. The tank's mounted on the wall now, beside the bed. Fitted the house up so they can send him home from hospital. Seems to be the way now. Pressure on beds. A home help calls once a day and he has a panic button in case of emergency. And there's Jean. And there's me. The mask hisses again.

Don't keep me. In suspense, he says.

I'm watching the boys in the street. The scooter is still, the rider saying something. The other boy listens and the stave swings from his hand like a makeshift pendulum.

Did you see it? he says.

Yes, I saw it. It was there all right. There was quite a crowd, too.

The pendulum tracks from side to side and rests in the middle. Then the boy pivots like a baseball pitcher and thrashes the scooter rider over the head with the stave. The younger lad sprawls on the floor, scooter clattering onto concrete and bewilderment on his face.

Dan, he says. The oxygen whispers. I didn't expect it. To get worse so soon. Jim isn't as friendly. As he was. I thought there would be another. Tick or two.

The boy lashes out again with the stave, but the other lad rolls out of the way and jumps to his feet and grabs the scooter. He scoots away out of range and then he turns and gives it large, the voice thin and yappy.

You can describe it anyway, he says. Sort of tick it for me. Vicariously.

Okay, I say. You know the Heugh Battery. You go through that tumbledown brick wall off the Headland. There's a plaque there. Something about the war.

It was shelled, he interrupts. By German battleships. Enormous great things. Must have seemed as terrible. As nuclear bombs. At the time.

The boy with the stave strides towards the other one and swings again but the scooter rider loops lazily back out of range, then sets off slowly down the street. The other boy walks purposefully after him, rangy and spare, twirling the stave.

You remember how it used to be? I continue. Overgrown with bushes and rubbish, them old gun emplacements like empty eye sockets, bunkers full of fly-tipped junk and all sorts. Condoms, druggy stuff.

Yan snorts.

In Hartlepool. We know the best. Places to take a lady.

He grins broadly.

Well, they've started clearing it up. A lot of the rubbish is gone, the bushes cut down, grass cut. I think they're going to refurbish the gun emplacements.

Fucking gentrification, he says. They don't realize. A bit of untidiness. Is what birds need. They'll make it sterile.

He's quiet for a minute, the oxygen tank clanking.

Tell me about the sea, he says.

I could tell him how the sea looks enormous from up there, how it quakes like corrugated iron in the wind, how it seems bleaker now the place is tidied up, less sheltered. You could get blown away.

You know about the sea, I say.

The two boys are receding into the distance and the rider's showboating on his scooter, blowing just out of reach of the stave. He's the one with all the moves, now that the shock has worn off. The other one looks plodding and predictable, wastes his strength on great scything strokes, connecting only with raw February air. They disappear, the two of them, behind the flaking frame of the window.

Who was there? he asks, craning towards me.

Well, the artillery was out in force, I laugh. Some of them scopes cost more than my house. It's all about the gear for some of them.

He chuckles croakily.

Frank was there. He sent his best wishes. Tommo and big Steve as well.

Is Tommo. Still with that lass? The traffic warden.

I don't know. She wasn't there today. Perhaps he's gone back to his first love. Yan grins.

Twitchers, he says. So. Hit me with the gravy stroke.

I look blank.

The bird, he says, impatiently. Make me see it.

I call it to mind, blowing about the top of an old emplacement like a little splinter of breezeblock. Never seen a bird shiver before, but I swear it was shaking with cold. Kept puffing up like a small grey cloud, a bleary dark eye popping open and shut. Looking for cover, angling itself against the wind, the sea rattling. And you could sense the discomfort and the cold air tugging at the plumage, at that shy sharp nightingale shape. It was blurred, somehow, like someone had smeared a rubber over the feathers and smudged everything. And it was yearning for a nice bit of deep thicket to get immersed in, like a warm tropical sea.

Not much to tell, I say. Thrush nightingale. It's the ultimate little brown job. It hopped around, flew towards that boundary wall. You should have seen the scopes all juddering round like Jodrell fucking Bank.

He laughs. Then he sucks at the oxygen and the tank clacks against the wall. And outside there's a clutch of young lasses striding up the street, deep in counsel, with stifled giggles and headlong glances.

You can't really do it second hand, he says. I guess you've got to be there. In the moment. That small life beating against yours. The tick.

I know what you mean, I say.

You see it doesn't care, he carries on. Hundreds of millions of years of evolution. The bird wears it lightly. It doesn't care. About the past. Just right now. The tick. The match flaring in the dark.

Human history is a piss in the sea, I say. When you think about it.

Birds are free. From all that, he croaks. Birds are liberating.

There's a long pause. Then he almost whispers.

And what about Paul?

Aye, I say wearily. I found him. But he wouldn't believe me. Wouldn't come back.

Didn't have a bunch of twitchers. On his tail.

No. Just the one.

What did he say?

If you were really his father, you'd have helped him out, when he was going down the pan. You'd have stopped it happening.

Yan doesn't say anything. Sits up in the bed, duvet at his chin, staring into space. Stays like that for a long time.

Jean looks worn out, grey circles around her eyes. She bends over the washing-up, suds rising around her slender forearms.

Didn't realize he ate so little, I say.

She shrugs.

Oh aye, love. Just picks at it now. Never has much of an appetite.

She rinses the petroleum sheen from a mug under the cold tap.

He's getting skinny, she says, pensive. Can't believe how much worse it's got, the last couple of month. He says it's like breathing through a straw. Christmas time he was like a rabbit.

She smiles.

Nowadays I even have to help him go to the bog. Laugh a minute. Might get one of them chemical ones for under the bed.

Her eyes are suddenly sprung with tears but I touch her arm and she steadies.

Anyway Danny. What's going on with you?

Don't ask.

I just did.

So I mop a plate with a damp teatowel, tell her about the letter from Martin. How Kelly left it lying around on the coffee table, the bright green envelope torn open.

You read her mail?

It was just a thank-you note, for the weekend. This one sentence though.

Go on.

'I can't help thinking you could do with a bit more excitement in your life.'

The words come out pat from where they're stored.

You think he was talking about you?

Of course he was talking about me. Don't know. We'll sort it out. Once things have settled down.

Jean looks at me hard.

Don't put it off, she says. Things might never settle down. Listen, I need to tell you something about your dad.

He's dying, I say. I know.

She laughs but her face is stark and desperate under the harsh overhead lighting.

He has night terrors, she says. More and more these nights. He likes me to be there if he wakes up in the dark.

Some grim stuff happened in the Falklands, I say. It doesn't lie down easy, that kind of shit.

It's not that so much. But he wakes up and he doesn't know who I am. Stares at me like a skull, like I'm a cockroach he's about to crush. I'm scared he might hurt me one of these nights. Don't know if I can take much more.

He won't hurt you, I say.

Twelve-bar blues playing on the stereo in his room.

Charlie Musselwhite, he says. One of my favourites.

The band is ripping through a guitar break. He takes a deep suck of oxygen, the white pyjama cuff falling back to reveal a painfully thin forearm.

Charlie isn't dead yet, he says.

He gasps painfully and spends a good minute behind the oxygen mask. The room is warm and the radiator throbbing out heat and the bedside lamp casts a pool of lucidity.

You spend years, he says. Watching birds. Each one a little separate being. A little world. No matter how hard you watch. You can't touch. There's always a windscreen between you. And you can put your fingers on the glass. But you can't reach through.

Sometimes, I say. I think there's more to birds. You know, when a flock moves like a twister, like it's one being made of all them little cells. A collective consciousness. Maybe the individual doesn't matter so much when it's wired in to so many others. When I was a kid I used to imagine I could do that. Sort of empty my brain out and let other people's thoughts and feelings move through me. Felt like I was connected to an endless grid of life.

Yan looks at me, the grey eyes mobile.

You're as much a loner as me, he says. Look at you. You're on your own inside your own head and your own dreams. And in there nobody else can touch you.

That's not true.

He looks at me. Flock behaviour, he says. It's an illusion of connectedness. It just suits the individual. Keeps it safer from predators. Like people, really.

There must be more than that.

He grins.

I was going to tell you, he says. About Mount Longdon.

Why?

Because you asked me.

But why now?

I told you I couldn't remember. Not strictly true. I told you I felt drunk. But I didn't. It was crystal-clear, that morning. One of them bell-like mornings. When your voice carries for miles. These fucking dago conscripts. Soaking wet and pale and shivering in them rain capes. I was shelling out fags. Wanted to share a smoke. And I never saw the kid go for his service pistol. Honestly Dan, I never did.

Barlow said he was only seventeen or eighteen.

None of them. Was much more than that. Secundino, his name was. Secundino Vargas.

How do you know?

Looked at his tags after. I never saw him go for the Beretta. And I never saw George pop him. Just heard the roar. You're fucking deaf that close up. Your ears singing.

George shot him through the eye, didn't he?

More like blew half his fucking head off. Only he wasn't dead.

Of course he was dead.

Only he wasn't. Fell on the floor with half his head missing. Started convulsing. Fitting. Jigging about with his feet fucking tapdancing. Boots banging a tattoo on the earth.

Christ.

Saw some kittens once. The tom had been at them. Eaten half their heads. Just dragging themselves round in circles. Crying. Had to drown them. And they fought against me. Fought to the fucking end.

So you put him out of his misery.

Aye, I did.

That's not so bad. Any human being would have done that.

It was the anger. Like a cold wall of sea. The stupid little bastard. Dancing that dance. I blew the rest of his stupid head off. Just to make him stop. The details you remember. Wisps of cloud high up and lonely. Cirrus and cirro-stratus. A little tic in the corner of my eye. Ears throbbing in the wind. And the little ratchet of the selfloader. As it racked up the next round. Like a polite cough. Ears throbbing. Joe had to stop me. Putting rounds into him. But by then the magazine. Was empty anyway.

I understand, I say. I understand why you walked away.

No, he says. You don't.

But then Charlie Musselwhite storms into a harmonica solo with the band swinging and stomping beneath him and Yan relaxes and beams and leans back on his pillow. Death is a cipher and past and future are mad dreams without interpretation, dead alphabets with no Rosetta Stone, and there is only the harp leaping and squealing and powered by Charlie's breath.

I fall asleep in the chair, an uneasy slumber peopled with wild dreams. His voice, when it comes, is harsh like a walnut cracking.

You.

I spring upright, don't know for a moment where I am. He flips the light on and I see him massing in the bed like a storm cloud.

Arse, I say. Must have fallen asleep. Long day at work.

I get up and yawn. He stares at me, eyes arctic.

Why did you come back? he says, glaring at me. After all these years.

I turn at the doorway and look at him and his eyes are those black coals at the centre of the fire.

I've always been here, I say. I'm not the one who came back.

He shuffles crablike across the bed towards me, like he wants to jump at my throat.

Don't come back now, he says. When it's too fucking late.

He fixes me with the boiling eyes, unblinking. Frustration inside me, cold and slow, and my voice haggard and roughened with sleep.

It's not too late, I say. I don't know why you left it till now, but even so it's not too late.

You pushed me away. Didn't want to know me.

I can't make sense of you. Never could. You wax lyrical over lapwings and then you leave a man to burn in a hotel room. You're a husband and father but you fuck some desperate barmaid in a car. You got to burn things up Yan, like some pyromaniac kid, just to watch the flames burning bright. And I pushed you away because I didn't understand – don't understand. But even now it's not too late. I'm here and you're here and you don't need flames to remind you you're alive. Just make me understand.

But he's lying back on the pillow, shrunken and dazed. Hasn't heard a word.

Dan, he says. Didn't know you were still here.

The eyes are calm and grey again. He's just a man. Walked around on the earth for a while. He happened to people and people happened to him. Not much walking to be done, now. To the toilet and back, a few more times.

You were talking in your sleep, I say. It's nothing. Nothing at all.

Downstairs, Jean is going out of the back door. Looks flustered when I come downstairs and see her, turns and stands framed in the light with a holdall in her hand like she's been caught.

I can't do this, she says.

The light on her hair, lifting out the silver threads.

It doesn't matter, I say. I understand.

Tell him, she says. Tell him I'll be thinking of him.

I will.

He's got you, she says. He's not on his own.

Aye.

She tries to smile, her face gaunt, and then she's gone. I go out and stand for a moment in the darkened yard, smelling the smoky air of February and listening to dogs bark in a hundred, in a thousand back yards, growing fainter and fainter across Hartlepool and dying away like smoke.

23. Eider

(Somateria mollissima)

Yan had a smell that was peculiar to him and real like an old sofa. It encompassed cigarettes and stale sweat, leather and blood. But it was more than those things and less. I'd more or less airbrushed the man out of the official photos. There was a gap on the balcony where he once stood, between me and Kate and Lenin. But I couldn't legislate for that smell and if he'd said something or done something right then I would have thrown myself on that smell and foundered upon it. But he didn't, and I didn't. We sat back down in the armchairs by the fire.

Dan, he said.

He began rolling up a cigarette, nimbly twisting the paper in the fingers of one hand, dispensing a wisp of tobacco and securing it with a dab of spit. A match flared and he sucked at the tiny roll-up. Clots of smoke dribbled from his nostrils.

I'll take one of them, I said.

He looked at me sharply.

It's a mug's game. You should give it up, before it does you some damage.

I will. Just not tonight.

He seemed to relax, handed me the tobacco pouch.

Keep forgetting you're seventeen.

Sixteen.

Aye. Sixteen.

I clumsily fashioned a cigarette and lit up. Smoke sprouted in the room as the day collapsed into exhaustion, and the coals of our cigarettes flared.

So, he said, tell me. How did you get your face rearranged? How's your mam?

I told him, as night gathered and rain still thrummed outside. About the afternoon on the beach, only hours ago but already dropping into eclipse. Watched his face grow gaunt and bleak and the firelight across his skin turn to ash. Thoughts in his head congealing into a cold hard mass like a neutron star and the smoke flickering from his mouth like dragon's breath. When I finished he ground the nub of his cigarette into the ashtray, mashing the filter right into the glass. Jonah appeared with two more cans. Yan took one and popped the ring pull with a hiss. Took a long gulp of the yeasty fluid.

Now you, I said.

He yawned and stretched. What?

Tell me about you.

We've got unfinished business, you and me. We'll get that out of the way first. Get my head down for a bit, and we'll go in the morning.

Jonah hovered.

You've kept the boy waiting three years, he said. We've got all night, and there's plenty of sleeping when you're dead.

Yan looked at him hard. It's a long story, he said. It can wait.

He rummaged in his pocket, held out a big old-fashioned lighter. Firelight trickled over the brass skin.

Brought this back from the Falklands. You can have it.

He dropped it into my hand. I tested its weight, shook it. Put it down on the arm of the chair.

It's empty, I said.

Here you go, said Jonah, standing by the bed. This'll keep you warm. Real eiderdown, this. Warm as toast. Used to belong to the old man. When he first came over from Barbados he didn't half feel the cold.

He tossed a thick maroon quilt down over me, threadbare but miraculously warm. I tucked it around me, up and over my aching head, the feathers of long-dead birds trapping my fugitive body heat in a secure cocoon.

So I slid into sleep and a curtain of rain swept aside and a raft of ducks huddled on the sea, wrinkles of grey water lifting and falling beneath the large soft bodies. Big vermiculated females like brindled cats in tabby and tortoiseshell, shrugging and shuffling their backs as the rain pockmarked the water, deep and watchful black eyes on the half-grown chicks clustered between. Rain craters grew and spread as the sea squall passed over, and the coast swam into view, the mouth of the Tees with the long sweep of pale sand to the north.

The estuary tide lifted and fell with a sleeper's breath and slipped back like a skin over miles of wet and metallic mudflats and mudbanks, creeks and runnels. And befuddling numbers of dunlin and sanderling, redshank and greenshank and knot, godwit and ruff, curlew and whimbrel and oystercatcher, grey plover and golden plover, scampered and delved like black ants and rose into the air and blew and twisted like hanks of dark smoke. The rain parted and I startled awake in a grey room in a grey house in Seaton Carew. A grey wind toyed with the window glass and it groaned like a wobbleboard. Everything hurt. I raised a hand to my throbbing face, felt the tracery of dried blood across my nose.

I lay for a while gazing at the ceiling of Jonah's box room. There was a broken patch in it. He must have slipped, up in the loft, put his foot through the ceiling. Cracks radiated from the point of impact like a star. I thought of the luminous stars I had stuck to my bedroom ceiling in the pub, how they glowed with a sick green light in the dark. A child's universe made of plastic. There wasn't much left of that universe. Less and less with each day.

Could you do with a cup of tea Dan? said Jonah, shouldering through the door and offering a mug to me, steam billowing. I rubbed my eyes and propped myself up on the pillows, then took the mug, cupping its heat between my palms. Sipped at the scalding liquid, felt the peaty tannins nibbling at my stomach.

It's nearly dinnertime, said Jonah. He's already up.

I'm not coming, I said. I've had enough of it.

You're coming, he said.

Grey eyes and a bald patch. Sparse and wispy hair. A cigarette clamped between his lips. Seized me by the upper arm, fingers like an iron grab. Propelled me out of the door into bitter morning light, into a car I'd never seen before. Then he was driving and I was in the passenger seat next to him.

Where did you get the car?

Cologne. She bought it for me.

Who?

I lost my soul. She helped me get it back.

The red car ran quietly along the edge of the estuary, across the reclaimed land, taut green fields lifting and falling in the wind, pylons striding out alongside. Ahead was the blue skeleton of the Transporter and the giant sheds of the Swan Hunter yards. We drove for years without speaking. On the southern shore, blast furnaces coughed themselves into life one by one, and a small town shimmered into being, reticent at first, then spreading in wrinkle upon wrinkle of terraced housing, rippling like a tattooed skin across the land until it broke against the dark flanks of the Eston Hills. From the outermost points of the estuary twin breakwaters grew like the shy horns of a snail, shaped from cold impurities shattered like brittle toffee. The swollen furnaces roared day and night and the sky bloomed orange. Tides lifted and fell, and behind the northern breakwater new sea walls snaked across the mud like varicose veins. Mudflats hardened into fields as green and square as stamps blowing in an album, and from the fields sprang a silver forest of metallic vines and creepers, mushrooms and tubers, stamens and stigmata, sepals and petals, breathing the sour spores of transpiration into the sky. Gas flares wove their delicate flames and the whole estuary was a living thing, hissing and humming and grumbling inside my head.

The car drifted up past the old shipyards to where a solitary building stood on the corner. Tired paintwork, peeling maroon gloss around the windows and the door. Turned onto the abandoned lot next door and the tyres crunched over gravel and cinder. The engine stopped and nothing happened for a long time. The man next to me sat drumming on the wheel with his thumbs.

One by one the furnaces blinked out, melting into landscapes of rubble and wire mesh. The metallic jungle was in retreat, whole swathes clear-felled and logged out, leaving isolated stands back-to-back in defiance. The concrete husk of a power station blew along the shore before gripping the marram grass and putting down roots.

You go in first, he said. Check it out. Don't acknowledge me when I come in. When it all kicks off, we'll get busy.

The room was busy. Sunday lunch, always a few in. The mouths of the drinkers flapped open and shut, disclosing pimpled and discoloured tongues, rows of uneven tobacco-stained teeth. Their faces distended in laughter, they gesticulated across the bar, clouds of smoke bloomed from them. Hagan and his mates were clustered around the pool tables, fagsmoke curdling beneath the overhead lights. Cue leapt into ball and ball thumped into pocket.

They didn't see me, and I sidled over to the bar. Michelle's rodent eyes flickered to me as she worked the pump but she didn't say nothing. The place felt clean and sharp, hard light on dark wood. Swept clean by sea and wind.

And a man came through the door. A tramp, or a pikey. He came to the bar and Michelle served him and his eyes moved over her, lingered on her bare legs. When he had his pint he knocked it back and put the glass back on the bar and rubbed tentatively at his bald spot. The dregs of the beer sank down the sides of the glass and pooled in the base. Then he walked over to the pool table and put some change down.

Magoo looked at him.

It's a closed table, he said. No pikeys.

He picked up the money and hurled it and it ricocheted from walls and tables in hailstones of light and metal. Franco pushed the tramp in the chest and he slipped and went down and sprawled on his arse on the floor. You could see it in his face, biting into the touchpaper, cold as the sea. Michelle was smirking behind the bar and he looked over at her, just for a moment. Then he got carefully to his feet and went over to where Hagan was leaning against one of the tables with them slabby arms crossed over his chest. Behind him Lovebite fed the jukebox and began to dance with an imaginary lass.

They looked at each other. The hardbitten derelict in the shabby leather jacket and Hagan inflated double his size with that steroid face and gelled hair and single gold hoop.

You ever play for proper money in here? said the derelict.

Hagan broke into a grin and slapped him on the back, one of the trimmed eyebrows rakishly raised.

What's your name pal?

Dermot.

That's a pikey name. You a gyppo?

If you say so.

Dermot produced a bundle of wedge and placed it down on the rail. Took a cue from the rack and rested the butt down with one fingernail tapping against the tip.

There's a couple of thou there, said Hagan.

Like I said, proper money.

Where d'you get it? Scrap metal? You must be the king of the gyppos mate.

If you say so.

Michelle shovelled notes from the till and handed them over to Hagan and he slapped them down on the table. Then he stepped up and put his ball on the break line and began.

I was sat at the bar but I couldn't taste the lager. They drew in around the table and Lovebite stopped his dance. They cast crisp shadows, sharp as a blade, in the white light streaming through the street windows. Dancing like moths.

Hagan started his usual routine, bullying the balls with muscle. Blasted the pack from the break and got two reds direct. He swaggered round the table and the onlookers gave him room. Started to put a break together but ran out of position and left one on the jaws. Raised his eyes to heaven. I followed his gaze, up to the artex ceiling. Whorls and scallops in the yellowing plaster, dagger-sharp.

Dermot came to the table, grinned.

You got to take them by surprise, he said. When they're not looking.

They laughed at him and he cued way off line and sent the ball squirting wide. Hagan smirked. Potted two more reds. There was a fly, trapped between two panels of the sash window. I watched it ricochet desperately from pane to pane. The bottle-green sheen of the body, the miraculous structure of the compound eye, the honeycomb of spiracles. Dead in a moment. Hagan planted the last red into the corner. Smiled broadly, the cue ball still scooting around the angles.

I looked at the security glass in the door, crazed and impact-rippled long ago but never replaced. Light crawled over the surface and rattled off a million facets, off the capillaries of wire mesh running through each shard. It seemed to resolve into a human face, mouth open and each tooth a talon of glass. Then it splintered into white noise.

The cue ball plopped into the middle pocket and the smile dropped from Hagan's face. He retrieved it and replaced it on the break line, not looking too bothered. He only had the black left and Dermot hadn't potted a ball. I gripped the bar stool beneath my backside, metal tubing and vinyl cladding. It gave an arthritic squeak, shifted and trembled under me.

Dermot hunkered down over the table and his grey eyes sparkled.

Charm, he said. Got to charm them in, not bully them.

But the white span comically off his cue again and missed all the yellows. The room dissolved into laughter and Hagan shook his head.

You taking the piss?

I'm trying me best son. Just getting me eye in, like.

An ashtray next to me on the bar, mounded high with cigarette butts, some still smouldering, others with smears of vermilion lipstick. Sour smoke rose, the agglomerated butts bristling like a hedgehog.

Hagan was on the black. He sighted on it and thumped the shot hard, but the ball rattled between the jaws like a beam of light refracted in a prism. Stopped. Hagan examined the baize and picked a tiny glittering fragment of something out of the nap. It was broken glass. He flicked it across the room.

Now I reckon my luck's in, said Dermot, twirling his cue.

He pinged the cue ball into a clutch of yellows and the balls leapt like a shoal of fish awakened by the sun. Two straight to pockets and another two on the jaws. More balls rattling home like wayward comets. At the window, net curtains shifted lazily on gentle draughts of air. Ethereal limbs, spun from nicotine-yellow material, floated out into the room, gesticulated, and sank.

Now he was on the black.

Come to daddy, he said, with a wink at Hagan. Dynamited the ball around the table from cushion to cushion, sucking the room towards it. The ball slowed, flopped lazily off the side cushion. There was an intake of breath. The black plopped square into the corner pocket.

Dermot grinned and picked up the pile of notes. Their mouths opened and closed. No words, just the sound of insects feeding, an army of locusts on the move. Trajan bounded into the bar with spittle lashing from his jowls and jumped straight at him with paws on his shoulders and muzzle in his face. Dermot pushed him down but Hagan was looking at him, looking deep into his eyes. Saw the clouds racing across the sea, saw the mountainous waves streaming in ranges towards the shore. Recognition dawned. Yan grinned like a loon and slammed the butt of his cue into Hagan's face.

I've seen any number of pub fights. It's a respectable pastime in this town. We play down the violence. Talk about a bit of chew, a barney.

That's rhyming slang, by the way. Barney Rubble. The chew explodes out of nowhere and subsides almost as quick, like a sudden squall of bitter weather. And five minutes later you might be shaking hands and looking sheepish over your pints. But this one was different. This one had to be pursued like a theorem, right down to the proof.

There was a welter of movement, pumped-up tattooed flesh thrashing and bellowing like cattle on the killing floor. Hagan collapsing like a slaughtered ox, Yan slamming Lovebite's head through the window and into the street, turning to thump a roundhouse into Magoo's guts. Drinkers were going for the door, knocking over furniture in panic. Yan grabbed Magoo by the ears and planted a knee into his face and Michelle was stock-still behind the bar, absolutely entranced.

His eyes, looking at me out of the middle of it. Open and grey and full of the sea, mobile as weather systems over the Baltic.

Franco backed Yan towards the juke box with a lager bottle in each hand. Burst each one against the pool table and thrust the jagged ends out in front.

The eyes were looking again. I stayed rooted to the stool. He wanted me to help. It bothered him. Then the door to the bar fluttered open and Paul O'Rourke stood there, grinning like a mule with his newly shaven head shining like the moon.

I love a barney, me, he said.

And he rampaged towards Franco, bisected them broken bottles and stuck the nut on him sweet and square as you ever saw. Franco's nose exploded like a barrage balloon and his blood and snot lashed across Paul's face.

But Hagan wasn't finished. He arose from his wreck on the floor and launched himself at Yan. The two of them in this staggering thrashing embrace, half fight and half fuck. Colour drained out of it and they carried on in monochrome, flickering like a silent film. Paul grabbed Hagan from behind and his teeth sought out that gold hoop and ripped it triumphantly from the lobe. Hagan bellowed and the back of his napper battered into Paul's face but Paul held on, twining his legs and arms round the thrashing body while Yan groped for a pool cue. He began to flog Hagan about the head and shoulders, the cue rising and falling like a scythe until it snapped and the tip clattered to the ground in slow motion, bouncing slow across the floor of the bar like it was the surface of the moon. And Yan belaboured Hagan with the splintered shaft, his jaw set in concentration and his muscles jumping and bunching with the effort, and Hagan lost consciousness and slumped down but Yan carried on. The bar became dark, splashes of light and shadow moving slow and attenuated. He was a broken spring, shuddering and flailing, the stump of the pool cue still moving like a pendulum in his hand.

When I got back to Jonah's I found him in the kitchen, peeling potatoes over the sink.

Thought I'd rustle up some chips, he said. Can't afford the oven ones. Anyway, I prefer it the old-fashioned way. No E numbers. Just good honest grease. The peeler flickered over the tubers, exposing the ghostly white flesh.

Don't you want to know what happened?

Jonah bent over the potatoes, brow furrowing.

I know what happened. He was always hard to handle, your old man. Burnt a short fuse. Many times I've been glad he was around, though.

I leaned heavily against the edge of the kitchen table, the wood grating uncomfortably into my coccyx.

Why were you glad?

Jonah's hands raced across potato after potato, dropping each naked vegetable into a bowl of cold water. They shimmered, like underwater corpses.

Imagine what it was like growing up half-caste around here, in the sixties. If people gave you chew you had to give it back. With interest. If you didn't teach them a lesson they wouldn't leave you alone. You couldn't opt out of it. That's why it was good having Yan around.

The potatoes were finished and he rinsed the sink out with scalding water, steam billowing from the stainless steel. He opened a drawer and produced a kitchen knife, dull and ominous. He chopped each potato in turn, first into thick slices driving down hard on the heel of the knife, and then quickly chipping each slice into long wedges, the blade rapping against the chopping board as he did so.

I can opt out, I said.

The blade clattered through another slice of potato.

How do you mean?

Yan's the same as Hagan. Stags goring each other with antlers. Tom cats ripping each other to shreds. Wild animals turning on each other in rage. We're more than that. We must be.

Jonah smiled, and laid the knife down flat for a moment, the blade dull with starch.

You're idealistic, he said. I was the same at your age.

I rolled up my sleeve, showed him the purple bruising around my bicep. The livid, metallic brand of a man's hand, where Yan had gripped my arm this morning.

Jonah placed the basket of chips into the deep fat fryer, and the golden oil simmered energetically, a deep rolling bubble.

I don't want to be like that, I said. Jonah looked at me sideways, sweat breaking out at his temples.

None of us want to be like that, he said. Not in the beginning, anyway.

We ate the scalding chips in silence on our laps with salt smeared across them and globules of deep red ketchup on each plate. Once, I looked up and caught Jonah's eye. He looked away.

I went back up to bed, though it was only mid-afternoon, pulled the eiderdown over my head. The scene in the pub came back. Paul stretched out a hand, grey as the dusk, and touched Yan's shoulder. Yan looked startled. He examined the cue in his hand like he was surprised to find it there, let it drop to the floor beside Hagan's body. As the light began to flicker, the projector slowing towards a halt, the strobe lamp caught his face, gaunt and bony. He turned towards the younger man and clapped him on the shoulder and the two of them locked eyes.

Breeze lifted the nets at the window and light roved over the shattered security glass in the door. And now Yan and Paul were struggling with a bundle between them. Black plastic like a rubbish sack, shimmering in folds and trussed with gaffer tape. Where the tape was stretched tight it revealed the shape of a man's face. Nostrils, the tip of a nose, the channel at the centre of the upper lip.

Give us a hand, Dan. He's fucking deadweight.

I stayed rooted to the stool. Yan caught sight of Michelle, still behind the bar, pale face turned towards him.

Get the fuck out of my pub, he said. You whore.

And then Kate was in the doorway. She stared at them, stared at me. Took in the broken glass and smashed furniture.

Yan, she said, her voice quavering.

Indulge me my sweet, he said. Some unfinished business, and then I am yours until the end of time.

She stood there, paralysed.

Outside in the yard they dumped the package inside the boot, Trajan jumping excitedly as Yan slammed the lid down. They were laughing, faces vibrant, and they lit cigarettes behind cupped hands, balloons of smoke rising from open mouths. Then the car started and they were gone. Rain moved in from the North Sea and hid them from view, and the projector finally jammed, the heat of the bulb melting through the frail acetate and consuming it in a pure flame of luminous white silence.

And I fled from them, out to where a raft of ducks huddled on the sea, wrinkles of grey water lifting and falling beneath them. The sea flowed into my ears and I could hear the eiders gabbling quietly, the black orbs becoming opaque with sleep. I moved close to the large, soft bodies, seeking their protection, and they shifted to accommodate me. Rain craters grew and spread as a sea squall passed over, and the coast swam into view, the mouth of the Tees with the long sweep of pale sand to the north.

24. **Raven**

(*Corvus corax*)

She's got another bloke, says Matt. In case you were wondering.

He's sat opposite me in the portakabin with a crinkly smile on his face and a roll-up wedged between his lips.

Clare, he continues. She don't hang around long, and apparently you didn't get in touch.

Seeing my confusion, he creases into a grin.

No secrets in our profession, you see. It's the long hours in the pub, steaming yourself dry. All comes out in the end.

Glad to have provided some amusement.

I manage a wry smile.

Well, he continues, conspiratorially, I'm not sure you even did that. Apparently you were a very poor shag.

He wiggles a little finger at me, eyes sparkling. A moment of silence while my cheeks begin to burn, and then Matt explodes with laughter, teeth glittering in his beard.

Just joking, he says. She didn't provide that much detail. But you should have seen your face.

I laugh along with him, relieved.

The webcam, he says. All packed up and ready to go. We'll just load it into the back of your van. I'll miss the old thing, you know. Got used to having my ugly coupon beamed around the world every day.

Your loss is the world's gain, I quip.

Matt chuckles.

Got something to show you, he says, before you go. Always happens on the last day.

He gets up from the table and I follow him outside into a gunmetal grey afternoon. We step gingerly across the site, mud squelching over shoes, rubbing up the insides of trouserlegs.

Remember having a rant at you, your first time on site, Matt says. About the past. Being a fucked-up place we'll never get our heads round. Something like that. Well, what Julie found this morning is the proof of the pudding.

Iron Age pit, says Julie, when we reach her. Bloody big one, too.

Her estuary accent twangs in the northern twilight, pale face like a moon beneath the hard hat.

Used 'em for storing grain, supposedly, Matt says. But when they'd finished, they filled them up with weird stuff. Broken pots, bits of animals, even bits of people. Not just rubbish. Kind of arranged in there, deliberately. Like it meant something.

A bit of insurance, Julie butts in. That's my theory. Putting something back, like planting little seeds, to make sure it all grew back again. Regenerated. People and crops and animals and pots.

Never seen anything like this but, says Matt.

We crane out over the deep pit, excavated into dark grey glacial clay, and look down. In the gloom, it appears that a huge bird has been crucified. It lies on its back on a plinth of black soil, wings outstretched to each side. The late-afternoon light ripples over the pure white bones, turning each one a pale arctic blue.

Dunno what species it is, Matt says. Bird of prey? Whatever, it's been laid out down there, freshly dead. Bones are still articulated. Then they covered it over with earth, and there it stayed for three thousand years.

It's a raven, I say. *Corvus corax*. Like a bloody big crow. Look at the size of the thing. Birds of prey have a hooked bill, for tearing at meat, but look at that one. It's just a bludgeon. An axe. Pure power.

Twitcher, beams Matt. Wouldn't ravens have evolved in the meantime, though?

No. Been the same for millions of years, millions of generations down the line. Ancients, they are. Not like us. We're the greenhorns on this planet. And they never forget. Got everything they need wired in, instinctive.

We're the buggers with collective amnesia, laughs Matt.

Even so, I say. The past doesn't trouble them. A single bright moment. That's all a bird worries about.

Better get on with it, says Julie. The light's going. Photos tomorrow?

Matt nods and Julie vaults back into the pit and hunches over the skeleton, brushing crumbs of soil from the eye sockets, the massive bill and broad sternum. The two of us stand in silence for a moment, looking out over the heavy fields and the gurgling lights of a newborn conurbation towards the muscular hills straining at the leash. Not very long ago, in the same place, somebody not so different from ourselves arranged a dead raven, still warm, in a half-filled pit. They took a shovelful of earth, then a second and a third, and emptied them over the coal black feathers, the crumbly loam mounting until the glossy body was hidden from view.

Just come. As soon as you can, he says, the voice urgent.

I sigh and look at Kelly, who's strenuously avoiding my glance.

I'm in the middle of something. I'll come as soon as I've finished here.

I snap the phone shut. Kelly sighs.

Was that really him on the phone? she says. Sometimes I think he's just inside your head.

He's dying, Kelly.

It's too convenient, she says. It's like you're having a conversation with yourself.

She's gathered in the corner of the sofa, thighs encased in tight denim, firmly crossed like a giant nutcracker. Looks at me incisively, blue eyes calm. That slight hint of a sneer about her upper lip.

Anyway, get your dinner, she says. There's some beer in the fridge as well. Then we need to talk.

Not hungry, I say. You can tell me now, whatever it is.

She sighs again, and sets her face.

I've made you some salad. You need to start eating properly.

I'm not sitting around noshing with *we need to talk* hanging over me. You've started it, so tell me what's going on.

At least have a beer, she says, in a small, tight voice, devoid of emotion. Unfolds herself and pads to the fridge, baggy shirt swirling around her curves. Hands me an ice-cold cylinder and I pop the ringpull before swigging the metallic liquid.

Real German lager, I say. Brewed in Luton.

She doesn't smile.

I'm moving out, she says.

It's like a blow in the stomach. I feel nauseous and light-headed, the beer rusty inside me.

There's a flat, she goes on, over Miriam's shop. She says I can have it in the short term, until I find somewhere permanent.

Hang on, I say. We can talk things through. It's like you haven't given me a chance.

She thinks for a moment before replying, twisted towards me on the sofa.

We don't want the same things any more Dan. I think it's had all the chance it's going to get.

'I can't help feeling you need a little more excitement in your life.'

You read my letter.

Yeah, so I read your letter. Add that to the list of grievances. Nice to know you discuss me with your friends.

I put the beer can down half drunk, no longer have the stomach for it.

I thought once we were through the IVF. Once we were through –

My voice rising desperately. She interrupts.

You'd have found something else. After your dad's dead, there'll be something else. A crisis at work, whatever. As long as it keeps you paralysed, stops you from acting.

It's not too late.

It's just not right. Not any more. We could go upstairs now and have sex, but it wouldn't be right. Something's broken.

I sit for a moment, rub my thumbnails together.

You haven't asked me whether there's someone else, she says.

I wondered. All the nights you've been away.

Well, there wasn't. Just stayed with a mate. Better than lying in that cold bed with you, back-to-back like bookends. Whereas you, she says, pointedly.

What?

Who is she Dan? Miranda saw her getting out of your car at the station. Nice little peck on the cheek, by all accounts. Someone classy, or just a whore from over the border?

Jesus, it's like the fucking Stasi, I groan. It happened once. All them nights you weren't here, the house cold and empty. I was lonely, I got drunk, and I slept with somebody. It was the first and last time.

She looks straight ahead, eyes boring into the wall.

Look, I say, I'll spare you the platitudes. I crossed the line. I stepped outside our marriage, and it scared me. Not a day goes by when it doesn't sicken me. And I know things haven't been right. But we haven't tried yet. Let's work through it, eh? Marriage guidance, counselling, whatever it takes. I thought we were in this for the long haul.

She's looking straight ahead, her face furrowed in concentration. She takes a deep breath.

We could spend a lot of time and effort working on it, she says, picking her words. And it might make things better. But it's not what I want any more.

She delivers this verdict like a stone dropped through a grille, into an abandoned mineshaft. I listen as it descends silently through acres of bitter darkness, and hear the dull and empty echo as it strikes bottom.

I've had enough, says the skeleton in the bed, abruptly.

He swallows and I can see the sinews and tendons in his jaw scrape together under the skin and hear the sand and gravel in the voice. He sucks deep at the oxygen mask, chest wheezing and rattling.

Pull the curtains, he says, eyes burning larger than ever in the emaciated face.

I scan for a nurse in the darkened ward, but all seems quiet. Draw the pastel pink curtains around the bed. Diffuse pink light softens Yan's expression.

It's time, he says. I want to go. To the hospice. Get a wheelchair.

Are you sure? I say. Hospital were talking about getting you stabilized again, sending you home. They don't think things are that far advanced.

His face cracks and a sharp laugh barks out.

Advanced. That's a good one. Try *drowning in my own fluids*. Slowly. Ask them to give me. A leaflet about that one.

Outside the drawn curtain a trolley rattles up the long ward, crockery rattling.

Before too long. I'm going to be incapable Dan. I can't let them have control over me. It's got to be now.

I can do it, he says, when I offer to help him. He levers his body, still in the hospital gown, across the gap, his chest rattling and veins jumping out on his temples. He settles into the wheelchair, breathing heavy and shallow.

I could murder. A fucking ciggy, he says, grinning. Get the oxygen.

I raise an eyebrow, detach the oxygen cylinder from the wall and hang it from the back of the chair. Hand him the mask.

You're still in your hospital gown, I say. You'll freeze.

There's a coat. In the locker, he says.

I open the door and pull out his old donkey jacket, huge and black and frayed. It gives off that sharp scent of old sweat and cigarettes. Tears spring to my eyes and I force them back. Drape the jacket around his thin shoulders, tuck it behind his back. He reaches out a hand and turns the collar up and we move out through the pink curtain and into the ward, heading for the lift.

Out in the car park the black bulk of the hospital juts into a night sky low and damp with the orange gloaming of Stockton. I look up at the windows, postage stamps of light in the flanks of the vast building. Yan transfers himself from the chair to the passenger seat, straining and grunting but accepting no help. I slot the oxygen cylinder into the footwell between his knees, hand him the mask.

Thanks Doris, he says. Fold up the chair and. Put it in the boot. Have you got a tyre lever? And a torch?

In the boot, I say. Why?

He smiles enigmatically, skin puckering like vellum.

At the Glebe shops he taps my arm and motions for me to pull over. I find a parking space.

Golden Virginia, he says. Green Rizla. You're paying.

I look at him in disbelief.

Last request of. A dying man, he croaks, eyes twinkling.

I get out of the car, swearing under my breath. Buy the tobacco and papers, dodge through a group of kids banging a football against the parade of shops. They look at me blankly with eyes like stones and I hurry back to the car and hand him the little bundle. He takes it and palms it into his jacket pocket with a wink. As we approach Norton roundabout he leans over.

Straight on here, he says, tapping my arm.

Hospice is right, I say, flipping the indicator on and drifting over into the right-hand lane.

We're going. Straight on, says Yan, in a firm metallic voice.

He flips the indicator off and I cut back into the middle lane. A horn blares behind me.

Where are we going? I say, irritated.

You'll see, he says. How's Kelly?

I fight back tears again, grimly.

She's fine, I say. More than fine. She's really sorting herself out.

Good, he says. She's a smart lass.

*

Julie levers her body down into the pit from above. It's another leaden day, still dark around the edges, and the developer's machines are at work on the plot next door, a flock of metal geese on the winter fields with yellow articulated necks rising and falling, taking huge bites of soil and subsoil and clay. She kneels down next to the skeleton, pulls a large finds bag from her pocket, and begins with the tip of her trowel to lift a bone at a time and slip it inside. Beginning at the feet. No reason, just personal preference. Jelly babies, chocolate santas, gingerbread men. Saving the best bit for last. The head, studded with sweets. The brute beak like a bludgeon. Tarsals and metatarsals first, the long toes and claws. Then she moves on to the legs, the strange flexures of ankle and knee, the bones flipping easily from the crumbly soil inside the pit.

The Cape of Good Hope, he says. Funny to see part of your life. Turned into archaeology.

He plonks himself down on the stump of the chimney breast. Surveys the rubble, wall footings poking out among the brick fragments, the chunks of concrete, the broken glass. I can see his bony legs under the gown, purple with varicose veins, hospital slippers still on his feet. The donkey jacket, now securely buttoned up, looks incongruous above this.

Ever been back Dan?

No. I've driven past, like. Never wanted to stop.

He produces a roll-up from his jacket pocket, already assembled into that characteristic matchstick-thin form. The lighter blossoms like a pallid moth in the darkness and I hear him cough gently. He pulls smoke wilfully into the ruined lungs, but not with the usual deep and satisfied inhalations. Instead, he takes short and furtive drags, the smoke emerging from mouth and nostrils almost immediately. I can't equate this little plot with the rambling building where I spent my childhood. Above us floats the space where we ate and slept and dreamed and argued, now liberated from earth and materiality.

Kate, he says. Used to see ghosts. Right where you're standing.

Me too, I think. They never hung around long enough to be sure. Always out of the corner of my eye. Something moving or shimmering. Turned out to be a fucking gas leak anyway.

Oh aye?

Yeah. That old boiler was pissing carbon monoxide. Not enough to kill us but enough to give you weird dreams. Hallucinations, like.

The ghosts were just gas dreams, he says. I'm almost sorry about that. Maybe we're just gas dreams Danny. The whole thing.

He shivers and the rain drifts across.

Time has moved past me, he says. Pretty soon I'll be marooned. Like some island you look back at. When you're steaming past on the ferry.

That'll be some island, I say. A dramatic landscape.

Oh aye. Contorted mountains and brooding lochs. Snowfields and glaciers. Volcanoes blasting lava.

That's the difference between you and me, I say. I'd settle for the warm house and the cat curled up on my lap, for a patch of garden and a patch of sky. I'd be watching a flock of starlings unfurl like a silk scarf. You'd be scouring the bushes for a Siberian vagrant.

Yan opens his mouth. Closes it again.

Remember Paul? I say. Coming through the door right there with that maniac smile on his face, steaming right into Franco.

Aye. I remember.

Tell me what you and Paul did with Hagan. You wrapped him in black plastic and you put him in the boot. You drove off and nobody saw him again.

Pest control, he says.

Did you kill him?

The question seems to spill from the ruined fabric of the pub.

He laughs, shakes his head.

All in good time.

And what about Michelle?

She was a smack rat.

Only after you kicked her out. They took her baby into care. Found

Michelle strung up from a light socket in the Social Club bogs.

I never made her sleep with them spare pricks, he snaps. Stupid bitch. And I never sold her the gear.

He gets painfully to his feet.

Danny, he says. I'm running out of breath.

I catch him by the arm and we totter back to the car where he drinks hungrily from the mask.

After the feet and legs, Julie moves on to the spine and the ribcage. The vertebrae come first, little knurled punctuation marks of bone knotted into one another like a jigsaw. She picks each one out separately, beginning at the tail end, revealing the empty channel where the spinal column of the bird once ran, where neural signals pulsed and jumped like a river of electricity. She drops the last of the vertebrae into the skeleton bag like a strange variety of boiled sweet. Then she moves on to the ribs, peeling them up from the ground, long and slender and easy.

Yan hunches in the car like an old feller with his spine sagging. We drive back along the northern edge of the site. It was once an impenetrable forest of steel and pipework but now it's much sparser, clearings of open ground between the surviving plantations, expanses of gravel and rubble where colonies of willow herb flutter in summer.

Pull over, he says. Into the car park.

But there are concrete blocks across the entrance so I stop on the roadside and we look up at the building, a cast concrete hulk eight storeys high. Used to be the main admin offices for the whole site, the largest chemical operation in Europe. Now it's derelict and surrounded by mesh fencing with the windows and doors boarded shut. Stark notices warn of dog patrols. Plants have got their roots in between the concrete panels in the car park and are prising them apart.

Billingham House, he says. Had my first job here, way back. Didn't last long, mind. Get the wheelchair. And the tyre lever.

He opens the door and begins to prise himself out. I grab at his sleeve.

Hang on, I say. What's going on?

He rights himself outside the car and bends creakily down to peer inside.

We're going. For a walk.

I kill the engine and walk wearily round to retrieve the chair. It snaps back into shape without putting up much of a struggle. Yan subsides into it.

Where to? I say.

He points into the car park like a maharajah directing an elephant.

It's locked up, I protest. There's security. Asbestos.

Asbestos, he barks. Now I'm fucking scared.

I make my way over to the fencing. The nuts joining the panels are only finger tight, so I fumble at the cold metal and free a panel to create a path for the chair. Then we're in the car park, wheels rumbling gently across the perishing concrete. We reach the base of the offices, where the barbed wire of bramble and elder is starting to coil from cracks and crevices.

Use the tyre lever, Yan says. Open some of the boarding. And we can get in.

This is mental, I blurt out in exasperation, passing a hand across my crown. It's dangerous in there. They've stripped out everything – there are open shafts from top to bottom, eight floors deep. And you're in no condition to go in. We'll get ourselves arrested.

A long pause. Yan raises himself slowly from the chair, hands braced against the frame, and stands facing me.

I need to die on my feet, he says. Not in a bed. Not swimming in a night sweat of morphine. On my feet, like a king in the Dark Ages. This has gone on too long. I've been letting you. Do it your way. But now I'm taking back control. I need to see the flames of the Chimera. One last time.

You can do what you like, I say, bitterly. You always did. But I don't have to be part of it. I'll be in the car.

I turn away and start to walk back towards the broken fence.

Danny.

The power of his voice stops me and I turn round. He is still standing, gaunt and unsupported, by the chair, the tails of his gown blowing about his ankles in the spare wind.

I can't get up there. Without you. If you help me, I'll finish the story. You'll know everything.

She looks at the outstretched wings and feels loath to disturb them. Once the wrists and fingerbones of an earthbound reptile, stretched by time into these miraculous structures. Birds don't even think about it, do they? The way crows just stroll into the air without thinking. You're about to hit the brakes, but they simply step backwards and gust into the air, out of harm's way. Julie begins to prise up the metacarpals and carpals, and then the delicate radius and ulna, entwined like creepers.

Inside the building I flip the torch on. Concentric circles of watery light illuminate the bare interior of a lobby with a concrete stair leading up towards the next floor. There's a corridor running away into darkness like a derelict mineral working, and the torch throws deep, startling shadows of Old Testament black. Yan points towards the stairwell and waves away my offer of help. He holds on to the banister and begins to drag himself up the stairs, lifting and placing each foot deliberately, veins standing out in his neck and sweat clustering at his temples. We reach the next landing and he pauses, gasping for breath. I flick the torch down abandoned galleries running away along the seams of the night, and we climb on, footfall echoing dully through the empty concrete halls.

By the sixth floor he's almost gone. Visibly diminished, shrivelling slowly into the night.

I knew, he says. I'd have to climb those stairs. In the end. Face what was at the top.

Your dream, I say.

Yes. It's funny. How you end up. In the same place. However much you struggle. Maybe that was the truth. I died there. And this track is shrivelling up now. Almost nothing left.

There's plenty left, I say.

I give him my arm and he grips it and we struggle up the last two flights and our shadows are mocking us in the deepest bitterest black.

Along here, he coughs, showing me the corridor.

We stumble along, looking for the service stairs up onto the roof. Halfway along the corridor two panes of darkness open up in the floor and I shine the torch into one of them and see the light ricochet down eight floors. The damp sides of the lift shaft glitter a dull metallic blue. I stand on the edge and look down and my insides are tingling and one more step would ensnare me in that long slow delicious tumble into the neutron star.

There's a limpid gust of flame as Yan sparks his lighter. The smell of petrol, shadows dancing.

Brought this all the way with me, he says. All the way from the Falklands.

Thought you didn't believe in talismans.

No. Didn't do Jonah no good. Can't believe he span you that line. About Schrödinger's cat.

Said we were caught between life and death. All I had to do was open the box.

It's still shut, he says. Did I die there, or do I die here? Am I a man or a ghost or a gas dream? You bring the hammer down and sparks fly up. Thousands of them. Tunnelling into the night. But every track cools and shrivels and dies.

You're real enough Yan.

Look, he says. What you got to remember is. You aren't in control. You aren't the egghead in the lab coat Danny.

What am I then?

You're the fucking cat boy. We both are. You can never open the box. Live your whole life. Trapped inside it.

Aye, I reckon.

Mind, he says. We can still wave our tails about. Let some fucking air in, eh?

He takes a step but the knotted purple legs give way and before I can reach him he crumples to the floor. I bend down and scoop him up, one arm under his knees and the other round his shoulders. He weighs fuck all and the flesh behind his knee is cold and scaly to the touch and his body close up gives off this sweet odour of decay. I find the doorway and the service stairs and lug him up, trying not to scrape his feet against the walls. He grunts and sighs and drops in and out of consciousness. And we emerge onto the roof, where the mouths of vent shafts and heating flues blossom from the concrete surface. At the edge I set him on his feet. He seems to wake up, supports himself.

The flames of the Chimera, he says.

We're looking out over the shimmering expanses of the Billingham site where constellations of white light are strewn across the transformers, the columns and the converters, sparkling saltily like the winter sky. I can hear the place breathing, a faint hiss and inrush of air followed by a deep contented exhalation. Clouds of vapour drift across the lights, backlit in ghostly white and orange. But above it all are the gas flares, luminous in the pure chemical colours of copper and sodium and potassium, green and turquoise and orange cat tongues flickering at the sky. We watch them silently for what seems like hours, father and son standing close together on the roof while molecules evaporate and burn in the mineral night.

Yan totters over to the rim of a ventilation shaft and perches on it like an emaciated gnome on the edge of a toadstool. Flare-light flickers over the fragile, concave skin of his cheeks. He sucks in a breath.

When me and Paul put Hagan in the car, he says. I was going to do him. No mistake. We took him down Back Saltholme. Off the road. Paul drags him out of the boot. Throws him on the ground. He's off his tits. What are we going to do with him Yan? he kept saying. What are we going to do with him?

His voice is ragged, a saw blade in the night, luminous flame leaping behind him.

Paul started it. Picks up a concrete slab from a pile of rubble. Lashes him over the head with it. He screams like a shrew. That's just seen the cat. And I thought. Yeah, we're going to kill him. Clear and cold, like sea water over me. Hagan's rolling around on the floor. The black bag over his head. Pleading like a snotty kid. Please Yan. Please no. Please mate.

I shivered. It was cold on the roof, heat leaking out into space.

I'm thinking. Grab a bit of slab. Hit him a hundred times. Hit him until the whimpering stops. And there's just a sick wet noise from inside the plastic. Rip his cock off, dripping black blood. And fucking throw it to the dog. I'm pottering about these piles of rubble. Looking for the right bit of slab. That's going to do the job. Try a couple in my hand.

A breeze lifts the sparse hair at his temples. I wait.

But then I thought about that kid. Secundino. What I felt when I plugged him. Plugged him till there was nowt left. When it was finished. That high-pitched whine in my ears. And I took his boots off. Peeled them off over his socks. With the white feet under. There wasn't a windscreen between us Dan. Not any more. Those white perfect feet. I touched them. They were my feet Danny. He was me and I was him. Or even worse than that. They were your feet. And I killed my own son.

Seems like we're hovering at the edge of space. Flames below us. The aurora borealis licking at the world.

I heard Hagan whining inside the bag. There were coot feeding in the lagoon. Redshank stalking through the shallows. A beautiful day. The tide going in and out. I thought about Secundino. His bare foot, in my bare hand. How I felt that warmth dying away. Through the thin skin of his feet. And I walked. Just walked away and left him lying there.

Like you walked away from Mount Longdon.

Just the same. The end and the beginning.

*

We stay there for minutes without talking, but it's getting cold. Yan tries to stand and I take his arm, steer him towards the stairwell. He subsides against me with relief and we work our way down the stairs, moving our limbs carefully and placing them in unison like one creature with four slow feet.

But what happened to Hagan, after you left him there?

Ended up in Pattaya, same as me, he mutters. Skin cancer got him in the end. Should have stayed off them sunbeds.

I wish I'd been there, instead of Paul.

Do you?

Inside the building I flip the torch back on but the batteries are dying and the faint light barely smudges walls and floor. We pick our way back to the open lift shafts, thick stains of shadow in the floor. Yan stops. Takes the brass lighter out of his pocket and holds it out, the metal almost liquid in the darkness.

Here, he says. Tried to give it you. That day at Jonah's.

I didn't want it then.

I always meant to clean it up. Get a new wick, refill it. Get it working again. All the time I was away. All the years in Pattaya. Never got round to it. Just sat in my pocket. It was only when I came back here. When I knew I was ill.

I take it from him, feel the weight. It's heavy, full. I close my hand around it.

Never brought me luck, he says. Maybe it'll bring you some.

He places both hands on my shoulders. The weight is negligible, tiny birds perching there. The warmth drains from his face.

What are you going to do?

I've never been afraid, he says. To jump in the dark. You see, we wrought the world. With our hands. Men like me. Miners, steelmakers, shipbuilders. Like the Greek heroes.

His face is a pale sheen in the dying torchlight, eyes and mouth swallowed in cavernous shadow.

We would rather be full. Of guilt and story. Than be empty and blameless. But our sons are afraid. Call-centre monkeys. And pizza boys. Get their kicks on a computer. Instead of for real.

Maybe we prefer it that way, I say, gently.

I've still got free will, he says. The dice are frozen in motion. Just like the painting. The deep mahogany sheen. Of the tabletop. See, I'm not going to be a lump. In a hospice. They're not going to give me. A fucking leaflet. About this.

He lifts his hands from my shoulders, birds gusting into the air.

Dad, I say. I don't want you to go.

I grab at his upper arms with both hands, but there is nothing under the jacket. The sleeves scrunch uselessly in my fists. Cigarettes and stale sweat, leather and blood. His face still floats there like a mask, beset by shadow.

We took their boots, he says. But it was only a lend. I reckon they'll be wanting them back now.

He glances up as if straining for a sound.

Let them in Danny, he whispers.

Then he steps back into the blackness of the shaft and is gone. And I can hear them thudding at the window boards. The stars are clubbing at the window with blackest boots. All the dark and pitiless boots of the universe, smelling of sweaty leather and banging out a tattoo of hate.

Julie lifts the calcified bubble of the skull, marvelling at its lightness. She turns it in her hand, admiring the stark and massive bill, imagining the brain that once burned behind the empty sockets. Then she slips it into the finds bag with the rest. She seals the bag, running her fingertips along its rim, and brushes stray crumbs of earth from the outside before climbing out of the pit for the last time. She looks down at where the raven lay. There's no imprint in the ground, no sign at all that it ever existed.

25. **Dunlin**

(Calidris alpina)

The summer pisses by like a gas leak only there's nobody left to make a spark. Kelly drops in for her stuff with Miriam's bloke and ends up taking most of the furniture. I haven't the heart to stop her. I'm in the kitchen with my head down on the worktop, sobbing great gobfuls of self-pity. And she stands in the front door with the clean air around her and the wind blowing through from the estuary.

See ya Danny, she says. And her voice is tender and embarrassed and sad and itching to get the hell out of there. Then she closes the door and it makes a good seal. It's one of them white plastic sealed units. Closes me in.

I stay here for an indeterminate time, drinking my own recycled air while the oxygen content dwindles. It's all I can do to get down the garage for a boil-in-the-bag curry and a few packets of dry roasted and a raft of wifebeater. Under the duvet my heart is too loud, whamming in my chest like a piledriver, reverberating through my stomach.

Let them in Danny. How many weeks is it?

Sooner or later the social will come round, because he discharged himself from hospital and didn't check in anywhere else. Sooner or later the police will come round, because they've finished stripping out Billingham House for redevelopment and found him there at the bottom of the shaft. There is a safety net. There are checks and balances. People don't just die and not get found.

It's a crap summer anyway, cold and wet with rain bearing down from the Atlantic in wave on wave. In the front garden the grass is on overdrive but it's never dry enough to cut. We never get them hot summers any more.

It was truer to what he wanted and I thought I owed him that. He wanted that fall into the dark to be the end. He didn't want them scraping around in the bottom of the shaft, didn't want the curtains at the crem and the crappy flowers outside lying on concrete, didn't want the smoke going up.

Didn't want them giving me a leaflet about bereavement.

But one morning the daylight nudges me awake and I don't turn my face back to the wall. One morning I can hear next door's dog above my own heartbeat, and their new baby roaring somewhere in between cat and gargoyle.

I'm starving hungry.

I told myself it was truer to what he wanted but the truth is I was afraid. I was afraid they'd search the bottom of the shaft and find nothing. Them white shinbones in the peat on East Falkland, after all. Would that have been better? Sparks flying up and the tracks dwindling in the darkness. Shrivelling away to nothing.

I crack that door open and the wind shoulders it against me. Green wind loping through from the estuary, brinefields and rain and the sea on its breath. That dog barking next door. Sounds like he's trying to batter his way out. I let myself into the front garden and breathe.

I'm in Tesco at White House Farm. Get myself a take-out from their coffee shop. Full-fat rocket fuel with an extra shot. It's proper flinty black stuff. Liquid obsidian. Thunder bangs overhead.

Shopping is dangerous when you're this hungry. I've got punnets of overripe strawberries with that blousy cream-soda smell, fresh flour-dusted bread from the bakery, biteable as Kelly's flesh. Two pots of crunchy peanut butter. I stand in line at the checkout behind an Asian woman with a little boy and a mountain of a weekly shop. The checkout monkey pings down her shopping too quick and she's getting flustered, struggling to keep up with the packing. The boy grabs a chocolate bar and puts it on the conveyor.

No Mahmoud, she says. Picks it up and puts it back. The boy starts whinging. Please mam. Away, go on.

I unload my stuff from the basket and she turns and looks at me. She's got too much eyeliner on. It's caked in the wrinkles round her eyes.

Hiya Danny, she says. Brings me up short and it takes me a minute to recognize her.

Raz. It's been a few year, like.

Away mam. It's only one chocky bar.

Go on, she says. Have your chocolate. Chucks the bar onto the conveyor with the rest.

Outside in the car park she manhandles her shopping bags.

You need a hand getting them to the car?

Nah, we're on the bus.

Let me give you a lift.

She looks at me, dark headscarf framing her sharp face. The eyes are weathered. Salt-glazed from the sea.

Go on then, she says.

I load the bags into the back of the van, open up the front for them to climb in.

It's only a two-seater, says Raz.

I'm riding shotgun, yells Mahmoud. Aren't I Danny? He climbs in and wedges himself between the seats, above the handbrake. Razia shrugs.

How old are you Mahmoud? I ask him as we drive. He's got a brown moon face and his hair spiked up with gel.

Eight and three-hundred-and-sixty-four three-hundred-and-sixty-fifths, he says.

Ah, right. So that means it's your birthday on Saturday.

No stupid. Tomorrow.

Tomorrow?

Yes.

Where are we going? I ask Raz.

Dad's house, she says.

I never knew you were back there.

He had a stroke a couple of month back. We moved in with him.

How's he getting on?

He's not good.

We pull up outside and I help them lug bags to the front door. She puts the Yale in the lock and cracks it open like a secret.

Shh, she says to Mahmoud. Don't wake your grandad.

I'll be off, I say. Turn to go.

Dan.

Her fingers are on my forearm, gripping the cuff of my jacket. I look down at them and she flushes.

How did we lose touch? she says.

Dunno. Guess it was when you and Sean moved away. Same sort of time I got together with Kelly. Both had other fish to fry.

We were both pretty crap at keeping in contact, she says, wrinkling her nose.

I thought your dad disapproved of Sean. More or less kicked you out, didn't he?

She grins at me, tongue between her teeth. The old Raz.

Yeah, well he needs me now. And he hasn't got any choice about it.

Well, give him my regards.

Dan.

The hand is still there.

He'd like to see you, she said. It'd do him good. Not that he'll be able to talk to you, but it'll still do him good.

Okay, I say.

She leads the way through the house and up to the front bedroom. The house hasn't changed much and it feels odd, just twenty years more threadbare. The thunderstorm that's been threatening suddenly breaks and it's hailing outside, door handles rattling and green stormlight at the window like ferns. I think of that afternoon at Jonah's.

Mr Shahid's propped up in the bed and there's a telly on in the corner but it's hard to tell whether he's looking at it or not. The eyes are dark and liquid but not particularly focused on anything.

Dad, says Raz. It's Danny, from the Cape. You remember Danny? Used to do his homework here, scoff the frozen pizzas out of the freezer.

Mmm, he says.

You took me to Darlo station once, I say. When I was doing a runner with the takings.

The limpid eyes move above the little moustache. I don't know where to look, end up half watching some bollocks on the telly. And then his hand slides into mine like a child's, the palm dry and crackling like brown paper. And above the miracle of his body working and the heat of his hand I don't need the Southern Ocean and I don't need crazy birds on South Georgia. We're going down with the ship, with the green fingers of the rain, and the house is drowning but it's a good sort of drowning.

We're going to the beach tomorrow, yells Mahmoud from the front room as I leave. For my birthday.

I peer round the door and find him plugged into some console game, wasting oversize space bugs.

What, in the rain?

It's going to be sunny, he says. We can have candy floss. You can give us a lift if you want.

So the next morning we're sat in the van on the front at Seaton watching rain bounce and boil on the bonnet and the steam from a flask of coffee grazing the windscreen. Stormclouds are bullying and brawling like cattle, blue heifers of the sea with splinters and rifts of pure brightness between. Cracks in the hairline of the world.

It's not fair, says Mahmoud.

He's bought a penny floater from one of the tat shops but it's sitting unused in the footwell.

Actually, I say. I'll tell you a secret.

What? he says.

No. Maybe I'd better not.

He thumps me on the arm and it hurts.

Tell me.

Ah, go on then. Human beings, you know, are actually waterproof. You can go out in the rain and all that happens is you get wet.

Right, he says.

Opens the door.

You be in goal, he says.

The beach and sea and sky are one surface running with silver tide and rain, the three of us walking on water, walking on a skin of mercury. Soaked to the fucking core. Mahmoud runs ahead, booting that penny floater around with the hair plastered down to his skull. I look at Raz, a triangle of face in the headscarf, her slap running in the rain. She looks like herself.

How's Sean? I say. I was surprised when you two got together. Always thought you'd go to university.

He left me. Some girl who worked in the cab office.

Right. Sorry.

Ah, it doesn't matter.

Remember how you used to say there were a zillion different maybes, all hanging around in the wind.

Aye. It feels like that when you're sixteen.

But not now.

She shrugs and smiles sideways.

Maybe there's just one, she says. And the others are make believe.

Or maybe you grab one, I say. And the rest just shrivel up.

It's the same difference, she says. In the end. A human being is just about the weirdest, most improbable thing you can get. The chance of me being in that bar at the same time as Sean, the chance of him deciding to come over. Millions to one. And without all that Mahmoud would never have been. He's improbability made solid.

Aye.

What happened to your dad? she said.

Well, you know he went out to Thailand.

I heard something about it.

He died out there, not long ago.

Sorry to hear that. What are you going to do now?

I dunno. Might buy a boat, take it down to Whitby.

You got the money?

Not really.

We carry on along the empty beach. Rain tatters our senses on a vacuous wind, sending car alarms off in the town. Raz slips her hand through my arm, pale fingers on my sodden sleeve. Mahmoud looks round.

Dan, he yells.

I finger the lighter in my pocket. Improbability made solid. I'd forgotten it was there.

The hand slips away from my arm.

Danny, she says. It's good to see you, but there's no way I'm looking for a relationship right now. No way.

Aye, I know, I say distractedly. I'm only just getting a divorce meself.

Oh. Right.

Dan, yells Mahmoud. He boots the floater and it lands in the sea.

You'll have to wade in, says Raz. People are waterproof, after all.

I grin at her. Plodge over towards Mahmoud with my hand in my pocket around the lighter. It's empty. The fluid must have evaporated away. It's been months since that night at Billingham House. The ball's bobbing on the waves, slowly drifting away from the beach.

Right, I say. I take my shoes and socks off and roll my trouserlegs up. Mahmoud laughs. Maybe the social will never ring and maybe the police will never turn up. I know the development's stalled because of the recession. Maybe there's no safety net after all, like Yan said. Don't get old in this country.

I wade into the sea, my feet white as dead things under the water and splinters of seacoal between my toes. It's hellish cold. I've half a mind to hurl that old brass lighter out as far as I can, but then I don't. Yan said talismans don't work. I drop it back down into my pocket but I know I'll never fill it up with fire again. Not even once.

One morning the daylight nudges me awake and I walk out of the door into the dog-barking, baby-crying dawn, pregnant with rain.

Down at Seal Sands hide I sit in the comfortable darkness for a few minutes. The smell of creosote, cracks of light winking between rough-hewn planks. Finally I rise, knees clicking quietly, and crack open the long shutter. Light floods into the hide but there's no epiphany, no slow-burning sunrise igniting the river. The light is white and constant and sober. Outside there are long expanses of wet mud glittering like melted chocolate and separated by fronds of water. A sharp scent of earth. And the chemical industry still hovers on the brink and the familiar shapes are dark and damp like exposed formations of wet rock and the long low humming underneath it all is just a quiet breathing.

I raise the bins and scan the flats. Plenty of waders feeding out there, pattering the shining surface with a tangled cryptography of footprints, punctuated by the looping casts of invertebrates. There are tiny pale sanderling and burly knot, nervous redshank with heads bobbing. But the dunlin are in for the winter and it's them I've come to see. Dunlin roving across the mudflat, worrying at the surface with bills like black dibbers. Standing still with one foot tucked for warmth into the soft belly fur. Nervous and mousy and neck-twisting to scan for danger. Dumpy and dowdy like harassed mums in the shopping centre. Sleepy, with the black button eyes blinking, hunched up with heads withdrawn, shuffling and reshuffling their scalloped backs like restless drifts of leaves. Drab and beautiful, familiar and alien, overlapping without touching. Mouse-grey dunlin, mudcoloured and ordinary. There are thousands of them.